DOCTORED VOWS

MARITAL PRIVILEGES
BOOK 1

SHANDI BOYES

COPYRIGHT

Photographer: Ren Saliba

Cover Design: SSB Covers & Design

Editor: Courtney Umphress

Proofreader: Crossbones Editing

Master Proofreader: Chavonne Eklund

Alpha Reader: Carolyn Wallace

WANT TO STAY IN TOUCH?

Facebook: facebook.com/authorshandi

Instagram: instagram.com/authorshandi

Email: authorshandi@gmail.com

Reader's Group: bit.ly/ShandiBookBabes

Website: authorshandi.com

Newsletter: https://www.subscribepage.com/AuthorShandi

DEDICATION

To Lauren,
For all those late nights we
endured discussing this book.
You, not me.
I was in bed by 9 every night.
If only Maksim had gotten the memo.
Shandi xx

CHAPTER ONE

A s I exit the medical equipment sterilization room at Myasnikov Private Hospital, I pull off my hairnet to dispose of it and my biodegradable hospital apron into an uncontaminated product waste receptacle. I'm taken aback when I catch sight of my watch while forcing part of my "uniform" into the overflowing bin. It is a little after 3 a.m.

I hadn't expected a position I accepted solely to pay student loans to take up so much time. Alas, with increased surgeries comes a demand for the sterilization of reusable medical equipment.

When accepted into medical school, I thought the most challenging part of the transition from college graduate to wannabe surgeon would be the long study sessions and textbooks that cost more than my first car.

I was poorly mistaken.

My tuition was more than I could afford. I barely get five hours of sleep a night, and although my studies have now switched to a somewhat paid position, I have to accept jobs on the side just to make ends meet.

By ends, I mean rent. My student loans are still in the red, and I'm drowning in personal credit card debt, but I have a roof over my head, and my family is taken care of, so I guess I shouldn't complain.

With the surgical department shockingly quiet, I detour through the space that smells like the chemicals that soak through my gloves each night while sterilizing the equipment used by this very department.

The rancid scent is the only reason my grandmother hasn't questioned my latest moonlighting position. As far as she is aware, I'm doing double shifts at the hospital every night.

I am—just not in the way she believes.

Although there's no shame in admitting you collect and sterilize medical equipment, I don't want anything to taint the gleam in her eyes when she tells her Bura teammates that I'm a soon-to-be world-renowned neurosurgeon.

I cringe when I cross theater three. There must have been a last-minute add-on to the surgical register outside the usual operating hours. The room is void of a soul, but used medical equipment is strewn from one side to the next.

My sluggish steps toward the mess slow when a voice from behind me says, "I'll get it."

Relief bombards me, but guilt quickly follows when I spin to face Alla.

She looks as exhausted as I feel.

"Are you sure? I don't mind helping."

She rolls her eyes before shooing off my offer with a wave of her hand. "I'm not the one scheduled to return here in a little over"—she checks her watch, which is still hidden by elbow-high gloves—"eight hours." When she returns her eyes to my face, she shoves her hands in her pockets and peers at me motheringly. Alla is only four years my senior, but since that places her in her thirties instead of her twenties, she acts like we have a two-decade age gap. "You can't keep running on fumes, Nikita. If you only dip the rag on the odd occasion, it will eventually run dry."

"I'm fine. I've only got..." My words trail off when I recall I only started the third year of my surgical residency three months ago. I've got a long way to go—especially if I want to specialize in pediatric neurosurgery.

When I finalize my reply with a groan, Alla twists me to face the exit. "I'll see you tomorrow." She barges me out of the OR with so much gall I crash into the nurses' station desk, bruising my hip. "And if you're good, there could be a *пончики* or two waiting for you when you finish your shift tomorrow."

Пончикис are Russia's version of doughnuts.

Alla smiles when I ask, "Glaze or sugarcoated?"

"Why can't we have both?"

I laugh. Her imitation of a famous commercial exposes that her English is as poor as my Russian was when I moved here nine years ago. I'm slowly learning the lingo, but I don't see myself mastering in it anytime soon.

"I'll bring *кофе*."

She jerks up her chin in appreciation half a second before her nose screws up. "Just not that latest craze the hobnobs are raving about. I don't care if it is the president's rat. I will not drink its droppings."

I'm still smiling about her disgust of the latest coffee craze in Russia while darting through the nurses' station for the interns' locker room at the back. My pace slows for the second time when I spot the surgical schedule slated to start at 6 a.m. My mother was Russian, so my given name is common around these parts, but my father is British, so my surname is rarely seen unless it is attached to a foreigner.

Hoffman shouldn't be on a surgical schedule, much less in the box that announces the lead surgeon for a patient's procedure.

"Ivanov," I murmur while trying to recall where I've heard the name before.

When my brief sort through the tumbleweeds in my head that always form when I'm running on zero comes up empty, I seek the patient's file from a stack on the nurses' desk.

Mrs. Irina Ivanov's ER paperwork exposes she was admitted five days ago. Her symptoms aren't what I would classify as life-threatening, so it has me curious as to why she is in an induced coma and scheduled for surgery first thing this morning.

After ensuring I haven't mistaken my name on both the surgical schedule and Mrs. Ivanov's admission writeup, I search her medical record for the correct medical officer so I can adjust the error.

Thirty minutes of searching awards me nothing but more confusion.

Mrs. Ivanov's patient record would have the most stringent medical insurance company convinced I am the surgeon increasing her premiums. It doesn't even say surgical resident. It appears as if I am the lead surgeon.

Even if that were the case, I would never seek a medical diagnosis by conducting a dangerous exploratory procedure. That is precisely what Mrs. Ivanov's surgery is. A risky and most likely unnecessary medical procedure that could detrimentally impact her chances of recovery.

With my unease too high to ignore and my anger at a possibly erroneous practice just as overflowing, I stuff Mrs. Ivanov's medical file under my arm before directing my steps to the surgical ward instead of the closest exit.

The usually bustling ward is as desolate of staff as the OR. A nurse is behind an unmanned nurses' station, but with a bowl of vomit in one hand and a used Foley catheter in the other, she isn't portraying a wish to be questioned.

Instead, I approach Mrs. Ivanov's room, hopeful a member of

her real medical team will arrive shortly to prepare her for surgery.

A peculiar sensation overwhelms me when I enter her room. I'm familiar with rooms as small as the curtained-off cubicles of the ER, but it isn't solely the impressive floor space of Mrs. Ivanov's private wing that has my heart breaking into a canter. It is finding a patient starkly contrasting to the notes in her file.

She is gaunt, her skin is pale, and her nails are brittle, but when you look past those points, you see a woman who takes care of herself. Her hair is glossy and voluptuous. Her muscle definition shows she works out, and not even being swamped by an oversized hospital bed and bulky medical equipment can hide the fighter inside her.

She reminds me of how my grandfather has defied the odds every single day for the past almost decade.

Confident that Mrs. Ivanov can do the same, I place down her file and commence a prolonged handwashing routine in the sink in her room.

"Mrs. Ivanov, my name is Dr. Hoffman. I'm a third-year surgical resident at Myasnikov." After ensuring my hands are more germ-free than the equipment I cleaned for the last several hours, I dry them with a paper towel before snapping on two powdered gloves from a box on the wall next to the sink.

While placing on the gloves, I say, "I know it's early, but with your surgery only hours away, I was hoping you would allow me to conduct a final assessment."

I look at the beautiful raven-haired lady who appears decades younger than the fifty-eight described on her medical record. She can't answer me. She was placed in a medically induced coma shortly after admittance, but after being the lead caregiver for my grandfather for the past four years, I soon learned that bedside manner is as important as the many other skills of a surgeon.

"It will only take a few minutes, and I promise it will not be invasive."

After smiling like the respirator breathing on her behalf answered for her, I walk to her bedside. Her fighting spirit is even more noticeable from this vantage point.

"I'm going to flash a light into your eyes. It will test your pupillary reflexes with a quick succession of flicks."

Again, I wait as if seeking permission before I raise her eyelids.

"That's good, Mrs. Ivanov. You did great. Your eyes are responding how they should."

After placing my penlight on the table at the side of her bed, I gently grasp her head.

"Now I need to pull down your eyelids to check their coloring."

I breathe out some of the unease in my chest before doing as stated. The skin beneath her eyelids is extremely pale, which is expected since her primary diagnosis is extreme anemia. However, I'm still not convinced going under the knife is the best option for her.

The severeness of anemia does not correspond with the severeness of her symptoms, so exploratory surgery could place Mrs. Ivanov's life at unnecessary risk. Surely the surgical consultant on her case knows this. Even a third-year intern can't mishear the warning sirens wailing in the distance.

After testing the movement of Mrs. Ivanov's joints and receiving the faintest groan of protest, I apologize for the discomfort before conducting my final test.

"The next test might cause a small bit of discomfort, but I assure you, I am only doing this because I have your best interests at heart."

After another big exhale, I open Mrs. Ivanov's mouth as gently as possible without compressing her breathing tube before assessing her tongue.

It is as smooth as anticipated.

"You did great, Mrs. Ivanov. Thank you so much for your assistance."

As I head back to her medical file on the table at the foot of her bed, eager to add some notes to the scarce number in her record, Mrs. Ivanov's room door shoots open, and Dr. Abdulov enters. He is the head of the surgical department at Myasnikov Private.

His squinted eyes dart from the medical file to Mrs. Ivanov before rocketing back to me.

"What are you doing?"

His tone should startle me, but I barely balk since it is thrown around at least ten times a day.

Dr. Abdulov can't say the same when I reply, "Assessing my *supposed* patient before surgery."

He *pffts*, scoffs, and sputters before he rips Mrs. Ivanov's file out of my hand. Even with my pulse beating in my ears, ripping paper can't be missed.

"You're a third-year resident—"

"Whose name is all over a patient's record I've never heard of until today." Since I still can't recall where I've heard the Ivanov name before, my tone dips in the middle of my statement, but only I am aware of the possible deceit in my reply.

Dr. Abdulov appears seconds from kicking me out of my residency, not solely Mrs. Ivanov's room, so I speak fast.

I don't take our conversation in a direction you'd expect from a person on the verge of homelessness.

"I believe Mrs. Ivanov has been misdiagnosed, and her surgery is gratuitous."

Sweat beads at my temples from his furious glare. "How dare you. I have years of experience."

"I'm not saying you don't. Your accomplishments are known across the globe, but a B12 deficiency is often overlooked. Even by the greats."

He scoffs so hard that his spit lands on my face. "B12 deficiency? That's your diagnosis?"

It is the fight of my life to nod with his mocking laugh booming around the room.

"She has muscle aches, pale eyelids, and a smooth tongue. All signs—"

"Of an anemic diagnosis."

"Severe anemia also demonstrates those signs, but her skin is scaly, and her nails are brittle. I also don't believe the bad hospital lighting is giving her skin that yellow hue."

I respond as if he physically slapped me instead of mentally slapping Mrs. Ivanov when he says with a laugh, "Perhaps she's a recovering alcoholic." Any chance of keeping things professional is lost when he adds, "Or a barely functioning one. She has all the signs of an addict."

"She has all the signs of a patient with an uncaring, arrogant, chauvinistic pig of a doctor misdiagnosing her. I get it. You have to straddle the line to please everyone, but a B12 deficiency is often overlooked because hospital administrators continually ride doctors' asses for the most billable procedures." I talk louder when he grabs my arm to remove me from the room. "If my diagnosis is correct, you will save your patient from an unnecessary medical procedure. Surely that is worth a slight dip in profits."

He appears seconds from saying no, but a deep, manly voice from the other side of the room forces any reply he's planning to give to the back of his throat. "Do the test she is suggesting."

My throat is on fire from ensuring I had my say before being tossed out of a patient's room, but it turns into the Sahara when the stranger's face is exposed. Chiseled cheekbones, plump lips, soul-searing eyes, and a defined jaw hidden under dark stubble wraps up a package that showcases danger and sexiness at the same time.

As my unnamed savior steps out of the shadows the above-bed lighting casts over the corners of all the patients' rooms, he folds his thick arms in front of his chest. Since a black A-shirt is the only clothing covering his chest, the cut lines of his arms stand out as evidently as the tic in his jaw when he drinks in Dr. Abdulov's clutch on my arm.

The stranger doesn't say anything. He doesn't need to. Within a second of his narrowed gaze scorching the skin high on my arm, Dr. Abdulov frees me from his grasp and takes a giant step back.

Even though it is clear who is now running the show, Dr. Abdulov tries to keep the playing field even. "The test Dr. Hoffman is suggesting is unnecessary. You have my word—"

"Your word means nothing to me."

The stranger steps closer, and my heart goes wild. I've never witnessed such an accurate display of raw arrogance before, and anyone who gave it a shot didn't have pulse-spiking good looks like this mysterious man.

"I said to do the test." His authority can't be denied. He is used to getting what he wants and doesn't care who he needs to trample to get it. "And I will not repeat myself for anyone."

Dr. Abdulov's head bobs in sync with his Adam's apple. "Very well. I will organize it now."

When he gestures for me to exit before him, I lock eyes with the stranger. I'm not seeking his permission to leave—though I'm sure he is accustomed to everyone in his realm doing precisely that. I am thanking him for his support before I lose the opportunity.

If the vein in Dr. Abdulov's neck is anything to go by, I won't just be marched out of the hospital for being insubordinate. My entire medical career is about to be trampled on. I doubt I'll even be allowed to sterilize equipment after my performance. Tell me one medical student who has called their supervisor a pig and continued to practice medicine. I can't think of a single incident.

Dr. Abdulov's brisk breaths fan my neck when the stranger stops him from shadowing my steps by asking to speak with him.

"In private," he adds when Dr. Abdulov's grip on my arm—which is nowhere near as grabby this time—hinders me from exiting.

"Of course."

Dr. Abdulov strives to wipe the riled expression from his face before he spins to face the dark-haired gent. Although Mrs. Ivanov's door closes quickly with me on the outside, nothing can override the putrid scent of fear leeching out of Dr. Abdulov. It is as potent as the sterile smell I scrub from my body every evening but barely strong enough to supersede the lusty aroma that engulfs me when the stranger watches me over Dr. Abdulov's shoulder for several heart-pumping seconds.

His watch is full of haughty arrogance, and it mists my skin with sweat.

I won't mention what other parts of my body get damp.

I'm meant to be celebrating a medical triumph that rarely occurs between a third-year surgical intern and a lead surgeon, not my body's insane reaction to a man whose looks alone would have him chewing through women as often as he does underwear.

Furthermore, I was on the verge of being homeless before I called my superior a pig.

Now "verge" looks set to be removed from the equation.

CHAPTER TWO

"Dr. Hoffman?"

Behind my locker door, I hide my grimace before removing it entirely.

Once I'm confident my expression represents a third-year surgical intern instead of the whiny brat it wants to portray, I answer, "Yes."

I know who's accosting me before I pop my head out of my locker. The head of the residency program at Myasnikov Private has the same burly tone as Dr. Abdulov, but since they pay him too much to socialize with the interns as often as his less-revered counterparts, I don't hear it as frequently.

I skipped the dressing down Dr. Abdulov no doubt planned to unleash earlier this morning. It wasn't by choice. When my grandmother called to say my grandfather was having a medical episode, I raced out of the hospital minus a lecture and my personal possessions—although I did gain another reason for my minimal sleep schedule.

The mystery stranger hasn't left my head since our eyes collided. His handsome face was pulled in a frown, but that didn't detract from his appeal. His first impression exuded down-right sexiness, and his smirk alone conjured up hundreds of wicked thoughts when I finally crawled into bed a little after six.

If I had an iota of energy left after helping my grandfather through a severe bout of respiratory insufficiency, I would have tried to put the visual to good use.

Alas, my nether regions remain as unbasted as my grand-mother's overcooked Christmas turkeys.

Although I had planned to arrive for my shift earlier than the assigned time, the alarm I swore I set didn't sound until minutes before my next double shift.

I nod like I have no clue what Dr. Sidorov could want to discuss when he asks, "Can I speak with you?" before I follow him into the hub of Myasnikov Private.

Top-of-the-line desks and bulky leather chairs are nothing out of the ordinary for private hospitals run with profits in mind more than integrity, but it still frustrates me.

Dr. Sidorov's desk cost far more than the B12 deficiency test they tried to deny Mrs. Ivanov.

When did possessions become more important than ethics?

My heart sinks when Dr. Sidorov gestures for me to sit across from him before he slides a multipage document across his desk. I put on a brave front when my grandmother planted her hands on each of my cheeks before she told me how proud she was of me, but I can no longer hold back my fear that I am about to lose my ability to practice medicine.

It's so prominent my vision is too blurred to read the thick black ink in front of me.

"I shouldn't have said what I said. It was a long, tiring week, and I acted like a brat. But I promise that the patient's best interest was *always* at the forefront of my mind. That's what we're about, isn't it? The patients?"

I wave my hand at his door like the wards filled with sick

people are outside, my heart sinking when my hand drifts past priceless paintings and collectible antiques on the way.

Defeated, I slump low before vying for another semi-paid position. "Will you at least consider deferring my residency to the general hospital? Their surgical roster won't be as demanding as Myasnikov Private, but I'm sure I will get an occasional sit-in when the time comes to defer my studies to a specialist position."

My eyes snap up from my hands when Dr. Sidorov replies, "And lose an upcoming neurosurgeon prodigy? Don't be absurd."

I couldn't be more shocked if he had slapped me.

"I... He..." I whisper my next set of words. "I called Dr. Abdulov a pig."

He checks a document before correcting, "An uncaring, arrogant, chauvinistic pig."

Since I have no defense, I remain quiet.

It is for the best. I may have missed his praise if I had tried to plead innocent.

"And you were right." Shock zips through me when he grins. "He is a pig." I haven't gotten over my first lot of disbelief when I'm hit with another dose. "Your diagnosis was also correct. Tests proved Mrs. Ivanov has a severe B12 deficiency. She was given her first dose of serum hours ago, and her prognosis has already drastically improved. We removed the ventilator and lowered the sedatives keeping her under. She woke two hours ago."

My mouth falls open, but other than that, it refuses to adhere to any other prompts my brain is giving. I knew her diagnosis could be unearthed without a scalpel. I'm just a novice at being told I was right by anyone, much less a supervisor.

Even when they're proven wrong, they rarely admit it.

"Her surgery?"

That's it. That is all I can get out—two measly words.

"Was canceled this morning. Her B12 levels were so low she will be rostered for bi-weekly serum injections..." His words trail off when an emotion I didn't mean to show leaps onto my face. "Do you disagree with my medical plan?"

"Umm..." Please excuse my idiocy. The genuine interest in his tone has left me a little dumbfounded. "I don't disagree with it. I just want to make sure the dosage level isn't too excessive. An overdose of B12 can be as dangerous as a deficiency. What was the level identified in her MMA test?"

"We conducted the homocysteine test. It was..."—again, he checks a document in front of him—"thirty-eight."

"Thirty-eight picomoles per liter?"

I sound shocked. Rightfully so. Those levels are dangerously low and are most likely the cause of Mrs. Ivanov's numerous neurological episodes. It would have made it seem as if she were having a stroke, or worse, it could have caused a stroke.

When you're deficient in B12, it causes an increase in homo-cysteine. Too much homocysteine causes inflammation of the blood vessels and oxidative stress—both significant contributors to strokes.

"Was an MRI conducted?"

When Dr. Sidorov nods, I hold my breath, waiting for him to elaborate. "It showed increased blood flow, but no dangerous clots were sighted."

I exhale deeply, relieved. "That's wonderful. I'm so grateful."

"As was Mr. Ivanov."

His words pique my attention as my heart rate soars. I don't know if it is a good or bad surge. It may be a bit of both. The "Mister" part of his comment instantly conjured up murky brown eyes and a devastatingly cut jaw, but it also proves a rela-tionship between the patient I assessed and the man who kept me awake half the night.

I can only hope it is a blood relation and not one founded by law, or my limbs will be weighed down with guilt instead of untapped sexual exhaustion.

My focus shifts back to Dr. Sidorov when he says, "You were

mentioned multiple times while he endorsed a check to fund the new wing slated for completion by the end of the year. The praise was so inspiring that it felt right to offer you this now instead of waiting for your residency to end."

When he nudges his head to the multipage document, I lift it from the desk. My eyes aren't as misted now, so the font is legible.

"You're offering me a promotion?" Before he can answer, my eyes bulge out of my head. The wages cited must be annually instead of monthly like my residency contract because the digits are excessive. "I think someone made an error. This amount can't be right."

Dr. Sidorov laughs when I twist the contract around to face him. "It is as stated and will be backdated to the day you began your third year."

I do a quick calculation and almost squeal when the figure means I can pay off my grandfather's latest medical insurance excess bill *and* some of my credit card debt. There isn't enough to put toward my student loans, but it far exceeds the internship hourly wage I was earning only hours ago.

"Are you sure this is allowed?" I ask, confident I'm dreaming. "I'm not yet a qualified surgeon."

Again, he nods. "Things are different in the private sector." His eyes gleam with excitement. "And if you continue to encourage endorsements like the one you secured this morning, this is just the beginning of an illustrious medical career with Myasnikov Private."

I almost fall over backward when the check Mr. Ivanov donated is exposed. Even with my new salary giving me indigestion, it would still take me working two jobs for over three decades to earn the figure cited on the handwritten check.

Doubt creeps in when Dr. Sidorov hands me his favorite pen out of the breast pocket of his jacket. He's been behind the scenes at this hospital for so long that he no longer wears a doctor's coat or scrubs.

"Would you mind if I take the contract home and read it before signing it? My mother always said you should never sign anything without reading it twice." My wet eyes are back, but more from fond memories than fear of unemployment. I loved my mother dearly, and I miss her every day.

Dr. Sidorov seems put off by my request, but he still obliges. "I guess that won't be a problem." He removes the document from his desk and places it into an envelope. "If you have any questions, you know where to reach me."

I nod until the possible inconvenience of his offer smacks into me. "Is there someone else I should call if I have any questions? I won't have time to review the offer until after my shifts tonight." I overexert the "s" at the end of shifts to ensure he knows I won't be heading home anytime within the next seventeen hours.

I'm tempted to pinch myself when he replies, "Why don't you take the day off so you can look over it... *twice*."

The humor at the end of his statement doesn't match his pinched expression.

He looks as uneasy as I feel.

"And draft your resignation to the sterilization contractor you've been working for the past four months while you're there."

His lips raise at the bewilderment on my face.

I wasn't aware he knew about my secondary employment.

"I've known for some time but figured you'd give it up when awarded a full-pay contract." He sees something I didn't mean to express. "Was I wrong?"

"No. I... ah..." I roll my shoulders before saying with more certainty, "No. You are correct. I just don't want to leave them short."

"They'll be fine." He sits in his big, bulky chair before raising his eyes to mine. "I'm sure you won't be hard to replace."

Ouch. There's a sting my ego never anticipated after being praised so highly.

"Still, I would like to finish my assigned shifts." When anger hardens his features, I add, "If that's okay with you?"

He breathes out his nose before finally giving in with the faintest head bob.

"Thank you." I gesture to the envelope in my hand. "For both. It is nice to have the belief of someone who doesn't share your blood."

He smiles at my praise before shifting his focus to a pile of documents in front of him. They're not patient records, more the calculated-to-the-penny reports of the mammoth debt most patients leave with once they're discharged.

With his focus elsewhere, I show myself out before immediately starting what I hope will be one of my last sixteen-hour-plus workdays.

With the ER overrun with another foodborne illness outbreak, this is the first five minutes I've had to myself in ages, and I use it by scrolling through patient records. I prefer a one-on-one approach, but there are too many overflowing vomit buckets to sneak a visit to the surgical ward, so I log into HIS (Myasnikov's health information system) and type my patients' names into the search bar.

Every name on my rounds roster shows a result except for Mrs. Ivanov.

"Is there an issue with HIS?" I ask a colleague, conscious it could be a software issue and not solely user error. I'm great with bedside manner, but I hate the computer side of my profession. Technology and I aren't friends.

A nurse whose name is skipping my mind joins me at the nurses' station. "I don't think so. Who are you looking for?"

"Irina Ivanov."

"Ivanov?" she asks, her tone as peaked as her manicured brow.

I nod. "She's a patient on the surgical ward. I wanted to check her current blood workup."

"Oh... umm..." She sounds more worried than daft. "Perhaps the report hasn't been added to her file yet." She clicks me out of the patient screen and logs me into the pathology mainframe we use when we're too impatient to wait for the pathology department to upload the results to the patient's record. "There you go."

"Thanks." My gratitude is short because she helped me find Mrs. Ivanov's latest blood workup, and the results are miraculous, but she completely overlooked the fact we have a patient in a ward who hasn't been admitted.

Mrs. Ivanov was brought in by an ambulance five days ago. That means the ER department should have handled her admission. If her time here was missed, and the department is not assigned the funds for her consultation and subsequent admission, they could lose even more medical officers than they lost the prior year.

"Who should I call to ensure Mrs. Ivanov's admission was done correctly?"

"You could ask the admissions clerk," answers the nurse, "but last I heard, she was off sick." When I huff in frustration, she promises to look into it if I assist her in administrating Ondansetron to a child in bay three. "She hasn't kept anything down in over twenty-four hours and has severe abdominal distension."

The worry on her face has me leaping up from my seat and following her into a curtained-off cubicle without further consultation.

CHAPTER THREE

B y the time I head for the room where underpaid hospital subcontractors sterilize medical equipment each night, ready for my second shift of the day, I've treated over three dozen patients with gastroenteritis and emesis symptoms, intubated two middle-aged women, and regretfully shadowed the honor walk of a patient who couldn't be saved.

He was an organ donor, so his legacy will live on for many years to come.

I'm exhausted but determined. You don't have much choice when you're relying on money you've not yet earned. The pharmacist allows me to place my grandfather's pricy medication on a tab, but the payment plan we agreed upon is due this Friday—the same day I get paid for the sterilization of instruments I plan to use one day. My salary from Myasnikov Private doesn't land in my bank account until Tuesday.

As I veer past the surgical ward, I pretend curiosity isn't gnawing at my stomach, begging for the chance to be heard. Mrs. Ivanov's latest blood workup shows her prognosis is significantly better than hours ago, but there's nothing like witnessing a miracle firsthand.

Confident that my half-hour break could be better utilized doing anything but gorging carbs I'll never work off, I veer my steps toward the surgical ward instead of the ORs our patients frequent.

Several nurses and doctors dip their chins in greeting when I stroll by, but none stop me to chat like they usually do when I do my rounds. They scatter more than socialize, meaning I make it to Mrs. Ivanov's room with twenty-seven minutes remaining on my break.

My brows stitch when I take in the made bed in the middle of the empty room. My scan of the patient board as I strolled past the nurses' station was quick, but Mrs. Ivanov was still assigned this room.

Concern slithers through me when I hear water running from the attached bathroom. Mrs. Ivanov's latest test results show a drastic improvement in her condition, but she shouldn't be showering without assistance. She could slip and hurt herself. Dizziness is a common side effect of a B_{12} deficiency.

After trying and failing to secure the assistance of a nurse, I enter Mrs. Ivanov's room, place the contract I was offered next to her patient file, and then make a beeline for the bathroom.

"Mrs. Ivanov," I call out while knocking softly. I don't want to startle her. That will increase the risk of a patient slip and a ton of paperwork I'd rather avoid. "Do you require assistance?"

When my question is answered with silence, I test the lock.

It is unlocked.

"Mrs. Ivanov, it is Dr. Hoffman from this morning," I announce while opening the door and directing my eyes toward the shower.

The chance of a slip hazard is a certainty when the person in the shower isn't who I'm expecting. He has the same inky-black hair and glowing tanned skin as Mrs. Ivanov, but his muscles are far more defined and covered with tattoos.

The stranger who took up my campaign this morning for Mrs. Ivanov to be tested for a B12 deficiency is drowning his head under a heavy flow of water. It flattens his slicked-back hair away from his gorgeous face and showcases the deep V in the middle of his prominent brows. His lips are parted as he sucks in shallow breaths, and his eyes are closed.

Well, they were until he senses my watch.

When his fists clench, the thick muscles in his forearms flex. I swear there's not an iota of unnecessary fat on him anywhere. He's all muscles and ink—and angry sneers.

"I'm so sorry," I blurt out before I divert my eyes to the floor.

I should have chosen the ceiling. It would have made my pledge of innocence more realistic since my dilated eyes wouldn't have needed to veer past his cock that grew larger the longer I stared.

"I thought you were Mrs. Ivanov, and I was worried she might have overestimated her mobility so soon after her recovery, so I-I came to help." I don't know who that blubbering idiot is, but she better quit right now.

"You came to help?"

Confident I'm not hearing the hope in his tone correctly, I nod before sheepishly raising my eyes. It is a challenging feat to direct them straight to his face, but I manage—somewhat.

The man I assume is Mr. Ivanov is still standing under the heavy flow of water, not attempting to cover himself. I understand his cockiness. The visual is spectacular, and it grows more mesmerizing when the appendage I'm trying to make out as if I see a hundred times a day steadily rises toward his belly button.

"If you want to help me, Doc, you'll need to come closer. My imagination is wondrous, but I only use it when the visual isn't appealing enough." His teeth catch his lower lip as he drags his eyes down my body. "You are more than fucking enticing."

I try to think of an appropriate response when his cock is the next thing caught. My mouth twitches, but not a peep sounds. Nothing forming in my head is suitable to say in any situation, much less when a deliriously handsome man is stroking his cock in front of me.

He doesn't look like the toothless patient who wanders the halls of the ER every long weekend, offering services none of the medical team want.

He's mind-bogglingly attractive and seemingly turned on by my hideous scrubs, makeup-free face, and messy bun combination.

"Are you gonna just stare, Doc?" He hardens more as the sides of his lips curl into a salacious grin. "Or are you going to join me?"

"I... umm... I—"

I don't know whether to stomp my feet in frustration or relief when my name is called by one of my colleagues. "Dr. Hoffman."

After responding to Mr. Ivanov's husky laugh about my childish pout with a stern stink eye, I spin to face Nurse Sharpe. She is wheeling in a now alert and conscious Mrs. Ivanov toward her bed. The cuffs of her hospital-issued uniform are damp, and Mrs. Ivanov's hair is glossy and smells recently shampooed.

Nurse Sharpe must have taken her to the bathroom in the corridor. Its wide doorframe allows patients to remain in a seated position while showering. You can't fit a wheelchair through the doorway of a patient bathroom. That's why I'm shocked Mr. Ivanov and his giant cock made it inside without incident.

"Is everything okay?" Nurse Sharpe asks when my shock is shown on my face.

Penises are a part of my medical studies. I'm not meant to look at them like normal women do. They should not differ from any other male appendage. But I devoured Mr. Ivanov's penis like my name is tattooed down the shaft and its sole function is to ensure my every whim is answered.

God, I wish that were the case.

It's been so long since I've orgasmed I couldn't fake it even if given the opportunity. And the last time I was this intrigued by a member of the opposite sex is an even more distant memory.

I'm the good girl. The safe date. The woman you bring home to meet your parents. So why does Mr. Ivanov look at me the way he does?

His watch as he stroked his cock has me heated up everywhere, and the sweaty situation worsens when I spot the patient's name above her bed.

Irina Ivanov.

Oh. My. God. Did I just eyeball a taken man? There'd have to be an age gap because Mr. Ivanov doesn't look a day over thirty, but my parents' difference in age exceeded fifteen years, so who's to say the same isn't happening here?

Sickened with guilt, I make an excuse to leave. "Yes. I was... ah..." With my head in too much of a daze to formulate a valid excuse, I settle for a pathetic one instead. "I'm going to—"

"Wait in the corridor for you to get situated," announces a voice from behind me—a voice so close the droplets of water I was envious of only seconds ago are absorbed by the thin material of my scrubs. He whispers his following sentence so it is only for my ears. "Because we're not finished yet, are we, Dr. Hoffman?"

With my knees close to buckling from the heat of Mr. Ivanov's breath on my ear and the uneasy stare of his possible wife, I briefly nod before sprinting for the closest exit.

CHAPTER FOUR

"**Y**ou're regretting your decision now, aren't you?" When I peer at Alla in bewilderment, she tosses a bag of contaminated waste at my feet. "Don't act surprised, Dr. Genius. Rumors of your promotion circulated the hospital hours before you arrived."

I sigh in relief. She isn't referencing my shameful cowardice in front of the most confident man I've ever met. She's talking about the promotion that was shoved to the back of my mind when a far more enticing package ripped it from my thoughts.

The event that will be forever referenced as the "shower incident" has kept my clit in a constant state of arousal all evening. It won't stop buzzing—which is concerning to admit since I've yet to work out how the man in the shower is connected to Mrs. Ivanov.

When Alla peers at me with an arched brow, waiting for a reply, I say, "Why gossip about something that may not occur?"

She gives me with the same look everyone gives when I enter the cafeteria with a packed-from-home lunch.

It is the look of pity.

She knows as well as I do that I could never turn down the offer Dr. Sidorov handed me this morning. It is the only lifeline available and still below what I need.

For future reference, anything with "medical" attached to it is expensive—for both the patient and soon-to-be doctor.

"I'm not regretting anything..." *Except not stepping into the bathroom thirty seconds earlier.*

I hide the disgust attempting to cross my face by lugging a second bag of biowaste that cannot be incinerated onto the cart so it can be disposed of into a landfill that will be uninhabitable for years to come.

"Not even the dozen or so donut holes I gorged."

Alla bumps me with her hip before locking her eyes with mine so I can see the truth in them when she says, "We could have survived without you tonight. It's been quiet."

"I know. I just..."

Since I'd rather look like an idiot than admit how desperate I am for this pay, I shrug. I'm burning the candle at both ends, and it is catching up to me. I'm one hour of overtime from burnout, but obligations don't stop because you're tired—*or horny.*

Once we have the cart loaded into the van hazardous waste is transported in, I peel off my gloves and hairnet, dump them into the trash, then turn to face Alla, who ditched the hazmat gear ten minutes ago. "I'll see you tomorrow."

"Not if I can help it." When my brows furrow, she explains, "When Mr. Bolderack heard you were leaving, he filled in the rest of your shifts with a person from the temp agency." My heart falters for only a second. "You'll still be paid as if you worked. You just don't need to show up."

This can't be my life. How did it switch from chaotic to surreal in a matter of hours?

Although I'm dying to sleep in, just like my patients will always come first, so will my morals. "I should still come in. It won't feel right to be paid and not work."

When Alla twists her lips, I assume she is considering my objection. I learn otherwise when she says, "If you show up, I'll tell Boris you said yes to his umpteenth request for a date."

My mouth slackens as my eyes widen. "You would never be so cruel."

Boris is lovely, but the name his mother chose for him matches his face.

He's a human bulldog.

Realizing she has me at her mercy, Alla says, "Enjoy the time off." She wheels a cart full of waste down the corridor. "And try to get some sun on those legs while you're at it. They're whiter than a hospital sheet and will look as red as the ones we collect from the OR if you don't prepare them for the sun bonanza they'll get hit with next month."

Giddiness flutters low in my stomach while I recall the three-day getaway I have planned with one of my oldest friends, but it doesn't alter the facts. "I'm not planning to spend the time sprawled on a pool lounge."

"Why not?" Alla asks, clearly disgusted.

"It's a hen party, not a vacation."

She cocks a brow. "A *destination* hen party. That screams margaritas by the pool and heatstroke that will put your head more in a tizzy than any orgasm you've ever had."

A groan rumbles in my chest when I fail to recall how giddy an orgasm should make me.

It's been so long that the memories are as dusty as the cobwebs between my legs.

I take a mental note to learn how to school my expressions better when Alla says, "Or perhaps you should work on whatever is going on with you right now." She leans in and takes a big whiff of my shirt. "Is that desperation I'm smelling?"

Yes, yes it is.

Since I can't say that, I return her hip bump before mouthing my thanks for a reason to leave guilt-free. I'll run from controversy before I will ever encourage it.

"I love you, girl, and don't act like you're about to become a stranger. Whenever you dump a clunky chest clamp on the OR floor and leave it there, you'll think of me."

"I will." I laugh, aware she is joking. After working with the department responsible for cleaning up a surgeon's mess, I will never leave any theater in disarray. "But if you think you're getting out of Donut Holes Thursdays, you're sadly mistaken."

Her smile competes with the OR light haloing her head. "I'll see you then."

"You will. Bye."

I wiggle my fingers in farewell. Alla uses her whole arm.

My steps are extra spirited as I walk toward the locker rooms all intern doctors use. Even with HosSterile having their own lockers for their staff to use, I keep my belongings in my hospital-issued locker. It saves taking up a space someone else may need.

When a severe bout of tiredness overwhelms me, I increase my speed. My apartment block is only a ten-minute walk from the hospital, so if I keep my focus on my bed and not a hope for a re-run of the event that's kept my pulse rampant for hours, I may achieve eight hours tonight instead of the four to five I usually get.

"Where are you?" I murmur when my dig through my locker fails to find the envelope Dr. Sidorov placed my offer in. I took it with me to the ER since my chat with Dr. Sidorov made me late for my shift, but I swear I left with it once my shift was over. I stuffed it under my arm before I...

My breath catches halfway to my lungs when I recall the last place I saw it.

I left it in Mrs. Ivanov's room.

When I close my locker door more abruptly than required, I apologize to the intern working the graveyard shift for startling him before making my way to the surgical ward. I'm not angry I need to visit Mrs. Ivanov again. I've been chomping at the bit to get an update on her condition all evening. I'm annoyed that excitement was the first emotion to blister through me—excitement that has nothing to do with the speed of Mrs. Ivanov's recovery.

My patient's health should be in the forefront of my mind, not my wailing libido.

"You didn't happen to pick up an envelope from Room 12A earlier tonight, did you?" I ask the nurse on duty at the desk. "It was white with a Myasnikov Private seal on the top corner."

"No, sorry." Before she can ask any of the questions in her eyes, a patient buzzes, demanding her attention.

I smile to assure her we're both fine before entering the corridor Mrs. Ivanov's room is located in. Since it is early, my knocks are faint. Most people are asleep at this time of the morning. I'm the only fool burning the night oil at all times of the day.

"Mrs. Ivanov?"

I brace the door's hinges so they only give out the slightest creak when opening before I tiptoe into the silent room.

I'm halfway in when I am startled by a light switching on. It beams from the corner Mr. Ivanov was shadowed by the night we met. Except it isn't Mr. Ivanov's almost sable eyes staring back at me. It is those belonging to my supervisor—the man I've been avoiding all day.

"Dr. Abdulov. You scared me." He leers at my skittish response but remains quiet, prompting me to ask, "Why are you sitting in a dark room?" I blame the late hour for my daftness. "And where is Mrs. Ivanov?" Her bed is empty, and not a single trickle of water can be heard.

My eyes snap back to Dr. Abdulov when he says, "She was discharged earlier this evening."

"Already?" When he nods, I ask, "Who authorized that?"

His glare leaves a sour taste in my mouth. He's clearly unappreciative of my line of questioning, but instead of calling me out on it, he lowers his eyes to the contract I came here to find. It is out of the envelope and ruffled like it has been flicked through. "Why haven't you signed that yet?"

I snatch up the document and place it back into the envelope before replying, "Because I'm unsure if this is the direction I want to take. I want to specialize in—"

"You specialize in whatever offers the biggest incentive." Again, he nudges his head to the contract. "That far exceeds anything you will receive in the public sector."

"Health isn't about profits."

He scoffs as if I am an imbecile. "Says every first-year intern."

"I'm a third-year surgical resident." His chin juts out sharply when I say, "Who would *never* let a patient's livelihood be jeopardized by undermining her medical condition." He attempts to interrupt me, so I speak faster. "A B12 deficiency isn't a joke. It can cause severe complications if not monitored and corrected by a team of medical professionals." I use my last word sparingly, because what I've witnessed the last three months under Dr. Abdulov's guidance hasn't been close to professional. "I will organize a discharge plan for Mrs. Ivanov this evening and forward it to her GP in the morning."

He slows my steps to the exit with a gravelly tone. "Mrs. Ivanov is *not* your patient."

"From what I'm hearing, she isn't yours either, because if she was, she'd still be admitted."

I crank my neck back to authenticate the anger in his snarled huff.

It is genuine. He looks seconds from ripping the contract out of my hand and tearing it in shreds, but for some reason, he doesn't.

He issues me a brief goodbye before he enters the corridor before me, leaving me utterly speechless that I dodged his wrath for the second time in under twenty-four hours.

CHAPTER FIVE

"You're still coming, right? We got our tickets with miles and are staying in a comped room, so accommodation and airfares are practically free. We just need to show up." Zoya stops, gulps, then starts again. "And maybe buy the occasional meal. I'm sure there will be a market close by. We can pick up some instant noodles. You still like those, right?"

The coffees I ducked out to purchase for Alla and me go cold when I move to the side of the entrance of Myasnikov Private to offer my best friend the support she's seeking. "I'm still technically a student, so even if I didn't like them, I'd still have to eat them."

She sighs in relief before getting down to the real reason she's panicked. "Do you think it's weird that I invited myself to her bachelorette party?"

"She's your sister, Zoya. Your invitation is automatic." Her breathing spikes again when I say, "Me, on the other hand..."

"You're *my* sister. That makes your invitation automatic."

"Maybe to your hen party, but I don't know if it counts for your sister."

"Our bond means she's practically your half-sister. That's close enough. I also really need you there. I don't know how I'll respond if *Mother* shows up." She says "mother" exactly how you'd expect any child with a loathing disdain for the woman who raised her to. "It will be bad enough having to deal with her at the wedding."

"She won't be there. The Trudny District isn't rich enough for her blood." She huffs but doesn't deny my claim. "And if she is, she can't get to you without first going through me."

"And this, ladies and gentlemen, is why she is my sister without sharing an iota of my blood." She shifts her focus from the imaginary people circling her to me. "I love you, Keet."

"I love you too, Z. I'll see you in a couple of hours. My bus should arrive around eight." When she grimaces, I say, "If I had any other option, I'd take it, but an Uber is too expensive with all the new taxes they've tacked on, and I sold Gigi's car last year to pay for Grampies' medication."

"I get it. I just..." When she realizes she is no better off than me, she tells me she loves me again before thanking me for always being there for her.

"Always. See you tonight."

"You will. Bye."

After storing my phone, I lift my eyes from the icy ground, startling when I spot Mr. Ivanov standing only a few feet across from me. He's dressed in far more clothing than the last time I saw him. His impeccably tailored suit and crisp business shirt combination adds to his commanding authority. It doesn't helm it.

He looks as in charge now as he did when he aided in my campaign to conduct Mrs. Ivanov's diagnosis without her going under a scalpel, like a business mogul who could hand over tens of millions of millions as easily as he did the accolades that saw me offered a new position.

I shouldn't say Dr. Sidorov's offer was a new position. If I had accepted it, I would have done the same things I've always done. I would have just been paid more to do it.

After checking the time and noticing I still have ten minutes left on my lunch break, I dump the cold coffees into the trash before storing the donuts purchased to go with them in my over-sized purse.

Once I'm sure my hair isn't a mess and my lipstick isn't smeared, I approach Mr. Ivanov. "Mr. Ivanov."

When he spins to face me, the frantic beat of my heart drops several inches lower.

Between my legs, to be precise.

He looks angry, and his unexpected response to being accosted has me blubbering out the first excuse that pops into my head. "Sorry. I won't take a minute of your time. I just wanted to—"

"Who is your friend, dear?"

Surprise blisters through me when Mrs. Ivanov's svelte frame clears the wide girth of Mr. Ivanov's shoulders. Then guilt settles in. With her coloring back to healthy and her eyes wide and bright, she is even more beautiful than first perceived. She could get any man she wants—even the one I've had numerous naughty dreams about over the past two weeks.

"This is Dr. Hoffman," Mr. Ivanov introduces, his tone far smoother than mine. "The doctor I told you about." His eyes are on me, hot and heavy. "Dr. Hoffman, this is my mother, Irina."

"Your mother?" I curse myself to hell when I vocalize my question instead of keeping it inside my head. When two pairs of identical eyes stare at me in shock, I blubber out, "I wasn't sure if she was your sister or your wife." *Mother! I meant to say mother.*

I'm saved from throwing myself into the trench I just dug when Mrs. Ivanov laughs. "I've been accused of being their sister many times, but this is the first time I've ever been mistaken for their wife."

She speaks as if more than just her son and me are standing across from her.

"Sorry," she apologizes when she spots the bewilderment on my face. My bedside manner is exemplary, but I need to work on schooling my expressions while trying to work out if a patient's quirks are neurological or part of their personality. "There was a time I could never get them apart. Now they're rarely together." Her eyes soften as they drift to her son. "Speaking of Matvei, you should probably give him an update. This development is no doubt interesting to all involved."

Dark hair falls into her son's eyes when he nods before he pulls a cell phone out of his pocket.

"Is everything okay?" I ask, too curious for my own good. "I tried to check up on you after you were discharged, but your contact information was as scarce as your admission paperwork."

I laugh like it's funny to lose a patient's admission.

Thankfully it makes me appear more caring than stalkerish.

"You checked up on me?" Mrs. Ivanov asks, her tone piqued.

I nod. "I organized your discharge plan and forwarded it to the GP cited on your online medical records. It was full of information on managing and living with a B12 deficiency." A frown crosses my face. "He wasn't overly interested when I spoke with him, but I was hopeful he'd pass on the information to you." I touch her arm before giving her the reassurance all practitioners should give their patients. "Your condition is manageable with the right management plan."

"He passed on some information," Mrs. Ivanov replies. "Although he failed to mention it came from you."

I want to act surprised by her admission, but I am not. Her confession is one reason I turned down Dr. Sidorov's promotion. I don't think the private sector is the right fit for me. I got into medicine to help people. Profits should never come into it—not even when you're struggling to rub two pennies together.

After looping her arm around my elbow, Mrs. Ivanov meanders us toward a taxi rank. "Come. Walk with me while Maksim takes care of business. We have much to discuss."

Her perfume is as powerful as the silent warning her son hits her with when he eyes her peculiarly. He doesn't exactly glare at her. He more gives her a look like the one I hit Zoya with whenever we went out drinking in college.

Once we're at a safe distance, Mrs. Ivanov says, "You'll have to excuse Maksim. He has a hard shell, but it is only to stop his gooey insides from spilling out."

Maksim proves he has supersonic hearing by scoffing.

With a smile that proves she likes ruffling her son's feathers, Mrs. Ivanov sits on a park bench edging the sidewalk before gesturing for me to join her. I move closer but remain standing. Benches are full of germs, and I need to save the sanitizing wipes in my purse for the bus trip I'm taking later tonight.

I remained living at my grandparents' apartment for a reason. It is close enough to the hospital that I'll never have to use public transport.

Public modes of transport give me the ick.

Their apartment is a little pricier than the other one-bedrooms in the area, but what I save in transport fees more than makes up the difference.

I've also not had a single sick day in the past three years.

Mrs. Ivanov mistakes my germ phobia as fear. "I won't bite, dear." She doesn't attempt to alter her volume when she adds, "Although from how highly Maksim has spoken of you the past two weeks, I may be the only Ivanov keeping their teeth sheathed."

Maksim's eyes shoot up from his cell phone while my eyes rocket to him. "Ma."

"What?" she replies, her eyes gleaming like she's proud she once again forced him to respond. "Was anything I said untrue?"

Heat creeps across my cheeks when Maksim remains quiet.

It returns my thoughts to when I walked in on him in the shower and has me hopeful for another spontaneous run-in.

My prayers appear as if they'll be left ungranted when a dark sedan pulls in behind the bench, completely ignoring the angry honk of the cab driver he cut off. The SUV is fancy and heavily tinted. I highly doubt it charges by the mile.

"That will be for me."

"Careful," I request when Mrs. Ivanov bounds off the bench like she has somewhere important to be. She may, but she'll end up back as my patient if she doesn't slow down.

When I say that to her, she blows a raspberry that doesn't match her style or sophistication. "You could never be so unlucky."

My heart melts when she wraps me up in a motherly hug like she's known me for years. Or perhaps she knows it's been years since I've been engulfed by a warmth only a mother can offer. I haven't experienced my mother's hugs in over eight years, and the last one we shared was as cold and unloving as the ground she was buried in only an hour later.

After thawing sections of my heart that froze when I lost both my parents within days of each other, Mrs. Ivanov caresses her son in the same manner. I don't know what she whispers in his ear, but his eyes flick to me numerous times, and he awards her the occasional nod.

Mrs. Ivanov's perfume whips up around me when she glides past me before slipping into the back of the SUV, passing a large black man holding open the door for her.

"Trust your instincts." I realize her request may not be solely for me when she adds, "They brought us back here for a reason, but they may not be all bad."

After waiting for Maksim to nod, she signals for the driver to go, leaving Maksim butting shoulders with me on the footpath.

My surprise is so high it takes her SUV melding into the

peak-hour traffic before my mouth will articulate anything. "Are you not going with her?"

"Eventually."

I feel Maksim's eyes on me for several long seconds before I build the courage to stop watching snow flurries fall around us and twist to face him.

He smirks as if he appreciates my strength. He shouldn't. My insides are in so much turmoil it is like the grade three dance recital all over again. I'm seconds from vomiting on my shoes.

"I have some matters I need to take care of here first."

"Here?" I don't give him the chance to reply. "I didn't realize your family's real estate portfolio extended this far inland."

I cringe at my inability to think on the spot. My reply disclosed my research didn't end when I unearthed his mother's medical history. I delved into their private affairs as well.

It didn't disclose much, only that the Ivanov name is attached to numerous development applications and structures across the globe.

After staring long enough for the snow to melt, Maksim says, "It hadn't previously." A ghost of a smile creeps onto his mouth, and it does wild things to my insides. They're definitely good jitters because they're the same ones that fluttered in my stomach when I walked in on him in the shower. "This is a new venture I recently unearthed an interest in."

"Cool."

Who the hell says "cool" anymore, Nikita?

"I hope it goes well for you."

He takes a moment to authenticate the sincerity in my tone before he dips his chin in gratitude.

Tension thickens the air with humidity, but before it can stick to my skin, Maksim glances over my shoulder. I miss who has caught his attention since they dart through foot traffic like they're attempting to outrun the Grim Reaper, but Maksim seems eager to catch up with them.

He mumbles a quick goodbye before he takes off after them, leaving me confused and devastated on the footpath.

CHAPTER SIX

"I'm on my way now." A valid excuse drowns out Zoya's shocked huff. "A patient came in with severe stomach cramps, and there was a rostering issue with the student doctors." I hustle past a patient wheeling his IV stand outside so he can get his daily hit of nicotine. "And then I called Gigi to make sure everything was okay. You know how much she loves to chat." I barely stop to suck in a much-needed breath. "I'll still be there in plenty of time, and I checked in online, so I can go straight to security."

"Okay."

Her calm response is shocking.

She is usually more vocal when stressed.

"Is she there?" I don't need to say her mother's name for her to know who I am referencing. My high pitch announces my worry without additional words needed.

I breathe a little easier when she replies, "No. It's just—"

She's interrupted by my cell phone sounding a long, annoying beep.

"Shit. I forgot to charge my phone." When I'm not riled about how even my cell is forced to operate with minimal recharges, I say, "Zoya...? Z...?"

I pull my phone from my ear and cuss when I notice it has begun its shutdown.

After storing it in my pocket, I sprint through the revolving door of Myasnikov Private Hospital. My speed is so brutal a woman is flung into the hospital foyer so forcefully she almost stumbles.

"Sorry."

I'd offer a more heartfelt apology if I had more than a minute to race to the bus stop half a block down. I can't miss this trip. It hasn't been in the works for months, but the instant it was brought up, I promised Zoya I'd be her plus-one.

The briskness of the evening air flapping my jacket out should be the first indicator of the slippery conditions I've merged into, but my brain doesn't register that the ground is icy until my stilettos lose traction with the slush-covered concrete.

I skid for several feet before I crash into a wall of hardness. The soles of my pumps are worn from hours of rounds. There's barely any tread left. So even with my skid ending, I still flap and wail like a chicken released from a coop when my feet continue to slip out from beneath me.

I'm saved from landing on my ass with a thud by digging my nails into the arm of the spicy-scented man keeping me upright. It is a cruel clutch that has me wishing I hadn't placed myself first.

"I'm so sorry..." The rest of my apology traps in my throat when I raise my eyes to my savior. His murky, almost black eyes are familiar, and just like every time I've caught their attention, they set my heart racing. "Maksim..." Like a freight train crashing, worry smacks into me hard and fast. "Is your mother okay? I tried to caution her to slow down, but she doesn't seem the type to—"

"Listen? Act her age? Continually change her mind on a

whim?" He smirks at me, and it has me as giddy as a teen girl meeting her idol. "If it is the latter, you may need to reevaluate your belief."

While smiling at the mirth in his tone, I correct my footing before placing a smidge of distance between us. Not a lot. Just enough to breathe without my erect nipples grazing his arm. "I was going to say she doesn't seem like the type to take unwanted medical advice. But if you need to vent, I've been told I'm a skilled listener."

His smirk turns into a smile. "Thank you for the offer, but there isn't enough time in the world to work through all my kinks."

With so much attraction firing in the air, my reply literally kills me. "I'd love to prove otherwise, but unfortunately, I can't. My bus"—my heart sinks when my eyes shoot down the street—"is leaving without me."

Shit.

It's the last bus to the downtown district. If I don't catch it, I won't be able to keep my promise to Zoya. That'll be worse than the corny lines I just tossed out. I've never been good at flirting, and tonight's attempt proves it is still a skill I lack.

The blows keep coming when I dig my cell phone out of my pocket to see if I can rummage up enough funds from an over-drawn credit card to pay an Uber fare.

I can't even order an Uber since my phone's battery is flat.

Double shit.

"Come with me."

Not waiting for me to reply, Maksim removes my carry-on bag from my grasp, flattens his spare hand on my lower back, and then guides me toward a foreign-plated car that is gaining nearly as many admiring stares as his animalistic walk.

He moves with such purpose, and before a single thought can conjure in my tired head, I'm seated in the back seat of the flashy ride next to him, and he instructs his driver to go.

As the driver finds an opening, I swallow to relieve my parched throat. The heat is at a nice setting, but it is impossible to sit next to a man with such pulse-setting good looks and not feel thirsty.

Maksim must also feel the heat. Two miles from the hospital, he adjusts the sleeves of the business suit he's now wearing minus the jacket. He only tugs them up an inch, but it exposes what I feared.

I was the only one saved from injury when he sheltered me from the icy ground.

My nails pierced into his wrists so brutally I punctured his skin.

"I'm so sorry—"

When Maksim's growl cuts off my apology, I use actions instead of words to express my sorrow. I dig a strip of Band-Aids and the sterile wipes I had planned to use on the bus out of my oversize purse before scooting to his half of the cab.

His scent is more pungent now, almost like he undertook strenuous activities during our time apart. It has my insides jittering like I'm submerged in below-freezing waters, but I act like the professional I'm meant to be. I wipe over the nail-width indents with the equivalent of a sterilized baby wipe before covering them with Band-Aids.

"At least they're not the Hello Kitty ones I've been using all week," I say when Maksim grunts about the superhero-themed Band-Aid I place on the angry red indents on his wrist. "They were pink and highly emasculating. The perfect accessory for the little princess warrior I took care of today."

My fondness for my profession can't be missed in my tone.

It is exhausting, but the rewards to come will forever make up for that.

"I thought you were studying to be a surgeon?"

"I am," I agree, my smile picking, knowing that he must have researched me like I did his family. "But the plan is to specialize in pediatric neurosurgery, so a few months in the pediatric ward will greatly assist with that plan."

Dr. Sidorov thought he was punishing me for being ungrateful when he placed me on the ped's roster. He couldn't have been further from the mark. This has been my goal since I was ten.

"Why pediatrics?" Maksim asks, his tone genuinely interested.

I give him the answer I gave in my college admission assessment. "There is substantial inequity in survival outcomes for pediatric brain tumor patients residing in high-income areas compared to low-and middle-income areas. I want to change that." I swallow to make sure my voice doesn't crack with emotions when I realize how close to home my statement hits. "A patient's care shouldn't be based on the tax bracket in which their parents reside. Healthcare should be the same across the board. Wealth shouldn't enter the equation."

"A million doctors and pharmaceutical companies disagree with you."

My huff ruffles a wisp of hair fallen from my bun. "If people stop thinking you must be rich to be successful, greed will only ever be an issue of the heart." I laugh like the donuts I purchased today for Alla and me aren't squashed in the bottom of my purse. "Although that could be just as dangerous. My heart always craves more donuts than my stomach can handle."

Once I peel off the protective strip of a fourth Band-Aid and set it into place on Maksim's left hand, I lift my eyes to gauge his response to his big, manly hands donning cartoon characters.

Air traps in my lungs when our eyes lock. I didn't realize I had scooted so close to him. Barely an inch of air is between us. I've practically crawled onto his lap during my assessment of his wounds.

"I'm so sor—"

I swallow the remainder of my apology with the spit his growl instigates. I've never heard such a brutish yet arousing sound. It could only be more delicious if it were vibrating through my clit instead of my lips.

I should pull back.

I should do anything but return his stare, but for the life of me, I can't get my body to cooperate with my head.

It refuses to budge since all its focus is devoted on how wild his hooded gaze makes me feel.

Ecstasy is trickling through every inch of me, and he isn't even touching me. I can only imagine how explosive it would be if he'd answer one of the shameful pleas beaming from my eyes.

I'm all but begging, and it fills me with so much shame. When I spot the bus I should have caught in front of us, I shift my eyes to the driver's beady pair watching us in the rearview mirror before saying, "If you pass the bus, I can get out at the next stop. I don't want to be an inconvenience."

When the driver strays his eyes to Maksim, seeking his thoughts on my proposal, Maksim waits a beat before he shakes his head.

"I'm also going to the airport, so it's no bother."

"We're going to the airport?" I can't see the driver's brows since they're hidden behind floppy, unkempt hair, but from the highness of his tone, I imagine they're cocked.

Maksim's glare is hot enough to melt ice when he returns the driver's watch. "Yes, we are."

The driver's gulp is audible before he signals to pull onto the freeway.

Although hostility is rife, I sink low into my chair before attempting to strike up a conversation. "Are you going home?" I ask at the same time Maksim queries, "Was the rest of your luggage pre-delivered to the airport?"

"Oh... No. This is all I need." I kick my carry-on he placed on the floor between us. "I'm only going away for the weekend, so I don't need much."

Maksim tugs down the sleeves of his shirt, covering most of the Band-Aids, before asking, "To Trudny Peninsula, right?"

I startle, dumbstruck he eavesdropped on my conversation with Zoya more than I realized. "Yes. I'm traveling with a friend. It is her little sister's hen party." When he replies with a simple nod, I ask, "Have you been to the Trudny Peninsula District before?"

He jerks up his chin. "A handful of times."

"Any recommendations?"

He wets his lips before aligning his eyes with mine. "For?"

"Places to eat. Visit. I don't have a lot of funds, but I've heard you don't need it at Nakhodka."

When his jaw tightens, I wonder if I said something wrong. Not everyone is a fan of penny-pinchers, but my budget consciousness has never caused such a severe reaction before.

Maksim takes our conversation in a direction I never anticipated. "What happened to the big payout you were recently offered?"

I swallow harshly, my throat drier than a desert.

How does everyone know about the promotion I was offered, but fail to keep abreast of it?

And I wouldn't exactly call it a big payout. If I had accepted the position, once income tax gobbled up a chunk of it, I would have only had enough to pay off one of my credit cards. My tuition and Grandfather's medication would have had to wait.

Although I don't owe Maksim an explanation, I give him one. I'd still be working in the ER if he hadn't funded the new wing at Myasnikov Private. "I turned down the placement."

He looks shocked, and his bewilderment jumps onto my face when he says, "So how can you afford to live in the Chrysler building not even half a mile from the hospital?"

The glitziness of his tone is highly inaccurate. Apartments in my building rent in the high six figures a month, but mine is the equivalent of a servant's quarters. It is cramped, dingy, and damp.

I often wonder if the moldy conditions are aggravating my grand-father's emphysema.

But despite this, it would still be outside my means if my grandparents didn't have a rent control agreement in place.

Housing in Myasnikov skyrocketed three years, pricing most people out of the built-up areas. Even dumps on the outskirts of town fetch top dollar.

"You do live there, right?"

"Yes," I reply, talking through the burn of a dry throat. "But it isn't as glamorous as it sounds."

With the tension turning awkward too fast for me to save, I've never been more grateful for the slow flow of traffic that always impedes the departure lanes of a local airport terminal.

After sliding to my half of the cab, I snatch up my bag, throw open my door with so much urgency the driver has no choice but to stop, and then hightail it out.

"Thank you so much for the ride."

I slam the door shut before Maksim can vocalize a reply, then suck in a relieved breath like I dodged a bullet I didn't realize was targeting me until now.

CHAPTER SEVEN

O utside departure gate 27, I crash into Zoya so viciously that I wind myself.

Since I exited Maksim's chauffeur-driven car at the Pobeda gates, I had to hustle through several other airlines' drop-off points before arriving at Aeroflot's terminal.

"I am so sorry I'm late. I—"

Zoya shushes me like she also loathes apologies. "You're here now, and that's all that matters." She steals the last of the air in my lungs with a big hug before inching back and twisting us to face the airline worker at the boarding station. "This is who we were waiting for."

"Wonderful." I wonder just how late I am when the air hostess gestures for us to walk down the gangway a second after scanning the paper boarding passes Zoya hands her.

"She didn't weigh my carry-on," I whisper to Zoya as we walk side by side.

Since we redeemed credit card points for our flight, we're not entitled to baggage—not even a carry-on. The rule is one personal item per passenger, such as a purse or a handbag. My carry-on is bigger than a gym bag and weighs over the two-pound limit stipulated on my ticket.

"I wasn't charged for a checked-in bag either." Zoya swivels around and walks backward before waggling her brows. "I thought it was because the baggage clerk was a breasts man."

I laugh when she wiggles her rack from side to side. Her DDs are natural and rarely saw us purchasing our own drinks throughout college.

"If only your tatas could pay off student loans."

She stops shaking her boobs before raking her teeth over her bottom lip.

"Z..." For one letter it drags out of my mouth for an extremely long time. "What did you do?"

"Nothing," she denies with a shrug.

I don't believe a word she speaks. Guilt crosses her features, as apparent as the deceitful flare darting through her impressive eyes.

She huffs at the mothering cock of my brow before announcing, "I got a new job."

I wait, confident that isn't the cause of the unease in her tone.

I'm right.

"It is at Le Rouge."

My eyes bulge as words crack out of my mouth like a whip. "The strip club?"

She shushes me with more than a wave of her hand this time. She clamps it over my mouth.

"Could you say it any louder? The losers in economy missed what you said."

I can't answer her since she has my mouth fastened, but the worry blistering through me must speak on my behalf.

"I've looked everywhere. No one is hiring."

When she removes her hand from my mouth with a heavy sigh, I say, "I could ask—"

"No, Nikita. You can't keep bailing me out."

"You seem to forget how often you do that for me."

She loops her arm around my elbow before continuing down the gangway. "I show up and sit with your grandma and grampies for a couple of hours. It's nothing."

"Seven hours isn't a couple." I air quote my last two words.

She brushes off my comment as if it is nothing. I learn why when she murmurs, "It's good for my soul. They ground me."

"Gigi will ground you for life if she finds out you're working at Le Rouge."

She tugs on her nonexistent collar before jumping a few steps ahead to hand the air hostess our boarding passes. She isn't panicked about my threat because she knows as well as I do that I won't expose her secret to anyone—not even my beloved grandparents.

Other than me, Zoya has no one in her corner.

I hate that even more than realizing her business degree could only secure her a position at an establishment owned by a criminal entity.

"Z..." My voice is as apprehensive now as when she said she works at Le Rogue when she commences walking toward the front of the plane instead of the back.

"I was as surprised as you when I collected our boarding passes," she replies when we're directed to lush cubicles with flat-lay beds, large monitors, and nooks filled with various snacks and beverages.

I removed a pair of jeans from the minimal selection of clothes I packed to ensure I had room for my Kindle since our ticket stated no inflight entertainment would be provided during the flight.

"This is me," Zoya says in the middle of the first-class section of the Boeing 737. "You're a few spots up."

After accepting the boarding pass she's holding out, I move to the suite marked next to my name on my ticket. It feels surreal—

even more so when I notice silk pajamas and an amenities kit have been left on my seat.

"Don't overthink it. Just enjoy," Zoya says, scaring the living daylights out of me.

Her airline-supplied pajamas tickle my arm when she scoots by me. She would never look a gift horse in the mouth and turn down its unexpected offerings.

We're so different. I'm shocked we've been friends for as long as we have.

Before she disappears behind a wall at the front of the plane, Zoya asks, "Do you think you'll sleep?"

My screwed-up nose should answer on my behalf, but my thumping head thinks I can be persuaded. "How long is the flight again?"

Zoya twists her lips. "Around six hours."

I mimic her nonchalant response before answering, "I guess it wouldn't hurt to try."

I give up on my endeavor to sleep five minutes after takeoff. With my hours drastically reduced over the past two weeks, I've secured approximately six hours a night. My body refuses more.

After dinner is served, I use the downtime well. I study with the online textbooks I downloaded illegally on my Kindle and ace the quiz on the inflight entertainment system.

I'm a little bored now, though. I don't usually have time to twiddle my thumbs. This is the first time I'm glad I don't have a lot of downtime. My life may be chaotic, but it is better than being bland.

I pretend to stretch, but I'm actually peering over at Zoya's cubicle to see if she's awake. She passed out before the hot towels were handed out.

When I notice she's still napping, I twist back to face the front of the plane. I'm about to plop back into my seat, when the quickest flash of a superhero Band-Aid peeking out the bottom of a cuff stops me in my tracks.

It can't be Maksim, surely. From what my Google search has unearthed, his family usually travels by private jet, so why would he be on a commercial flight? The first-class suites are more luxurious than anything I've experienced, but wouldn't compare to a chartered jet.

Too curious for my own good, I slip out of my cubicle and go to the front of the plane. The bar for business class travelers is as showy and varnished as the cubicles that offer unexpected privacy when traveling long distances. Bottles of expensive liquor line the wall behind the glossed bar, and a handful of travelers fill the stools in front of the oak counter.

The décor is the only thing of value in this section of the plane, though.

Most of the men seated around the bar are drunk and eyeballing me like I'm more appealing than the three-course meal they were served at the commencement of our flight.

"What can I get you?" asks the bartender, foiling my quick getaway.

His question catches me off guard. I was snooping, not looking for a drink, but I reply remarkably fast for someone not adept at thinking on the spot. "Bourbon and Diet Coke, please."

When he dips his chin, I continue to scan my fellow travelers.

I must have been hallucinating. A man with an aura like Maksim's would stand out in a crowd, so it should be almost suffocating in the small confines of a plane's bar.

"There you go." The bartender places my order between two men with bulky shoulders and seedy mustaches.

"Thank you."

My breasts squash against one of the man's shoulders when he fails to budge so I can collect my drink. His breaths quicken like my budded nipples are from his demoralizing gawk instead of the cool conditions, and when he licks his lips with a zealous amount of spit, it is the fight of my life not to barf.

"Where are you going, sweetheart?" the stranger asks with a laugh when I veer for the exit. "The bathroom is in the other direction." His tone could only be more insinuating if he spoke while removing his wrinkled dick from his pants. "That's where you want us to meet, isn't it?"

My eye roll stops halfway when an unexpected pocket of turbulence shakes the plane. Its shudder is so firm the chuckles of the drunk travelers dull to a simmer, and half of my bourbon and coke splatters onto the crisp white shirt of the passenger in Seat 1A.

Not even proof that I'm not going mad will stop me from apologizing to the man with soul-stealing eyes and a dislike of apologies. "I'm so sorry. Your shirt. It's... ah..." My reply veers in another direction when I spot a bottle of soda water in the selection of beverages in his travel cubicle. "Fixable. Soda water will draw that stain right out. It can remove bloodstains, so I'm sure it can handle some bourbon."

Maksim remains quiet when I pluck him from his seat and veer him toward the bathroom the drunk passenger nudged his head at earlier. The rowdy crowd quietens so ruefully when we walk past them that you'd swear the seat belt sign had been illuminated.

My mouth falls open when we enter the bathroom. It isn't the standard washroom you find on most commercial planes. It's three times the length and double the width. The vanity has sample-sized lotions, perfumes, and aftershaves available, and to the far left is a shower.

A shower!

I remember the reason I forced a man into a bathroom with

me when Maksim snickers at my parted lips and hued cheeks. He's clearly accustomed to the finer things in life.

His dislike of my earlier request for some penny-saving tips is a surefire sign of this.

After walking to the vanity, I snag a handful of paper towels from the dispenser. Except they're not paper towels. They're rich and luxuriously soft cotton towels that deserve more than one brush before soaking them with soda water.

"This was the first skill I picked up at medical school. I went through socks more than any other clothes my first month." Once the cloths are damp enough to compete with the stain on Maksim's shirt, I spin to face him. "The big clamps they use to open the chest plate during surgery are super clunky. They're dropped during almost every operation..." My words fade for a moan when the image that confronts me far exceeds the extravagance of a ten-thousand-dollar airline ticket.

Maksim has removed his button-up shirt, and even though he is wearing an A-shirt like the night we met, since it is white and fitted, it clings to every cut line of his pectoral muscles, stomach, and arms as if he were shirtless.

The visual is enticing. So much so that I almost choke on my swelling tongue.

My eyes shoot up from the bumps in Maksim's midsection to his face when he says, "What are you going to do now, Doc?" My mind goes instantly to the gutter. I fantasize about the many places I'd love to run my tongue across but realize that isn't what his question was referencing when he mutters, "There's nowhere for you to run this time."

"I wasn't running last time," I lie.

His sultry grin sends a pulse straight to my needy pussy. "Really?"

He steps closer until I'm crowded against the vanity, and his lips brush the shell of my ear.

I won't lie. The briefest contact has me on the edge of combustion.

"You're a shit liar. It's almost on par with your ability to issue a heartfelt apology."

I sense his eyes on me as I stammer out a reply. "My apologies are based on the severity of my crime, so I rarely need to fall to my knees and beg for forgiveness."

My nostrils flare when he leans in so deep it announces I'm not the only one turned on by our closeness. He's hard.

"Is that so?"

I can't speak, so I nod.

He inches back and locks our eyes. I see anger there, but that isn't all they're displaying. "What if I believe you should?"

I bounce my eyes between his, which are more hooded now than earlier, before asking, "Should what?"

I melt like a popsicle when he answers, "Get on your knees and beg for forgiveness."

"You'd first need to tell me what I'm meant to be apologizing for."

The smoothness of my reply would have you convinced I'm not seconds from falling to my knees as requested. They're already buckled. It is just the placement of Maksim's thigh between my legs that has stopped me from toppling.

My pulse beats in my ears when he spins me to face the mirror stretched across one wall. "Why don't you tell me, Doc?"

"I have nothing to... *tell*." The gap in my reply is compliments to one of Maksim's hands gripping my throat while the other moves to the waistband of my stretchy black pants.

If his hold is meant to be threatening, he needs to try another tactic.

I only see it as erotic. My pants are thin enough for him to feel the heat of my pussy, and his aggressive hold on my neck has wetness pooling between my legs at a rate I'm certain will dampen his fingers in mere seconds.

I'm not the only one recognizing the sudden cause of my red cheeks and dilated eyes. After flaring his nostrils like his nose is an inch from my pussy, Maksim loosens his grip on my throat, opens my pants with a flick of his wrist, and then slips his hand inside the cotton panties I'm now wishing were lacy and scant.

An unladylike moan rips from my throat when he braces two girthy fingers against the opening of my recently waxed pussy. They're not deep enough to break the seal no one has pierced for over three years but intrusive enough to announce how wet he's made me.

"Fuck, Doc. You're saturated."

As he locks eyes with me in the mirror, he glides one finger between the folds of my pussy, opening and preparing me, before he slowly pushes it inside me.

His growl slicks his hand with wetness. "I knew you'd be tight. How long has it been?"

"A while," I gasp out as the spasms of my clit extend to my thighs.

"How. Long?"

I whimper when his thumb circles my clit, before answering, "Th-three years. Coming up three years."

With a pleasing moan, he increases the speed and length of his pumps. He finger fucks me for several long minutes, and the friction is delicious. It takes everything I have not to come on the spot. I'm only holding back because an unexpected pocket of turbulence reminds me of the unusual location where I decided to re-find my libido. If we were anywhere but in a washroom at thirty thousand feet in the air, I would have crumbled by now.

When Maksim adds a second finger into the mix and curls the tips to milk my G-spot in rhythm to the frantic throbs of my clit, the furious pulse raging through my body almost has me missing what he breathes into my neck. "Do you have any fucking clue how many times I've imagined seeing you exactly like this the past two weeks?" Wetness slicks between my legs when he rocks his hips forward, grinding his thick cock against my ass. "Every. Fucking. Day. Your face forced me to seek release with my hand every day for two weeks straight."

His punctured words exhibit anger, but since they're also delivered with precise swivels of his thumb on my clit, I push them to the back of my mind. I can't talk. Think. I can't do anything but surrender to the madness engulfing me.

I'm losing control. Consumed.

I am mere seconds from climax.

"Please..."

I feel too good to be embarrassed that I'm begging.

I'm feeling nothing but pleasure.

"Oh god, Maksim, I'm going to come."

"No."

I freeze as the fantasy surrounding me crashes back to reality.

"No?" I ask, certain I heard him wrong.

I didn't.

"Not yet. I want to be inside you when you come." He removes his hand from inside my panties and cleans his fingers with his tongue before he yanks my pants and modest cotton underwear to my knees.

I'm naked from the waist down, so I should feel exposed, but when he pops open the button on his pricy trousers and frees his fat cock, I can't conjure up spit, let alone an emotion no woman could ever experience when being eyed with so much zeal.

While returning my needy stare, Maksim grips the base of his lengthy cock before giving it a teasing stroke. "This is what you wanted when you walked in on me in the shower, isn't it, Doc?"

Strands of dark hair cling to my sweaty neck when I shake my head. "I... I..."

Talking is still above me. Watching him stroke his cock is better than I could have possibly imagined. It beads the crown with pre-cum and pushes my moans from husky mewls to wheezy screams.

After using the pre-cum pooled at the end of his gloriously long cock to wet the girthy head, Maksim says with a smirk, "You're still a shit liar, Doc. You've imagined this as often as I've pictured you on your knees, sucking my cock."

Now is not the time to be professional. I'm naked from the waist down in a washroom, for crying out loud, but I can't help but bite back when riled about disregarding an oath I pledged many years ago. "I thought you were a patient in need of assistance." My dainty laugh echoes around the washroom. "I thought you were your mother."

Bringing up his mother during sexual escapades probably wasn't the best idea I've ever had, but I could have never fathomed Maksim's response. Instead of responding with the self-assuredness he oozes by the bucketload, his cock softens as the angry glint his eyes had earlier returns more potent than ever.

"That's right. You were there to help *my* mother." He licks his lips like they're as dry as my throat, his nostrils flaring when he tastes me on his mouth. Don't ask if it is a good or bad flare, as I couldn't tell you. "The woman who birthed me. The woman who raised me. The same woman whose admission was never documented on *any* official paperwork. My mother was as fit as an ox before she arrived at *your* hospital." He steps back before tugging up his pants with the same aggression he used to remove mine. "I can't believe I forgot that's what started all of this." When he gestures his hand between us, he doesn't look at me like he did only moments ago. I would say he hates me, but since he's looking past me, not at me, I'm going to assume some of the fury is directed at himself. "I've often been told I put my cock before anyone." His eyes are back on me, hot and angry. "Never believed it until now."

Disappointment flashes through his eyes for the quickest second before he exits the washroom without glancing back my way.

CHAPTER EIGHT

"Are you sure you're okay?" Zoya asks as we exit the plane on the heels of the first-class passengers who glowered and snickered at me when I made my way to my seat after the pilot announced we were about to begin the descent. I would have never left the washroom if given the choice, but my options were limited. "You've been quiet." She leans into my side and lowers her voice. "I didn't snore, did I?"

"No." I gulp before correcting, "I don't think."

I haven't told her about what happened in the washroom. I'm clueless about how it went from exhilarating to disastrous in seconds, so how can I explain it to anyone else?

She probably wouldn't believe me anyway. My cheeks are still flushed, my panties are still saturated, and lust is still beaming from my eyes. Not even the flight attendant believed my mumbled excuse that I'd been in the washroom for so long because I was cleaning Maksim's shirt as initially planned.

It was wet from a soda water sponge bath and folded over my arm, but she still *tsked* me.

Her scorn took me back to my pre-med days and how the head professor was harder on me than everyone else. I thought it was because he wanted me to succeed, but I learned otherwise when my father was convicted to life behind bars.

His constant ridicule almost had me leaving medical school. I only stayed because Zoya got him off my back.

Married men will do anything for their wives not to find out that they're adulterers.

I'm drawn from sordid memories when the woman who will go to hell and back for me suddenly stops walking. After cocking her brow, Zoya fans her hands across her tiny waist. "Why do you smell like a hot hunk of a man with too much testosterone?" A second after her eyes lower to my neck, her mouth gapes like a fish out of water. "And what caused that red mark on your neck? Neither it nor that expensive aftershave I'm smelling were present when we boarded."

"Everyone on our flight now smells like a hunky man. It is the airline's preferred scent." I'm only good for one lie. It is all downhill after that. "And what mark? My neck feels fine. It isn't the slightest bit achy."

When I stupidly shoot my hand up to rub the stubble burn Maksim's beard left, Zoya's mouth no longer hangs open. It hits the floor. "You're the woman they were talking about in first class! You stamped your mile-high card in the bathroom during the flight. Who was it?" She twirls to face the people exiting the plane with us, making a spectacle of herself. "Which one of you horny fuckers claimed my BFF's airplane virginity?"

"I'm so sorry," I apologize to the men close enough to hear her before I clamp my hand over her mouth like she did mine earlier and drag her toward the baggage carousel. Once we're at a safe distance from prying eyes, I say, "I didn't lose my airplane virginity." When her nostrils flare like she is dying to call me out as a liar, I add quickly, "He would have had to fuck me for that to happen, and he didn't. He left me hanging." My next words are barely whispers. "I didn't even get to orgasm."

Her nostrils flare for an entirely different reason now.

She is disgusted.

Mercifully, she is more subdued when confused by the actions of the opposite sex.

After warning her that I know how to dismantle her voice box permanently, I slowly lower my hand from her mouth.

It takes her a moment to find her bases, but her voice is more respectable once she does. "One, who the hell would walk away from that?" While whistling like a construction worker on a building site, she glides her hand up and down my body. "And two, was penetration involved? Because if something was poked, it could be classed as virginity popping." She pays my gaped mouth and wide eyes no attention. "Remember Alekstar Quinovic? He had that issue where down there didn't work unless he was being poked in his..." She pulls a face I can read with no issues, and it has the tension tightening my shoulders easing a smidge. "He didn't class that as losing his virginity, but when it was multiple fingers and a handful of kitchen gadgets, my opinion on virginity popping changed."

Since she looks settled for a long conversation on a card she stamped far too young, I wrap my arm around her shoulders and escort her toward the luggage carousel our fellow passengers are surrounding. It is late—or early depending on whether you're a sun chaser—and I'm more than eager to get out of the clothes I've been wearing for almost twenty-four hours and wash off the funk of a long flight.

During the short trek, Zoya continues reminding me of the horrifying men she's met in her jam-packed twenty-eight years. Her trip down memory lane ends when we reach the baggage carousel assigned by the airline.

"What the..." She storms away from me with the determination of a momma bear about to protect her cubs. Her possessions are the only thing of value she has, so to see her clothing shredded and strewn across the conveyor belt of the carousel is devastating for her. "Someone is about to get a new asshole... and don't go looking at her." She points to the lady behind the lost baggage claim desk. "Because she's sick of cleaning up your guys' mess just like the rest of us."

I've never seen Zoya so quiet. Anyone would swear the 3,800-dollar compensation check she got for her ruined luggage was a million dollars. She wouldn't have gotten a single cent if our tickets hadn't been upgraded, but since she was first-class, she got the max and is tickled pink.

"Imagine how many margaritas this will buy." She grips my arm as her eyes widen. "Or maybe I could book us a private pool-side cabana. Then you'd have no excuse not to come swimming with me."

"Cabanas don't offer shelter from the sun's harsh rays in the pool."

She slaps my arm before she returns to daydreaming about the luxurious life she could live with her small windfall. I'm not as appreciative of the silence as you'd think. It gives my head too much time to wander back to my exchange with Maksim in the washroom and the possible cause of his rejection.

Twenty minutes of deliberation only awards me more confusion.

I am completely lost as to where his anger stems, and out of time to deliberate further.

We've finally arrived at our hotel.

"Wow. This place looks nicer than the online brochures."

Still accustomed to tipping from spending her formative years in the American schooling system, Zoya hands the driver a few low-domination bills from her purse before slipping out the back of his cab.

"It doesn't even look like the same hotel," I say after joining her on the footpath outside the massive steel-and-glass architectural structure. "Are you sure you said the right address? Your Russian is better than mine, but maybe you fudged an important detail."

"I did no such thing." She barges me away from her before I can search for the reservation she printed out this morning, then moseys into the elaborate foyer.

We added "Doctor" to my name during the booking process, hopeful it might award us an upgrade, but I doubt we will need it here. This place is so stylish. We stand out like a sore thumb in scrubs, shorts, and midriff T-shirts.

Zoya ribs me with her elbow halfway across the glistening marble floor that stretches from one side of the resort-like hotel to the next. "Act like we belong so we don't get kicked out."

My reply is barely a whisper. "They can't kick us out if we're guests."

Although I'm telling her no, I straighten my spine, roll back my shoulders, and tilt my nose.

We look ridiculous, but the check-in clerk acts oblivious. "Welcome to Signiel. How can I help you?"

"We're checking in," I reply when Zoya fails to acknowledge she was addressed. She's frozen at my side, gasping like a fish out of water.

"Wonderful. What name is on the booking?"

I remove the reservation Zoya pulled out of her pocket during our trek across the elegant foyer before handing it to the clerk. "Nikita Hoffman. Doctor Nikita Hoffman."

"Welcome, Dr. Hoffman." The clerk dips her head in greeting before punching my name into the computer.

I hold my breath, convinced we are seconds from being asked to leave.

My worry isn't warranted.

After a handful of taps, the clerk says, "We have you as our guest for three nights. Is that correct?"

"Yes. We leave Sunday."

"Wonderful." She bounces her eyes between a still-frozen Zoya and me. "How many keycards would you like for your room?"

"Two, please," I reply after ribbing Zoya, soundlessly requesting that she get with the program. She looks like she's seen a ghost. Her cheeks are as white as my legs, and her pupils are massive. "Does this hotel offer a buffet breakfast?"

When the clerk nods, I slip her a twenty with the hope it will get us on the buffet list for free.

She peers down at the crinkled note before returning her eyes to my face. "That isn't necessary." My disappointment doesn't linger for long. "Breakfast is included with your reservation."

With Zoya back on planet Earth, she taps the low-five I'm holding out for her. With breakfast included, we won't need to purchase hardly any meals during our mini getaway. Smuggled muffins and yogurt aren't a feast fit for a king, but they'll get us through the day with only the slightest grumbles from our stomachs.

"The elevators are left of the bar." The clerk slips two keycards into a mini envelope before handing it to me. "You will need to scan your card to select your floor." Her eyes once again bounce between Zoya and me. "If you need anything during your stay, my cell number is on the back of your keycard."

Surprise resonates in my tone. "Great. Thank you."

She smiles before asking if we need a bellhop to assist with our luggage.

"No. This is it." I gesture to my carry-on and Zoya's luggage, now housed in a garbage bag. "This is all we have."

The clerk hides her grimace well, but I don't need to see it to know of its arrival.

Eager to leave before we get any more looks of pity, I slip the keycard envelope into my pocket before helming our walk to the elevators.

The further we walk, the more fraudulent I feel. This place is impressive, with vaulted ceilings, chandeliers, and the aroma of wealth.

I hope one day to match the level of sophistication in this room, but I don't know if I will ever become accustomed to it. I didn't lie when I hinted to Maksim that I want my heart to be my only greedy organ.

"Shit," I mumble under my breath when a co-rider in the packed elevator asks what floor we need. She is closest to the panel, so she's hogging it like it's a slice of my grandmother's famous *ptichye moloko*. "I didn't check the room number the clerk wrote down."

"The ninetieth floor," announces a voice at the back before he leans over my shoulder to scan his room card and select the button at the top of many.

Even if I hadn't recognized his commanding rumble, there's no way I could mistake his scent—even more so since his cologne is now mixed with my perfume.

I'm proud that I make it to floor thirty-three before my curiosity gets the better of me.

I only peer back at Maksim for a second, but my gawk is long enough to announce he's replaced the button-up shirt I stuffed on top of my clothes a second before they commenced deboarding the plane.

He must travel with a selection of shirts, because this is the third one he's donned in less than twenty-four hours.

With the turmoil in Maksim's eyes as strong as it was in the seconds prior to him leaving me in the washroom, I return my focus front and center.

Not even a nanosecond later, Zoya leans into my side and whispers, "He wants to fuck you." She's quiet, but not enough for a lady with a hearing aid and an apparent disdain for personal space.

The hotel guest who popped my bubble within a second of entering the elevator coughs to demand our attention before she hits us with a cranky glare.

Over narrow-minded people, I crank my neck to Zoya and say, "He did." I don't care that we have eavesdroppers. I'm too confused to continue going at it alone. I need help, and who better to get that from than my best friend? "But he doesn't seem interested anymore."

"Because...?" Zoya leaves her question open for me to finish on her behalf.

"Because..." I'm clueless. Maksim announced at the start of our exchange that he used my face as inspiration while masturbating the past two weeks, but then he left me on the edge of orgasmic bliss instead of helping me over it. "Because he's a... patient's son?" My confusion makes the last half of my reply sound like a question.

I'm not the only one bewildered. Zoya looks constipated as she tries to follow the minimal crumbs I'm laying out. "And that matters how?"

"Because he... I..."

I'm saved from portraying a brain-dead idiot by a likely source.

We are here for her bachelorette party.

"Zoya?" Zoya's younger sister, Aleena, forms her mouth into an O as tears flood her bloodshot eyes. "You came?" When strands of platinum-blonde hair bounce in the aftermath of Zoya's nod, Aleena squeals so loud it could shatter glass, before repeating, "You came!"

When she bounds into the elevator with her giggling and

bouncing bridesmaids in tow, I'm no longer worried about homicide being cited on my death certificate as it was my mother's.

Death in a plunging elevator, though. That is now at the top of my list.

And perhaps the narrowed glare of a patient's unappreciative son.

CHAPTER NINE

The creak of a door slowly closing breaks into the living room of the monstrous suite I've been milling in for the past hour.

Zoya cringes about the noise similar to someone dragging their nails down a chalkboard before tiptoeing across the room. "That came many years later than expected, but followed a similar path to what I had envisioned."

She spent the last hour convincing her sister and her tipsy bridesmaids that 4 a.m. isn't the best time to go clubbing. That is usually when the good half of society returns from the club scene.

After filling a whiskey glass with a generous serving of vodka, Zoya spins to face me. "Are you sure you're okay with them staying here with us?"

"I'm sure," I reply, still unconvinced this is our room.

You can't really call our hotel room a room. It is more of an apartment with a kitchen, two bedrooms, a grand piano, and an endless supply of liquor.

"Are you sure you didn't mix up our keycards with Aleena's? A destination bachelorette party screams old money, and only someone spending their daddy's money could afford this room."

Zoya rolls her eyes at the unease in my tone. "I'm reasonably sure Aleena's room is on the floor she entered the elevator, but it's hard to get anything out of her when she's a blubbering idiot."

There's no malice in her tone. She is simply trying to act like she's not delighted by her sister's excitement that she arrived at her bachelorette party without an official invitation.

"I told you you had nothing to worry about." After removing the glass from her hand, I wrap her up in a warm hug. "I'm sure she understands why you left." When her exhale beads condensation on my neck, I add, "And if she doesn't, I'm not opposed to convincing her otherwise."

That gets a smile out of her. "I love you, Kita."

"I love you too... enough I'm willing to share a bed with you."

She wiggles out of my hold when I drag her toward the untouched bedroom on our right. "The last time we shared a bed, you humped my leg."

"That was you!"

She *pffts* me. "Whoever it was, girl-on-girl action isn't on the agenda this weekend." She moseys to her bag and removes a small package. "And to make sure it stays off, I bought this for you."

When she tosses me the box, I catch it. "What is it?"

Not looking at me, she replies, "Sleeping pills."

I cock a brow before rattling the box. "It doesn't sound like sleeping pills."

When she gestures for me to open my unexpected gift, I rip it open like I've never received a present. My cheeks turn the color of beets when my sluggish head clues in to what the small silicone device is.

"You bought me a sex toy?" I don't give her the chance to reply. "How the hell is this supposed to help me sleep?"

Zoya stares at me like I have a second head. "You use it to orgasm yourself into the sexual coma the limp dick on the plane should have placed you in." With shock keeping me quiet, she moseys my way, her hips swinging, her smile bright. "When was the last time you got a solid eight hours?"

I attempt to lie.

I don't know why. Zoya sees it from a mile out and squashes it like a bug.

"In that little cabin at Kolomna. Demyan had a peanut for a cock, but made up for what it lacked with a magic tongue and gifted fingers." She secures the trickle of desire the memory caused by adding, "I heard your screams from the lake, but I had to wait to tease you about it since you were passed out for eight... *whole...* hours." She says her final three words as dramatically as you're imagining.

"I was zonked from the alcohol we drank."

She gives me her best don't-fuck-with-me look. "You never drank when we went out. You didn't want to face the repercussions of underage drinking with your father, and none of the boys we hung out with were stupid enough to give you alcohol. Not if they wanted to live." She freezes before she cusses under her breath. "I'm an asshole who doesn't dese—"

I don't want to fight, especially since everything she said is gospel, so I interrupt her. "You're right. I did wonder what his response would have been, which is exactly why I didn't drink." I jingle the package in my hand. "But I still don't see this helping."

Zoya shrugs. "You won't know unless you try." She pulls her 'luggage' off the sofa she dumped it on before pulling out the made-up bed beneath. "Look at that, a fancy-schmancy bed solely for me."

"Remember those words when you're whining about a sore back in the morning."

She shoos off my warning with a wave of her hand like a bad back isn't a regular grumble of hers. Zoya is only twenty-eight, but she has the joints of an eighty-year-old.

"Are you sure you don't want to share a bed with me?" I raise the package in my hand. "I could test this out in the bathroom. It seems to be my venue of choice of late."

Zoya looks tempted to nibble on the bait I just threw out but thinks better of it when she spots the dark circles plaguing my eyes. "I'm sure. Sleep well. I'll see you in the morning."

Since she seems just as eager for some alone time, I tell her I love her before entering the main bedroom of our suite.

It is as opulent as the rest of the hotel. The king-size bed looks tiny in front of a wall that hides his-and-her walk-in closets. The bathroom is bigger than my entire apartment, and there is a jetted tub next to a double-headed shower.

"You should see the size of the bathroom, Z. It is massive." I assume I miss Zoya's reply because my voice is echoing in the bathroom, but I am proven wrong when my return to the living room unearths an empty space. The sheets on the foldout bed aren't even ruffled. It appears Zoya left the instant I was out of eyesight.

"Maybe she wanted to give you some privacy," I murmur to myself.

I love Zoya, but I'd rather dig a pen in my ear than hear her in ecstasy.

Perhaps she feels the same.

After showering and setting my alarm clock, I climb into a bed that is as soft as a cloud. It should take me no time to fall asleep. It is almost dawn, I'm mentally exhausted, and my body is acting like I underwent eight grueling rounds with World Champion Jacob Walters. Still, no amount of pleading sees me falling asleep.

I do the trick my sleep therapist suggested when my mother took me to her for advice during my senior year of high school. I pretend each limb in my body is weighed down and heavy from my toes to my neck, but the instant I reach my face, a thought pops into my head, and my muscles loosen up.

Zoya's gift catches my attention when I roll onto my side to rest on the cool half of my pillow. It isn't close to heatwave temperature here, but it is far nicer than the weather we've been experiencing in Myasnikov.

Zoya wasn't lying when she said that night ten years ago was the last time I slept solid. I haven't had over six hours in a decade.

Although I'm skeptical about her theory, with how weighed down my limbs have been since Maksim left the washroom, I test it by sliding my hand beneath the panties and silky pajama shorts combination I'm wearing under a loose T-shirt.

Shockingly, my clit is still firm and buzzing with excitement.

I swallow the thick knot of anxiety lodged in my throat before brushing my fingertip over the nervy bud. Excitement bubbles through me when the briefest touch elicits a ton of friction. It reminds me of the waves that rolled through my stomach when Maksim touched me for the first time, and how euphoric it felt when he slipped his finger inside me.

Within seconds, my fingertips dampen, and a faint lust-inspiring scent streams through my nostrils.

Pleasure skitters through me when I roll the tips of my index and middle fingers over my clit. I stimulate it until there's no doubt of my aroused state, and my limbs sink deeper into the mattress.

My shoulder blades almost join when I switch my fingers for my thumb. I swivel my clit like Maksim did while fucking me with his fingers before lowering my fingertips to the wet crevice between my legs.

"Please," I plead when a sensation I've never experienced when attempting to self-pleasure commences forming. It isn't as blistering as it was when Maksim brought me to the brink of climax, but its intensity can't be denied.

I've tried to get myself off many times in the past decade. This is the closest I've come to experiencing anything near enjoyable.

I groan when tingles race across my pussy before I lift my

hips, seeking firmer contact. I pretend that the thumb toying with my clit doesn't belong to me. That it is a part of someone far more appealing—someone far more dangerous.

"Yes..."

The knuckles on my hand not driving me to the brink turn white as my grip on the bedding firms.

I'm so close to the edge that I may break a record. It usually takes a lot to make me come, but I've not even been stimulating myself for two minutes, and I'm on the verge of combusting.

I don't deserve all the accolades. I'm not even sure I should receive a mention. Nothing happening to my body right now is because of anything I'm doing.

Maksim deserves all the praise.

I remember his words and how good it felt to have his hands on me.

I think back to how he growled when he felt how wet I was for him.

Fuck, Doc. You're saturated.

As similar stars form now as they did then, I finger fuck myself faster. I plunge them in and out of my pussy over and over again while I use the heel of my hand to incite my clit.

Waves of pleasure roll through me, making me pant and my thighs shake, but I don't fully surrender to the bliss I'm seeking.

"Please."

When I curl the tips of my fingers like Maksim did, I almost vault off the bed.

There's the extra pressure I need—the fuel I'm seeking to get this fire fully lit.

"Oh..."

I whimper desperately when the fingers inside my pussy and my thumb on the outside massage my clit simultaneously. The friction is addictive, but it isn't the sole cause of the sheets growing sticky. It is recalling that Maksim replaced the shirt I stole but didn't remove my scent from his skin.

He still smelled like me, and the memory has my knees pulling together and stars blistering behind my tightly snapped-shut eyes.

As my thighs tremble, I picture him using the feminine scent I left on his hand to stimulate himself. Is he stroking his cock with the same hand? Moaning my name as I am his? Is my face once again the sole motivator of his release?

You wouldn't think I knew the word "rejection" with how tightly coiled my body is. It felt how mouthwateringly thick and long his cock was when he pushed me up against the vanity of the washroom and then when he pulled it out and the lighting above caught the glistening droplet on the end.

"Ohhh..."

Desire burns through me when I pretend it is Maksim's head between my legs, lapping up my arousal, instead of the silky bottoms of my pajamas. I imagine him peering up at me occasionally because he doesn't want to miss witnessing my face in ecstasy, but his desire to taste me returns his mouth to my pussy often. He fucks me with his mouth. Punishes me with his tongue. Then he...

"Oh... oh... *oh*..."

I slam my hand over my mouth to lessen my moans as shockwaves dart through me. My orgasm is long and draining. It steals the last of my energy and reminds my limbs of the blissful heaviness they were denied earlier until I fall into a peaceful slumber.

CHAPTER TEN

My hands itch to pull up the covers, to stay asleep for a few minutes more, but my grumbling stomach refuses to accept no as an answer.

It is starving, and so am I.

Its rumbles are understandable. My unexpected run-in with Maksim and his mother kept my mind occupied, so I haven't eaten since lunchtime yesterday. Although I have an extra twenty dollars I didn't anticipate having after check-in, it could be used on something better than the food we could get for free at breakfast.

After a leisurely stretch, I sling my eyes to my cell to calculate how long I slept. My eyes bulge when I notice it is almost eleven. It isn't a record, but I set my alarm for ten, so why am I two minutes away from missing breakfast?

"Z!" I shriek while diving out of the bed and racing into the living room. "We're about to miss breakfast!"

"Huh? What?" She rubs her eyes before flopping her head back onto the pillow and covering her ears with its overhang. "Why are you yelling? It's too early to yell."

"Breakfast! We forgot breakfast."

With the alertness of the alarm that didn't go off, she jack-knifes into a half-seated position before gulping. "Breakfast?"

"Yes. We have two minutes." I check my watch, grimacing when I notice how close the hour hand is to the twelve. "If that." I throw her the denim shorts discarded haphazardly on the floor before hightailing it to the door. "I'll meet you down there. Hopefully I can stall them."

"Okay," she shouts through the rapidly closing door of our suite.

I jab the elevator button multiple times. If we weren't on the top floor of the hotel, I'd be tempted to take the stairs, but the rapid climb of the elevator closest to me saves me from an early-morning cardio session.

"Yes," I praise when it arrives in a record-breaking three seconds.

I slip inside before selecting the button for the foyer.

The doors are almost closed when a hand darts between them, forcing them back open.

"No..."

I realize I articulated my gripe out loud when Maksim's handsome features harden a second before he steps into the almost-empty elevator.

"Sor—"

A low rumble in his throat cuts me off.

When he spins to push the close-door button, my eyes drop to the spectacular curves of his lower back. His suit jacket is impeccably tailored and made from a thick woolen material most Russians are accustomed to, but it does little to hide the ridges and planes I pictured while bringing myself to climax.

Heated eyes steal my focus. Maksim is watching me in the brushed steel material of the elevator dashboard. He appears unappreciative of my prolonged gawk of his ass, so I try to think of something respectable to say.

When my comb through the limited supply of excuses in my head fails to yield anything decent, I shift my search to a part of my brain that rarely gets used—the personal side.

"Late brunch?" I ask when I notice he selected level two. That is where the restaurants and spa are located.

I don't know why I'm making small talk. He is displaying clear signs that he's disinterested in a conversation. I'm just struggling with guilt that I used his face to bring myself to climax. I either pretend he is my friend or blurt out a confession I don't want even my best friend to know.

She'd never let me live down the fact I climaxed over a man who rejected me.

I don't even know if I'll get over it.

It feels like Earth circles the sun a million times before Maksim finally replies, "Hoping to still catch breakfast."

"Same. I could have sworn I set my alarm, but this week has been such a clusterf..."—when his eyes connect with mine in the steel dashboard, and he glares at me with the same intensity as when I tried to apologize, I switch out my cuss word for one that's more appropriate, like I am speaking with my grandmother—"fudge, I'd forget my head if it wasn't screwed on."

His smirk is barely visible, but I act like I got a standing ovation from the audience at a comedy club. My insides gleam as brightly as my cheeks when my deviant head stores his facial quirks for future self-pleasuring expeditions.

I squirm like I'm busting to use the restroom, and the undeniable aroma of lust fills the elevator, which is awkward when we're joined by a couple on the thirty-third floor.

"Morning," I mumble before moving to the back of the elevator, fighting not to apologize for the atrocious conditions I forced them into.

When the elevator finally arrives on level two, Maksim gestures for the couple and me to exit before him. He could be being cordial because we're not alone, but it makes my heart beat a little faster.

Maksim's brow arches when I fail to follow the couple out.

"I'm going to the buffet," I announce, struggling not to gleam like a pig about to eat out of a trough. That's usually how I describe Zoya's and my eating habits when treated to an endless stream of food.

Maksim's crimped lips are more noticeable this time around. "The buffet is on the second floor."

"Oh." When I step out of the elevator, the undeniable scent of bacon, eggs, and sausages can't be missed—and neither can the concerned face of my best friend.

How did she beat me? We only stopped to collect one set of passengers.

"They're not letting us in," Zoya announces, heading my way. "They said the cutoff is eleven, and there are no exceptions for anyone." Her disappointed huff ruffles my unbrushed hair. "I think I have some mints in my bag."

I butt shoulders with her before joining her watch of the dismantling of the food we were hoping to consume. "It's okay. I have that twenty dollars I had planned to use for an upgrade. We could grab a day's worth of supplies with that."

It dawns on me that our penny-counting ways are being witnessed by the last person I want to subject them to when Maksim's demanding tone prickles the hairs on my nape. "Wait here."

Zoya eyeballs me as if my reaction to Maksim approaching the restaurant hostess will be more entertaining than their exchange.

She isn't far off the mark. I'm more jealous than pleased when Maksim's presence switches the hostess's personality from bitchy to bubbly in under a second.

She practically fawns over him, her gloating only ending

when she tilts out of his shadow and signals for us to enter the restaurant behind Maksim and her.

"Don't be jelly," Zoya teases as we enter a space that could seat hundreds. "Even if the buffet weren't included in his room package, I'd let him in too. He's hot!"

"Shut up," Zoya demands when her waddle out of the restaurant has her midsection swaying like she's in the last month of pregnancy. "I had to sneak in extra because you forgot to bring your coat to breakfast."

We're high-end grifters. We don't steal buffet food by walking it out in our hands. We hide it in our clothes. I just can't today because my sleepwear leaves little to the imagination.

I can't even hide a banana.

Well, I could, but that could gain me even more questioning looks than I got throughout breakfast.

The flirty hostess left shortly after seating us, but the staff required to replace the supplies they began dismantling when the clock struck eleven didn't conceal their surprise.

You'd swear they've never worked a minute of overtime.

I'm reminded why my maturity has dropped into an abyss the past twenty-four hours when Zoya says, "I've heard Greek yogurt is good for thrush, but I thought you were meant to eat it, not have it dribble down your thighs."

She often tells me doctors mature backward since they endure twelve years of nonstop studying and exams. I'm not meant to hit the teenage rebellion I missed out on during high school for another two years.

When Zoya grimaces, I inch back and lower my eyes to the back of her coat. "Are you leaking?"

I stop checking for any slip hazards she may have left for unsuspecting hotel guests when she replies, "Not any worse than you." She nudges her head to the cleanup crew once again dismantling the buffet. "They're not mopping up apple juice." Since I know her better than I know myself, I rib her with my elbow. It silences her for barely a second. "I get it. He's hot, and his leave-me-the-fuck-alone vibes only make me want to gawk at him more. But when he scowls..."—a moan vibrates her lips—"even my panties get sticky."

I almost laugh until I remember it will encourage more nosy-Nancying. "You need to stop bringing your panties into every conversation we have." Shockingly, my voice is professional, without the quiver of the giggles in my chest.

Zoya appears disgusted. "Why? I have a best friend for a reason."

When we reach the elevators, the closest one is open but packed with hotel guests.

Zoya wiggles her brows when one of the male riders exits so the "heavily pregnant lady" can take his spot. "I'll meet you up there."

I nod, and once the elevator carting her away reaches the third floor, I push the button to call another.

It arrives in under ten seconds.

"Ladies first," croons the unnamed man who gave up his spot for a fraudster.

I'll give credit where credit is due. He has charm by the mile and a face that matches his gentlemanly ways. He could be quite the catch. I just don't see his charm rubbing off on me. He seems a little too nice, and I learned fast during medical school that a saintly title rarely equates to its owner being an upstanding member of society.

After cursing my inability to let bygones be bygones, I enter the elevator first, as offered, before praising the stranger for his thoughtfulness. If I can forgive Maksim for leaving me hanging, I can forgive Dr. Schloss for not calling after a "thorough medical examination" of my vagina.

"Thank you. That is very chivalrous of you."

Shockingly, the hairs on my arm stand to attention when he shadows me into the elevator.

I realize the error of my ways when a stern demand quickly follows the elevator car's brief dip. "You can get the next one."

When my eyes shoot to the unnamed man, who is still stationed outside the elevator, he tries to fire off an objection, but Maksim's warning glare proves why the good guys need to scheme their way into a woman's panties.

They can't compete against men who unequivocally don't care about the consequences of their actions.

It is how my father won over my mother.

He always said it is safer to side with a wolf than a wolf in sheep's clothing because you know what you're getting with a man who doesn't hide his intentions.

I stop recalling the number of wolves in sheep's clothing working in the medical field when Maksim says, "Your friend dropped this."

A smile creeps onto my face when his twist exposes a banana, but since I don't want to look more pathetic than I already do, I ask, "Are you sure it was hers? Maybe it was one of the many other patrons at the buffet with us."

"I'm sure," he answers, following my ruse that the buffet wasn't solely re-opened for us. "It fell out of her coat halfway to the elevators."

"Oh..." I snatch the banana out of his hand. "Then that would be my lunch."

He either misses the humor in my tone or loathes budget-conscious people.

I'd say it is a bit of both.

When I issue him my thanks in a more respectable manner,

with a smile, he dips his chin before he turns back to face the elevator dashboard.

We climb eleven floors before I break the silence this time around. "Are you here on business?"

I hear him swallow before he answers, "You could say that."

"Will you be here long?"

Thud, thud, thud. That is the only noise I hear while waiting for him to reply.

For how long he delays in answering, I expect more than a one-word response. "Depends."

I wait, hopeful for more.

I get a smidge, but nowhere near as much as I want.

"Some contracts barely last a minute. Others can stretch into weeks."

"What are you hoping for? Minutes, days, or weeks?"

His tone is clipped when he answers, "What I want doesn't matter."

"Yes, it does. Your wants are as important as anyone else's, Maksim." My voice comes out huskier than intended. It can't be helped. The temperature in the elevator is roasting, and it has me conjuring up the many ways we could achieve the same sweat-slicked skin scent outside of this tin box.

It takes him half a lifetime to answer. "Do you know what I want?" He isn't looking at me but must spot my nod because he continues rather quickly. "I want to know why I think I'd know if you were lying when I don't even know you. I want to know why you won't leave my fucking head after everything you did."

Everything I did? What did I do?

Before I can articulate my questions to the person capable of answering them, Maksim crowds me against the wall and sneers through clenched teeth, "But more than anything, I want to know what hand you used."

His anger worries me, but since I'd need more than eight

hours of sleep to give it any justice, I veer for the nonviolent checkbox on his wish list. "Hand I used for what?"

When his eyes lift from my chest to my face, my breath catches. He's angry, but his fury isn't directed at me. He seems furious at himself, so you can picture my shock when his response is nothing like I am anticipating.

"Which hand you used to climax while pretending it was my head buried between your legs."

My eyes widen as my throat dries.

The situation between my legs is on the opposite end of the humidity scale, but I won't let him know that.

The only time a wolf isn't dangerous is when it is standing across from one.

"I did no such thing."

"You're a shit liar, Doc." My heart races when he snatches up my left hand. He removes the banana I'm clutching for dear life with so much force it turns to mash. "You're ambidextrous. You use your right hand as often as your left, so I kept jumping between the two when I pretended it was your hand stroking my cock last night."

My thighs shake when he unballs my hand and drags his nose down my sweaty palm.

His growl sets my skin on fire, but instead of taking a second whiff as my wicked head is hoping, he drops my hand back to my side before gathering up my right.

I don't object when he follows the same routine as earlier. I'm too mesmerized by the lusty glint in his eyes to do anything. I don't even pay attention to the elevator arriving at our floor.

Maksim looks as hungry as I felt before I gorged my weight in greasy breakfast food, but the only item on his menu is me.

I like that more than I should admit.

"You used your right hand," he murmurs a second after sniffing the palm of my right hand.

"I don't know what you're talking about. I didn't do anything last *night*."

I choke on my last word when he tugs me forward so fast that I crash into his chest. Then I moan his name like I did last night when he slides my hand down the front of his pants. He's hard, veiny, and the tip of his cut penis is weeping with pre-cum.

The silky droplets coat my palm in no time.

The same can be said for my panties.

I'm drenched, but before I can ashamedly beg for Maksim to finish what he started last night, he pulls my hand out of his pants and says, "Now I'll be able to hear and smell you next time," then exits the elevator like his head isn't spinning as ruefully as mine.

CHAPTER ELEVEN

Zoya's lips twitch, but not a peep escapes them. She's confused. I understand why. I just dumped all my bewilderment onto her, and I don't feel the slightest bit relieved.

"Nope. You need to go over it again," she requests a short time later. "He called you a liar before shoving your hand down his pants to intermingle your scents." She points to me as she says "your" and hooks her thumb at the matching penthouse next to us when she reaches "his."

"That's not what he did." When she glares at me while folding her arms over her chest, I backtrack on my fabricated statement. "Yes. Then he left."

"Because he..." Her words are delivered slowly as she struggles to sort through my brief yet confusing exchanges with Maksim. After a beat, the confusion clouding her eyes clears before they open wide. "He doesn't think you're married, does he?"

"No. But even if he did, would that stop him?"

Zoya shrugs. "Maybe he's married to some bigshot lady boss,

and she'd force him to kill anyone he cheats with. He could be protecting you." When I glare at her, she snorts in my face. "What? His suits scream mafia, and it is something I'd do if I were the Godmother of the Bratva."

I wish she were lying. Zoya has a mile-long jealousy streak and enough boxing hours under her belt to make any cheating spouse regret their stupidity.

"You'd be a terrible mafia boss. You would recruit anyone in a suit." She laughs but doesn't deny my claim. "Even Mr. Alcadoz."

That switches the laugh lines on her face to sprouts of annoyance. "My theories about his extracurricular activities haven't been discredited."

"He works in the morgue at our university."

Zoya gives me a look as if to say, *Exactly!* "Where do you think he gets all the cadavers from?"

I try to hold back my laughter. I bite on the inside of my cheek and pinch my thigh, but the instant she stares at me like she is expecting me to take her theory seriously, my resolve breaks.

I laugh like a hyena, and Zoya joins me.

"Oh my god," she breathes out several long minutes later. "I haven't laughed like that in forever."

"Same," I admit, pouting. "My life sucks."

If she glares any harder, she will pop a vein in her neck.

"I'm not looking for sympathy, Z. I just—"

"Seem to have forgotten you've got a hot hunk of a man losing his ever-loving mind over you." She stands like she can't continue without giving her lungs room to expand. "You're a doctor... a fucking good one, and you look like that." She thrusts her hand at me. "So don't give me the *my life sucks* line. Your life is awesome. You're fucking awesome. We just need to find a way for Mr. Grumpy Pants to pull his finger out of his ass before one of the many other men who'd donate their left nut to have you in their life snatches you up."

"I don't want to force him to do anything he doesn't want to do."

Zoya's glare is hot enough to melt ice. "You like him."

"Yeah. And?"

"And?" She wiggles her ear like something is affecting her hearing before repeating, "And?"

When I nod, she *pffts* me before telling me to get up.

"Where are we going?"

She ignores me, still focusing on the "and?" part of my reply.

"And?" She shifts her eyes to her baby sister. "Can you believe this girl? And?"

Aleena giggles like she's more clued in to Zoya's quirks than I am before joining us in the main room of the suite.

Over an hour later, while wobbling in sky-high stilettos, I drift my eyes to Zoya. "This is ridiculous. Who goes swimming in heels?"

Zoya finishes applying a gloss to her fire-engine-red lips before twisting her torso to face me. "Don't act like you were going to swim even if we were going to the pool."

Her reply stumps me.

If we're not going to the pool, why am I wearing a super skimpy bikini I plan to hide with an oversized T-shirt?

When I ask Zoya that, my answer comes from her baby sister, who is entering our room wearing a gorgeous crisscross one-piece swimsuit that is far more risqué than it sounds. Inches upon inches of Aleena's skin is on display, and she looks amazing. "Because that's what people wear at a bikini competition."

My eyes bulge as my throat becomes scratchy. "This is your grand plan? A bikini competition?" When Zoya nods, I shake my head. "Nope. Nuh-uh. I'm out." Stuff a tee that could become see-through with the slightest splash. I need a coverup my grand-mother would approve of. "I'm a doctor. I don't participate in bikini competitions."

My hand freezes halfway into my carry-on when Aleena says, "The prize money is twenty big ones."

"Twenty thousand *US* dollars?" I clarify, caught off guard by a Galdean before.

Zoya is very much one of those people who thinks "twenty bucks is twenty bucks." I guess that's why I shouldn't have been shocked when she admitted she works at Le Rogue.

When Zoya and Aleena nod in sync, my throat works through a stern swallow.

"Who the hell puts up a twenty-thousand-dollar pot for a bikini competition?"

My pulse doesn't know which area in my body to thud first when Zoya tosses a pamphlet for today's activities onto my rumpled luggage. "A real estate mogul who wants his guests to use the outdoor facilities of his fancy-schmancy new hotel even while it's cold enough for them to freeze their tits off." She shrugs like the rest of her reply isn't as important as the former. "And it's for charity. Even Gigi would get her nips out for charity."

I can't deny her accusation this time around, so I focus on the brochure she gave me. Although it is more about the charity swimsuit competition occurring today, the hotelier's business name under the sponsorship section can't be denied—Ivanov Industries—much less the name of one of the judges.

"Maksim is judging this event?" My eyes pop when my slug-gish head finally absorbs all the facts. "His family owns this hotel?"

Zoya looks at me like I didn't ace my college admission test. "Did that not click when he got us into a closed restaurant in under three seconds?"

"No." I hate admitting I'm an idiot, so finalizing my reply

takes me a minute. "I thought the hostess wanted to sleep with him."

"She did." Zoya laughs like anything she says is funny. "But I doubt all the servers did. Well, not all the male ones, anyway."

I stop hitting her with the stink eye to rival all stink eyes when Aleena says, "You know Maksim Ivanov?"

My reply stings my ego more than I care to admit. "Not exactly."

"She's being modest," Zoya interrupts, hating my inability to gloat even more than my inability not to apologize. "She saved his mother's life."

Aleena steps closer, and for once, is more interested in me than her sister. "You saved Irina's life?"

When Zoya nods, I mimic her movement—just more hesitantly.

I don't get the "wow" I'm anticipating.

Confusion is the gasoline of Aleena's interrogation. "When?"

"Two weeks ago." When I glare at Zoya, silently pleading for her to shut her gigantic trap, she deflects Aleena's interest in a patient of mine by asking if she has any last-minute bachelorette party wishes. "I'm hoping to finalize all the plans today, so speak now or forever hold your peace."

When Aleena's focus immediately shifts, I mouth my thanks to Zoya. Although I would love to ease Aleena's confusion, I can't. My patients' medical records aren't for public consumption. Accidentally telling Zoya Mrs. Ivanov was a patient of mine during my purge is bad enough. I don't want more wood tossed onto the dumpster fire I could face if anyone finds out I broke practician/patient confidentiality.

My hunt for a frumpy T-shirt is interrupted when Aleena's head bridesmaid's perfume tickles my nose. She's a little excessive with how much spray she uses, and it has me wondering if that's why she suffers so many sinus issues. "Weird question, but do you know if the elevators are monitored?"

"The elevators in the hotel?" Footage of Maksim shoving my hand down the front of his pants rolls through my head like a movie when Shevi nods. "Um. I'm not sure." When her nose screws up like a rabbit, I say, "We could check?"

Ignorant to the fact I could require her support more than she needs mine if the elevators are monitored, Shevi says, "That would be great. Thank you so much."

When she gets straight down to business, I rummage through my carry-on like it is double its size. I could have sworn I packed three baggy tees, but can't find one. There's nothing in my bag but a skimpy pair of panties and a clubbing outfit not respectable for daytime activities. Everything else has vanished.

"Are you coming?" Shevi asks, shouting to project her voice through the massive living room separating us.

"Yes. I just..." I swallow the rest of my reply before marching to the foyer. I'll have more pressing matters to handle than looking like I'm going for a swim if cameras are in the elevator. I could face charges for being a public nuisance. Or worse, committing a lewd act in public. A criminal record will have me stripped of my medical license before it is officially mine.

When Shevi races into the hallway, I follow her, clueless that I'm stepping into a trap until my foot is almost snared by the rapid close of the suite's door, and I bump into a snickering, heavy-breasted lady.

"Oh no," Zoya says, her pout as fake as the sincerity in her tone. "You left our room in only a bikini, and our keycard is still inside. Whatever will we do?"

When Shevi backs away with her hands in the air, mumbling that Aleena and Zoya forced her to join their ruse, I shift my focus to my soon-to-be ex-best friend. "This isn't funny. We're not freshmen anymore." I step closer before seething through clenched teeth, "Let me back into our room."

Zoya tries to pull off the picture of innocence. "I would if I could, but I can't."

It isn't a ruse she can pull off.

She looks like a cat who caught a mouse.

"Zoya..." The shortness of my reply can't hide the scratchiness of my throat. I'm on the verge of hyperventilating. I wear scrubs twenty-four-seven for a reason. They hide a lot of skin.

Zoya laughs when I pat her down like she's smuggling narcotics. "I honestly don't have it."

I wish she were lying, but her bikini is as skimpy as mine. There's nowhere to hide a grain of rice, much less a keycard.

That leaves me only one lifeline.

Aleena mimics Shevi's defense by portraying a woman on the verge of arrest before saying, "Don't look at me. I only asked if we could host part of the bachelorette party here. I didn't demand unlimited access."

"Oh poo." Zoya doesn't even attempt to act upset this time. "I guess that means we'll have to go down to the foyer and ask for another key."

Her smile grows when I mutter, "The foyer wouldn't happen to be next to the bikini competition area, would it?"

"No." I stare at her in shock. I should save my expressions. She doesn't deserve them. "But the registration desk for the bikini competition is right next door."

When she jabs the call button on the elevator, I fold my arms over my barely covered chest and firm my stance. "I'll wait for you here."

She enters the elevator behind Aleena and Shevi before spinning to face me. "Okay. But if my hand ends up down a billionaire's pants, I won't be held accountable for my actions."

Aleena's voice is so loud that I hear it twice when it echoes. "You put your hand down Maksim Ivanov's pants?"

"No," I deny, the solo word whipped from my mouth. "He put my hand down there."

Aleena's eyes pop before she turns into a mini version of her sister. "Get in. *Now!*"

She yanks me into the elevator by the strap of my micro bikini bottoms, cracking the elastic against my skin as ruefully as my heart strums my ribs.

CHAPTER TWELVE

I stop pretending my hands are a shawl to wordlessly ask the hotel receptionist where I'm meant to conceal my purse in my outfit—if you can call it an outfit.

"My purse is in my room with my room card. If it were with me, I'd give you my ID."

"I'm sorry, Ms.—"

"It's Doctor. Doctor Nikita Hoffman."

I hate the person I am being, but I also hate the gawks I've been getting for the past ten minutes when I refused Zoya, Aleena, and Shevi's begs for me to join them as a contestant at the bikini competition, so I had to leave the "competitors only" section of the hotel's outdoor facilities.

Our ride in the elevator exposed that they are monitored, so now I am wondering if I'm being eyeballed because I'm wearing dental floss in the foyer of a five-star hotel or because rumors are already circulating about how I got a penthouse suite comped for next to nothing.

"If someone could grant me access to my room, I will gladly...

show... them... my..." My words are spaced more and more when a man with a devastatingly handsome face enters my peripheral vision.

Maksim is approaching the guarded door Zoya, Aleena, and Shevi were ushered through seconds after I wished them good luck. He isn't alone. A beautiful blonde is at his right. They look cozy, like they could possibly know each other intimately.

It has me worried that Zoya is right.

Perhaps he is married, and I just gave up the opportunity to find out.

"Is it too late to enter the bikini competition?" When the clerk's lips tilt, I say, "I haven't done nowhere near as much charity work this year."

"I can check for you, Dr. Hoffman."

"Please call me Nikita." When her bewildered expression grows, I lower my chin and balance it above my chest. "And I guess a doctorate in medicine is charitable enough. It isn't like I'm doing it for the money." I laugh like my bank account isn't down to its last dollar. "Not yet, anyway. Hopefully never." Loathing the imbecile I am portraying, I hook my thumb to the bar. "I'll wait over there for my friends. Hopefully one of their bikinis has a hidden pocket sewn into it somewhere."

If researchers need more proof that sleep deprivation is the equivalent of being under the influence, they just got it.

I make it halfway to the bar before a dozen immoral stares have me twirling like a ballerina.

"The pool entrance?" I ask the clerk while pointing to the door Maksim walked through only moments ago.

"That is the entrance for the competitors," the clerk advises, her tone apologetic. "If you wish to attend as a spectator, you'll need to enter via the guest entrance." Her following words are barely whispers. "And pay an entrance fee." Her throat bobs before she says, "I can place it on your room tab."

"Of a room I don't have access to?"

She acts as if I never spoke. "It's two thousand rubles and tax deductible. I will forward a receipt for your donation to your email." She works so fast that the whoosh of an email being sent sounds from her computer a second before she signals for a man waiting in the roped-off section to move forward.

After breathing out my annoyance—and perhaps a smidge of nerves—I cross the foyer that appears far larger than it did when I checked in.

"It is okay. You're fine *and* dressed." My last word is solely for my swirling-down-the-drain confidence. I've never felt more naked, and I've had sex. It was just under the covers with the lights out like my self-pleasing expedition last night.

I didn't even feel this exposed when Maksim yanked my pants to my knees in a well-lit bathroom.

The heaviness on my shoulders slackens when I'm buzzed into a tropical paradise worthy of its hefty price tag. The land-scaped grounds are brimming with people of all genders and ages, and the lazy river has several hotel guests floating by on inflatable pool toys.

The further I merge into the bustling space, the more I smile. I thought the event would be as tactless as its stigma implies, but the vibe is more happening than sleazy. People are laughing and talking, a DJ is playing the latest hits in the far corner of the beau-tifully landscaped gardens, and a handful of women with heads of silver strands are tacking competition numbers onto their sequined bikini tops. The leader of the pack has a rocking body for a person her age, and her confidence makes the signs of age on her face nonexistent.

"Good luck," I encourage her as I veer past.

Her eyes twinkle with kindness when she replies, "I would offer you the same, but I don't think you'll need it, sweetheart. You are beautiful."

Her praise isn't the first I've heard today, but it is the first time I've believed it since it wasn't delivered with a sexual proposition. "Thank you, but I'm not entering. I am here supporting my friends."

I smile when she pretends to wipe sweat from her brow, and then I force my hands to my sides.

"Much better," she assures me, clearly missing the nerves fluttering in my stomach.

When the contestants are called to the stage area, I make a beeline for a bar to its left. It looks like it belongs on a beach in Bali. Leis hang from the thatched roof, and coconuts are spread across the battered wood surface. It looks so worn you would swear it has been here for years, not the two months this hotel has been operating.

"What can I get you?" asks a bartender with a cute smile and shaggy, surfer-boy hair.

"Ah..." As he places a coaster down in front of me, I scan the shelves behind him like I don't know I will only order tap water. I learned the hard way how expensive bottled water is when I graduated with honors. "I think I'll stick with water. I don't want to become dehydrated." My confidence takes another hit when I'm forced to ask, "It's free, right?"

I breathe a little easier when he jerks up his chin.

After filling a cocktail glass with water and adding two olives so I don't look like a loser, he places it in front of me and then angles his head. "You're the girl from the buffet, right? The one who arrived late with her friend?"

My balk is louder than my reply. "Yes. That's me."

He steps back before fanning his arms wide. "Then why the hell are you drinking tap water? The bar is your oyster, baby. You can have anything your heart desires."

"Huh?"

He smiles like my daftness is cute. "You're staying in the penthouse. That means everything in the hotel is free."

The thudding of my penny-pinching heart echoes in my reply. "Everything?" When he nods, I ask, "What about the steakhouse restaurant on the second floor?"

"*Everything.*" He says one word as if it is several. "You can have anything your heart desires, and it'll be at the Ivanovs' expense."

Like a genie being summoned from a lamp, Maksim exits a poolside cabana closest to the stage. An unlit cigarette hangs from his mouth, and his business attire has been switched for board shorts and a black T-shirt. He's casual, sexy, and dangerous—the very epitome of what I imagined while bringing myself to climax.

My pulse spikes when his head suddenly cranks to the side. His lips quirk around his cigarette when he unearths the owner of the heated stare. I would like to say that is his only response to my presence. Regretfully, it isn't. His brows also knit, which scours his forehead with a scowling groove.

After dragging his eyes down my body, he lights his cigarette and takes in a long draw, hopeful it will hide the tic his jaw got when his eyes landed on my almost naked derriere.

I usually loathe anything that causes unnecessary stress on your body, but I can't help but be mesmerized by the chain of smoke that leaves his mouth as he drinks in the bottom half of my bikini for the second time. Since I've yet to take a seat, my ass is hanging out for the world to see, and the balling of Maksim's hands announces he finds that as unacceptable as I do.

He looks seconds from fetching me the towel I've been seeking since I left the suite, but before he can, the blonde he was with earlier parts the thick, curtained walls of the cabana he just left before she steps through them. Her hair is fluffed out, her cheeks are rosy, and her bikini is as minuscule as mine. She is gorgeous—and she knows it.

After plonking onto a barstool in defeat, I set to work on drowning my sorrows. "Bourbon on the rocks, please." When my sneaky glance at the poolside cabana fails to have my eyes landing on Maksim and his friend, I add, "And my friend will have...?"

When I twist to face the unnamed man waiting to be served, he smirks like he knows jealousy is fueling my motives before saying, "Make them a double, and hold the ice."

CHAPTER THIRTEEN

"Last-minute nerves, or did you wait too long to start downing liquid courage?" The unnamed man making a dent in the Ivanovs' profits with me the past two hours thanks the bartender for his latest refill with a chin lift before swiveling in his barstool to face me. "You could have given any of these contestants a run for their money."

I don't find his comment sleazy. He speaks as matter-of-factly as Zoya and doesn't appear to sugarcoat anything for anyone.

He's also kept his eyes from my shoulders up the entire time we've been socializing. His lack of interest would have scolded my ego if Maksim's narrowed glare hadn't softened it. He's meant to be judging the competition. If I were a contestant, I'd ask for a recount. He's barely taken his eyes off me for a second, and I'm not the only one noticing.

His blonde companion has tried to shift his focus from me several times. She raked her nails on his arm, gushed and raved about the contestants, and squeezed his thigh. The last point irks me the most and is the sole reason I've downed so many drinks in quick succession.

When my drinking partner coughs, reminding me he asked a question, I reply, "I never planned to participate. I'm here supporting some friends."

Talking about friends, I leap from my seat when Aleena prances onto the stage seconds after Shevi. They work the stage together like I could have with Zoya if I weren't such a chicken, and the crowd gobbles up their enthusiasm.

"Yes!" I wolf whistle like it isn't insulting coming from a member of the same sex and drum my hands against the bar. "Work it, girls!"

If you haven't realized this yet, the stranger and I have been going drink for drink.

I'm well on the way to intoxicated.

When Aleena wiggles her fingers at the gent next to me longer than she does toward the judges, I shoot him a riled look.

He smirks with wolfish satisfaction before introducing himself. "Kazimir Dokovic."

I sober up a smidge when the familiarity of his name smacks into me like a freight train. "You're Aleena's fiancé!" When he nods like I was asking a question instead of stating a fact, I slap his arm like we're long-lost friends. "You can't be here. This is her hen's weekend. It is meant to be her last hurrah to single life before the shackles are brought out."

I shoot my eyes to Maksim when a delicious growl rumbles through my body. He's still scowling, but the crowd's hollers are too loud for even a fire alarm to be heard, so the source of the rumble must be closer to me.

Next to me, to be precise.

Kazimir looks seconds from blowing his top.

When it dawns on me where his anger could stem from, I say, "Aleena hasn't stopped talking about you all weekend. That's why your name was instantly familiar."

My lie doesn't offer him any comfort. His jaw tightens to the point of cracking, but since it is now my best friend's turn to strut the stage in a white stringed bikini, any further assurances will have to wait.

Zoya looks hot, and everyone in a five-mile radius knows that, but I still shout and holler her name like I did for Aleena and Shevi. She deserves my support and could use the prize money even more than I could.

"How friggin' gorgeous is my best friend?" I ask while sinking back into the highbacked barstool and gathering my recently refilled drink to replenish my dry throat. I screamed my praise so loud three blocks over would have heard me.

The burn of bourbon worsens the tender conditions, but it has nothing to do with the dryness Kazimir's silence invokes.

He's no longer seated next to me. No one is. I have the entire bar to myself.

The bartender reminds me that he only mixes drinks and does not offer advice when I peer at him with a raised brow. "Another?"

I barely jerk up my chin when I'm startled from the side.

"Hey." Aleena's heated cheeks and glossy eyes expose she liked the attention she got on stage. "Where did Kazimir go?"

"Ah..."

I once again seek the bartender's help.

He leaves me hanging.

"He had to..." I want to blame the alcohol sloshing in my veins for the sudden backflip on my lie, but I can't. I hate liars, so I try not to be one unless absolutely necessary. Telling a teenage girl she isn't going to die the night of her prom is absolutely necessary. "I think I scared him off."

Aleena pouts before plopping into the seat her fiancé vacated in a hurry. "Oh."

"I'm sorry. I jokingly told him he shouldn't be here because it is your last hurrah of single life." I cuss under my breath when it sounds worse explaining it than it did when I blurted it out. "I didn't mean it in the way he took it. I just—"

"It's fine, Nikita. I know what you meant." She orders a drink before explaining there's a lot of infidelity in Kazimir's family and it's made his trust low.

"But he knows you'd never do anything like that to him, right?"

"Yeah... I think so." She doesn't sound as confident as she was aiming for. "I just hope I'm enough."

"Of course you are. Did you not hear the crowd's roar? It almost deafened me."

She downs the double nip of vodka the bartender places down in front of her like it is water before dragging her hand across her red-painted lips. "They were pretty wild." She breathes heavily out of her nose. "But I would have preferred for the praise to come from Kazimir."

"He looked smitten to me when you worked the stage."

She looks up at me with love in her eyes. "Yeah?"

I nod. "A hundred percent."

Her confusion is exposed when she asks, "Then why did he run?"

I try to make light of the situation. "Once again, did you hear the crowd's roar? The lazy river is about to become overloaded with floaters." That was hard for me to say, but I can't explain why while intoxicated. It isn't something I like to discuss when sober, either, but beggars can't be choosers.

With a giggle that shows she appreciates my commentary, Aleena clinks her shot glass against mine, throws back the double nip, and then signals for another.

Although I am grateful to have secured another drinking partner, Aleena is needed elsewhere. The bikini competition is over, and the beautiful women who graced the stage over the past two and a half hours are being requested to return to the stage.

"You better get back up there. There could be twenty K with your name on it."

Aleena peers in the direction I gestured before shaking her

head. "You heard the crowd. Zoya has this in the bag." Her low tone announces her confidence has slid off a cliff again.

"You're just as beautiful, Aleena." When she sighs like she doesn't believe me, I say, "There's just something about Zoya that draws people to her. She's a flame, and they're—"

"The stupid moths who should know better?"

She's already kicking herself for being petty about a woman who would give her the clothes on her back if asked, so I won't add more jabs while she's feeling down. I'll simply remind her not every issue in life belongs on our shoulders.

"It isn't our fault men's brains are between their legs."

That gets a smile out of her. "They are?"

"Uh-huh. I've studied all parts of the male anatomy, and every time I think I'm on the verge of a medical miracle... *bam!* Their brains are back between their legs."

Aleena laughs so hard that she snorts. "I wish we had met sooner."

I throw my arm around her shoulders and tug her in close. "Me too."

We down another three rounds before the winner of the main competition is announced.

It is Zoya, as anticipated.

"Zoya?" the MC repeats, louder this time.

I scan the crowd with hundreds of participants and spectators when Zoya fails to claim her oversized check.

Zoya's aura shines as brightly as Maksim's, so it doesn't take me long to deduce that she is nowhere to be seen.

The MC's dark brows join before he squashes his lips to the microphone. "This is a first. I've never had a winner not claim their prize. Ah..." He seeks advice from the judges, who appear as dumbfounded as him. Well, except Maksim. He looks more smug than annoyed. "Should we go with the runner-up?"

"No!" I shout before I can stop myself. That money could greatly benefit Zoya. She could even give up her job at Le Rogue.

I can't let it be taken from her without putting up a fight. "She had to use the bathroom." I point behind me like Zoya darted past me only seconds ago. "She is literally two minutes away." When the MC looks eager to wrap things up by giving her prize to someone else, I suggest, "Can I accept the check on her behalf?"

Gratitude fills me when the MC seeks Maksim's approval of my suggestion. He isn't as petty as me when trampled by jealousy. He dips his chin remarkably quick, but regretfully, it is only after seeking the opinion of the blonde who hasn't left his side all afternoon.

I'm treated like a contestant when I mosey up to the stage to collect Zoya's prize. Since I'm tipsy, I don't respond like the prude my best friend assures me I am. I return the tempting grins of a handful of spectators before adding an extra swing to my hips at the request of the rowdy college-aged men in the front row.

By the time I make it onto the stage, my confidence is sky high, and Maksim's jaw is as tight as Kazimir's was when I made out Aleena may act single during her hen's weekend.

Kazimir has a reason to be snooty. Maksim does not, and the realization has me snatching Zoya's check out of his hand more aggressively than necessary.

"Don't run away just yet," the MC says when I turn back to face the audience that is so enthralled you'd swear they can feel the tension crackling and hissing between Maksim and me when he can't hide his anger at my rudeness. "We need photos of the winner collecting her prize."

"I'm not the winner."

"You are now," the MC replies before forcing me to stand next to Maksim. "Your friend is wild, and the crowd went nuts, but this..." He scans the crowd surging closer to the stage, even with the contestants dwindling by the second. "They *love* you." The rake of his teeth over his bottom lip is sexy, but it has nothing on Maksim's angry scowl. "They've got a soft spot for shy girls."

A second after he positions me next to Maksim, I'm blinded

by camera flashes. The media covering the event takes hundreds of stills in less than a minute before acting like the Amazon River is wedged between Maksim and me.

"Can you move closer?"

"Maksim, stop acting like you're not enjoying this."

That gets a laugh from the masses.

"Lower the check and tilt in closer."

Their shouts become nothing but a buzz when Maksim bands his arm around my back and rests his hand low on my waist. His fingertips tickle the skin barely covered by the strings of my bikini bottoms and send a throb of excitement through my pussy.

"Perfect."

"Yes."

"Just like that."

A stern voice breaks over the journalists' approving chants, and it cakes my skin with sweat. "If you wish to continue using the facilities once the competition ends, do it in the cabana closest to the stage."

When Maksim nudges his head to the cabana he exited mere seconds before a blonde with sex-mussed hair, I attempt to walk away.

He snatches up my wrist before I can, tugs me back until my breasts are squashed against his chest, then tilts in so close he looks seconds from kissing me like one journalist continually demands.

His minty breath fans my lips when he continues barking out orders. "It comes with a private bartender. Order drinks from that bartender and *only* that bartender." His fingers on the hand still circling my wrist flex before he adds, "I will have a coverup delivered shortly. Use it."

"Or what?" I ask, shocking myself.

I never knew I had a rebellious side until now.

I shouldn't find Maksim's flaring nostrils and thumping neck veins attractive, but I do. "Or I'll make sure you pay your dues in ways you would have never considered when you decided to test just how far my leniencies stretch."

The sneer of his words would have you convinced his reply is a threat. However, my body doesn't agree. It thrums with excitement as my eyes beg for him to make true on his pledge.

When he remains standing firm, my slaughtered ego speaks on my behalf. "Why are you acting like this? You had your shot, and you blew it."

"Because that prick"—he nudges his head to the bartender who's been serving me for the past two-plus hours—"doesn't deserve an ounce of your time."

"That prick"—my tone dips when I mimic his scorn—"has been nothing but kind to me. Unlike you." His silence announces he's being cruel on purpose, and it snaps my last nerve. "I don't know what the fuck your issue is, Maksim, but you need to get over yourself. I saved your mother—"

"After nearly ending it!" he roars loud enough to silence the paparazzi going crazy.

"What?" That's all I can get out. One measly word. I was referencing how I saved his mother from going under the scalpel, but his interruption makes it seem far more sinister than that. He's acting like her life was dangling precariously off a cliff.

I guess he isn't that far off the mark. They were planning to do an investigational surgical procedure before I arrived on the scene. But shouldn't that place me in his good books, not out in the cold, wondering what the hell I did wrong?

"I wasn't—"

Before I can get out another word, the paparazzi click on to the cause of the tension hissing between us.

"What did you save his mother from?" a reporter asks after shoving a mini microphone my way.

"Maksim, are you confirming reports that your mother was missing were true?"

As the crowd is shoved out of the way, another reporter asks, "What is Irina's current prognosis?"

"Did anyone catch her name?" That question isn't for Maksim or me. It is from one reporter to the dozen surrounding him. "I don't recall seeing it on the contestant sheet."

The blonde responsible for the uprising of my attitude tries to subdue the boisterous paparazzi. She informs them that they will be forwarded a statement about today's charity event and Irina's condition later this afternoon before ushering them toward the exit.

When they fail to budge, too caught up in the hostility bristling between Maksim and me, beefy guys with security batons move them on the blonde's behalf. They don't belt into them like riot police most likely would. Their sneers alone get the reporters' feet moving.

I wish I could say the same. Maksim is glaring at me as well, but instead of racing for the closest exit, I return his stare. So much pain reflects in his beautiful dark eyes, but it is barely seen behind the confusion clouding them.

He appears as lost as I am.

With the media at a safe distance, the blonde strives to simmer the rage in me by attempting to hand me a smaller version of the check I'm clutching for dear life.

I say attempt because I don't accept it.

I can't do anything but stare if I want to unearth the secrets Maksim's narrowed gaze is displaying.

He doesn't hate me.

He hates my profession.

What the?

After a beat, the blonde says, "You can't cash that check. It's a prop." When her attempt to ignite a conversation remains one-sided for several long seconds, she asks, "Do you two need a minute?"

"Yes," I answer at the same time Maksim says, "No."

When I balk at the dismissiveness in his tone, my blink steals more than my dignity. I also lose the ability to continue reading the truth from his eyes. I'm once again in the dark, and it annoys the living shit out of me.

As Maksim scrubs at his stubble, he shifts on his feet to face the blonde. "Let her keep the check." Arrogance clogs the air with humidity before he adds, "Then she can use it to cover herself until her shawl arrives."

His last two words come out with a grunt when I shove the check into his chest before I leave the stage with so much spring in my step, my bouncing bosom mesmerizes a throng of thirsty men.

They offer to purchase me drinks before announcing they're more than happy for me to prance around without a shawl.

I pretend I'm interested in their offers. I'm not. I am merely doing everything in my power to make Maksim snap, because it may be the only way I'll unearth the cause of his angst.

"You know you're playing with fire, right?" Aleena asks when I return to the bar and order a double bourbon on the rocks.

An agreeing hum vibrates my lips.

"All right." She fills her shot glass with vodka like she's had a gig as a bartender before, then clinks it against my recently refilled glass. "As long as you are aware, I can both drink and support that."

With the wink of a woman eager to cause trouble, she downs the generous serving before asking the men circling us what their beverage of choice is.

"Don't be shy. It's not my bank balance you're hurting," she assures them when they hesitate.

When my eyes shoot to the bartender, he shrugs before he commences prepping the orders he's being inundated with like his boss is glaring this way to ensure he does the job he's paid to do.

CHAPTER FOURTEEN

"Zoya..." I stumble across a cabana littered with plastic cups and empty beer cans before wrapping my best friend up in a hug. "Where have you been? You missed the celebration." I jump up and down like Aleena's bridesmaids did when Aleena told them to order anything they wanted at the bar after they barged through the hundreds of guests depleting the Ivanovs' profits by thousands in literally minutes. "You won! You got twenty big ones." My nose screws up. "Well, more like ten after I borrow a tiny bit to fix *that*." I thrust my hand at the bar that was shut down by hotel security a minute after I returned to it. "They didn't have long, but they almost drank the bar dry. They won't tell me the final tally, but I can't leave all that mess to Maksim's family. Especially because I was acting like a jealous twit." The crinkles in my nose smooth. "He deserved it, though. He's being weird." I brush off my comment as if I didn't speak it. "Anyway, you won!"

"Wow."

When that is the entirety of her reply, I inch back and stare at her like she's a stranger. "Who are you, and what did you do with"—hiccup—"my best friend? You sound like Aleena when I reminded her that her wedding is only a few short weeks away." With my tact tossed out the window along with my sobriety, I say, "She's not giving off blushing virginal bride vibes tonight."

Zoya tries to hide her smile before asking, "Where is she?"

"Um..." I scan the two dozen or so drunk women—and just as many sober hotel security personnel—scattered throughout the cabana. "There." I cringe when I realize how glazed over her eyes are. "She's pretty wasted." An unexpected giggle rumbles up my chest. "We're all pretty wasted." As quickly as my giddiness comes, I'm hit with an equal amount of unease. "I don't think the eggs in the brownies were fresh. I've been feeling a little off since I ate them."

Zoya lifts my downcast head before peering into my eyes. "Are you high?"

"No. I don't think." My eyes bulge when my symptoms finally make sense. "Do I look high?"

"Yeah, you do." Her lips tug at one side. "And you smell like a brewery."

"That would be my fault." I gleam excitedly when Riccardo, the bartender whose shift ended shortly after I was marched into Maksim's pool cabana by his head of security, props his elbow on the cabana's bar before he waves hello to Zoya.

"Zoya, this is Riccardo." I drag Riccardo into the cabana like I wasn't ordered to stay away from him by Maksim's head security guy. He didn't say the order came directly from Maksim, but he didn't deny it, either. "Riccardo, this is my deliciously gorgeous friend Zoya."

When I push them together, then stare at them with loved-up eyes, Zoya clicks on to my plan faster than Riccardo. "Oh... ah. I'm not looking for anything permanent right now."

"Good, because from what I can tell, neither is Riccardo." I apologize for the loudness of my voice before clamping my hand over my mouth and waiting for the fireworks to start.

Regretfully, every single one I thought I'd secretly planted turns out to be a dud.

Not a single spark fires between Zoya and Riccardo.

"I'm sorry for asking you to come back after your shift. I could have sworn you were her type." When I attempt to add to my condolences with a hug, I trip over my feet and crash into Riccardo's chest. His extremely developed chest. "Are you sure there's nothing?" I ask Zoya. "Maybe you should feel his chest. It is all rigid and tanned, with only the slightest smattering of dark hairs."

After snapping her eyes to Riccardo's smooth and white chest, Zoya rockets them to my face. "I think it's time to call it a night."

"No. It's still early. The sun hasn't even gone to bed yet, so I don't want to either." I sound like a brat who hasn't been drinking since midday.

"Kita—"

"Please, Z. I promise I'll be good."

She drinks in my puppy-dog eyes and drooped lip for a few seconds before asking, "How many bottles can you fit under your..." She tugs on the garment only a frumpy grandma would wear. "What even is this?"

"It is the ugly coverup Maksim told me I had to wear." I flop onto a couch and cradle my blurry head in my hands. "He didn't like that my ass was showing. Well, he didn't actually say that. Aleena just thinks that is what he meant. He's so confusing. *I want to see you come. You won't leave my fucking head.*" My impersonation of Maksim's accent is atrocious. "Then, the next minute, he pushes me away. I just wish he'd give me a straight answer like you did Riccardo. Not... fucking... interested." My stomach rolls before I shoot my eyes up to Riccardo. "Sorry."

"It's all good." His smile makes my dizziness worse. "I'd rather be honest than strung along."

"That's what he's doing. He's stringing me along like my feelings don't matter." With drunkenness comes honesty. "And I think I know why." I lock my teary eyes with my best friend. "I think he's suing the hospital for malpractice. In all honesty, they deserve it. Their plan to diagnose his mother's condition was preposterous. They were stabbing at theories that made no sense for her symptoms, and when that didn't work, they conjured up an even more absurd way to justify their stupidity. Her diagnosis was so simple a third-year resident worked it out in minutes, so how could seasoned doctors not do the same?"

My eyes snap to Aleena when she unexpectedly joins our conversation. "Because their brains are wrinkly lards of flabby skin between their legs."

Zoya's laugh pierces my ears before her voice soothes the sting. "You gave her the *men are stupid because their brains are in their dicks* speech, didn't you?"

"Maybe." I shrug. "It's my go-to material when someone is feeling down."

I realize I said too much when concern hardens Zoya's features. "Aleena was feeling down?" I only hold my pointer finger and middle finger half an inch apart, but she acts like my arms are stretched from one side of the cabana to the next. "What happened?"

"Nothing happened. She just seemed a little—"

Before I can find an appropriate word, Aleena rejoins our conversation. "To men who think with their dicks." When she holds up her glass, ready to toast, I accept one of the shot glasses Riccardo recently refilled. Zoya declines. "And the women stupid enough to fall for their tricks."

My double shot of bourbon almost slides down my windpipe when Aleena clinks her glass against Shevi's with enough force it shatters. When she tries to down the shards as if they're ice, I forcefully swallow the liquid burning my throat and then shift on my feet to face Zoya. "It's time to call it a night."

She sighs in relief before making a beeline for her little sister.

Aleena is so drunk it takes Riccardo, Zoya, Shevi, and me to get her to our room and then just as many limbs to direct her to the secondary suite instead of the in-room bar.

I'm not the greatest help since I'm just as intoxicated, but I'm well-versed on pretending my head isn't muddled and my limbs aren't the weight of trunks.

While Zoya switches Aleena's clothes for pajamas, Aleena mumbles something about how not all men think with their penises and that if given the chance, we could show them how they could have the best of both worlds.

"They could have love and money. We-we could give them that." She shoots her bloodshot eyes to me, then swallows like the brisk movement almost causes her to vomit. "You just need to tell Maksim the truth. That you'd never intentionally hurt his mother."

"He knows. He was there."

She stumbles away too quickly for Zoya to hinder. "No, he doesn't. They told him it was a ruse"—a smelly burp breaks up her reply—"and that you knew he was there. They're putting all the blame on you." She grips my arm firm enough to bruise. "You have to tell him the truth. They need to be told when they're wrong." This could be my drunk head talking, but I feel like a lot of what she is saying resonates with her as much as it does me. Her next lot of words proves my theory. "They only treat us this way because we let them." Her spine straightens as determination sparks in her eyes. "If we don't like how we're treated, we should stand up for ourselves. Tell them to either ship up or ship out." Her grit rises along with the sturdiness of her legs. "And we should do it now."

"Now?" Zoya and I radio in sync.

"Uh-huh." She gets so up in my face that my intoxication level rises from the alcohol on her breath. "Let's get it out of the way. That way, if he's not interested in what we're offering, we can do whatever the hell we like all day tomorrow. Stuff the consequences."

"Stuff the consequences," I echo, too drunk to realize I am accepting the advice of an intoxicated woman. "I'm going to confront him and give him a piece of my mind. If it weren't for me, his mother would most likely still be admitted." My leap of determination almost ends my campaign, but I swallow down the vomit surging up my throat before chickening out with more dignity. "Tomorrow. I'll talk to him tomorrow."

"No! Not tomorrow," Aleena says. "We need to do this now before it's too late."

For someone who could barely stand minutes ago, she charges for the door without a single stumble Shevi uses to trace her steps.

"What do I do?" Zoya asks, unversed in dealing with family issues since she left home at fifteen.

"Go with her," I suggest when Aleena disappears into the hallway and takes a left instead of the expected right. Maksim's suite is on the right. "I'll be right behind you. I just need to grab my bag. It is the equivalent of a first-aid kit. It may come in handy." When Zoya groans, I push her toward the door, almost stumbling when dizziness overwhelms me. "I'm joking. Go." I'm not, but she doesn't need to know that. "Your baby sister needs you."

Since they're the words she's needed to hear for years, she throws her arms around my neck and breathes in my scent before sprinting after Aleena. "I'll meet you down there!"

"I'm right behind you."

When the entryway door of our suite slams closed, I flatten my palms on the drawers and suck in some big breaths. I'm not feeling well at all, and although my symptoms mimic ones similar to someone who has drunk too much, I don't believe excessive alcohol consumption is solely to blame for my woozy state. I'm having memory issues of events that happened earlier, such as, why am I wearing a frumpy coverup?

After checking my pulse and noticing it is dangerously high, I veer toward the suite's kitchen for a glass of water. Dehydration doesn't excuse all my symptoms, but alleviating it could reduce some of them.

I startle out of my skin when my stumble through the living room is met with a manly voice. "How are you feeling, Nikita?"

It takes me a few seconds to remember the name of the blond gent in front of me. That's how woozy my head is.

"Riccardo..." I lower my voice from ear-piercing before repeating, "I... ah..."

His smirk reminds me of how drunk I am. I didn't find it attractive earlier. "You forgot my name."

"No. Not at all. I just..." I wish I weren't so honest when drunk. "I'm sorry."

"It's all good. It proves the second dose is working better than the first. I was starting to worry that I'd have to improv."

He rubs his hands together but makes no attempts to leave, lumping the task onto me. "I'm not feeling the best, and Zoya will probably be gone awhile, so..." I nudge my head to the door, soundlessly giving him his marching orders.

He can't take a hint.

After his teeth catch his lower lip, he glides his hooded eyes down my body. "I usually hate when the party loses steam early, but I'm glad it's just us this time around." When he steps closer, exposing the lusty glint his perusal of my body caused his eyes, the vomit I forced down earlier burns my throat. "Gives us plenty of time to—"

"Play Scrabble?"

He laughs like I'm joking.

I'm not.

That is the only game we will ever play.

I thought he was a good match for Zoya. That means he is the opposite of what I am seeking. She likes them wild and danger-ous. I usually only ever look for the safe option.

Well, until Maksim entered my life.

"I think you should go."

As I walk to the door, disgustingly stumbling, Riccardo replies, "I'd rather stay."

"I don't care what you want. I asked you to leave, so leave." I sound rude, but I don't care. I'm unwell, and he's acting like a dick.

After yanking open the door, I crank my neck back to Riccardo. He hasn't budged an inch, and his threatening snarl exposes he has no intention of going anywhere.

"I wouldn't test me. I know where every artery in your body is and which are vital."

I assume his whitening cheeks are from the honesty in my statement, but I learn otherwise when a voice I immediately recognize rumbles over my shoulder. "She asked you to leave." After returning my stare long enough to convince me he feels my gratitude, Maksim shifts his narrowed eyes to a brute of a man on his left. "Get him the fuck out of here."

"I'm going," Riccardo assures, holding his hands in the air in defeat.

The brute doesn't listen. He grabs him by the scruff of his shirt and pulls him out of the suite fast enough that a knife similar to the one he used to slice limes earlier today falls out of the back of his jeans.

"Oh my god."

I feel even more sick now—incredibly ill.

"Was he...? Did he come here to...?" As my stupidity steamrolls me into a blubbering, teary mess, the chaos I almost introduced into my best friend's life smacks into me. "I brought him into her life. Despite your security officers' warnings, I told him to come back. I-I introduced him to my best friend."

Maksim steadies my swaying movements by gripping the tops of my arms before staring at me with stern yet worried eyes. "Did he hurt you?"

I shake my head so fast that I almost vomit. "No. I thought

he-he'd be a good match for Zoya. I-I tried to set them up. What if he had hurt her like... like... like... What if he'd...?"

Bile races up my esophagus between my stammered words. I try to swallow it down, but several gulps offer little relief. I'm going to be sick, and since Maksim's grip on my arms is too firm to dislodge, it lands on his shoes.

CHAPTER FIFTEEN

"I swear to God, if you're not juggling a gallon of coffee, you're not welcome."

I usually love Zoya's girlie giggles, but this morning, they represent a knife being stabbed into my ears on repeat. I'm hungover, dehydrated, and having a hard time remembering a single thing that occurred after she tricked me out of our suite.

"You won, right? That wasn't a dream."

When my question is answered with silence, I carefully crack open my eyes, blink to lubricate them, and then move them in the direction Zoya's voice projected from. She's arrived with gifts, a gigantic mug of coffee, and a wholegrain muffin, but instead of seeking the praise she usually demands when she brings treats, her focus is on the far corner of the room.

I shoot up to a half-seated position too fast for my hungover head when I follow the direction of her gaze. Maksim is seated on the winged-back chair I dumped my bag on not long after checking in.

He looks tired, like his sleep schedule has been as lagging as mine the past two weeks, but he is still incredibly handsome.

"Why are you in my room?" When my hand shoots up to make sure my pounding heart remains in my chest, another crazy fact smacks into me. "And why am I naked?"

"You—"

Maksim cuts Zoya off by slicing his hand through the air. And even more shocking than that is the fact she lets him.

She sinks back like she's happy for him to take the lead, which he does without hesitation crossing his features. "You vomited."

"Okay," I reply, struggling not to cringe. "And that led to me being naked how?"

"You got it on your clothes, so I helped you change them."

"You helped me change them?" When he nods nonchalantly, I squeal, "You saw me naked? Like naked *naked*, not the little preview you had in the washroom."

He smiles in wolfish satisfaction before he dips his chin. "Yes."

I curse my lack of confidence to hell when I mumble, "And you're still here?"

Maksim's smirk does wicked things to my insides when he drags his eyes down my body before he repeats, "Yes." He returns them to my face. They're more heated now. "Does that bother you?"

"No," I answer far too quickly.

"Good." His reply flips my stomach in a way I'm not anticipating, but it is pushed aside for confusion when he adds, "Because it would have been awkward if you'd changed your mind after we'd made things official."

Official? What is he talking about? He's acting as if I couldn't get rid of him even if I wanted to.

I realize that is precisely what he's implying when the high-hanging sun streaming through the curtains of my room reflects off a giant rock on my left hand.

"What the hell is that?" I shoot my eyes to Zoya, panting and with a crinkled nose. "You let me get married!" I don't give her the chance to answer. "You let me get married to a man who hates me?"

"I don't hate you."

My breathing announces I'm on the verge of a panic attack even while delighted by Maksim's comment, so Zoya sets to work on trying to calm me. "I tried to stop you." She gives Maksim a sympathetic look before moving closer to my bedside. "But by the time I returned to our suite, you had already decided. You were so determined to go through with it that you organized a late-night visit from a local minister."

"No. I wouldn't do that. I went to the foyer for a room key and watched you shake your ass, and then I... I... I..." When my memories are nothing but black pools of despair, I bring my eyes back to meet with Maksim's and murmur, "I married you."

His grin is the most arrogant to date. "You did."

"Because...?" I know there's more to this. Strangers don't marry strangers unless they're in Vegas, and they wouldn't tie the knot with someone they don't like. Maksim dislikes me so much he walked out when my pants were huddled around my knees and my pussy was exposed.

When I say that to Maksim, he says, "I didn't—"

"Want to miss out on a big inheritance."

That didn't come from Zoya or me. It came from Aleena, who's entering my room, looking more presentable than the bear-with-a-sore-head guise I'm working.

Maksim's, Zoya's, and my eyes snap to her in sync. Maksim appears as confused as Zoya and I do, but he hides it better with an angry scowl.

Aleena takes his narrowed glare in stride like this isn't the first time she's been at its mercy. "When I accidentally let slip to Maksim about your excessive student loans, he mentioned an inheritance he'd never see if he didn't wed. Putting two and two together, I realized how ideal *this* could be." She waves her hand between Maksim and me while saying "this." "You need money, and Maksim needs a wife to get it. This"—her hand is back between us—"fixes both dilemmas."

Nothing she says makes any sense. "Zoya just said I had already decided before either of you had returned to our suite." She nods, unwillingly inching toward the trap I'm laying out for her. "But now you're saying you helped cook up a scheme that would have me believing marrying a stranger was a good idea?"

"No, that isn't what happened," Zoya jumps in. "She... I... I brought you coffee."

She shoves a takeaway cup into my chest so fast I either grab it or wear it.

I grab it, almost exposing my breasts at the same time.

"Shit. Sorry."

When Maksim's low growl rumbles through Zoya's chest, her mouth falls open as her loved-up eyes shift to Maksim. "You loathe that too?" She backhands his chest like there won't be a single consequence for her action. "Aleena is right. You are a perfect match."

"Z!"

Her eyes are back on me, full of mischief. "What? Don't act like you can't feel the sparks. You've been panting like a dog in heat since we got here."

"And you thought he was married, so you should have muzzled my mouth."

When Maksim bounces his eyes between Zoya and me, his brows crinkling more the longer he stares, she discloses, "The blonde."

"Slatvena?" Maksim asks, awakening my jealousy. Slatvena's name rolled off his tongue in a seductive purr, and it has my claws out even without them having a single thing to sink into.

Maksim takes a moment to enjoy the anger burning me alive from the inside out before saying, "She is my assistant."

The honesty in his tone doesn't ease my jealousy in the slightest. If anything, it makes it worse. I've read many steamy stories about bosses and secretaries.

"She also wasn't forced to attend yesterday's festivities. She was there for the same reason every other spectator was."

"For charity," I assume.

Maksim laughs. Its rumble has me wanting to gloss over the part where I was drunk when we wed. I've never heard a more panty-wetting noise. "She went to enjoy the view."

Zoya clicks on faster than me. "Oh..."

When she gives me a look that no one over sixteen should be able to read, I mimic her reply but with more shock. "*Oh.*" With my jealousy contained but my confusion still apparent, I ask, "Then why not marry her?"

With Maksim and Zoya stumped, Aleena jumps back in. "It needs to look authentic." Her face screws up like she sucked a lemon. "If it doesn't appear legitimate, the inheritance will be voided." When she realizes my concern is growing instead of dissipating, she shifts on her feet to face Zoya and then hooks her thumb to the door. "We should probably go. This is a private matter. We don't want to intrude."

When Zoya nods in agreement, I glower at her.

Who is this alien, and what did she do with my best friend?

When she leans in to hug me, I hold on tight. "If you leave me now, I'll disown you for life."

"He won't hurt you, Keet," she breathes into my neck, announcing she understands the catalyst of my worry. It isn't physical harm I'm afraid of. I am terrified as to what this man could do to my heart. He's had it in a flutter since the day we met, and I see it worsening now. "He only wants to help you."

Before I can ask why he would want to do that, she wiggles out of my hold and makes a beeline for the door, hot on Aleena's tail.

I'd take off after them if I weren't naked.

I feel Maksim's eyes on me, and despite the alarm bells

sounding in my head, I bring my eyes back to his. His almost sable eyes have lost the icy brutality they held in the washroom. They're hooded as he awards me a sultry gaze.

"Did we...?"

I'm grateful he can understand me without the rude gestures Zoya forever requires. "No." I flinch, waiting for the brutal slap my ego is about to get hit with. It never arrives. "Not for a lack of want. You were drunk." He drags his hand along his jaw, tracing a tremor there. "And possibly drugged."

"Drugged?"

He drops his hand from his jaw before working it side to side. "I knew Riccardo wouldn't try anything while Kazimir was with you, so I allowed my security team to continue their operation."

Riccardo? Kazimir? I have no clue who these people are, but I have more pressing matters to address. "Was I alone with Riccardo long?"

I breathe a little easier when Maksim shakes his head. "As soon as I was alerted of his re-appearance by my security team, I immediately returned to the hotel." He looks impressed while saying, "When I arrived at your suite, you were in the process of threatening him if he didn't leave."

The smile I'm struggling to hide radiates in my tone when I ask, "Arteries or dismembering?" When he arches a brow, seeking further explanation, my smile breaks free. "They're my go-to threats. Arteries for the men who have no fear of living without their penises. Dismembering for the men who couldn't think of a more torturous way to live. Sounds like he would be the former."

"He was." He stops, pulls an expression I can't quite read, then asks, "What category do I belong in?"

"Depends," I reply.

Maksim's firm jaw reveals he doesn't like extracting answers from people, but he plays along for my benefit. The more we interact, the less I'm freaking out about waking up married to a man who is practically a stranger. "On what?"

"On how you explain me waking up naked. If we didn't have... *sex*, why am I without a stitch of clothing?"

His leer over my stumble of the word "sex" sends the pounding in my skull several inches lower. "You told me you didn't want your dress to get crushed." He waves his hand to a beautiful white lace dress hanging on the hook behind the door Zoya and Aleena recently fled through. "So you removed it while I showered, and climbed under the sheets." He moves so close we breathe as one. "These were held far higher on your chest when I exited the bathroom. I wasn't granted the slightest peek of your skin." A scarlet hue creeps across my chest when he traces a figure-eight pattern on my cleavage. "It was for the best. I may have never left if you had added a teasing amount of skin to your numerous wordless begs."

Wheezy breaths break up my reply. "Symptoms of GHB and Rohypnol absorption can last for several hours. My actions were not my own. If they were, I wouldn't have woken up married."

Would you listen to me? I'm acting as if I wouldn't marry this man if he tossed me half a bone with hardly any meat on it. He's gorgeous, successful, and staring at me like he'd burn the world to find me if I were out of his reach for even a minute. I'd be insane to act like a little part of me isn't excited that I've finally secured his attention.

I'm just confused as to what caused his sudden backflip. It could be the inheritance Aleena stated earlier, but I'm skeptical. Maksim seemed as surprised as me when she blurted it out, and he's already immensely wealthy, so why marry a woman he's pushed away as often as he's pulled in for a bit of extra coin?

He could end up worse off when he learns my debt isn't chump change. I am hundreds of thousands of dollars in the hole, and the shame associated with not wanting to admit that to anyone, much less a man I've had a fascination about since the moment we met, has me blurting out, "I think we should organize an annulment."

Maksim recoils as if I slapped him across the face. "No." The swiftness of his denial is shocking, but his quick exodus from the bed is more devastating than alarming. "What's done is done, and it is too late to change it."

"You honestly can't want to go through with this. I'm a stranger. A fucking mess." When none of my concerns cause a single snippet of worry to flare through his eyes, I give honesty a whirl. "I am up to my eyeballs in debt."

"Not anymore, you're not." He misses my O-formed mouth since he spins to gather his crumpled suit jacket from the back of the chair. "Your credit cards were paid in full this morning, and your student loans will be handled first thing Monday." I wonder just how much I shared with this man last night when he adds, "The other matter will take a little longer to sort out, but I'm hopeful it will be finalized as soon as possible."

"Your generosity is appreciated, but I can't accept it."

He puts on a dark pinstriped jacket that matches his pants and then spins to face me, fiddling with the lapels on the way. "Why?" His expression is deadpanned, like he can't understand my apprehension.

"Because..." It takes me a minute to sort through the slosh in my head to find anything decent. "Because this isn't how negotiations work. Even in an arranged marriage, both parties are supposed to benefit from the agreement. It isn't meant to be one-sided."

"Then there isn't an issue, because our *arrangement*"—he snarls his last word—"isn't one-sided."

"How isn't it one-sided? I get my loans wiped, and you get—"

"You," Maksim interrupts, his tone as stern as the firm line of his lips. "I get you."

I can't respond to that. What woman in their right mind could? He just placed me onto a pedestal so high I'm not sure I will ever get back down.

Although I can now blame some of my dizziness on altitude

sickness, not even the heights of Mt. Everest could have me forgetting my obligations.

"My grandparents live in Myasnikov. I can't leave them, and they're not well enough to travel."

The tears I'm struggling to hold back come close to falling when Maksim replies, "I know, and they won't need to go anywhere. I will make arrangements to work out of Myasnikov this morning."

"You would do that for me?" The words are out of my mouth before I can stop them. Shock does that to you. It has you speaking without fear of repercussions—*and waking up married to a stranger.*

I'd rather Maksim vocalize his decision than use a gesture, but I am still delighted when he nods. "It was part of the terms we negotiated last night."

It hurts to be reminded that our marriage is a sham for benefits, but I hide my disappointment well. "What other terms did we agree to?"

"We wrote them down." He pulls a sheet of paper out of the breast pocket of his suit jacket and hands it to me. "Your terms are written in pen at the top. Mine is in pencil at the bottom."

My heart whacks my chest when I open the folded-up piece of paper. My terms are lengthy but not overly demanding after remembering this is an arranged marriage. They're more necessities of life than dramatic diva demands, but Maksim's minimal requests make them seem obsessive.

Well, I shouldn't really say requests since he only has one.

He wants us to share the same bed every night.

The surge in my pulse thuds in my voice when I ask the motive behind his demand.

Cockiness is the first emotion he expresses.

It is quickly changed for deceit.

"We need our marriage to appear legitimate." His eyes ping-pong between mine for a handful of seconds before he says, "I will organize someone to move your things to my suite by this afternoon."

He waits for me to nod before he farewells me with an awkward forehead kiss, and then he heads for the door.

Just before he exits, he twists back to face me. "Riccardo's drug of choice was Ketamine." My pulse races through my body so fast I almost miss what he says next. "So although your actions were not your own for the first hour or two of our exchange, you were alert and responsive for several hours before you became my wife." His smirk is more confident than arrogant. "You said last night was the first time your heart has won. Perhaps your lack of memories this morning is your head's way of fighting back."

He waits until I read the message the menacing glint in his eyes is relaying—that he has no intention of going down without a fight—before he finalizes his exit.

Half a second later, Zoya pops her head into the room. "How dead am I?"

I purse my lips before answering, "Critical enough that I don't think even I can save you."

CHAPTER SIXTEEN

"Still freaking out?"

As Zoya flops belly-first onto the sunlounge next to me, I stop admiring the way the midday sun reflects off the diamonds of my engagement and wedding rings and put all my focus on my "supposed" best friend. The title is negotiable after last night. Her hair is wet and flopped on top of her head in a messy bun, and the tropical paradise she missed yesterday since she was shaking her ass on a stage has removed almost all her makeup.

She could still stop traffic, though.

"A little," I reply, being honest. "I'm more worried what Gigi's reaction will be than anything else."

"I think I can help with that." She breathes out slowly before saying, "Tell her you did it for me. That I made a deal I had no intention to keep, ran with the money negotiated for said deal, then convinced you it was a good idea to marry a sugar daddy so you could lend me the money to pay back the fool I tried to swindle."

I laugh, assuming she is joking.

I'm so far off the mark my dart doesn't even hit the board. "Z—"

"I fucked up. I got cocky thinking he wouldn't go through with it. Then when he did, that was a lot of money to walk away from."

"So you walked away with it instead?" When she nods, I give her my best motherly scold. "Zoya."

"It's okay. It isn't as bad as it seems. *Now*. Maksim is squaring everything up as we speak." When worry flares through my eyes that I'll owe Maksim far more than the six figures he's already shelled out to pay off my credit cards, she says quickly, "I spent hardly any of it. I just upgraded our flights and paid for us to stay in the penthouse. I'm sorry." She pushes out a sob when she can't miss the disappointment on my face. "I wanted to make Aleena's hen night special."

"What's that got to do with first-class tickets?"

I want to remain angry, but she makes it almost impossible when she replies, "I was hoping you'd sleep. You were coming off a double, and I knew you wouldn't rest in economy since you'd be freaking about the germs, so I splurged a little."

"Z..." This one is nowhere near as scolding as my previous one. I love how much she loves me. I just wish she'd do it in a less dangerous manner.

She looks up at me with begging eyes like the cat in *Puss N' Boots*. Her stare is pleading but also filled with remorse. "Do you hate me?"

"No. I could never. I just wish you would have told me."

"I had planned to come clean last night." She lowers her eyes to the wedding set on my left hand. "We all know how that turned out." She laughs at my rolling eyes before saying, "He picked well. That set is gorgeous."

My pulse doubles when my sluggish head clicks on to what she just said. "Maksim picked my rings?"

She rolls over and rests her cheek onto her folded hands

before nodding. "Uh-huh. He said something about a carat for each lie he believed." Her breathy giggles echo even with the cabana's walls being made of material. "He must have trusted the wrong people." If life was a cartoon, love hearts would bounce from her eyes as she says, "Because that is a heap of please-forgive-me carats."

"Please-forgive-me carats because he thought I should have been a part of the malpractice suit he's planning to pursue against Myasnikov Private?"

Zoya props herself onto her elbows, her expression unreadable. "You remember what happened last night?"

I wish I could nod, but unfortunately, I can't. "No. I just have a feeling it centers around that." This kills me to say, but I'm hopeful a purge will chip through some of the confusion muddling in my head. "I mentioned his mother when we were about to..." I make a gesture someone as deviant as Zoya should be able to understand. However, she acts clueless. "When we were about to... *fuck*."

"Sweetie, I didn't think we needed to have this talk, but clearly we do." Zoya gathers my hands in hers, then looks me straight in the eyes. "You never bring up a man's momma during sexual activities. It lets the air straight out of the balloon." She holds her arm in the air, straight and rigid like a flagpole, before she drops it to represent a floppy elephant's trunk. "Penetration is hard when his manhood isn't."

"That wasn't the issue." When she soundlessly mocks me like she doesn't believe me, denials tumble from my mouth. "It wasn't. He was hard. And veiny. And long. So *very* long." I mentally slap myself before getting back on track. "He said things to me he should have said to his mother's medical team. Things Myasnikov Private should pay careful attention to if they want to avoid multiple malpractice claims. But he said it as if I was as much to blame for his mother's misdiagnosis as Dr. Abdulov."

"That's what she meant," Zoya murmurs to herself, her words

whispers. She takes a moment to sort through the facts before she halves the load by sharing them with me. "Aleena mentioned last night that Maksim didn't know the truth because they were placing all the blame on you. She said something about them telling him you knew he was there and that you were acting."

Bewilderment colors my tone. "Acting? The only acting I did that night was pretend I didn't want to slap Dr. Abdulov across the face."

Zoya laughs. "I wish you would have. That creep needs to be taught a lesson." She flattens her back to the sunlounge and covers her eyes with sunglasses like she's about to catch as many z's as she is rays. "But Maksim knows the truth now, and that's all that matters. He can live out his insta-love fantasy full throttle without a damn thing in the way." When I choke on my spit during the middle of her last sentence, she rips off her sunglasses with the dramatics of a small-screen actress. "You, of all people, are dissing insta-love? What would your momma say?" She shoves her hand in my face before I can respond. "You can't use the dead mom ruse for this. Not when she was the biggest advocator for falling in love at first sight. She loved your daddy from the moment she laid eyes on him. And he loved her so much—"

"He went to jail for killing the men who took her from him."

"No, Keet," Zoya denies, shaking her head. "He went to jail for killing the men who took her from you." Tears prick in my eyes so hard and fast it stings when she says, "Because he knew from the moment he laid eyes on you that your momma's claims of insta-love were true." I wipe a tear from my cheek fast enough that she shouldn't be able to see it, but she does. "Don't..." Her voice cracks with emotions. "If you start, I'll start."

"I'm not... I won't." I exhale quickly before staring up at the cabana's ceiling and fluttering my lashes, hopeful it will dry my tears. "I just miss him."

I haven't seen my dad in over seven years. When he was convicted to life behind bars, he made me promise I'd never visit him. He said the Russian prison system was no place for a woman, that it is more corrupt than a foreigner trying to defend himself during an unjust trial.

I tried a handful of times to see him, but he forever refused my requests. I want to believe he is doing it to protect me, but part of me wonders if it is because I look too much like my mother. We have the same pale porcelain skin and opposing almost-raven hair. She just had green eyes, whereas mine are hazel.

I stop recalling the pain in my father's eyes the last time I saw him, when Zoya says, "Scoot." She is no longer on her sunlounge; she's hovering over mine, shadowing me from the sun I've been protected from all morning.

When I move as requested, she slips onto the sunlounge with me and pulls me into her chest. My heart melts, but since I'm still fighting not to cry, I'll never let her know that.

"I thought you said there was no girl-on-girl action on the agenda this weekend."

Her laughs have my head bouncing off her ample chest like a bronco rider vying for a podium spot. "I did..."—just like me, she keeps the tension low—"but then I remembered how much guys love it, so I thought, what the hell, why not give them what they came here to see."

Giggles bubble in my chest until the heaviness weighing it down has no choice but to lighten and the only wetness in my eyes are laughter tears. "I love you, Z."

"I love you too, Keet." She could leave it there, but she wouldn't be Zoya if she did. "Just like I know you're going to love him too. You just need to stop looking at this as if it is a bad thing."

"I'm trying. It's just hard with no memories." Small snippets are starting to filter through the dark, like Maksim on his knees, peering up at me with dilated eyes, but other than that, I'm wandering in the dark, unable to find the light switch.

Zoya jackknifes into a half-seated position so fast she almost sends me flying off our shared sunlounge. "I have pictures. I took a ton of them." After snatching our room keycard off the table wedged between our daybeds, she twists to face me. "I'll be back!" She's halfway out of the cabana before she twirls back around. "Can you keep an eye on Aleena for me? I'm trying to tell her to pace herself, but she's like..."

"You?" I fill in when she struggles to find an appropriate comparison.

She nods as if delighted before air-blowing me a kiss and leaving.

After wrapping a sarong around the lower half of my swimsuit and protecting my eyes with sunglasses, I shadow her exit. With everything going on, it is easy for me to forget this weekend is meant to be about Aleena. I just refuse to be that woman. I loathe people who make everything about them.

I find Aleena at a bar near the wave pool.

"Hey, Keet. I'm glad you've finally joined us."

Her dilated eyes reveal she is on her way to tipsy but far from being drunk.

"Hey. Are you having fun?"

She wiggles her brows before eyeing the line of shot glasses in front of her. "I sure am."

When Shevi holds out one for me, I shake my head. "I think I'll stick with water today."

"Are you sure?" checks the bartender after refilling the glasses Aleena and her bridesmaids down. "I can mix a mean cocktail."

"The bartender last night said the same." While cringing, I slip onto a barstool. "It wasn't good."

The bartender's rumbling laugh rolls through my chest as I freeze. That's the first memory I've had of last night that didn't involve Maksim. It's so hazy it is more an audible clip than a video montage, but it is a memory, nonetheless.

"Were you working the bar yesterday?"

"During the bikini competition?" When I nod, dark hair falls into his eyes as he shakes his head. "No. That was Riccardo. Last I heard, he was let go." When I can't hide my shock that he said the same name Maksim mentioned this morning when advising I was drugged, his smile grows. He's clearly mistaken my panicked face as disappointment. "I can get his number for you, if you want. You're just his type." He bites his lower lip before murmuring, "Actually, you're everyone's type."

"Oh. I'm flattered but—"

"She's married," Aleena interrupts before lifting my left hand in the air, blinding him with my new bling.

"To who?" the bartender asks, shaping up like he's willing to fight for my affection.

Aleena's expression is just as glitzy when she replies, "To him."

When she nudges her head to the left, I follow the direction of her nudge so fast my neck muscles scream in protest. Maksim is entering the pool area via the staff-only entrance. He's wearing the same suit he left my suite in this morning, but instead of confusion scouring his forehead, anger is.

His forehead groove represents a V when he's angry.

It is as straight as a line when he's confused.

Since I'm surprised I've already mastered some of his facial quirks, when Maksim presses his lips to my temple a second before he flattens his hand low on my waist, I startle.

It isn't in repulsion, but Maksim's low, simpering growl would have convinced others otherwise. The groove between his dark brows deepens as his grip on my waist turns possessive.

When it becomes obvious Maksim isn't the only one who noticed my balk, I try to lie my way out of an awkward situation. "I think I've been in the sun too long. My skin is a little tender. I should probably head back to the cabana before I turn into a lobster." I thank the bartender for the bottle of water he placed down a second before Maksim arrived, before peering up at Maksim. "Would you care to join me?"

I ensure my voice is as seductive as the pleading look I hit him with. I've never been overly good at flirting, but I give today's shot the performance of my life. It is only right. The credit card debt Maksim took care of this morning wasn't small fry.

I'll find a way to pay him back, but since it won't be until after I've finalized my residency, I must play the part I agreed to last night.

I can only pray my heart will survive being in his presence that long.

Having above average smarts is wonderful until you realize your heart governs all your decisions. The fact I woke up married proves this without doubt.

Maksim's eyes dance between mine for several long seconds before he eventually jerks up his chin. As he assists me off the barstool, the air hisses and cracks with electricity. It is the same fiery heat I felt in the bathroom weeks ago, and it augments when Shevi tosses a bottle of sunscreen into Maksim's chest.

"We don't want one of the newlyweds out of action so soon into their honeymoon."

She hides her mammoth smile with a cocktail before it's stolen from my view entirely by Maksim escorting me away from the giggling group.

The reason for Maksim's unexpected arrival is unearthed when our walk through the lush paradise is stalked by numerous pairs of eyes. Some stare in fascination—even wearing a suit to a pool party can't detract from Maksim's sexiness—but a handful are more inquisitive than fascinated. They don't hide their snooping ways, not even when we enter the cabana Zoya booked for the commencement of Aleena's bachelorette party.

"I'm sorry," I whisper to Maksim as I make a beeline for the sunlounge with the most shade and plop onto the edge. "I'll do better. My head is still a little foggy, and then Zoya overloaded it." I glance up at him. "I hope she didn't cause you too much trouble today."

"It wasn't anything I haven't handled before."

"Negotiating for a woman's time with money nothing new for you?"

I sound jealous. Rightfully so. I am.

Maksim plucks the SPF 50+ sunscreen off the table he dumped it on before joining me on the sunlounge. It creaks when placed under the strain of his six-foot-four height half a second before a cool substance coats my right shoulder.

"I've never bartered for a woman's time." I almost correct him, but he continues talking before I can. "And I never will."

"We—"

"Are here because we want to be," he interrupts, his tone stern yet honest. "Both of us."

When I glance back at him, he holds my gaze for several heart-stuttering seconds before he smirks, squeezes a generous blob of sunscreen onto his palm, and then smears it across my left shoulder so it will be as sun protected as my right.

As he dotes on me like a husband would his new bride, I wonder if he took my defense as literal, or is he making sure Shevi's warning that I could be out of action tonight with heat-stroke won't be an issue?

My shoulders don't have the slightest bit of coloring, so I want to believe it is the latter, but the gawk of a man seated across from us makes me hesitant.

If he eyeballs us any harder, I won't blame the sun for any damage caused to my skin today.

"Do you know who that man is?" My words are huskier than I'd like. It can't be helped. Maksim is more massaging my shoulders than slapping on sun protection in the quickest means possible, and every swipe of his hand diverts the throb of my pulse to between my legs.

"Who?" His voice is as breathless as mine, and the need in it has me tilting back so his fingers brush my neck and collarbone more than my shoulders.

Multiple times, I try to reply, but when Maksim's fingertips dip so low they're close to tracing the triangular outline of my bikini top, I can't concentrate on anything but how wild his simplest touch makes me feel. His fingers are right there, inches from my nipples, yet not close enough to excuse the wet patch slowly darkening my bikini bottoms.

"Don't even think about it," Maksim growls when I swivel my hips, hopeful my sarong will stop him from seeing how turned on his basic touch has made me. "If just my hands on you make you this wet, I want to see what happens when I answer one of the many pleas you hit me with last night."

My back bends when one of his hands slips beneath my bikini and he squeezes and caresses my breast.

"Do you have any idea how hard it was to turn you down?" He takes his anger out on my nipple, tweaking and twisting it into a hard bud. "I had to sleep on a fucking armchair while *my wife* was naked in my bed."

The way he growls "my wife" has my legs scissoring and plea-sure crushing through me, making me hot.

He runs his nose down the throb in my throat before saying on a moan, "I almost buckled when you moaned my name in your sleep."

There's no deceit in his tone, no dishonesty, but I still look up at him like I don't believe him.

The need in his eyes drives me wild. I whimper, unashamed to display I'm desperate for any morsel of affection he's willing to give me. I've craved this man from the moment I met him, and for the first time since the "shower incident," he's not staring at me like he should hate himself for wanting the same.

He wants this as badly as I do.

"Please," I beg, speaking through the pulse in my throat.

The sunscreen my skin has yet to absorb smears his business

clothes when he tugs me back while asking, "Tell me what you want, Doc. I'll give you anything you want."

"You." I breathe out a moan, arching up when his hand slithers down my stomach. "Everywhere."

I balance my head on his shoulder and snap my eyes shut when the sunscreen on his fingers adds to the dampness between my legs. It acts as lubricant when he stuffs two fingers inside me before he stimulates my aching clit with his palm.

The pounding in my head is gone. My hangover no longer exists. I feel nothing but jolts of electricity coursing through me as he brings me to the peak of climax.

"Do you like that, Doc? My fingers in you? My cock braced against your back?" His thumb gets in on the action, flicking and circling my clit. "You're going to look so good filled with my cock."

His words cause my heart to pound, and they rush my orgasm to the surface quicker than I can force it down. My thighs tremble as I fight to hold it back, but their shudders only make Maksim work harder.

He spreads my legs wider and gently tilts my hips, opening me for him, before he strokes, twangs, and finger fucks me until stars ignite and my skin slicks with sweat.

"Give it to me," he demands, like he's as desperate for me to come as I am.

No man has ever put me first.

No man has ever placed my needs before his.

No man has ever made me feel so desired.

So instead of clamming up like I should, I sink into him deeper before twisting up to align our lips.

With one hand down my bikini bottoms and the other curled around my throat, Maksim kisses me with a hunger I've never experienced. He duels our tongues and bites my lips before he speaks over my now-bruised mouth. "Make my fingers sticky, Doc. Smear them with my wife's cum."

I break.

With the cry of a woman who has forgotten she is in public, I grip the edges of the sunlounge and come. My orgasm is so uncontrollable I scream loudly.

So loud my best friend races into the cabana with the speed of a bullet being fired from a gun.

"Fuck." I assume Maksim's cuss is in response to Zoya interrupting us, but I am proven wrong when it is quickly chased by him demanding Zoya take me back to our suite as if I am a teenager sneaking in hours past curfew.

"But—"

"Now, Nikita!"

His roar is commanding enough that I jump up from my seat, snatch up my belongings, and race for the exit so fast I almost knock over Zoya on my way past.

CHAPTER SEVENTEEN

Zoya's eyes narrow into thin slits when I mutter, "It's my fault. He asked me to pretend to be his wife, not a hussy who opens her legs after the slightest bit of attention. I should have never let him touch me like that in public."

"You were in the privacy of a walled cabana."

"That had one of its walls pinned back. Anyone could have seen us." I breathe out slowly before confessing, "Someone did see us."

Zoya's eyes widen as she moves to the edge of her seat. "Who?"

"I don't think I've seen him before. The deep scar along his jaw kind of makes him memorable." I slump into the sofa before resting my arms above my head. I want to excuse my aching muscles on a lack of use, but that would be a lie. They're still reeling in the delightful tightness of a blistering orgasm. "I tried to tell Maksim we had a gawker, but I..." Too ashamed to continue, I finalize my reply with a groan.

Zoya would never let me off so easily. "But you...?" Her

mouth falls open when I slant my head and arch a brow. "Maybe you should tell Maksim exhibitionism is your kink. Then he won't go psycho when a guy eyeballs you. He'll take full advantage."

"Exhibitionism isn't my... *kink*. And as if he'd go psycho." *I'm not worth the fight.*

You'd swear I vocalized my inner thoughts when Zoya whacks me upside the head with a pillow. She mushes it with my face so well the static the velour material makes with my hair almost drowns out the buzz of our suite's doorbell.

"Do you think it's Maksim returning to finish what he started?" Zoya asks like she's aware I'm using Aleena's pending hen party as an excuse to hide in our suite instead of the one next door.

"He didn't start anything." She hits me with a look I will never live down. My best friend witnessed me orgasming. Trying to pretend I'm not mortified, I say, "But I guess there's only one way to find out."

After rolling my shoulders and fixing my hair like my low self-esteem hasn't tried to convince me my facial expressions when climaxing were the cause of Maksim's abrupt departure, I mosey to the door and open it.

"Hi..." I breathe out slowly, my confidence dipping when the person on the other side isn't who I am expecting.

It isn't one person. Multiple bodies are cramming the once spacious hallway.

The lady Aleena is meant to meet with this afternoon to get glammed up for her night out begins the parade of women and men of all shapes and sizes. A middle-aged woman with a rack of designer clothes ends it.

"Can we come in?" asks the pack leader. I think her name is Sandra.

"Of course." When I move out of the doorway and gesture for

them to enter, they pile in one by one, filling the space in under a minute. "Was this you?" I whisper to Zoya when the team commences setting up a glamour station suitable for an A-list star. It reminds me of the behind-the-scenes clips Zoya watches while waiting for the Oscars to start.

Zoya shakes her head before joining me at the side of the living room that now feels half its size. "All my party funds went to Maksim so he wouldn't be out of pocket for my stuff up." She bumps me with her hip. "And because I wanted to make sure you stayed with him purely for your greedy little self." Her lips curl into a wicked grin. "Seems as if I misjudged your greediest organ. I thought it was your heart, not your—" I clamp a hand over her mouth before she can say another word.

Only once the flare of her nostrils announces she is a mouth breather do I release her from my hold.

For several minutes, we watch the team set up a glam station that would have any woman frothing at the mouth to participate before Zoya eventually saunters away from me, her hips swinging.

"Whoever organized this has class and money." She waves her hand at the case of champagne a delivery man dumped just inside the suite's door, not brave enough to enter a room that appears seconds from being overwhelmed by estrogen. "They wholesale for three thousand US dollars a bottle. I'd hate to see their retail value."

Even announcing how pricy the bottles are doesn't stop her from snagging one from a crate and cracking it open. She takes a generous swig before tilting the bottle my way.

"Are you sure?" she asks when I shake my head.

"I'm sure. The last time I drank, I woke up married. Enough said."

After tossing her head back and laughing, she takes another hefty swallow and then passes the bottle to Aleena, who has entered the living room with her mouth ajar and her eyes misted.

Her excited response to being spoiled by her husband-to-be makes me wish Zoya would keep the gift giver's identity a secret. Alas, she's too giddy to keep quiet. "The last time you got drunk, you woke up married to a man who could easily afford this." She twists the lock I wish her lips had and throws away the key before saying, "Maksim made me promise not to say anything."

Aleena's shoulders slump as fast as my heart rate climbs. "You just told me this was Maksim."

"I did no such thing," she denies. "I implied it was him. Totally different." Before I can utter a single defense, she pokes me in the chest and cocks a brow. "And before you get all worked up, this has nothing to do with your eagerness to get freaky with him in a cabana in the middle of the day." I want to crawl under a cushion and die when her words reach the women setting up a manicure station on our left. "He organized this before we went to the pool." Guilt crosses her features for barely a second before it is overrun by sassiness. "I may have hinted that this is the best way to get over a hangover."

"Z!"

"What? I had no clue he'd take my hints for a mini spa day this far." Even if she were lying as straight as a line, her smile makes her appear as crooked as her bottom teeth before she got braces. "I'm kinda glad he did, though. Who doesn't want to be treated like a princess?" She drags Aleena and me to stand in front of multiple stations you'd expect to find at a high-end spa, before asking, "What shall we do first? Pedi, mani, or a full-body massage?" When she notices the masseuse is tall, wide, and male, the devil on her shoulder decides on her behalf. "Him. Definitely him." When I don't follow Aleena and her to the Swedish giant, she cranks her neck back to peer at me. "Come on, Keet. Don't be a party pooper."

"I'm fine here." When her bottom lip drops, I add, "This day isn't about me. It is about Aleena and ensuring she has the best hen party known to mankind."

"That's true," Zoya immediately fires back, doubling Aleena's smile. "But I have a feeling your denial is more because you'd rather your husband rub out your kinks than a stranger."

"They're pretty much the same thing."

She laughs, taking my comment as intended—playfully—before she's lost to the magic of a gifted pair of hands.

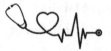

I use the unexpected silence I rarely get in Zoya's presence well. I read about the social and political aspects of the development of neurosurgery in the late nineteenth century and how meningioma terminology was the subject of nationalistic pride.

It is an interesting piece, but I've barely given it an ounce of attention the past twenty minutes. I've spent more time glancing longingly at the wall that separates my suite from Maksim's than my Kindle.

Although I shouldn't be able to hear anything over the clink of champagne glasses and the laughter a few glasses of bubbly instigate, I'm reasonably sure Maksim returned to his suite twenty minutes ago. A door creaked, and then, barely a minute later, running water trickled through the wallpapered divider between us.

Understandably, I've been in an inferno ever since.

Images of Maksim in the shower at Myasnikov Private are rolling through my head on repeat, so you can imagine how tense the situation between my legs became when I recalled his confession on how he used my face as inspiration while masturbating the past two weeks.

Add those two points to the euphoria I was experiencing in the cabana, and the tiny snippets of memories breaking through the fog in my head, and you have the perfect recipe for disaster.

I've been straying my eyes to Zoya's gift too often to brush it off as curiosity.

I'm horny—extremely—and fighting not to march into Maksim's suite and pretend his request for us to share the same bed each night includes sexual activities.

"Nikita?"

I snap my eyes away from the wall dividing my suite from Maksim's before straying them to the entryway of my room. Zoya has her shoulder propped on the doorjamb. She looks relaxed but sexually frustrated.

I'm not going to lie. I'm glad it is finally on her face instead of mine.

That doesn't mean I won't try to act like I'm not a harlot lusting over a man I've only just met, though.

"It's not nice to be teased, is it?"

She groans before slowly pacing into my room. "I swear I was this close"—she holds her thumb and forefinger a millimeter apart—"but I just couldn't quite get over the line."

"Orgasming with an audience is hard."

She looks at me as if I lost my marbles. "It wasn't that. I just..."

When she goes quiet, I'm confident I do not know the woman across from me. Zoya doesn't shy away from anything, much less something as unthreatening as controversy.

My heart thuds in my ears when a reason for her peculiar response smacks into me. "You have feelings for the guy you duped!"

"Don't be ridiculous. I'd never fall for a guy like that." She holds back her truth for two whole seconds. "His son, though... I wish he wasn't so damn sexy. He would be a lot easier to forget if he were butt ugly." When she flops onto my bed, the study snacks I downed like a piggy crinkle beneath her.

I cringe when she pulls out the multiple wrappers I was hiding under a thick duvet.

"You didn't eat all of these, right?"

I snatch them from her hands and stuff them back under the bedding. "We're not discussing my poor eating habits while studying. We're discussing you and the unbelievable notion that you may have developed feelings for someone."

"But those aren't normal chocolates—"

"No buts. Tell me about this guy and why you thought running was better than seeing if he feels the same way?"

My back molars crunch when the first reason she smacks me with is highly valid. "He's married or soon-to-be married. Something like that."

"Z—"

"I didn't know that when we started messing around." She rolls over and props herself on her elbows. "He says that they're not sexually involved."

"They all say that."

"I know," she grinds out, dramatically sobbing. "But he's so convincing I almost believe him."

"Only almost?"

She breathes out of her nose before peering up at me with pleading-for-forgiveness eyes.

"Z..."

"It's not my fault. That man can swoon, and when he's jealous..." I could have lived without seeing her hued cheeks and glossed-over eyes. "Fuck. I've never known someone so cocky."

"Have you met my husband?"

Her laugh is nice to hear considering the tenseness of our conversation. "I have." She locks her eyes with me. "That's one of the reasons I asked for his help. If I had to return the money to Andrik this morning, I may not have survived." Fear crosses my face, but she's quick to douse it. "Not like that. I mean, I may have become the other woman... *permanently*."

"His hold over you is that strong?"

It kills her, but she nods. "If he weren't taken, maybe you

wouldn't be the only one shacked up with a hot hunk of a man you barely know."

I try to think of something to say, either witty or helpful, but I'm genuinely stumped. Zoya lives life in the fast lane, but I knew it would eventually slow for the right person. I just never fathomed that that person would be already taken.

After squeezing her hand, soundlessly promising I will always be there for her, I ask, "Do you want to go back to the chocolates now?"

She smiles, grateful for the diversion, before replying, "In a minute."

I eye her curiously, shocked she's not jumping at the opportunity to steer the attention away from her. She loves demanding the focus of a room, but only when that room is full of men.

"With everything going on"—she wiggles her hand at the lower half of my body so I can't miss what she means—"I completely forgot why I left you in the hands of a genius who clearly knows what he's doing." She gets off track remarkably quick for someone with a GPA as high as mine. "Was that a new record? Surely it was a new record. I had to go up and down ninety floors, but you were done by the time I got back."

She laughs when I whisper, "I wasn't in the right head space to set my stopwatch... but yeah, I think it was." For the first time in over a decade, I remember my ability to have fun didn't end when my baby sister died. "His skills are mind-blowing. They kind of make me..."

"Jealous?" Zoya answers when words elude me.

"I was going to say horny, but yeah, jealous could be used too."

She laughs again, and it is infectious. "That might have more to do with the chocolates you gorged while studying, but let's focus on one matter at a time." With a megawatt smile, she tosses her phone into my lap. "I cleaned the album up for you. You should be able to go back at least three days and be safe of any vulgarities."

"Only three days?" I jest while logging into her phone and opening her photo album.

Because I click on the first photo displayed, the events of last night play in reverse. They start from me tossing the bouquet—and purposely aiming it at an ashen-faced Zoya—to my best friend holding the dress Maksim pointed out this morning against herself and snapping a hundred selfies.

"What?" Zoya says with a laugh when my flicks make her move like a cartoon. "That dress was gorgeous. Even I was wondering what it would be like to get married in it." She nudges me with her elbow before she switches the photo album for videos. "This one is my favorite," she says, stopping on a video that registers as familiar even with my memories clouded.

"I remember that," I murmur more to myself than Zoya when it commences playing.

She peers down at the footage that's bordered by the door and doorframe she must have shoved her phone between to capture the private moment between a groom and his bride-to-be, but remains quiet, leaving the floor to me.

"All day today, I've been seeing images of Maksim kneeling in front of me and peering up. I thought maybe he was proposing." I trace the garter Maksim is placing high on my thigh before whispering, "The way he was looking at me should have sobered me up, but it made me worse. I was intoxicated..."

"By him," Zoya and I say at the same time.

When I snap my eyes to her, she smiles. "You said the same thing last night, and in an instant, everything made sense. Drugs weren't speaking on your behalf. It was that big fat heart you tried to lock away when your mother died." Wetness pools in her eyes, making me panicked. "You told him everything, Kita. About your sister and your mom and how their deaths drove your dad insane." She tries to bring out some playfulness to ensure our tears remain at bay. "Your hate of pistachio nuts and anything associated with them." There's no jealousy in her tone when she admits, "You even told him things I didn't know." There's nothing but love and admiration. "I've never seen you like that before. You were so free, and since he gave you that, I stepped back and let you do what you wanted to do. Will you hate me for it in the future? Maybe. But for now, I get to watch you live for you instead of everyone else."

"It's my job," I try to defend, loathing that I've done such a terrible job of making out that I'm okay when I'm barely surviving. "I'm meant to help people."

"It is. I agree. But occasionally you have to accept help as well. If the well is empty, no one will be able to drink from it." She aligns our eyes so I can see the honesty in them. "Not even you." When I screw up my face so hard I'm afraid of a new wrinkle, she gives me the same out I gave her earlier. "Do you want to go back to the chocolates now?"

I nod, almost sending sentimental tears rolling down my face. "Please."

"Okay." She squeezes my hand before pulling out the wrappers I hid.

It dawns on me that I was more gluttonous than first perceived when my quick head count announces I consumed more sugar today than I do during Donut Holes Thursday. It is dark chocolate, which makes it not as bad as regular chocolate, but the flavanols found in dark chocolate are meant to lower your blood pressure.

This batch did the opposite.

I'm buzzing all over and don't feel the slightest bit tired.

"I'll probably pay a hefty penalty for my gluttony tonight."

"We can only hope," Zoya replies, her voice husky with concealed laughter. "Because they're not standard chocolates. I had these especially shipped in for Aleena's honeymoon."

My throat works through a dry swallow when she turns over

the lid of the box I didn't pay attention to when my hunger got the better of me.

Break. Bite. **Bang.** *Pleasure-boosting dark chocolate to increase your sexual performance.*

When my eyes snap to Zoya, she waggles her brows before saying, "You're welcome."

CHAPTER EIGHTEEN

A s I wipe sweat from the back of my neck, my grandmother asks, "Are you sure you're okay? You sound a little restless."

"I'm fine. I just... ah..." *Ate my weight in the female equivalent of Viagra and can't stop having naughty thoughts about the stranger I married*, but since I can't say that to my sweet old grandmother, I reply, "I'm just a little tired. It's been a big day."

Usually, I ring my grandmother every night to check in. I missed our call last night, so I'm doing tonight's early so I won't make the same mistake twice.

"I can imagine." Her joyful sigh whistles through her dentures. "This must have taken a lot of planning."

I drift my eyes back to Aleena and her bridesmaids still getting glammed up for a night on the town. "Zoya organized everything. I just showed up."

"Not the bachelorette party, darling, although I'm glad things are going well. I am talking about moving us into an apartment upstairs."

Assuming the chatter between Aleena and her friends who

could only attend the official bachelorette part of her destination hen party has me mishearing her, I slip into the corridor before asking, "What did you say?"

"The move. It must have taken a lot of work to plan it while you were away. The apartment is gorgeous, Kita. The rooms are spacious and mold-free, and the kitchen is bigger than any I've seen. I'll be able to bake for days in there. Do you remember how I used to bake when you visited as a child?" She doesn't wait for me to answer. "I'll be able to make you all your favorite treats again."

Her excitement is felt from thousands of miles away, but it doesn't change the facts. I have no clue what she is referencing. I can't afford the rent in the basement apartment they get at a steal because they've lived there for over two decades.

"Gigi, I don't know what you're talking about. I didn't organize anything."

"Oh..." She goes quiet for a second before saying, "There's a medical team here preparing to move your grandfather. Maybe one of them will know more."

"Ah... hello," says a deep voice a second after a whoosh sounds down the line. "This is Dr. Muhamed. How can I help you?"

"I'm sorry, my grandmother has a bad habit of forcing her issues onto unsuspecting victims." I love my grandmother with all my heart, but her belief that she couldn't take care of my grandfather after he was diagnosed with emphysema is the sole reason my family moved to Russia. My mother was seventeen years my father's senior, so they faced ailing parental health long before my father's parents reached retirement age. "My grandmother mentioned they were in the process of being moved into another apartment?"

"Yes," Dr. Muhamed answers quickly. "It is in the same building, just several floors up."

"Who organized that?"

"We were contracted by"—papers ruffle before he says—"Ivanov..."

"Industries," we say at the same time.

I have a million questions to ask, but since they can't be answered by the medical contractor Maksim hired, I focus on what is most important right now. "My grandfather has stage four chronic obstruction pulmonary disease with limited cardiopulmonary reserve. He cannot be moved without proper equipment and planning."

"We've arrived with portable oxygen, oximeters, and corticosteroid medication we will only use if necessary."

"Fluticasone or Budesonide?"

I step back, shocked when he answers, "Both."

I've never had the option of choosing my grandfather's medication.

It was whichever option was the cheapest.

"He was administered oral steroids earlier this week, so please limit them unless also necessary, and he's—"

"On a single dose of Azithromycin for pneumonia. I read his medical report before agreeing to this assignment, Dr. Hoffman. I assure you we will make the move as safe and as uncomplicated as possible."

The assurance in his tone is encouraging, but I can't help but worry. My grandparents are the only family I have left. My father was sentenced to life, and his parents want nothing to do with me since they believe I am the only reason my father married my mother. "Has someone checked the new apartment for any aggravators of COPD?"

"Yes," Dr. Muhamed answers. "I went over it myself. Not a single dust bunny or speck of ash could be seen. It is as clean as its hefty price tag demands."

"Okay. Good." I would like to say more, but I'm too shocked to function. I feel like I'm living in a dream and everything I've ever wanted is finally coming true.

"Is that all?" Dr. Muhamed asks, his tone uneasy.

"Yes." I wipe at my cheeks like it will stop my words from cracking with emotion. "But can you please take down my number? I would like to be informed of any changes to my grandfather's condition during the relocation."

"I already have your number stored. I will keep you updated, though I doubt it will be in regard to declining markers." He sounds surprised while saying, "His stats are exceptional for his prognosis. His care far exceeds any I've seen from other palliative care patients, and I only see that improving with the new ventilation and ECOM unit currently being installed in his new apartment."

There's no hiding my sob this time around. I've been saving for a new extracorporeal membrane oxygenation unit for several years. The one we've been using is on loan from the hospital. It is old and outdated and often shuts down in the middle of the night. That's why my sleep is so lagging even when I don't work a double shift.

"Dr. Hoffman? Are you still there?" Dr. Muhamed asks.

"Yes, sorry." I wipe at my cheeks that are now wet. "I think the connection is bad. If you need me—"

"You're only a phone call away."

I smile like it won't make me look psychotic. My tears are tears of happiness, but you wouldn't know that for how many are streaming down my face.

Dr. Muhamed must hear my smile, as he says, "Enjoy your honeymoon, Dr. Hoffman. I'll be in touch if I have any questions."

He disconnects our call before I can reply. If only he were half a second faster, then maybe I would have missed my grandmother's surprised gasp when he assumed I am on my honeymoon.

I had planned to tell my grandparents about my arrangement with Maksim in person.

I don't have a choice now.

My finger hovers over the number at the top of my recently called list when a creak sounds over my big exhalation of nerves. It didn't come from the door opposite me. It came from one down the corridor—from Maksim's suite.

When he notices me, a smirk curls his lips before he bridges the gap between us. His hair is wet like his shower was long for the exact reason my deviant head believes, and he's replaced his sunscreen-ruined suit for one that is navy blue and cut to show-case every perfect ridge of his body.

His walk is predatory. Claiming. It activates every one of my hot buttons and has me remembering the sticky mess I was before Zoya interrupted my stalk of the wall separating our suites.

A mannish cologne wafts up around me when he swoops down to kiss my forehead like he did in the video I've watched on repeat the past twenty minutes. It was closely followed by him falling to his knees to slide my garter up my leg.

"I was just coming to find you..." His words trail off as fury hardens his features. "What happened? Are you hurt? Did someone hurt you?" He stops seeking the apparent perp in the hallway when I shake my head, but not even my silent pledge that I'm fine lessens the anger in his tone when he asks, "Then why are you crying?"

His protectiveness takes my breath away when it unearths a memory of him wiping away my tears when I told him how I lost both my parents within days of each other. My father is still breathing, but since he refuses to meet with me, his loss was as painful as my mother and sister's.

When my delay causes more angst for Maksim, I wet my mouth to loosen up my words before saying, "I just spoke with my grandmother." My words flutter as wildly out of control as my heart does when his possessiveness has me wanting to run into his arms instead of away from him. "She told me about the apartment." My voice breaks when I add, "And the medical equipment."

He brushes a tear off my cheek with a gentleness I'd forgotten he had until I watched the videos of last night before he mutters, "They weren't supposed to tell you until you returned home." Unexpected laughter bubbles in my chest when he says more clearly, "I didn't want to be accused of bartering for sexual favors... even if that is what I am doing." He leers as if pleased I took his comment as intended. Playfully.

His spirited nature clears my nerves and has me acting how I did in the many videos and images Zoya snapped of me last night. "I think you've mistaken the terminology of negotiating, Mr. Ivanov."

Maksim's voice holds the same husky edge as mine when he steps closer and says, "And how did you come to that belief, *Mrs. Ivanov?*"

Sweet lord, that is even sexier than "my wife."

I swallow to lube my throat with much-needed spit before replying, "Because when you're the payee of the barter, you're also meant to be the recipient of any benefits sought." Lust hangs heavy in the air, forcing a brief interlude in my reply. "I've been the sole beneficiary of our arrangement. That isn't exactly fair."

"It isn't?"

When I shake my head, he crowds me against the wall, then angles his head until our lips are half an inch apart.

I bake under the intensity of his hooded gaze, but I play it cool. I want him to kiss me again, desperately, but solely with the hope it will unlock more memories like our kiss in the cabana did.

Yeah, right.

I want him to kiss me so badly that I'm on the verge of falling to my knees and begging.

I won't, though.

If I don't keep things even between us, I will be eaten alive.

Maksim's eyes flicker like he mistook my worry as a challenge before he finally breaks the tension that's so hot I'm overcooked. "If things aren't even, and you're all about equality, how are you going to fix the injustice, Mrs.—"

I propel onto my tippy-toes and kiss him before he can finalize his reply, and before my head can get in a single word over the numerous shouted demands of my heart.

My boldness eggs Maksim on as much as it did in the video from last night. After banding my legs around his waist, he weaves his fingers through my hair and tugs my head back. He takes all the control, and I give it to him.

This time, since we're not interrupted, our kiss lasts far longer than the thirty-second grind-up Zoya promised she'd remove from her phone after forwarding it to me.

Maksim's kiss is deep and messy. *Desperate.* It is better than the one we shared in the cabana but makes me just as needy and hot. I want his hands roaming my body like they were then, groping and exploring me. I want to feel his erection squashed against me, and the roughness of his stubble on my collarbone when he suckles on the delicate skin of my neck.

I want him everywhere.

And I want it now.

With one swoop, I use the legs circling his waist to yank him over the half an inch separating us before I grind down on the thickness his zipper is struggling to contain.

"Fuck, Doc. You've got my cock acting like I don't have an ounce of control over it." He cups my ass in his hands before he guides my hips forward, rocking me against him. It is the equivalent of a prom night grind-up behind bleachers, but it has me burning up everywhere. My skin sets on fire as my panties dampen. "You're making me lose my fucking mind, and I don't want to do a damn thing about it."

He kisses me again until I am as drunk on excitement as I was last night, and then he inches back.

It isn't as bad as it seems.

A second after he steals a longing glance, he cranks his neck to the side and tells a man standing at the end to continue without him. "Make sure he is found. I want this public."

"Yes, boss," the man replies, his voice as rumbling as predicted when you take in his broad shoulders and gigantic height.

He's barely entered the elevator before Maksim reacquaints our lips. While walking us toward his suite, he kisses me like he can't breathe without my mouth on him, like the chemistry that's burned between us since day one will never disintegrate.

He kisses me like he loves me, which is utterly ridiculous to even consider. We barely know each other, but that doesn't mean I'm not going to relish every snippet of attention he awards me.

I'd be insane to turn this down.

As Maksim drags his tongue along the roof of my mouth, his hand slips beneath my shirt. Just his fingertips brushing across my skin sends a torrent of excitement to the area between my legs.

My pussy, to be precise.

My body's response to his simplest touch makes me frantic to experience the same. I want to feel the heat of his skin under my hands, to see if it bunches and contracts like mine does when awarded simple brushes and urgent gropes. I want to feel every inch of him, and I don't know if I can wait until we're in the safety of the bedroom to do that.

Maksim chuckles when I push him into the first solid object I see. Luckily for him, it is a bulky sofa.

His laughter is switched for a moan when I fall to my knees between his splayed thighs and shoot my hands to the waistband of his pants. I pull at his belt, *hard*, and work it through the loops with urgency.

Maksim's pace is slower than mine. With a lazy smile like he has all the time in the world, he unknots his tie and tosses it aside before he unbuttons his pants and lowers the zipper just enough to expose the designer brand name of his boxer briefs.

When his thumb hooks into the stretchy black material, I balance my backside on my heels and wait for what I know will be a spectacular visual. His cock will be phenomenal from any angle, but there's something more exciting about the prospect of facing it head-on. It is almost intimidating.

"Tell me how much you want my cock, Doc," Maksim demands, his words as punctured as the throbs of the veins in his neck when our eyes lock and hold. "Tell me how much you want me."

Lust rolls through my stomach like a wave, and I lose all cognitive thoughts.

"How about I show you instead?"

His cock bounces when I tug down on the black material incapable of concealing the enormity of his package. Then I hiss when I realize I am in way over my head.

I thought his penis was glorious before, but it has nothing on the silky pre-cum-tipped cock I've pulled out. It is long and thick, the nicest-looking penis I've ever seen, but I don't know what I'm doing.

The amount of pre-cum leaking from Maksim's cock exposes he believes differently.

His hooded watch as I struggle to comprehend the scale of his cock gifts me so much confidence, I grip the base of his shaft, wet my lips, then slide them over the crown.

My moan when I taste him for the first time sees him threading his fingers through my hair and encouraging me to take him deeper. The corners of my mouth burn when they're forced to accommodate his girth, and my eyes water, but excitement is my most notable emotion.

"Fuck, Doc," he groans when I take him to the back of my throat. "Look how beautiful you look swallowing my cock. You're doing so well. Just a little more." He thrusts his hips slightly, bulging my eyes. "Yes," he hisses like a snake. "Just like that. So fucking good."

I breathe through my nose while following his silent prompts. I take him deeper when his tugs on my hair turn violent, then flatten my tongue and dedicate the attention of my lips to the rim circling his crown when his ass sinks into the sofa.

I work him over and over again until his grunts leave no doubt that he is on the verge of release, and my panties are drenched through.

"You're going to make me come."

He groans in pleasure when I swirl my tongue around his knob, working him with enough determination he knows I'm not going anywhere.

I want him to come in my mouth.

"And you're going to swallow it all, aren't you, Doc. Every last drop."

Don't misconstrue. He isn't asking a question. He's stating a fact. He knows I'm desperate to taste him, and that my hunger can only be quenched one way, but I still murmur my agreement because I don't want anything to derail this train now.

The tension is so white-hot that I completely forget this is the first time I've ever considered swallowing a man's cum, much less encouraged it.

"Scoot back a bit and tilt your head up. I want to watch my cum slide down your throat," Maksim requests a short time later.

My thighs press together when he edges off the sofa far enough that he towers over me. Then I meow when he directs his cock in and out of my mouth another handful of times before he demands my eyes to his.

I try to follow his orders, but the image of him stroking his cock while dipping the crown in and out of my mouth is too enticing to give up.

"I said, *look* at me."

Our eyes lock a mere second before a beading of cum pumps

out of his cock and hits the back of my throat. I swallow it down immediately, moaning through every delicious drop.

After ensuring not a single morsel has been missed, Maksim plucks me from the floor and positions me until my knees cuddle his thighs, and my clit is acutely aware his release hasn't deflated his cock in the slightest.

Unable to stop myself, I grind down on him. His cum lingering on my taste buds already has my thighs shuddering, so I won't mention how wild the rim of his cock makes me when it flicks past my clit.

"Fuck," I pant, mimicking Maksim's praise.

I feel his lips rise against my neck before he says, "I knew there was a heap of naughtiness hidden in your wholesome package the moment I laid eyes on you."

When he tilts up his hips, matching my grinds, pleasure courses through my veins like a drug.

I grind against him until I'm so drunk on lust, I talk freely.

"What gave it away?" I don't wait for him to answer. "Watching a man I hadn't officially met stroke his cock? Or marrying him only weeks later?"

"It would have been days if they hadn't tried to fool me." His hand slides between us, and my brain fritzes so thoroughly he could say anything and I wouldn't stop this. "But you're here now, heating my cock with a cunt that smells so fucking good I'm glad I skipped breakfast."

I giggle like a schoolgirl when he tosses me onto the other half of the springy sofa with enough force that I bounce. That's where my childish antics end, though. The instant he mimics my kneeled position and slides his hands under my skirt to hook his thumbs into my panties, things turn so serious I almost clam up.

I'm nervous as hell, but also horny, so I nod when Maksim wordlessly asks permission to remove the one pair of lacy panties I threw in my bag in case of an emergency. They were the only pair Zoya left when she hid my granny panties and baggy tees under my bed so I couldn't change out of the swimwear she lent me.

After sliding my panties down my thighs and guiding them past my almost soleless shoes, Maksim lifts them to his nose.

His moan when he breathes in the scent darkening the crotch pulls my knees together.

"I fucked my hand to that smell so many times the past two weeks." He takes another whiff. "It is even better than I remembered." He drops his eyes to the slit between my legs. "I bet it tastes even more delicious than it smells."

His mouth lands on the cleft of my pussy with the accuracy of a missile not even a second later. Electricity jolts through me when his tongue flicks my clit before he swivels it around it, and then my hands seek something to grab when his gritty tone vibrating through my pussy almost makes me combust on the spot. "Best. Fucking. Meal. I've. Ever. Tasted."

He works my pussy so well I'm in a frenzy in under a minute. My clit thumps louder than my heart, and the scent he is sampling strengthens.

I'm putty in the hands of a genius.

"Oh my god," I grit out when he overwhelms my senses by pushing two fingers inside me and scissoring them wide.

"I knew you'd be tight." While toying my clit with his tongue, he continues to stretch my pussy with his fingers. "Could have never predicted this, though." He looks at me over my thrusting chest and a stomach that won't quit quivering even though pain is associated with our exchange. "I've got to stretch you, Doc, or I'll tear you."

His eyes speak the words his mouth won't.

This isn't about pleasure right now.

It is about making sure he'll fit when we move on to the next stage.

"Relax a bit for me. It's going to feel real good real soon. I just need you to relax." He adds extra pressure to my clit with his tongue when I loosen the clench of my thighs and sweep them open a little more. "That's it. You are doing so well. You're going to be swallowing my cock in no time."

Once Maksim is certain my pussy will be more accommodating to a man of his girth, he curls his fingers stuffed inside me upward, creating an immense amount of pressure between his mouth and his fingertips.

He flicks his tongue over my clit and milks my G-spot for several long minutes, sprinting my orgasm toward an imminent release.

This is no longer about making sure he'll fit.

It is about pleasure and how a snippet of pain can gain you a ton of rewards.

A hot, wet trail slides from my pussy to my ass when Maksim pulls me onto his mouth and swirls his tongue over my clit again and again and again. He draws it into his mouth, curling my toes with the power of his sucks.

My thighs shake as every muscle in my body tightens.

"I'm going to come," I warn like it's a bad thing.

How could anything that feels this good be bad?

I feel Maksim's lips rise against my pussy before he increases the pressure of his tongue on my clit. He flicks the nervy bud on repeat while guiding his fingers in and out of my pussy in tempo to the rock of my hips.

His dedication blisters stars before my eyes and shoves me to within an inch of the finish line.

I'm right there.

Right on the edge.

I just need him to move to fully surrender to the wave tumbling into me.

"Wait..."

I claw at his head, desperate to move him away from the carnage.

This isn't how it's meant to be. His head isn't meant to be

between my legs when I climax. He's meant to be gathering the washcloth while I finish myself off.

That's how it always worked with my other bed partners.

"You can't... I'm about to—"

I lose the fight when Maksim seizes my wrists and pins them to my sides. He holds nothing back as he unravels me with his mouth. He eats me like he is starved of taste, and I crumble under the intensity.

My orgasm is strong. Intense. *Dangerous.* I thrash against Maksim's mouth until the pull becomes too great and I sink into the sofa like I'm plunging backward off a cliff, moaning nonstop.

"Look at you making a mess of my sofa. You're so fucking beautiful when you're creating a ruckus."

His praise extends my orgasm and drains me of energy. I'm a sticky, floppy mess when he scoops me into his arms and positions me until I'm once again straddling his lap.

His pants are hanging lower down his legs now, past his ass and almost at his knees, and his sheathed cock is nudging at the opening of my pussy.

Don't ask me where he got a condom from. It must have been sometime between me being catapulted into hysteria and slowly floating back to Earth.

Although I'm exhausted, I rock my hips forward, welcoming him in when he rubs his head through the folds of my pussy.

Maksim accepts my invitation with a brief nod before he thrusts inside me.

He prepared my body for him, but a whimper still escapes me. I've never been filled like this before. It's almost too much, but I grit my teeth and breathe through the pain.

"Wait." His one word is forced through a tight jaw and grinding teeth. "Lean back. If I pull out now, there is a possibility I could still tear you." I'd give anything to have all my memories returned when he locks his eyes with mine and mutters, "I can't hurt you, Doc. I don't care how badly I want you; I'll never force you to do anything you don't want to do. Not after what you told me last night."

After tilting me back far enough I can't miss the intimate way our bodies are joined, he lowers his hand between my legs.

With my clit still sensitive from two orgasms in a matter of hours, it only takes a handful of rotations to loosen the walls of my vagina clamped around him.

"Oh god," I moan when a familiar sensation builds low in my stomach again.

"We can do better than that," Maksim murmurs before he whips my shirt off over my head and tugs down on the cup of my bra.

My knees hug his thick thighs when he toys with my nipple and clit at the same time.

I'm on the verge of climaxing again in a shamefully quick amount of time, but too horny to care.

I want to come again, and I want Maksim to know how wild his attention makes me.

"Yes, Doc. Ride me," he hisses against my breast when the tingles racing through me see me rolling my hips in rhythm to the pulse of my clit.

Like it can get any bigger, his cock flexes when I rise to my knees before I pull them out from beneath me.

When I fall back onto him with a thud, his groan is as loud as the slap my ass makes with his thighs.

"Naughty, naughty girl," he grits out before he encourages my reckless pace by gripping my hair at the nape and thrusting his hips upward. "I knew you'd be wild. That's why I was so cocky when you walked in on me in the shower. When you looked at me all wide-eyed and needy, I wanted to take you where you stood... right on the floor of my mother's hospital room."

His confession makes him angry.

He fucks even harder when he's mad, and in no time, another orgasm pulses through me.

I'm barely back from the clouds when Maksim's dirty mouth has me racing for the finish line again. "Your cunt looks so good swallowing my cock. You're taking me so well." He pushes down on the middle of my stomach. "I am so fucking deep. I've never been so hard. That's all you, Doc. Those eyes... them lips... that big ass brain of yours." He thrusts harder, pushing past the inches hidden because of his seated position. "I hadn't even looked at you and I already knew I needed to make you scream my name. Then I saw you..." His grunt vibrates all the way to his balls. "Fucking kneecapped."

He screws me senseless until I scream so loud, if Zoya didn't know where I disappeared to, she does now.

"Say my name, Doc. Scream it. Let everyone know who is fucking you."

A snippet of defiance blisters through me as I strive to keep my moans generic. It isn't that I don't appreciate how well Maksim fucks. He fucks like a god. I'd just rather he be the only one who knows what I sound like when I come.

"Fucking say it."

He pulls at my hair, tugging the roots away from the scalp, but I can't get enough. I love how filthy he's making me feel. How unhinged.

"Say. It!"

He slams into me over and over again until his name rips from my throat in a long, mangled roar and I collapse onto his chest from exhaustion.

CHAPTER NINETEEN

"**D**oc."

Consistent, dull pounding wakes me every day. Today is no different. It is just the location of the *thud, thud, thud* that's changed. My head is demanding more sleep, but the throbbing pulse is several inches lower than my temples.

It is between my legs, and the delicious ache rushes memories of the event I was undertaking before I collapsed from exhaustion to the forefront of my mind.

Touching.

Groping.

More orgasms than I can count.

I consummated my vows as if they were legitimate instead of the arrangement they are.

I shouldn't be so hard on myself. I knew my heart wouldn't survive a second in Maksim's presence, so why did I expect anything different from my body? I guess I could excuse it on the fact my body usually demands less. It is the vessel of my heart and brain. It never gets a say in any decisions I make.

I can't say that anymore.

It wanted Maksim almost as much as my heart did.

My tongue briefly skims over a delicious salty palette when I wet my lips. It is only the quickest sample, but it heightens my senses as rapidly as the fullness between my legs grows.

I open my eyes before snapping them shut again.

They were barely open for a second, but it was long enough to announce to Maksim that I am awake. His cock—that is still inside me—thickens as he brushes off a strand of hair that fell across my eye.

"I'd let you continue sleeping if I could, Doc."

As his gravelly tone brings me out of my zombie state, the horror of the situation smacks into me.

I fell asleep on him after he awarded me the best sex of my life.

Was it before he came?

After?

Did I drool on him?

When I inch back, too horrified by the possibility not to check, Maksim's groan rolls through me. "Easy. If you want me to keep my word to Zoya, you need to quit wiggling. A man can only take so much teasing."

Confusion rolls through me. "Zoya is here?"

I stop scanning the living room of Maksim's suite when his growl announces he wouldn't even allow my best friend to see me in such a compromising position. I'm somewhat dressed. My skirt is just now a belt, and my bra is a midriff top.

"No. Zoya messaged your phone not long after you crashed." He nudges his head to my phone, which is dumped on a side table next to the sofa we got freaky on. "I messaged her back so she wouldn't worry."

I gulp hard when I notice the time on my phone.

I napped for more than a few minutes.

I've been sleeping for almost three hours.

My eyes bulge when I flick through the planner in my head and land on an important task I was meant to undertake this evening.

"I have to go." Maksim's groan when I dismount him makes me want to forget the promises I made. If they were pledged to anyone but Zoya, I would. As my skirt slips down my thighs, covering me, I snatch up my shirt and place it on before diving for my phone. "I'm meant to be preparing pre-club... snacks... and... cocktails." The gasping delay between my words is easily excusable. Maksim is naked from the waist down. His cock—still sheathed by a condom that exposes he mercifully finished before I collapsed from exhaustion—is impressive enough to hang heavy on his thigh, and unlike earlier, his chest is exposed since the buttons on his dress shirt are undone. "No undershirt today?"

I realize I spoke my inner monologue out loud when Maksim's eyes stray to a white A-frame shirt dumped near the pants he kicked off during our escapades, and he says, "I knew you had plans, so I didn't want you to have a sleep crinkle in your cheek."

My throat dries when I take in the ridges and bumps of his stomach a second after his smooth pecs. "I guess it's lucky I slept on your chest and not your stomach."

His smirk reveals he appreciates my underhanded compliment, but he keeps my focus where it needs to be, which also exposes he understands Zoya's importance in my life. "Doc?"

"Yeah?" I reply while fighting to take my eyes off his delicious body.

He waits for me to finish my long appraisal, before saying, "Get a move on before I add more items to my terms."

I snap my eyes to his face so fast I make myself dizzy. "We can add more?"

His agreeing murmur isn't something I'll ever hear and not squirm. "Especially if it entails anything similar to what we just did."

I can't talk. Think. I can't do anything.

I'm too busy calculating how much paper I'll need for the terms I want to add.

A clink of laughter from next door snaps me from my wicked thoughts.

"I should go?" I grit my teeth before changing my question to an affirmation. "I better go." My second attempt shows progress, but I give it another shot since it's still imperfect. "I'm going."

When I lean in to farewell Maksim like he did me this morning, I fight with all my might not to drop my eyes to his cock.

I miserably fail, and the chuckle of my husband when I limp for the door, groaning like a child, proclaims how satisfied he is with my devastation.

When Zoya exits Aleena's room, I pretend I didn't max out all my phone storage by airdropping her photos of my "wedding" to my phone.

"All settled?"

She looks as exhausted as I feel. "Finally." Her flop onto the sofa wafts up her familiar scent before her deep exhale blows it away. "Today was..."—a hundred words roll through my head as she takes time to find the right one—"amazing." Her eyes are on me, heartfelt and misted. "Thank you so much."

"Don't thank me. I didn't do anything."

She smacks my words back into my mouth with a cushion before saying, "No prenup, baby. So any gift from Maksim today was also a gift from you."

I'd groan over her reminder Maksim didn't protect his assets with a prenuptial agreement if I wasn't so damn appreciative of how special he made Aleena's day. He didn't just assist in the pre-hen party preparation. He went all out for the entire event. Food. Drinks. Limousine transfers to and from a DJ gig at a night-club that's been sold out for months. He even had four of the hotel's security team escort us, so if anyone got out of hand, they were moved on before Aleena's friends and bridal party felt uncomfortable.

"I've seriously had the best day of my life. I never would have predicted that would be the statement that ended my day when I woke up this morning."

Zoya hums in agreement as if she had similar thoughts before she nudges me with her shoulder. "Then what are you still doing here? Why aren't you taking full advantage of the alone time before we fly home tomorrow? I love Gigi, but you know as well as I do that if Maksim makes you scream like you did earlier today, she'll take his head off with a baseball bat."

"Z!"

"What? It was so hot I'm seriously reconsidering my stance on sex club parties." She stands on the couch, arches over it, then shakes her ass. "You don't have to participate, but what are your thoughts on this pose? Too risqué or tastefully nasty?"

Laughing, I spank her backside before leaping up from the sofa and making a beeline for my room.

"Are you seriously staying here? He had one request, Keet." She holds her pointer finger in the air to emphasize her state-ment. "One!"

"It's late."

Zoya scoffs at me. "Don't act like he isn't awake, awaiting your return."

When she follows me to my room, I press my finger to my lips, wordlessly requesting she be quiet before squashing my ear to the wall dividing my suite from Maksim's. "I don't want to wake him if he's asleep."

"He isn't asleep." Even though she's arguing, she presses her ear to the wall, mimicking me.

I can tell the exact moment she hears the same thing as me, as her brows scrunch before worry settles on her face.

Maksim isn't alone, and his visitor is female and most likely under the age of thirty-five.

"Maybe it's the TV?" Zoya defends.

"That isn't the TV," I reply when the female laughs at something Maksim says. "There's nothing but infomercials on at this time of the night, and her voice is too young to be an infomercial host." I almost say too seductive, but my jealousy won't let me.

My theory is proven accurate when Maksim's voice breaks over the thud of my heart in my throat. "I appreciate you coming, Raya. I know it is late, and you've traveled a long way, but hopefully I made the trip worthwhile."

"Of course you did." I gag on the seductive purr of her reply.

I hear Maksim's smirk when he says, "Let me know if you need anything."

"I wouldn't say no to a chaperon to my car."

When footsteps move away from us, Zoya and I lock eyes, sharing a million words without a single one escaping our lips, before we sprint for the entryway of our suite like we're competitors in a marathon.

I curse Zoya's long legs to hell when she beats me to the peephole. It isn't a long scold. It only lasts as long as it takes for her throat to work through a stern swallow.

A second after she inches back from the peephole, I spot the cause of her unease. Maksim is guiding a beautiful redhead down the corridor. She would be of similar age to Zoya and me, but her clothing makes her appear far more mature. Her dress hugs her curves—particularly the one Maksim's hand is hovering near—and her stilettos are the red-bottom ones every woman dreams of owning one day.

When they disappear from view, I spin away from the door and flatten my back against it. I honestly don't know what emotion to express first. I'm hurt, angry, and so very jealous, but I'm also confused.

Why do all the wonderful things he did tonight and throw them away before getting any accolades for them?

"Maybe he wasn't expecting me to give it up so easily," I answer my thoughts.

"No, Nikita. This isn't on you. And we don't even know what this is. She could be an acquaintance? Maybe she helped him arrange all the things he did today?" Zoya tries to rationalize.

"His hand was on her ass. They're more than colleagues."

"No, it wasn't. It was near it but not on it." When I glare at her in disbelief, shocked she's defending him, she says, "You don't see how he looks at you. He's crazy about you."

"The only thing he's crazy about is thinking I will let this slide." When I walk away, her eyes follow me. "It is two in the morning. No one has business meetings at two in the morning."

Zoya's giggle when I snag a dining room chair out from under the dining room table frustrates me, but I act like I don't hear it while shoving the chair under the lock that jangles two seconds after I barricade it.

I beat Zoya to the peephole this time, and I'm glad. She may not have survived the death stare Maksim hits the peephole with when a second swipe of his keycard on the electronic lock fails to disengage the lock.

"Nikita, open the door." His voice is far calmer than the tightness pinching his face. I inch back from the door when he locks his eyes with the peephole and says, "I know you're there. I can see your shadow under the door."

Zoya and I are smart enough not to move—forcing the shadows under the door to dance is the oldest trick in the book—but there's little we can do to settle our breaths when Maksim says, "You have twenty minutes. If you're not in *my* bed in twenty minutes, I will come get you."

It takes thirty seconds for Maksim's shadow to move from

underneath the door and another thirty seconds for Zoya's breathing to regulate enough for her to speak. "What are you going to do?"

"Nothing. I'm not going to do a damn thing."

She stares at me with a dazed look for several long seconds before finally realizing one thing is more capable of stealing my maturity than she is.

My wish to be placed first.

"You want him to fight for your attention." She thrusts her hand at the door. "You're disappointed he didn't knock down that door and drag you to his bed."

"Don't be ridiculous. Why would I want to sleep on the same sheets he just messed with another woman?"

"Because you know he didn't do anything." I scoff, but she continues talking as if I didn't react. "I get it. I understand why you feel this way." She hits the nail on the head when she says, "But you need to stop punishing every guy you meet for something your dad did. He chose to go after the people who hurt your mom, knowing it would take him away from you as well. Maksim—"

"Is a stranger! So stop acting like he isn't."

Over the same conversation we have whenever I end a date early because the guy is an ass, I storm into my room and slam the door so hard I wake Aleena.

I hear her ask Zoya if everything is okay. At the same time a deep voice behind me says, "Twenty minutes was far too generous."

My hand shoots for the door handle as I twist to face it, but Maksim crowds me against it before I can race through it. "We can either do this the easy way or the hard way, Doc. I'm open to either."

"I'm not going anywhere with you," I seethe, more annoyed that Zoya's accusation was more truthful than deceitful. My mother and sister were taken from me, but my father chose to leave.

That hurts.

My lungs can fill again when Maksim steps back, shockingly giving up.

I realize the error of my ways when he growls, "Hard way it is." Five seconds later, he pulls me away from the door with a tug on my wrist, bobs down, and then tosses me over his shoulder.

Zoya and Aleena freeze when he throws open my door like I'm not whacking into his back like a psycho, but they do nothing to help me get free of his hold.

They just watch as he kicks the chair I stuffed under the door and walks me down the corridor separating the penthouse suites before they're stolen from my view by Maksim walking me into his room, acting oblivious to how many times I kick and punch him.

"Let me go, Maksim," I shout. "If you don't let me go, I'll scream so loud everyone will know you're holding me against my will."

"And then what will they do, Doc? Try to take you away from me? Try to *save* you from me?" His voice is as hostile as mine, his anger just as apparent. "They'd never be so stupid."

Even him walking us toward a bed with sheets pulled tight enough that you could bounce a nickel on them doesn't calm my anger. This isn't about jealousy anymore. This is about how quickly your life can change and how rarely it is a good mix-up.

For now, Maksim's influence is good, but what happens when he decides I'm no longer enough, and I'm once again left to fend for myself?

These fears are why I haven't extended my inner circle once in the past eight years.

Zoya is my one and only friend by choice.

"I can do this all night, Doc," Maksim warns a second before placing me on the bed and caging me with his arms. "All. Fucking. Night," He waits for me to accept the promise in his eyes before asking, "So are we going to do this with words or actions?"

"Fuck you."

His smirk makes me hate myself more than I already do. "We will get to that... eventually. But first, we need to work out what the hell has your panties in such a twist you can't abide by my sole term in our agreement. My bed, Doc. My bed every night—"

"Even after it's been heated by someone else?"

When my jealousy shocks him, I slip under his arm and race for the door.

He once again beats me to it, but this time, he crowds me against it until I have no misgivings of what he meant when he said he could use actions instead of words.

He's hard and bulging, and the thickness that hasn't left my head for a single second tonight, even while dancing amongst a group of sweaty bodies, sends my head into a tailspin.

"Don't," I plea when he grinds against me, simmering my anger by replacing it with lust.

He ignores my demand. "Do you feel how hard you make me? How fucking crazy?" He rocks his hips forward another four times, firmer and deeper each time. "I fucked my hand for two weeks straight because no one could hold my interest long enough for me to even look at them." He drops one of the hands he's using to keep my arms pinned above my head to my waist before he tugs me back so the swell of my ass nestles his cock. "Why would I give this up so soon after discovering you were worth every single second I tormented myself by denying myself of you?" He answers on my behalf. "I wouldn't. I won't." His following four words are the ones I need to hear the most. "I'm not going anywhere."

"But—"

"No fucking buts." The hand he flattened against my stomach slips beneath my panties. "I don't want anything but this." He strums my clit like a musician would a guitar, making me even more desperate than a fool with abandonment issues. "No one but you."

When he licks my shoulder, I moan, my defenses weakening. It isn't solely his pledge slackening my worry. It's also the cool breeze floating in from outside.

It discloses that he scaled a balcony ninety floors high to get to me.

Ninety. Floors!

His eagerness to reach me has me wondering if maybe there's more to this than just lust. Perhaps he was brought into my life for a reason.

I arch back from the door, giving him more access to the areas of my body dying for his attention. Maksim accepts my wordless offer with a breathy groan before the hand between my legs becomes more teasing than tormenting. He places pressure on my clit with his thumb before sliding two fingers between the lines of my pussy.

"Already so wet for me," he groans against my sticky neck before he slips two fingers inside me, making me moan. "But I think we can do better."

He pumps into me enough times to dampen his palm before he withdraws his fingers, twists me around, and then flattens my back to the door. My breath hitches halfway to my lungs when he falls to his knees in front of me.

The lusty stare he hits me with is similar to the one in the video I watched earlier today, but instead of holding back his desire to devour me whole, he does the exact opposite.

He slips down my panties, which are shadowed with wetness, before he makes my dress even more immodest by shoving it up until it wraps around my quivering stomach.

"You have such an enticing cunt, Nikita. So pretty and pink." His words alone build a familiar sensation low in my stomach, so you can imagine how potent the spasms become when he moves his mouth to within an inch of my pussy. "Why would I want anything else?"

Before I can answer him, his tongue flicks my clit, and my knees almost buckle. I feel his lips rise more than I witness his grin. He loves making me so needy I can't think, speak, or breathe. And I'm too horny to care if it makes me look like a lovesick idiot.

A sex god is kneeling in front of me, licking, biting, and teasing my pussy with a mouth as sinful as his devilish good looks.

I'd be insane to give this up.

As Maksim makes love to my pussy with his mouth, I brace myself against the door and flutter my eyes shut. Waves of ecstasy roll through me as my limbs tighten in preparation for release.

I should be horrified by how quickly he makes me come undone, but I'm not. His talents are wondrous, and I'm limp and pliable within minutes. If it weren't for his big hand gripping my ass, holding me hostage to his mouth, I would have stumbled by now.

"Look at me," Maksim demands as I tighten around him, racing toward release.

As I rake my teeth over my lower lip, striving to calm the hysteria roaring through me with a smidge of pain, I flutter open my eyes and lower them.

Our eyes make contact, and I hiss. The tilt of my hips means I can see everything he's doing to me. His tongue connecting with my clit. His fingers coated in my arousal as he thrusts them in and out of me. A thickness not even the sturdiest material could conceal. I can see every wicked detail, and the naughtiness is my undoing.

My hands search for something to tether to as the tingles rushing through me redden my skin. One settles on Maksim's hair, and the other twists around the doorknob.

I tug on his shiny locks, messing up their slicked-back design as my thighs clench his head.

My climax is long, and my tugs are cruel, but Maksim acts like he can't get enough. He continually flicks his tongue over my clit and groans like the pleasure pouring through me is also engulfing him.

I love how much he enjoys giving head. I grunt and grind like I'm possessed.

Then I fully surrender.

"Yes," Maksim hisses against my soaked sex, his grip on my ass more pleasing than painful. "You're so fucking beautiful when you come, Doc. So fucking delicious." He sucks on the sensitive skin that pulled me under once more before he stands, wipes his mouth with the back of his hand, then seals his lips over mine.

I can taste myself on his mouth, but instead of being repulsed, I'm turned on.

Some of the mess between my legs is transferred to his suit jacket when he bands his arm around my ass and hoists me against him. While I return the lashes of his tongue and his playful bites, he walks us back to the bed that looks like it hasn't been slept in for days.

We kiss at the foot of the mattress for several long minutes before Maksim eventually inches back. He nips at the lip I protrude in disappointment before he places me on the bed and takes another step back.

I'm mesmerized in under a second when his hand shoots to his cufflinks. There's something sexy about his unhurried pace. He makes it seem like not even a hurricane could come between us. He has all the time in the world, and if I want to hog every second of it, I can have them all.

I love that more than anything.

My breathing stalls when the removal of his cuffs and suit jacket is closely followed by the unbuttoning of his business shirt.

His shoulders are bulky and defined, stacked onto pecs that display peak physical fitness and a midsection I'd trace with my tongue even if he'd spent his day aboard public transport.

His body is divine, and it is taking everything I have not to reach out and touch every spectacular dip, ridge, and bulge.

"If you wanna touch, Doc, touch. I won't stop you."

Desire overwhelms me when his belt clatters to the floor a second before the designer brand of his briefs is exposed by a slow, careless tug on the waistband of his pants. I've felt what's hiding beneath the black material, traced the veins feeding it with my tongue. I know exactly how magnificent it is, but I'm still eyeballing his crotch as if it is the first time I've ever seen a penis.

"So fucking impatient," Maksim murmurs with a groan when my needy breaths have him lowering his pants faster than he removed his shirt and jacket.

His cock bobs when it's freed from his briefs, and the tip is already wet with pre-cum, but before my tongue can answer the deviant plans of both my head and heart, Maksim ends my campaign with two little words. "Your turn."

When I stare at him, clueless, he drops his eyes to my dress, which is barely club appropriate. It is skimpy and risqué—a dress you'd usually find on Zoya's sexy frame instead of mine. It isn't a look I can pull off, but since I was feeling airy and free after back-to-back orgasms, I threw caution to the wind and let Zoya and Aleena dress me as if I were a Barbie doll.

"I—"

Maksim shoves my denial to the back of my throat before snatching up my wrist and plucking me from the bed. I crash into his chest with enough force to wind me. However, it is not the cause of my sudden breathlessness. It is from feeling how he thickens when he spins me to face a freestanding mirror in the corner of the room. It is one of those antique-looking gold-leafed mirrors you can buy at IKEA for a couple of hundred, except it seems genuine instead of a cheap knockoff.

My confidence slithers off a cliff when Maksim commences walking us to the mirror. His gorgeous tan skin reflects the overhead lighting illuminating his suite like Hollywood stage lights. It makes it even more tempting, whereas my pasty-white skin absorbs the light more than it bounces it. It increases its gaunt appearance, and even from a distance, you can tell my muscles aren't defined like Maksim's. They are forced to keep moving. Maksim's move with purpose.

"I'm—"

"So fucking beautiful." He drags my hair away from my neck and pulls it behind my shoulders. "So fucking sexy. Christ"—he grinds himself against me like he can't wait a second longer to feel my skin against him—"I could come just from looking at you."

When his hand on my waist lowers to the dangerously high-riding hem of my dress, I brace one of my hands on the mirror and drop my head. His fingers are so long, even with his hand not officially slipping under my dress, they brush my pussy.

My clit is still thrumming and hard, desperate for any morsel of attention he wishes to award it.

"Look at me," Maksim demands, his voice husky with lust.

He awards my submissiveness by placing a delicious amount of pressure on my clit with his thumb before he slowly inches two fingers inside me.

He finger fucks me for several long minutes, teasing and stimulating me until I am on the edge of hysteria before he cruelly pulls me back to reality. "Now look at her."

When his eyes dart to the side, mine instinctively follow. Instead of the troll I'm anticipating, I am confronted by a lady with wide, lusty eyes, glistening kiss-swollen lips, and enough heat on her cheeks to convince her she should go without makeup more often.

I look presentable—desirable, even.

And since I feel so completely different, I don't cringe when Maksim's tug on my dress sends my bosom spilling out the top.

My nipples are rosy and strained, begging for attention, and my skin is so flawlessly unblemished it could only look better if covered in Maksim's marks.

"Now she understands," Maksim groans out slowly, his hand as teasing as his hot breaths on my neck. He traces them across my collarbone, tickling my shoulder blade with his stubble. "My wife is a fucking goddess."

When he steps back, I almost wilt like a picked flower left on a windowsill. The only reason I don't is there is no denying his attraction when our eyes lock in the mirror. He's as drunk as I am, just as snowed under. He truly appears as if his every wish has been granted, and for some strange reason, that gift is me.

When I spin to face him, almost stumbling since his painfully erect cock is the first thing my eyes land on, the air hisses and cracks with sexual chemistry. It humidifies the air so well I'm glad Maksim was too impatient to close the door he stormed through before scaling the balconies between our rooms.

I'm hot all over.

Even more so when Maksim rolls his tongue over his lips, his eyes flaring when he tastes me on his mouth before he repeats his earlier demand. "Your turn."

I don't hesitate for a second. Who would? I've never been looked at with so much need. So much hunger.

Once I unzip the dress all the way down, it slips off my body with only the slightest whoosh. I'm naked now—fully naked head to toe except for my scuffed-to-within-an-inch-of-their-life stilettos—but so fixated on how much pre-cum drips from Maksim's cock as he drags his eyes over my body, you'd swear I was draped in diamonds.

My eyes lift from Maksim's cock to his face when he whispers, "You make me forget how to breathe. One glance, and I forgot every instinct I was born with. Every moral. Every principle. I forgot *anything* that wasn't associated with you."

With my self-loathing obliterated and my confidence at an

all-time high, I become the woman I swore I'd grow up to be. I throw myself into Maksim's arms before kissing him as if his mouth is the secret weapon to bring me out of my shell.

Hands, arms, and legs go in all directions as I attack him with the savagery of a bear. We're naked and wet but clawing at each other as if there are layers of clothes between us.

"Not yet," Maksim breathes over my kiss-swollen lips when I grip his cock and lead it to the opening of my pussy. "You're not wet enough yet." The wooden flooring offers relief to my over-heated skin when he rolls me over before tracing a slow yet desperate kiss down my quivering stomach. "I need you fucking drenched."

My shoulder blades meet when he spears his tongue inside a second after he swivels it around my aching clit. He stuffs it deep inside, urging me toward the finish line with frantic licks and sucks before ensuring a climax is imminent by adding fingers to the mix.

He places so much pressure between his fingers and my clit, before I can warn him of its arrival, I fall into pieces, and his name rips from my throat.

"Fuck... God... Please."

Sentences are above me.

Breathing is above me.

And so is Maksim.

His giant, brooding frame hovers over me a second before he tilts my hips, lines up for a home run, and then enters me with one ardent thrust.

I call out, the sensation almost overwhelming.

I've never felt so full and content at the same time. I'm stretched beyond my limit, my vagina burning as it struggles to accommodate his size, but ecstatic to have reached this stage of our exchange for the second time.

Lust thickens my veins when Maksim drags his cock all the way out before he slams back in. He takes me so deep that I ride the crest between pain and pleasure for several long seconds before it veers in one direction—pleasure.

"Oh god, you're so..."

"Deep."

He thrusts into me harder.

"Hard."

I clamp around him when he adds a flick to his hips that drives me wild.

"Striving not to lose control." He aligns our eyes, his pupils widening when I don't attempt to hide how he makes me feel. "I'll burn down the entire world and everyone in it before I will ever give this up. I won't let *anyone* take this from me."

He waits for me to see the honesty in his eyes before he screws me senseless. He takes charge of my body, commands every inch, and I let him.

Maksim's toes dig into the wooden floorboards as the wave in my stomach crests. He drives into me on repeat, fucking me as I've never been fucked. He acts like it is his mission to unravel me, to have me screaming his name loud enough for all the guests at his hotel to hear.

He fucks like a machine designed solely to make me come.

And that is precisely what I do two seconds later.

As an orgasm crashes into me, Maksim's name tears from my throat. I quiver around him, my thighs trembling as frequently as the moans bellowing around the sex-scented space, but his pace doesn't slow in the slightest. He continues driving into me, grunting, panting, and increasing my screams until they reach an ear-piercing level.

"Yes, Doc. Scream my name. Say it so loud I'll hear it for a week."

When he tilts my ass higher, giving himself unrestricted access to my pussy, a familiar tightening in the lower half of my stomach builds again. It forms like a wildfire—out of control and with no chance of being diminished.

He pumps into me on repeat, caking my skin with sweat with every perfect thrust. I'm overcome in an instant, clawing and panting as fireworks detonate through me for the umpteenth time tonight.

As a ruckus of devastation scorches my veins, I still before throwing my head back and moaning through the stars blistering before me.

The tingles spreading from the tips of my toes to the roots of my hair augment when Maksim grinds out his release. He thrusts into me another three times before the hot spurts of cum erupting from his cock extend my orgasm.

"Fuck, Doc," he groans between frantic breaths as he struggles to fill his lungs with air. "How is this even real?" He bites at my lips and licks up a droplet of sweat before he rolls over, taking me with him.

We lay entangled for several long minutes, the heat never lessening despite our nakedness.

How could it when the most intimate parts of our bodies are still joined?

"No," Maksim murmurs a short time later when I attempt to wiggle out of his embrace. I'd rather stay wrapped up in his warmth, but even if I hadn't studied the female anatomy, I'd still know the importance of using the facilities after sexual activities. "Let him stay. My cock loves being surrounded by your heat."

His groggy voice is so sexy nothing but need fuels my tone when I ask, "Even when we're not doing anything?"

Maksim lowers the arm he threw over his eyes before peering at me. I smile when I notice how at peace he seems. There's no crinkle between his brows, and his eyes still shimmer with danger, but more because of the damage they could inflict on my heart than anything else.

"Even when we're not doing anything." His cock twitches, and the fire that has barely simmered reignites all over again.

"Though I doubt that will be a regular occurrence. It seems to have a mind of its own when it comes to you."

"Oh sweet Jesus," I murmur when he shows inhumane strength by rising to his feet without losing our connection. He doesn't even strain under the pressure of our conjoined weights as he exposes that the bumps in his midsection aren't for show. He has impressive core strength.

As he walks us toward the attached bathroom, he says, "I'll get you cleaned up like your germ phobia is rubbing off on me, Doc, but we may get a little dirty in the meantime."

I'd be a liar if I said I wasn't hopeful.

CHAPTER TWENTY

I f anyone tells you flying first class is the epitome of wealth, they're lying. First class is everything you think your heart desires until you're spoiled by a private jet.

Ivanov Industries' private jet is massive. It has rows of plush leather recliners, a marble kitchen full to the brim with snacks and expensive bottles of champagne, and a bedroom that could have been put to good use if Maksim hadn't offered for Zoya to fly back with us.

She heard me orgasm multiple times through a wall. I don't want to subject her to more torture since the jet's walls are thinner than the hotel's.

Furthermore, Maksim has been a little preoccupied for the past six hours. He made sure Zoya and I had everything we needed for our flight and gave me the same forehead kiss he did this morning when he slipped out of me after sleeping inside me all night, but he's being different. I wouldn't exactly say cold, but something is definitely occupying his time.

As the jet taxis toward a private hangar, Zoya shifts my focus away from the door Maksim disappeared behind hours ago to her.

"I honestly didn't think your husband could get any hotter." When paper crinkles in her hand, my mouth falls open. She has the terms Maksim and I agreed to before we wed in her hand. "Cock warming..." She moans in a way I wish never to hear again. "That's like top tier in the alpha stakes."

By snatching our contract out of her hand, I act as if I am not as equally turned on by the slight alteration Maksim made to his one term. "Where did you get this? You're such a snoop."

"I am not. It was sitting out for the world to see."

I glare at her, calling her a liar without words.

It buckles her lie in less than thirty seconds. "It was in the breast pocket of Maksim's suit jacket. Since that's where all men file their important documents, it was pretty much begging for me to take a look at it." She waits for me to tuck away that little tidbit of information before she twists her torso to face me. "You've got to admit, it is pretty hot that he wants to be up in your business as often as possible."

"It's not solely about sex," I try to defend. "It's about connection and—"

"Your naughty bits being stuffed to the brim as often as possible?"

She laughs like a hyena when I smash a pillow in her face but doesn't attempt to apologize to the air hostess, who startled at the derogative tone, lumping the task onto me.

"I'm so sorry—"

"She stole the man you so desperately want you're still hopeful you can sink your hooks into him even now." Zoya lifts my hand, sending rainbow hues bouncing across the dark wood grain the jet is fitted with. "This isn't a I-might-take-you-for-a-ride-when-my-wife-isn't-looking ring. This is the real deal. The ring you give your wife when you're so fucking obsessed with her you don't just want to sleep next to her every night—you want to sleep inside her too."

The air hostess scoffs, *pffts*, and glowers at us before her shock is replaced with anger. "If I wanted him, I could have had him."

Jealousy rears its ugly head, but before I can act on it, a voice that could only sound gruffer if he were coming sounds from behind my shoulder. "Get the fuck off my plane."

"Mr. Ivanov." The air hostess breathes out heavily. "I was just coming to wake you—"

"Get. *The. Fuck.* Off. My. Plane." As the air hostess hurries for the exit, Maksim locks his eyes with a gentleman over her shoulder. "And you can go with her."

"Maksim, Maria was out of line but unaware of your recent nuptials."

His use of Maksim's first name indicates he knows him more than a standard staff member, but that doesn't lessen Maksim's frustration. "She may not have, but you did." The male air hostess tries to interrupt, but Maksim continues talking before he can. "Yet you sat back and watched her belittle *my wife.*" Even Zoya almost faints from how he growls "my wife."

With how much tension is firing in the air, I am shocked when the man backs down with an apology. "You are right. I am sorry." He drifts his eyes to me. "I apologize for any discomfort caused, Mrs. Ivanov."

I barely dip my chin when he sinks into the plane's galley and disappears from view.

The hostility is rife, so of course Zoya tries to barge through it. "If you ever grow tired of him, toss him my way. There's no such thing as sloppy seconds when it comes to men." She kisses my forehead like Maksim did at the start of our flight, hopeful it will hide her grin about my narrowed glance before she thanks Maksim for letting her tag along.

"Are you not traveling with us?" My pleading eyes say what my mouth can't. *Don't force me to face Gigi's wrath alone.*

"Gigi is going to love him," she says, proving she has mind-reading capabilities. "And I've got some matters I need to wrap up before commencing my new job on Monday." She locks eyes with Maksim. "Ten, right?"

He jerks up his chin before telling her he will forward a job offer to her inbox later today.

She smiles like she has the world at her feet before she gallops down the jet's stairs.

I don't wait a second before stating the obvious. "You hired Zoya?"

Again, he lifts his chin. His reply is so nonchalant it seems as if it is only a big deal for me. "Does that bother you?"

"No," I immediately answer. "I just..." With words eluding me, I try not to look a gift horse in the mouth. "It makes me wish we still had hours left in the air." When I stray my eyes to the back of the plane, Maksim's eyes follow their route. "The bedroom has a bed, right?"

"It does," he answers as the front of his pants tighten. "And enough aviation fuel to get us halfway across the globe." My skin flushes with heat when he smirks. "But I think *my wife*"—he growls my title again as if he's aware of how wild it makes me— "would rather be ravished in an empty hangar than thirty thousand feet in the air."

He doesn't wait for me to confirm his assumption. He thanks the pilots for a smooth flight before he shows them the way out.

I'm naked and sprawled across the queen bed in his private jet not even thirty seconds later.

It is dark by the time we enter the apartment building where I reside with my grandparents. Although not quite dark enough to mistake the look of surprise on the doorman's face when Maksim guides me through the main doors of the building instead of down the cracked walkway I usually take.

The shocked looks continue when we enter the elevator, and the attendant is told to take us to the penthouse suite.

I already feel like I'm dreaming, and Maksim makes my beliefs worse. "I had originally purchased the penthouse for us, but better ventilation could be installed on the top floor. Your grandfather will be more comfortable there."

"Thank you." My praise is not enough, but it is all I have to offer him right now. Once my grandmother is no longer eyeballing me, I will find a more sufficient way to thank him.

"Darling, you look so refreshed." She tugs me out of the elevator that opens directly into the penthouse apartment before wrapping me up in one of her famously warm hugs. "I've missed you. You haven't been away this long since..." She inches back, adjusts the collar of my shirt, and then brushes off her reply like she wasn't about to say my last absence was when I sat in the morgue with my badly battered and mutilated mother's body.

She was no longer there—I like to pretend her soul left her body seconds into her assault—but I promised my father I would stay with her, so I remained at her side until she was placed in her final resting place.

With haunted memories holding my responses hostage, it takes Maksim coughing to remind me I've yet to offer an introduction.

"Gigi, this is Maksim Iv—"

"I knew you'd be back." She greets Maksim like they're long-lost friends.

Their hug doesn't last as long as the one we shared, but she speaks to him freely in Russian, making me envious of her fluency. I'd give anything to know what they're discussing. I catch portions of their conversation but nothing that makes any sense. Something about needing sleep and hoping I will never find out.

Maksim laughs during her last sentence before promising her

that will be highly unlikely. "A man knows ways to encourage his wife to sleep." I'm grateful he's returned to using English so I can keep up, but he needs to keep the desires of my lust-driven heart out of the conversation when he's talking with family. "She slept like a baby for almost three hours in the plane."

He fails to mention I slept so long because he forced so many orgasms out of me I either collapsed from exhaustion or died—*thank god.*

"Wife?" Gigi questions, forever only hearing what's important.

A tingle spreads across my chest, and my stomach clenches before I sheepishly nod.

You can't miss the size of the diamond on my hand, but I raise it in the air as if you can.

Gigi gasps before stumbling back.

I prepare my ears to be slaughtered, and although they're hammered by hundreds of words spoken in seconds, they don't follow the path I'm anticipating. She isn't upset I married without a single family member present. She's delighted.

What the?

"Come." She waves us into the apartment she's made homely with the trinkets she's collected over the years. "We must update Grampies. He's been waiting for this for some time." She cranks her neck to Maksim. "He knew it would be only a matter of time before someone snatched up his beautiful granddaughter. He just didn't want it to be one of those *козы* she works with."

"*Capre? Più che altro dei codardi,*" Maksim answers as his hand flattens against my back instead of hovering above it. I don't know if he's gauging my response to him being multilingual or ensuring I don't stumble like my grandmother did when he spoke in her native tongue. "*Codardi che stanno per ricevere una lezione.*"

My grandmother peers at me and then back at Maksim

before she spits out, "Good. *Anche dopo anni di studio, la trattano ancora come facevano con sua madre. Come spazzatura."*

The only part of her reply I understand is mother, and it is enough to spring tears to my eyes, much less what Maksim replies, "That is done with now." He isn't looking at my grandmother. He is staring straight at me and speaking in a language I understand. "No one will ever hurt her again."

Needing to do something before I maul my husband in front of my elderly grandparents, I shift my eyes in the direction I hear my grandfather's respirator, then gasp like my lungs are as airless as his when I see his aging eyes smiling a grin his oxygen mask covers.

"Grampies." I sprint to the man who has loved me as much as my father has.

"Missy Moo," he breathes out slowly when a handful of tears I can't hold back soak his gown. "The only sunshine in the world is you."

"Before you go."

My tears dried hours ago, replaced with laughter only ever released when your heart is so full it is about to spill over. There's a chance of them returning when Dr. Muhamed steps out from the portable workstation at the side of my grandfather's bed. Maksim didn't solely contract him to safely move my grandfather. He is his new full-time caregiver.

"I thought you'd like to see these before calling it a night." He hands me my grandfather's latest stats and markers. "You would swear he is in the early stages of his diagnosis."

"I wish he was." I take in the stats that show a drastic increase in lung capacity. "His VTs and IRVs are exceptional. Are you sure these are correct?"

"Yes," he answers, his voice choked with laughter. "I ran them twice just in case."

I try to think with my head instead of my heart. "It's not the surge, is it?"

Terminal lucidity, or death surge as some medical staff call it, is when terminally ill patients have abrupt and unexpected increases in alertness and energy. It often fills their family with false hope. I don't want that to be the case, but it is a phenomenon I'm anticipating undertaking in the next six months.

"Perhaps if he were on his death bed, but he still has a long way to go, Dr. Hoffman. If this is terminal lucidity, I will hand in my license to practice medicine." When he realizes he is filling me with the false hope a grandchild of a terminally ill patient should never receive, he adds, "But I will continue testing and keep you abreast."

"Thank you. I appreciate that."

He farewells me with a smile before dipping his chin to Maksim standing behind me. I can't see him. He is directly behind me. However, I detected his presence a second after Dr. Muhamed had requested to speak with me.

I take a moment to consider how much more energetic my grandfather was today before I spin to face Maksim. "Would it be okay if I sat with him for a little longer?"

I almost say "alone," but Maksim's head bob announces he is aware of my wishes before he confirms them by saying, "I will come get you in around an hour."

He presses his lips to my forehead, breathes in my scent for barely a second, and then heads for the elevator. He announced earlier that he had purchased the two three-bedroom apartments below the penthouse. When I joked that he'd never require six bedrooms, he gave me a heated look that made me wish we were alone before he said he was transforming one into a home office so he can be close to me no matter my rostered shifts.

I'm not going to lie. I melted into a puddle when he said that.

Everything he's done for my family has me shouting his name before he enters the elevator. "Maksim." He stores his cell before spinning to face me. "Thank you."

Again, my praise isn't enough, but when they're all you have, they are all you can give.

His sultry watch tells me I will pay my restitution with far more than words, but since I'm not worried, I mouth goodnight before tiptoeing toward the bed my grandfather is resting on.

I don't know how much time passed before I fell asleep on the bulky leather chair beside my grandfather's bed. It was long enough for Dr. Muhamed to conduct another set of stats on my grandfather's oxygen levels and hum in approval, but the heaviness of my limbs and the thump of my temples make it seem as if I didn't crawl into bed until after the sun woke up.

That can't be the case, because even with my vision partially blocked by the spicy-scented man pulling me into his chest, I can see the large window that spans one wall of my grandfather's room. It is pitch black outside.

"I can walk," I murmur to Maksim as he steers me away from my grandfather and the night duty nurse who arrived to relieve Dr. Muhamed shortly after Maksim left.

A hint of the cigarette he must have consumed while we were apart filters in my nose when he replies, "You can, but I'd rather carry you."

I lean in closer, using his pecs to hide my smile. He smells divine. He's a little sweaty, but that can be expected since he's carrying me down a flight of stairs instead of using the elevator.

"I didn't know these apartments had stairs."

"They're all interconnected by servants' hallways." His love of architecture is exposed when he tells me how this building was once owned by a Russian aristocrat who built it for his first wife. "The top level was hers to do whatever she pleased with." My groan vibrates through his chest when he says, "The other sixteen were for his mistresses. He snuck between each floor using the servants stairwell."

"Then why not call it the mistresses' stairwell?"

The laughter I hear in his chest isn't released, but I see it twinkling in his eyes when he lowers them to me and says, "Because, to him, they were the same thing."

"Ah..." I reply, my one word long. "The aristocrat part of your statement threw me off the scent. If you had said he was Bratva, I would have clicked on quicker."

"Because...?" He leaves his question open for me to answer how I see fit.

"Because that's the norm in the Bratva. The men cheat, lie, and steal, and the women—"

"Are worshipped like gods," he interrupts, his tone stern.

"Not in any of the stories I've read."

"Because they were fictional." He nods his head to a man standing guard at the end of the hall, dismissing him from his watch before he enters an apartment on our right. "It is far different in real life." His next set of words are barely whispers. "Well, they will be."

I try to respond to his murmured comment but lose the chance to do anything but gawp when we enter the opulent apartment. There's hardly any difference from the penthouse, except the room sizes are halved, and the furniture appears more modern since it isn't decorated with ornaments my grandmother should have thrown away in her forties.

"Maksim, this place is..." I almost say too much. Too expensive. Too worthy. But I settle on, "It's beautiful." As quickly as my praise leaves my mouth, guilt smacks into me. "But we don't need to stay here. My grandparents' apartment downstairs is—"

"A rat-infested dump."

"There are no rats. The building supervisor had exterminators come in every three months as per our rental agreement."

My lips twitch when he murmurs, "You're still a shit liar, Doc," but I refuse to smile. He's right. My grandparents' old apartment is a rat-infested dump full of germs and mold, and God knows what else, but it was also home.

As we enter the main bedroom, Maksim toes off his shoes before making a beeline for the bed. "We will shower in the morning. I'm fucking beat." When an unexpected groan rolls up my chest, I pray for light to break through the drapes covering the floor-to-roof window. "Don't worry. You'll be taken care of first. I have no intention to sleep until you've screamed my name at least twice."

He tosses me onto the mattress like he counted the steps from the door of our room to the bed before he hooks my ankle and drags me down until my ass dangles near the edge.

"Jesus... Christ..." I push out between big breaths when his mouth lands on my pussy with the accuracy of a missile.

"Making you go without panties was a shit move on my behalf," he murmurs against my clit, stimulating it more with his raspy tone. "I sat through a meeting with my dick pressed against my zipper."

He's devouring me like I'm the most delicious dessert he's ever tasted, yet jealousy still sneaks through the cracks. "Were there any women in attendance at your meeting?"

"Doc..." He pauses like he needs a minute to fully absorb my jealousy before he sucks, licks, and toys with my clit until nothing but the thrill of the chase is on my mind. "I fuckin' love when you get jealous."

"I'd have no reason to get jealous if you gave me a straight answer."

You have no idea how hard it is to talk. Every word I speak is forced through trembling thighs and moans loud enough to wake the dead. Maksim doesn't get angry when questioned. He gets hungry—and the only feast he wants to consume is me.

"You said you'd come back in an hour. You were gone for"—I stray my eyes to the clock on a remote that looks like it could land a jumbo jet—"three hours."

Three hours? Who the hell has a meeting for three hours at this time of night?

Before I can demand answers, Maksim says between licks, "It took longer than planned, but believe me, you were on my mind the entire time."

Pleasure hums through me, but it won't stop my interrogation. "Who... were... you... with?"

"Mm," Maksim moans against my clit, almost causing me to unravel. "I can taste myself in you." He stabs his tongue inside me, then does a long lick before saying with a moan, "I bet you'll be able to taste yourself on my cock too." He looks at me over the swell of my breasts, our eyes locking since they've adjusted to the dark conditions. "Do you want to check, Doc? Or can I return to the only dessert I'll ever select on any menu handed to me?"

His reply appeases my worry, but I wouldn't be me if I gave in without a little bit of sassiness. "What if it is one of those hole-in-the-wall joints that don't hand out menus?"

He backhands my clit, sending a fiery warmth across my midsection. "They don't have any desserts this tasty." His mouth is back on me in an instant, and I'm steamrolling toward release.

"Oh god..."

"Close," Maksim murmurs against my clit. "But we can do better than that."

He slips two fingers inside me and curls them at the end, milking me in rhythm to the flicks he does to my clit.

I grind against him, desperate for more friction.

My bucks drive him wild. He fucks me with his mouth faster, stretching the sensation making me a shaky, sticky mess.

Every nerve ending tingles as a long, breathy moan ripples through my lips. "Maksim... Oh... please."

"Closer."

He eats me harder and faster, feasting on my pussy like it is the only meal he has consumed today. I know that isn't the case. We shared a late breakfast in bed before he ordered enough takeout to feed an army. My grandmother is adamant she won't need to cook for a week.

"Fuck, Maksim," I hiss out with a scream when the sensation becomes too much. I'm blinded by lust, hot all over. I'm so horny I am feral with need. "Make me come. *Please.* I need you to make me come."

"Better. *So* much better."

He hits my G-spot and clit at the same time with an intense amount of pressure. I break into pieces, moaning and clawing as stars flicker above me. I can't breathe or speak. I can't do anything but fall into a bliss so chaotic and draining that my limbs feel as heavy as my eyelids.

Running water sounds into the room a second before a warm cloth is placed between my legs.

"Shh," Maksim murmurs when I stir.

He washes me with a tenderness I'm still not anticipating before he strips out of his clothes and slips beneath the sheets. I melt into a gooey puddle when he gathers me in his arms until his torso heats my back, and his cock rests between my butt cheeks—his rock-hard cock.

I want to return the favor, but I'm the most exhausted I've

ever been. Maksim and I barely slept last night, and my next shift at the hospital is only five hours away. A lack of sleep is more dangerous than drinking on the clock. I can't risk my patients' lives no matter how much I wish to stay in the lusty bubble Maksim placed me in days ago.

When Maksim positions me so my upper leg is slightly bent and his cock's head notches at the opening of my pussy, I groan before saying words I hope never to speak again. "I can't. I'm—"

"Sleep, baby."

Baby? That's new.

"I'm not going to keep you awake. I just want to be inside you while you sleep."

I want him to be proven a liar when his slow and tortuous entrance does crazy things to me. There's something sexy about a rough brute of a man going slow. It is almost as wicked as when he loses control.

"Doc," Maksim growls out in warning when my hips naturally roll. "You need to sleep. It wasn't the first item on your terms, but it is the only thing guaranteeing I can maintain number one."

My first term, and the focus of a majority of our contract, is that I continue my surgical residency.

When my silence announces I can't think of a way for both of our terms to be met, Maksim slowly withdraws.

"No," I shout a little too loudly considering the hour. I clamp around him, thickening him more. "I just need a little time to adjust. I'm so... *full.*" When I feel Maksim's lips rise, I rib him with my elbow. "It wouldn't be an issue if you'd let me help you."

His cock flexes before he replies, "It would still be an issue. Even when I was being lied to, I got hard anytime your name was mentioned." He laughs as if he is joking. I know he isn't. His jaw tightened so fast I heard its crack.

"I didn't lie to you."

"I know," he replies before he firms his grip like he knows I'm going to move. "But they did, and I need you to remember that when you return to work tomorrow." I'd give anything to roll over and face him head-on when the angst in his voice becomes too raw to bear. "They made costly mistakes, but instead of owning them, they tried to cover them up with lies."

I let his words sink in before steering him in a direction he has every right to explore. "There are steps you can take. It won't change what happened or lower the anguish, but it could stop it from happening to anyone else." I peer back at him the best I can from my little spoon position. "I know people you can speak with. They usually work pro-bono, but I'm sure they won't say no to a client who can afford to pay."

He takes my comment as intended—playfully. I hate the tension in the air, even more so since my employer is responsible, so I'll do anything to ease it.

After watching me for several heart-thumping seconds, Maksim says, "I've already spoken with someone. She gave me some advice on how to move forward from this."

I never thought I'd be a woman constantly stricken down with jealousy, but Maksim's arrival in my life is proving a liar out of me. "I'm glad *she* was able to help you."

I swear I only scoot half an inch away, but when Maksim tugs me back, I learn it is closer to nine inches.

Nine.

Glorious.

Inches.

And that doesn't include the parts of his cock hidden by his sturdy thighs.

When Maksim hears the moan I can't hold back, he presses his lips to my ear while lowering his hand between my legs. "Since term one of our agreement is important to you, it is important to me. But be warned..." He waits long enough for the tension to turn excruciating before he finishes his reply. "This will be the only time I will fuck the jealousy out of you in under an hour. Every other time—"

"It won't occur again."

He acts as if I didn't speak. "Every other time, you'll be on your knees longer than that."

Before I can conjure up a single scenario to force him to make true on his threat, he twangs my clit with his thumb, stealing my devotion from anything but him.

CHAPTER TWENTY-ONE

Maksim made his target, *just*, but when my phone buzzed, announcing a change in my roster from an early shift to a daytime shift, he switched off my alarm, then returned to fucking me like he hadn't found release only five minutes earlier.

It was a glorious night of orgasms and, shockingly, six-plus hours of sleep.

I've never felt more alive.

I freeze mid-stretch when a familiar voice warns, "If you keep moaning like that, I'm going to shove a blunt object into my ear." Zoya waits for our eyes to align before grinning. "I love you, girl, but I heard you moan enough the past weekend to last me a lifetime."

Her grin doubles when I match her maturity with a tongue poke.

After finalizing my stretch, I ask, "What are you doing here, Z? Miss me already?"

A restful slumber isn't responsible for my cheery mood. I'm a new woman solely from more orgasms than I can count.

Zoya wiggles her brows. "Always." She moves closer to my bed. "I also thought I should check that you're okay with me working with Maksim. You say I have a mile-long jealous streak, but you seem to have forgotten I learned all my best tricks from you." I scoff but don't get a single word in. "Don't scoff me. You were about ready to tear that air hostess a new butthole before Maksim took out the trash." She flops onto the bed, sending pillows and bedding flying into the air. "And I saw your stage storm-off at the bikini comp. That was gold-class jealousy."

"He was being a twit."

She rolls onto her stomach and kicks her legs in the air. "He was, but for a good reason." As quickly as my confusion arrives, she leaps off my bed and gets back to business. "Anyhoo, when Maksim offered me a job, I accepted it without considering how you'd feel about me being at your man's side more than you. You know I'd never do anything." Her smile quickly fades. "I would never disrespect you like that. But I still should have asked you." She looks seconds from falling to her knees as the glint in her eyes turns pleading. "Do you hate me?"

"Never, Z." I try to hold in my spitefulness, but it rears its head too quickly for me to shut down. "How could I when you'll keep the skanks away from my husband."

She fans her hands out in front of herself. "Why do you think I accepted his offer?"

I laugh, wishing she was joking but aware she isn't.

With my shift not starting for another hour, I pretend I have all the time in the world for girl talk. "What exactly does your new position entail?"

Zoya twists her lips. "I'm not exactly sure. I think it has more to do with you than Maksim, but we haven't hammered out all the details yet."

"Me?" I ask, too shocked to articulate more.

"Uh-huh. This kind of gave it away." She moseys to my open door, thanks someone on the other side, then wheels in a breakfast feast fit for a king. It is brimming with every breakfast treat you could think of and enough coffee to keep me awake for a week. "He also asked me to give you this."

I drag my eyes away from a massive stack of pancakes when she hands me an envelope. The card inside is basic, but the worth of the black card that falls out couldn't be mistaken even by someone without a cent to their name.

My heart flutters when I read Maksim's message.

For whatever your heart desires.
M xx

When Zoya reads the message, she moans before adding words to the disturbing sound. "I'm seriously getting a lady boner for your husband."

I give her a look as if to say, *Keep your mitts off my husband,* before I place the credit card onto the bedside table and offer for her to join me for breakfast. She crosses her heart like she does anytime she makes a promise before she beats me to the stack of pancakes I was eyeing off.

We're almost in a carbohydrate coma by the time Maksim returns to my room. He hands Zoya a sheet of paper that smells recently printed before his eyes stray to me. He drags them down my body like my wrinkled scrubs, messy bun, and makeup-free face are more appealing than the skimpy dress and fully made-up face I donned at Aleena's hen night.

"Are you ready?" His voice is husky and deep and has me wishing I had more than fifteen minutes before my shift starts.

"Almost." I spritz myself with deodorant and slip my feet into the pumps I've almost worn to death, before saying, "Now I'm ready." I wiggle my fingers at Zoya while making my way to Maksim, who is standing at the entrance of the room. My nostrils flare when I press my lips to the edge of his mouth. He smells like coffee, buttered toast, and me. "I'll see you tonight."

He jerks up his chin before kissing my temple and then stepping back. "Ano is waiting for you downstairs." Confusion must cross my features, as Maksim is quick to remove it. "He will drive you to work."

"It's half a mile down the street."

Zoya sits back and watches the fireworks when Maksim replies, "That I don't want you walking."

"With traffic, it will take longer to drive."

"I. Don't. Care," Maksim bites out, his temper rising. "Your shift finishes at nine. It will be dark by then."

Over being babied, I skirt past him while saying, "Then Ano can pick me up tonight."

"Nikita."

"Goodbye, Maksim."

My race for the exit means the click of my heels almost drowns out Zoya's breathy laugh. "And you thought getting her to agree to marry you would be the hardest part of your marriage."

Her comment lowers my speed but only long enough for the clomp of Maksim's boots to overtake the pounding of my pulse. He's hot on my tail, and even though his scowl should frighten me, my body reacts on the opposite end of the spectrum.

I'm so turned on by his possessive stalk I don't give him a chance to voice any of his grievances.

I kiss him instead.

It is a fumbling, messy embrace that makes a bird nest of my hair in under ten seconds and makes me wish a pledge didn't require putting in the hard yards.

I've enjoyed being in Maksim's bubble so much the past few days, for the first time, I'm dreading going to work.

After nipping at my lips, Maksim slowly pulls back before murmuring, "You play dirty, Doc."

"Says the guy whose kisses alone have me wanting to back-track on every promise I've ever made." Since I don't have time to settle his confusion, I ask, "Is Ano waiting for me in the garage or the foyer?"

His smile makes my backflip easy to swallow. "The garage."

With no more words needed, he flattens his hand against my back and guides me to the elevator. The eyes of the man he excused last night peek up over a newspaper when he notices our approach before he hits the call button and returns to reading. Since his suit jacket has been removed, it is impossible to miss the two-gun holster bulking out his large frame.

"Is this much security necessary?"

Maksim escorts me inside the elevator and selects the floor for the garage before instructing the attendant that he can take it from here.

He waits for him to leave before answering my question. "Being married to someone like me has as many disadvantages as perks. Security can seem like a disadvantage until you need it."

"So they're here for you?" You can hear the confusion in my voice.

Maksim's smirk makes my heart race. "No. I can take care of myself."

"And you think I can't?" Not looking for a fight, I continue talking. "I wasn't lying when I said I know exactly which arteries are vital."

"I'd ask for tips if cutting off a guy's cock was my forte."

As the elevator dings, announcing we've arrived at the garage, I reply, "The male appendage doesn't contain vital arteries."

"It does when it comes to you, Doc. Even when you're slicing through his junk with a scalpel, all his blood would still be rushing to the area you're groping. He'd bleed out in seconds."

I laugh. It is a far nicer way to end our conversation than the argument we were inching toward earlier.

After pressing my lips to the corner of his mouth for the second time this morning, I slip through the car door Maksim holds open for me, before latching my seat belt.

"Straight to Myasnikov Private," Maksim demands to the driver before he closes the back door of a blacked-out SUV and taps the roof, signaling for the driver to leave.

Traffic is atrocious, but Maksim's wish for me to be driven to work makes sense when I spot the number of media vans clogging the streets. They're lined up outside my building and remind me of the number of gossip articles I found about Maksim while trying to track down his mother's details.

He was featured in glossy magazines like he's a celebrity, and was one of Russia's most eligible bachelors, so I guess I shouldn't be surprised at the media's interest in discovering who removed the prestigious title they assured its readers would never occur.

Things are as hectic at Myasnikov Private as at my building. The staff are overrun with another gastroenteritis outbreak, and although I'm no longer on the roster in the ER, the number of cases has also flooded into the pediatric ward.

"Where do you need me?"

Dr. Lipovsky, my now supervisor, sighs in relief when she spots me before suggesting Room 3A. "Yulia Petrovitch was brought in this morning with severe abdominal cramps and distension."

"Was she scanned?"

She nods before handing off a patient chart to a nurse. "Nothing was found. Her bowels are clear, and all organs are of normal size and appearance. We're thinking food poisoning." She flicks her eyes to the curtained-off room. "Her father arrived an hour ago. I've not yet had the chance to speak with him."

"I will do it now."

She thanks me with a smile before she assists a nurse with a patient transfer.

After running my eyes over Yulia's blood workup that just arrived and the scans taken while I slept, I enter her room. "Mr. Petrovitch, my name is Nikita Hoffman. I am one of the residents at Myasnikov Private. I—" When I look up and notice Mr. Petrovitch removing the IV line of his ashen-faced daughter, my words entomb in my throat. "What are you doing? Your daughter is severely dehydrated. Without fluids, she could become very unwell."

Guilt is the first emotion he expresses. It is chased by panic. "I-I lost my job. I don't know when our insurance expires." He speaks in Russian, so I struggle to keep up, but I get the gist of what he is saying. "I may not be able to pay."

I stop his tugs on the cannula by asking, "Was she admitted by the ER team?"

His stitched brows indicate he's uncomfortable with our language barrier, but his nod reveals he understands me.

"Then her admission is already taken care of." I place my hand over his, stilling his fidgeting movements further before saying, "They would not have admitted her if she had inadequate health coverage." Relief floods his eyes with wetness. "Let me help your daughter, Mr. Petrovitch. That's why you brought her here, isn't it? You want her to get better."

"Yes," he breathes out slowly, struggling not to let his tears fall. "She's my baby. My darling." He runs his hand over her hair that sticks to her sweaty scalp. "I can't lose her."

"You won't." He shoots his eyes to mine to see the promise in them. "But I need you to step back so I can assess her properly."

His head bobs like a bobblehead toy before he eventually moves into the shadows Maksim hid in when I assessed his mother.

"Hello, sweetheart," I greet Yulia, who is peering up at me

wide-eyed and responsive. Her cheeks are white, and she appears unwell, but she is a cute little cherub. "Is it okay if I listen to your chest? It won't hurt, but the bell at the end might be a little cold."

She checks with her dad before nodding.

"How long has she been unwell?" I ask her father while plugging a stethoscope into my ears to listen to Yulia's heart and check her vitals.

"Th-three days," he admits, his words stuttering with shame.

Her heart sounds healthy, and her vitals are decent, considering how unwell she has been.

"Now I'm going to push down on your stomach." I wait for her to nod again before starting my assessment near her ribs and then lowering it to her stomach. "I'm sorry, sweetheart. Just a little longer, okay?" She nods again, but it breaks my heart when little tears form in her eyes. "There we go, all done." I pull down her hospital gown before spinning to face her father. "Her pain could be caused by a gastroenteritis bug or perhaps even a parasite, but her pain intolerance increased when I pressed near her kidneys, so I would like to test her urine to ensure there isn't an infection in her kidneys."

"Will that cost anything?"

I shake my head. "No. It is part of her admission." With money at the forefront of his mind, I can't help but ask, "Did Yulia eat anything unusual before she became unwell? Raw food? Or did she handle uncooked poultry?"

"No. Nothing like that. I always make sure her food is cooked properly. I'm a chef." He stops, cusses, then corrects himself. "I was a chef. I know food preparation. I go through anything given to us. I would never serve her scraps. You have to believe me."

"I believe you." I step toward him with kind, caring eyes. "We just need to make sure we cover all our bases to ensure the best prognosis for Yulia." When he nods, still fighting not to cry, I twist back around to face Yulia. "I know your tummy is very sore, but if I brought you something special, do you think you could try to eat a little bit of it for me?" I laugh when her eyes stray to the horrid hospital food no one wants to eat. "Not that disgusting stuff. Something more special."

That piques her interest, but she still gets her father's approval before she nods.

Her need to seek permission would be concerning if I didn't understand.

She isn't making sure she follows his every command. She is vying for the best possible outcome because she knows no one will protect and love her more than her father.

How do I know this if we've only just met?

I once did the same with my father.

And I can see the same thing happening with Maksim.

CHAPTER TWENTY-TWO

"I don't know how you do it, Dr. Hoffman, but you have a way of looking past the gobbledygook to find the real source of the issue under the mess."

I smile at Dr. Lipovsky's praise before farewelling her with a wave and pushing through the door of the interns' locker room. Today has been a good day. With food in her stomach and a course of antibiotics for a urinary infection, Yulia's recovery was swift enough for her to be discharged earlier tonight.

I doubt Dr. Lipovsky's praise would have been as high if she knew how I had tempted Yulia to eat. Donut holes should never be a staple in anyone's household, but you run with them when they can tempt a child to eat after days of sickness.

It felt good watching Yulia enjoy the treats I had Alla purchase on her way in, and since I made out it was on the hospital's dime, her father didn't hesitate to assist me in devouring the leftovers.

During our carb fest, some of the causes for Yulia's symptoms were unearthed. With Lev's position made redundant before the latest winter storms, most of his family's food budget went to keep the heat on in their home. When his pantry stock got low, he started using a local food bank to top off supplies.

Although they're a godsend for people short on funds, I personally know their stock isn't the best on offer. Most produce is usually a week or more old and rarely stored correctly.

There are fewer issues consuming incorrectly stored food products in the winter months, but the same can't be said in spring and summer. It can cause a range of stomach issues and can eventually do more harm than good.

When I explained to Lev that even products that appear fresh can still house parasites, he promised he would be more selective with the foods he accepted from the food bank.

I genuinely believe he has Yulia's best interests at heart, so I shared the items I accepted at food banks during my first two years of college. It was more breads, cereals, and dried pasta instead of the vegetables, fruits, and meats most people seek help with, but Lev was confident it would only be a matter of time until he found a new position, so his family could survive on less for the time being.

His praise for my help is why I wanted to become a doctor. It's never been about the money. It has always been about helping people who have none.

Bewilderment swamps me when I open my locker. The black credit card I left on the bedside table this morning is propped up against my purse, in direct eyesight.

"Ready, Mrs. Ivanov?"

I jump out of my skin before spinning to face the voice. "Ano." I clutch my chest to ensure my heart remains in its rightful place. "You scared the poop out of me."

Ano is far younger than most of Maksim's staff. His shaven face could be leading me off the scent, but he appears to be in his late teens, if not younger. He is as tall as Maksim but not as bulky, and instead of donning tailored suits, he favors designer sweats and jeans and a cap he wears backward even while inside.

Ano smiles for barely a second about my fright before it is replaced with worry. "I wasn't sure if you knew where the underground garage was since I dropped you off at the side entrance, so I thought I should meet with you. Was that wrong of me to do?"

"No, not at all." He exhales deeply, the panic scouring his face softening. "But maybe next time, warn a girl before you sneak up on her."

"Perhaps I could place a bell around my neck?" I smile when he murmurs, "That's Maksim's suggestion any time I sneak up on him unaware."

After watching me gather my belongings out of my locker, he leads us to the underground parking. During our brief walk, I strive to learn more about the man who's always seen in the background but rarely takes center stage. "Have you worked with Maksim long?"

He hums like he's unsure how to answer my question rather than murmuring in agreement. "I've known him for about six years."

"How old were you when you met?"

He smothers my curiosity nicely. "Sixteen." He chuckles when I can't hold back my shocked huff that he is older than perceived. "It's the baby face. I've tried to grow a beard, but I hate the itchy stage and end up shaving it off before it can cast a shadow."

We enter the elevator, and although he gains many admiring eyes, he loses them just as fast. It isn't because he is ugly. He has a cut jaw, icy-blue eyes, and a swagger that announces a ton of trouble. He just appears too young for people who have attended medical school for four years to lust over.

No one wants to be accused of cradle snatching.

"Guess I might have to give it another whirl."

"Wouldn't hurt," I murmur in agreement when I shadow him out of the elevator and into the underground garage. "Is Ano short for anything?"

He opens the back door of the SUV like his baseball cap is a chauffeur's hat before his throat works through a slow swallow. After I'm seated, he murmurs, "Anonymous."

"Your mother called you Anonymous?" I hate myself the instant the question leaves my mouth. He clearly feels uncomfortable with the direction our conversation has taken, but I continue to push.

I'm a cow.

"No," Ano answers. "It's what Maksim called me when he found me naked, beaten, and with no recollection of my prior sixteen years in the back alley of one of his clubs." He smiles to assure me my sympathies aren't needed before he shrugs like it's no big deal. "It kinda stuck."

He closes my door before I can ask another violating question, and then he slips into the driver's seat and commences our short trip home.

"Are you not coming in?" I ask Ano when he closes the door I opened for myself, but he doesn't trace my steps to the elevator.

"No. I've still got a few more hours on my shift."

"And then you'll go...?" I can't help but mother him. It is a natural instinct of anyone in the health profession.

He rubs his hands together like he appreciates my smothering ways before he says, "Then I'll come up."

"You're staying here?" Once again, the words leave my mouth before I can stop them.

His smile is brighter than the light haloing his head. "Oh, you still think Maksim only bought the top two floors of this building?" When I nod, too shocked for a worded response, he murmurs, "That's cute." Before I can grill him further, he ends the possibility. "Goodnight, Mrs. Ivanov."

I could push him, but since I know I'll get more answers from Maksim than from him, I tell him to call me Nikita, return his farewell, and then enter the elevator once again manned by an attendant.

He doesn't ask me what floor. He selects the penthouse suite before announcing, "Mr. Ivanov suggested you should visit your grandparents before joining him for dinner." A hue hits both of our cheeks when he finalizes his statement. "Since you will be preoccupied for the remainder of the evening, he doesn't want you to miss seeing them."

"Thank you. That... works." I grimace at my poor choice of words before watching the elevator climb the many floors from the garage to the top floor. "Have you worked here long?" Since my apartment was in the basement, I only associated with the doorman.

"For several years now."

"So you know most of the occupants?"

He smiles as fondness glistens in his eyes. "Yes. Almost all of them."

"What is the ratio of tenants to owners?"

The elevator attendant seems put off by my question. "Umm... I'm not entirely sure."

"I don't need exact numbers. Just a ballpark figure."

Before he can speak, a deliciously raspy voice sounds out of the emergency speaker on the elevator panel. "Is there something you want to know, Doc?"

My eyes bounce around the elevator cabin before they stop at the blinking red contraption on the far front corner. Maksim could be solely listening in, but I feel his gaze on me, so I stare at the camera while asking, "Did you buy every apartment in my building?"

"Yes," he answers without pause for thought, shocking both me and the attendant.

"Why?"

There's no delay in this answer, either. "Because I like to know who is surrounding me. Are they good people who don't turn their noses down at others not as well off as them? Or are they leeches who'd walk past a boy lying lifeless without a stitch of clothing and not do a damn thing to help him." His reply exposes he isn't solely watching my ride in the elevator. He has eyes on me everywhere. "Do you have any more questions?"

"Just a few." I wait for his exhale to stop rustling through the speaker before asking, "Can you see my grandfather?"

Two clicks sound before he answers, "Yes."

"Is he sleeping?"

You shouldn't be able to hear a smirk, but I swear I hear Maksim's before he answers, "Yes."

"Good." There's no doubt you can hear someone's grin when I lean across the attendant to select the floor below the penthouse.

"Have a pleasant evening," the attendant murmurs when the elevator arrives at the floor of the apartment I share with Maksim.

I almost veer for the door on the right but instead take a left. My instincts have never steered me wrong, so I don't see that changing anytime soon.

My heart beats double time when I enter the area a construction crew is transforming into an office space. The floor plan has been completely reworked, and numerous walls have been removed or replaced. There are even a handful of new access points.

I startle when a rich, velvety voice says, "That will be a secondary entrance to our apartment." With the agility a man his size shouldn't have, Maksim sneaks up on me, pulls back the strands that fell from my bun, and then replaces their tickling presence on my neck with his lips. "Then I'll have immediate access to you as often as my heart desires."

"One hallway too much distance?" I ask, pretending I'm not loving his neediness.

"Yes." He kisses my neck and breathes in my scent before he walks us to the door I was staring at when he interrupted my perusal of his space.

I gasp in an excited breath when he pushes open the door. It doesn't just give him access to our apartment. It takes him directly to the primary suite.

"It feels naughty," I murmur, smiling when I realize the desperation I showcased only seconds ago has nothing on Maksim's level of need. His groping hands and wandering mouth expose that our time apart was as painful for him as it was for me. "I like it."

"Good, because it is staying even if you didn't." Moving us closer to the bed, he confesses, "I had planned to take down the entire wall, but Zoya said it was a bad idea." He unlatches his lips from my neck and then peers down at me. "For some strange reason, she seems to think you're shy."

"I *am* shy."

He flattens his hand on my chest and pushes me onto the mattress before placing his knee between the large gap of my splayed thighs. "Still a shit liar, Doc." He searches for the heat he knows my cheeks are about to get as he says, "I'm barely touching you, and I already know you're ready for me." He tilts in so close a fire burns through me. "I can smell how aroused you are."

"What has that got to do with being shy?" I roll my shoulders back, thrusting my chest out before saying with a confidence I never thought I'd have, "I'm wet for *you*. That has nothing to do with anyone else."

He lunges for me in an instant, groping, kissing, and stroking his length against the damp patch in the crotch of my scrubs.

Our speed is reckless, our needs too great to ignore.

In under a minute, the pants of my uniform are tugged to my knees, and Maksim's fat cock is notching at the opening of my vagina.

When he enters me as fast as he stripped me bare, I call out.

I suck in a deep breath, feeling divinely stretched, before digging the heels of my shoes into his ass, encouraging him to go faster.

I want to be ravished by him.

Claimed.

I want to feel where he's been for days.

When I say that to Maksim, he bites out a cuss word before he pulls out to the tip and then slams back in. Spasms dart across my womb and zap up my spine when he's deep enough to bruise my uterus, but I continue to encourage his recklessness by squeezing the walls of my vagina around him.

"Christ, Doc. You're so fucking tight."

He pounds into me on repeat, slapping my ass with his balls before he adds a flick to his hips that drives me crazy.

"Yes. Please. Oh god."

He grips my ass firmer, marking me. "Almost, but we're not quite there yet."

Tingles skate across my skin when he flattens his hand low on my stomach before his thumb toys with my clit. It is so responsive to his touch that within seconds I'm chanting his name so loud it will ring in his ears for a week.

"Better." His gasped word exposes his restraint is holding on by barely a thread.

He is as aroused as I am, as hot and as tender.

"You just need a little bit more."

I clench around him when he doubles the effort of his thumb while thrusting in and out of me hard enough for stars to form. His pumps are perfect and precise. Without warning, I freefall into ecstasy.

He watches every pleasing jerk of my body while praising how beautiful I look when I come.

"You're so fucking perfect, Doc. So sexy, beautiful, and smart."

His thigh muscles flex and release as he prolongs the sparks of passion burning through my veins.

"Look at how well you're taking me."

His beautiful body moves with such primal, animalistic traits that expose he was designed for precisely this.

To unravel me.

"You're doing so well. I just need a little more."

My back arches, and my head is tossed back when he unexpectedly withdraws before he buries his head between my legs. The sensation is almost too much. It is overwhelming, but for the life of me, I weave my fingers through his hair and hold him hostage to my pussy instead of yanking him away.

My clit pounds in rhythm to my raging heart as he licks, pokes, and teases me with his mouth. Everything tightens as the hungry, needy storm in my lower stomach builds again.

I flatten my body into the mattress when he draws my clit into his mouth and sucks it gently. His controlled pace is my undoing. I writhe against the sheets and his mouth as another orgasm jolts through me.

Maksim doesn't stop, though. He continues nuzzling my aching flesh with his lips and tongue, forcing my orgasm to never let go.

"No," I push out on a breathless moan when he replaces his tongue with his fingers. He slides them inside me, not facing an ounce of resistance, before he sets the pace somewhere between the manic fucking we were doing before he commenced eating me and the slow, leisured pace that saw me climaxing so hard and long the bedding under my backside is wet. "No more. I... can't."

"One more," he demands, still groping, still teasing. "Then we'll fuck, you'll nap on me for an hour while I'm still inside you, and then we'll eat."

"I can't..."

His words battering my swollen flesh almost make an instant liar out of me. "Yeah, you can, Doc. Because I'm not going to stop until you do."

My knuckles go white when he returns his mouth to my clit. He blows a hot breath over the nervy bud before he suckles it into his mouth.

His pace should be too slow to get me off, too gentle, but the orgasm it coerces from me is just as leisured. It pulses through me like liquid ecstasy, tensing and relaxing every limb that brought it to life.

Its slow, tortuous pace doesn't make it any less energy-draining. I'm a sticky, floppy mess when Maksim crawls up my body with a lazy, Sunday-afternoon-drive smile spread across his face.

He knows he won, and I'm too exhausted to try to pretend he didn't.

He parts me with his fingers, his thumb hovering over my clit, before he slowly inches inside me. "Christ," he bites out as he adjusts my legs wrapped around his waist, angling my hips so he can slide in even deeper. "It just gets better and better."

While moaning in agreement, I swivel my hips to lessen the fragment of pain associated with taking a man of his length and girth. He's the biggest I've ever been with, and even if everything falls to pieces between us, I don't see that ever changing.

He'd have to have a monster dick to top Maksim, and even then, I still don't see it being enough.

His cock is as savagely beautiful as the rest of him.

My legs shake as he pushes in deep, stretching me more.

"You're so deep," I breathe out, dangerously close to climaxing again.

He pumps into me while staring down at me, his closeness almost too intimate to bear. Every light in our apartment is on. There isn't a single shadow to hide in, but I relish the brightness instead of hating that there is no coverage.

I can see every lash fanning Maksim's dark eyes. Every perfect pore producing the sweat glistening on his panty-wetting face and body. I watch his muscles contract and release as he uses them to make me come undone. And how his gorgeous face strains when he gets as close to the edge as I am.

I drink in every devastating feature until I climax with a cry, my entire body shaking.

My vision distorts as moans roll up my chest and escape my gaped mouth.

My moans set Maksim off. He grinds into me another three times before he pins my hips to the mattress and grunts through a release so fiery and hot that we undertake a second round before collapsing from exhaustion.

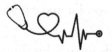

Maksim glances at me over his shoulder when I say, "I've been meaning to ask how your mother is." He scrapes our leftovers into the trash, his back moving as elegantly as it did when he fucked me into a state of unconsciousness. "Did she experience any side effects from the B12 serum she was administered today?"

He continues clearing away the dishes before replying, "Not as far as I am aware. She appears to be handling them well." He stacks the scraped clean plates into the dishwasher before drying his hands with a tea towel. "Is there anything specific I should look for?"

"There are no visual indicators of a B12 deficiency or surplus until the levels are either extremely low or high, but there are indicators that could expose which way her levels are moving. She would have to share those symptoms, though. They're more felt by the patient than physically visual."

After tossing down the tea towel, he huffs. "Then your guess will be as good as mine."

"Stubborn?" I ask, reading between the lines.

Maksim smiles, taking my comment as intended. "Who do you think I inherited it from?" He plucks me from the floor, sits on the couch our backs braced against while eating, and then pulls me into his chest. "If you say my father, I may kill you."

There's an edge of malice in his tone, but since it appears more directed at his father than me, I let his threat slide. "The main indicators are weakness, tiredness, and lightheadedness. Constipation, diarrhea, loss of appetite..." My words trail off when many of the symptoms I spout off match the ones shared with me today.

Maksim groans when I leap off him and race into the room where I dumped my purse when he started ravishing my neck, but remains quiet when I tug my cell phone out of my purse and select a frequently called number.

A nurse in the pediatric ward answers a short time later. "Pediatric department, Nurse Kelley speaking."

"Was Yulia Petrovitch's insurance company billed for an MMA or homocysteine test?"

"I beg your pardon?"

"Yulia Petrovitch, the patient from Room 3A, were her B12 levels checked?"

I groan in frustration when she asks, "Who is this?"

"It is Dr. Hoffman." Maksim's growl is deeper and sterner than my bark when a department nurse fails to keep abreast with the patients in the ward. "Yulia was brought in with severe stomach cramps and abdominal distention. Her initial diagnosis was food poisoning with cystitis of the lower tract, but her symptoms are mimicking ones of a patient I diagnosed earlier this month. She could also have a B12 deficiency."

Nurse Kelley takes her time replying, so I expect more than a blasé response. "Yulia was discharged this evening."

"I am aware of that. I wrote her discharge paperwork. But that isn't what I'm asking. Did her blood workup include the MMA or homocysteine tests?"

"No. There is no indication either of those tests were performed."

Her tone indicates she doesn't like being shouted at, but since it is effective, I don't offer an apology. I simply lower the volume of my voice to a respectable level. "Can you please request the additional tests."

She assumes I am asking a question. I am not. "The patient has been discharged—"

"So? That doesn't mean our medical care ends the instant she leaves the hospital."

"With all due respect, Dr. Hoffman, I believe you are wrong." No buzzes of patients' bells or code blue alarms sound, but she acts like they're ringing off the hook. "I have patients who require my assistance."

She hangs up on me, making me fuming mad.

"She... That... Ugh!" I grip my cell phone hard enough that I almost crack the screen. "Can you believe the hide of that woman? She's one of those people who should leave the profession the instant she no longer cares. They're the people giving the rest of us a bad..." My words trail off when my twist to face Maksim unearths that he is on a call. I didn't hear him dial a number, much less speak.

I mouth an apology before slumping onto a couch that's so new I wouldn't be surprised to learn it still has its price tag attached.

I've only just cradled my head in my hands when Maksim crouches down in front of me. "Which test does the hospital generally use?"

When I peer at him, lost, a unique accent sounds out of his iPhone. "It will be less suspicious to the insurance assessor if we use the standard billing code Myasnikov Private uses."

I'm completely and utterly lost, and my stupidity deepens when Maksim opens his laptop and spins it to face me. He's logged into HIS, Myasnikov Private's health information system, and in the program where doctors and nurses order blood workups for inpatients.

"Which one?" Maksim asks as the cursor bounces between the MMA and homocysteine check boxes.

He isn't moving the cursor. His finger isn't close to the trackpad of his MacBook Pro, so it must be being controlled remotely.

Too shocked not to interrogate, I ask, "How do you have access to HIS? That is a private server."

"A private server with shit security. It didn't even take me two seconds to bypass their outdated firewall," answers a southern voice from Maksim's cell.

After bouncing his eyes between my wide gaze for several heart-thumping seconds, Maksim asks, "Do you want to test Yulia for a B12 deficiency?"

"Yes," I answer, since it is the truth.

But I don't know if I can do it like this.

I don't know if I can break the law to help a patient.

When my heart calls me a liar two seconds before my head, I say, "The second one. These tests are rarely approved, but that's the one they used to diagnose your mother's condition."

"Irina is s—"

"Order the test, and if you face any trouble with the billing side of things, make sure those inquiries are forwarded directly to me," Maksim interrupts, his tone stern.

"There won't be any issues." Keys being clicked sound out of Maksim's phone before the unnamed man says, "You know where to reach me if you need me."

He hangs up on Maksim as quickly as the nurse did me, but Maksim seems more relieved than annoyed.

In the silence, the reality of what we just did crashes down on me.

"Did we just break the law?"

Maksim squashes his finger against my lips. "We helped a patient. That's *all* we did."

The simplicity of his reply doesn't alter the honesty of it.

That is precisely what we did.

We helped someone—someone extremely deserving of our assistance.

The reminder instantly removes any angst I'm feeling. I am more ecstatic than worried. It is nice to know I have more than me on my patients' side. If there had been someone like Maksim on Stefania's side when she got sick, maybe she would still be here.

With a smirk that makes me needy, Maksim nudges his head to the primary suite. "Your alarm is set to go off in a little over six hours. You should head to bed."

"I'm not tired."

My lie tumbles from my mouth so fast you'd have no clue it is a lie if Maksim wasn't the master of detecting deceit. "You're a shit liar, Doc."

He marches me into our room and turns down the sheets someone must have snuck in to make after we messed them, before he nudges his head to the opening, wordlessly demanding my entrance.

I bow to his demand, exhausted from multiple orgasms.

"Are you not coming to bed?" I ask when he presses his lips to my temple like he does anytime he's planning to leave me alone for longer than five minutes.

He heads to the door before spinning back around. "I have some stuff I need to take care of. I'll join you shortly."

I try not to pout like a whiny baby.

It is a hard feat I only achieve because Maksim adds, "Take your panties off. I don't want anything in my way when I come back."

Since he appears to be struggling as much as I am, I don't object when he commences closing the door a second after I slide my panties down my thighs.

"Maksim," I blurt out just before the door shuts.

"Yeah."

I can't see his face, but I feel his smile when I reply, "Thank you."

CHAPTER TWENTY-THREE

D r. Lipovsky's relieved huff rustles a strand of hair fallen from my bun when she takes in Yulia's latest blood workup. "Her levels are good."

"They are," I agree, relieved a child won't need to undertake regular blood workups and serum injections. "Although something is off with her results." I highlight two agents I've not seen before. They appear to be chemical, but the foreign language on the report could be leading me astray. "Do you know what could have caused this?"

Dr. Lipovsky screws up her button nose before suggesting I request a full toxicology report on her sample.

"Shouldn't that have already been done?"

Blonde tresses of hair slap her cheeks when she shakes her head. "Her original blood workup was pretty basic. A resident would be shot if they ordered the works from the get-go." She laughs when I grimace. "You got the B12 test approved. Perhaps you'll get lucky again?"

"Yeah, maybe," I murmur, my tone as uneasy as my facial expression.

After ordering an X-ray for a child with similar symptoms to Yulia, Dr. Lipovsky reminds me I wasn't the only person running on fumes last week. She slips one hundred rubles my way while hitting me with pleading *I-need-caffeine* eyes.

"This round is on me," I say while logging out of HIS and snagging a jacket from the rack to cover my scrubs. It isn't winter yet, but you wouldn't know that with how cold it is today.

"Are you sure?" she double-checks, aware I didn't regularly seek overtime for no reason. "I'm willing to pay premium prices to escape that disaster."

My lips twist up when I follow the direction of her head nudge. Snow flurries coat the overhead windows, and the fog is heavy enough to decrease visibility to barely a foot.

Although I'd rather go home and snuggle up in bed with the man who makes me warm inside and out, today is Donut Holes Thursday, so I have to brave the weather no matter how much I wish to avoid it.

"I'm sure. I still owe you from last time." My heart rate kicks up a gear when the rustles of my coat pick up a familiar scent. Just being housed in the same closet as Maksim's clothing has allowed it to capture his scent. It is a deliciously manly smell that always makes me hot enough to forgo a jacket.

I pull out the collar from beneath the bulky jacket before spinning to face Dr. Lipovsky. "White and two, right?"

"Please." She slips the note back into the pocket of her white doctor's coat. "But if they're short on that, I'll take anything. This place is always crazy, but it's been worse since Nurse Kelley failed to show up for her shifts."

"Is she sick?" I ask, my interest piqued.

If she is hiding because of our run-in nights ago, she shouldn't bother. My bark is far more vicious than my bite.

Dr. Lipovsky shrugs before she is called into a patient's room by a nurse.

"Go. I'll be back as soon as possible."

My shift is technically over, but since we're short on staff, I should work some overtime.

Dr. Lipovsky smiles in thanks before power walking down the corridor.

I also hustle, but I head in the opposite direction.

My puffy winter coat is almost overwhelming in the tight confines of the elevator, and the sticky situation worsens when the elevator stops at the second level of Myasnikov Private to collect a rider from the surgical ward.

"Dr. Hoffman," Dr. Sidorov greets me from outside the elevator. This is the first time I've seen him since I turned down his proposal, and it appears as if he is not ready to let bygones be bygones. "I'll get the next one."

I stare at him peculiarly. The elevator could carry twenty riders, and I am the only person in it, so why does he want to wait?

I cuss my stupidity when he pulls his ringing cell phone out of his pocket and presses it to his ear. He must have felt its vibrations.

Ghastly winds whip through the revolving door of Myasnikov Private ruefully enough that I have to push against them to get out. The conditions are so horrendous I contemplate fetching our coffees at the hospital cafeteria, but then Alla would have to make it through a nine-hour shift without the carbs she needs to survive it unscathed.

Some good comes from the icy elements. Hardly anyone is willing to brave them, so I make it to the donut shop half a block down without bumping into anyone.

"Three large whites and a bucket of glaze donut holes, please," I request to the person serving. "Actually, can I add a single glaze donut to my order as well?" Dr. Lipovsky looks like she could use more than an IV of caffeine.

After paying the total and grimacing about the recent upsurge in pricing, I move to the side of the glass cabinets to collect the sugar packets needed to make the pre-brewed coffee decent enough to digest.

I've barely stuffed the packets into my pocket when a glossy printout is slapped down on the counter in front of me. It is a grainy photograph of Dr. Abdulov. I'm not well-versed on the multiple entry and exit points of Myasnikov Private, but this exit point is easily identifiable since it is the main one most doctors and nurses use.

I lift my eyes from Dr. Abdulov's ashen face when a badge and Myasnikov PD credentials are placed on top of it.

I've been anticipating repercussions for the words we exchanged weeks ago, but I would have never anticipated for it to take this route.

Why bring in the authorities on a case that should be handled by the hospital board?

I realize I have the situation all wrong when a second photograph is placed on top of the first one. This one isn't as grainy, and I somewhat recognize the man with snow-white hair and an arrogant smile but not enough to put a name to his face.

He'd be mid-to-late fifties and has the aura of wealth, not someone I generally associate with. He is approximately thirty years older than the third, and what I hope, final man photographed. His face is also registering as familiar, but I can't pinpoint exactly how I know him.

"Who are these men?" I ask as my wide gaze bounces between two plain-clothed officers.

The female half of the duo is approximately the same age and build as me. Her hair is glossy and inky, pairing well with her almost-black eyes, and her frame is several sizes smaller than her male partner, who is glaring at me with so much disdain I'll need to check for burns once freed from his gawk.

"Are you trying to tell me you don't know who they are?" asks the male officer, scoffing.

"I know who Dr. Abdulov is, obviously, but the names of the

other two gentlemen have me stumped." Frustration bubbles in my veins, but I try not to let it be seen or heard. Even with the male officer choosing the role of bad cop, it isn't his fault he's been brought into a fight he doesn't belong in. "If these men are patients of mine—"

I choke on my words when the gray-haired man snaps out, "These men are dead."

"Allegedly," the female officer jumps in, lowering my blood pressure by a smidge. "Dr. Hoffman, I'm Detective Lara Sonova from Trudny PD, and this is Detective Ivan Mutz, lead investigator at Myasnikov PD." Ivan practically grunts at me when Lara waves her hand at him in introduction. "We've joined taskforces to investigate the disappearance of three individuals we believe you may have come in contact with last weekend."

Forever willing to assist, and desperate to hide my shock that I do know these men, I say, "Dr. Abdulov and I work together, but I can't recall where I associated with the other two gentlemen."

In under a second, some of my confusion lifts—not a lot. Just a little.

The gate number on the surveillance image Ivan places down matches the gate number Zoya and I used last week, and the air hostess scanning the middle-aged man's ticket is the same one who ushered us down the gangway when I arrived late.

It is clear we shared the same flight, but that doesn't alter the facts.

"I boarded late. My fellow passengers had already embarked."

My eyes shoot to Ivan when he says, "He was seated two rows in front of you."

I don't appreciate his tone, and it has my reply coming out as snappily as his expression. "Two *cubicles* in front of me. Visibility is far lower in first class compared to economy."

"I'm sure it is. Though I'll have to take your word on it since

I've never flown first class." Ivan steps closer, attempting to intimidate me with his large frame. "Is flying across the country first class something you do often, *Doctor*?" He spits out the title I've worked hard for as if it is trash.

"It isn't a luxury I often seek out, but a friend purchased us an upgrade—"

"Friend? Ha!"

His rudeness shocks me, but I've handled my fair share of arrogant, conceited men, so I take his unprofessionalism in stride —mostly. "Yes, friend." With the curtesy I usually offer fellow public servants obliterated, I look him straight in the eyes before saying, "If you're trying to imply her generosity was something more lurid than it was, you better have more than a sliver of conjecture."

I can take the hits of life better than anyone, but when it comes to people I care about, all bets are off. I will protect them until my last breath.

I stumble back, shocked when Ivan snarls, "I have enough to issue an arrest warrant right now."

"For what? Booking the same flight as another two-hundred-plus people?"

"Accessory after the fact can be liable for twenty-five to life." He's once again up in my face, his breath heavy on my cheek. "Three men were murdered, and you were on the scene before every single hit."

I can't breathe, speak, or move when he slams down image after image after image. My recollection of the third man is basic, but it is clear I associated with him more than a doctor would a patient when half of the shots show him standing directly across from me.

A Tahiti-style bar separates us in a majority of the time-stamped images until the last three. It shows him in an elevator with Zoya, Aleena, Shevi, and me.

Although she appears remorseful, Lara can't continue

playing the good cop when Ivan stacks evidence against Zoya and me. Except this time, it isn't solely my best friend being thrown in the fire with me. Maksim is tossed into the flames as well.

"Dr. Abdulov was last seen entering an alleyway that borders Myasnikov Private on Thursday, September third at 2:58 p.m." He places down a time-stamped image that shows Dr. Abdulov entering the alleyway mere seconds before a man who shelters his face from numerous surveillance cameras by tilting his chin. *If only he could hide the tailored cut of his suit just as easily.* "This image was collected at 3:08 p.m."

The face of the man in an Armani suit is still concealed during his exit, but since he is holding a cell phone to his ear, parts of his hand is visible.

"Are they—"

"The nail indents of a man fighting for his life?" Ivan interrupts. "Yes, that is what they are."

My throat is already burning from the amount of bile sitting there, but the scald becomes unmanageable when a camera above the cockpit of the plane shows frame by frame footage of me dragging Maksim into the bathroom of our transportation.

This isn't about Zoya accepting money she didn't earn.

This is about Maksim and me.

Ivan angles his head to bring us eye to eye. "Need to clean up after bludgeoning a fellow passenger to death?"

"I spilled my drink."

"That he served you?" He taps on the third man's image. "Is that what got him killed? Did he not mix your cocktail how you like it?"

"I—"

"Am not speaking another word," says a voice from behind my shoulder.

I can't hide my shock when the woman Maksim chaperoned out of his room at two in the morning arrives out of nowhere. Raya looks dressed to impress in a fitted pantsuit and minimal makeup, but her angry scowl is what I pay the most attention to.

"All your so-called evidence is inadmissible. You have no bodies, no motive, and no witnesses—"

"According to your client's alibis, Dr. Fernandez was present at every murder. We can also convict in absentee of a body."

I assume they have the wrong person until Raya corrects, "Dr. *Ivanov* attended an event with her friends and her *husband*" —she annunciates her last word to ensure its importance can't be missed—"where some unfortunate fools had too much to drink and forgot to check in with their wives. That is a regular occurrence in the Trudny District. It does *not* warrant a murder investigation, much less three."

Detective Lara rejoins our conversation. "Her husband is a known Bratva boss. The Fernandezes have been at the top of Russia's most wanted list for years. And although there are no bodies, the slash mark in Dr. Azores's seat is enough to rule foul play." She turns her eyes to mine. They're brimming with remorse; however, it is hardly visible through the distrust clouding them. "You have to understand our suspicions. Your husband isn't who he says he is."

Before I can demand proof, Raya shoves her hand in Lara's face, silencing me. "If you're concerned about some torn fabric in a passenger's seat, perhaps investigate the airline who places dangerous weapons in the hands of their travelers simply because they can afford a first-class ticket." I wonder who Raya is here to defend when she says, "Furthermore, my client spent most of the flight in the washroom, entertaining a fellow passenger, as per your evidence."

I choke on my spit when she nudges her head to the frame-by-frame footage that is timestamped incorrectly. It appears as if Maksim and I went into the washroom earlier than we did. Almost thirty minutes sooner.

With my silence making Detective Lara believe I am

supporting Raya's alibi claims, she gathers up the images before saying, "We will be in contact."

"If you wish to waste your resources on a dead end, go ahead." Raya's tone is neither mocking nor angry. It is more unrepentant than arrogant. "But if you have time to waste, I suggest taking a moment to familiarize yourself with marital privilege laws." I listen as eagerly as Lara and Ivan when my stupidity is unearthed for the world to see. "They render a witness immunity from giving information that may criminate their spouse. So even if *Mrs.* Ivanov can't corroborate the statement *Mr.* Ivanov issued your department this morning, she is under no obligation to announce that."

"So you're insinuating he did it? Maksim Fernandez killed three men *for her.*" Ivan shoots daggers at me during the "for her" part of his reply. "Possibly more." His glare intensifies along with the volume of his voice. "There is taking down the competition, and then there is this."

"Perhaps you should start on client–attorney confidentiality clauses before pleading for a judge to ignore a spousal privilege that has been upheld in this country for hundreds of years," Raya bites back, smiling vindictively. "You have my number. Use it before *ever* approaching either of my clients again."

I'm so stunned by the turn of events that I'm guided out of the donut shop and into the back seat of Maksim's SUV before I can sort through a single fact.

My husband is a suspected Russian gangster, and I was allegedly used as his alibi for each murder he is accused of.

That's pretty much what the detectives were insinuating, right? I'm not jumbling things up. I've slept six-plus hours every night for a week. My head is the clearest it's ever been.

Well, it was.

Now it is a clusterfuck of confusion.

The turmoil grows when Raya locks her eyes with Ano's in the rearview mirror and snarls, "You were supposed to keep them away from her both during commute to and from the hospital and her shifts. How did you fuck this up so badly?"

Ano thrusts his hand at the windscreen. "Can you see two feet in front of you?"

"If you couldn't see, you should have gotten out of your car! Maksim didn't want her to find out this way."

"I did get out. Still couldn't see shit—"

Ano's defense cuts off when I ask, "Didn't want me to find out what? That he is a Russian gangster or that his last name isn't Ivanov?" I can't bring up the prospect of him killing people. I'm too stunned to let that fully sink in right now.

Raya and Ano hold each other's gazes for several terrifying seconds before Raya breaks their stare down first with an honesty I'm not expecting. "Maksim hasn't used the Fernandez name in years, not since his father left his family without two pennies to rub together, and a heap of debt. He *legally* operates under his mother's maiden name."

Her confession and Maksim's obvious disdain of his father settles that debate in a heartbeat, but it doesn't answer all my questions.

"And the rest?"

It only takes half a second for me to unearth the truth in her eyes.

Everything the detectives allege is true.

Maksim is a murderer, and I'm the lead witness in the case they're attempting to build against him.

"Is that why he married me?" When Raya seeks Ano's opinion on how to answer my question, I ask it again, louder this time. "Is that why he married me!"

The contrite glint that flares through her eyes has the truth smacking into me like a ton of bricks.

The nail indents I mended because I thought I had caused them.

Our time together in the airplane bathroom.

The vows we exchanged.

They were all for a purpose, and it isn't close to what Maksim and Aleena made out.

He doesn't want an inheritance.

He wants to get off murder charges.

And I'm his scapegoat.

"Nikita!" Ano shouts when I throw open the back door of the SUV, slip out, and then sprint down the icy sidewalk.

He could be chasing after me on foot, but I can't hear anything over the thuds of my heart in my ears. I thought what Maksim and I had was special, that it was fast because it was right. You don't need to stay in the slow lane when there's nothing to be fearful of.

I've never felt more stupid.

I'm taken aback when my entrance into the foyer of my building occurs at the same time Maksim exits the elevator. He's surrounded by men in powerhouse suits that scream importance, but his aura trumps them all. He is the clear alpha of the room, and after everything I've just learned, it should make me scared to approach him.

Regretfully, I inherited my stubbornness from my mother.

"Did you marry me so I wouldn't be able to testify against you?"

Maksim balks for barely a second before he forces his expression back to impassive, and then he continues showing his guests the way out.

I'm too hurt to wait for privacy.

I want answers, and I want them now.

"Answer me! Did you marry me so I couldn't testify against you?"

Maksim's jaw gains a tic. I don't know if it is from my line of questioning in front of dignitaries, some I now realize are foreign since they appear oblivious to my accusations, or because two of his guests are barged out of the way by Ano sprinting into the foyer, red-faced and out of breath.

Ano believes it is the latter. "I'm sorry, boss, she—"

Maksim cuts him off by slicing his hand through the air before he requests for the building to be placed into lockdown. "No one is to come in or out until we have a handle on the *situation*."

He glares at me during his last word, and it announces my ankle wasn't solely ensnared the night we wed. The trap tonight is pronged with just as many maiming stakes.

"Don't even think about it," Maksim mutters in a low tone when I attempt to skirt past him and follow his straggling guests out.

He grabs my arm forcefully enough that instincts have me rearing up to defend myself. I slap him hard enough that the crack of my hit echoes in the silence of the foyer. We're surrounded by a handful of the tenants Maksim allowed to stay and construction crew members, but the tension is so white hot they're not willing to breathe in case it forces them to miss a snippet of the action.

"Let me go, Maksim," I scream when he walks me toward the elevator while I struggle to be freed from his hold.

When he ignores my demand, I stray my eyes across the people watching me being forcefully placed into the elevator.

Not a single one comes to my defense—not even the security guards paid to protect the occupants of this building.

"Cowards," I mutter, too angry at myself not to deflect it onto someone else.

"They're not cowards, Doc. They're smart." Maksim lowers his massively dilated eyes to me. "Smart enough to know I would rip them to shreds if they even considered coming between us."

"Because you'd hate for anyone to wedge a gap between you and your guarantee of continued freedom."

The fact he doesn't try to deny my claim hurts more than anything.

"Did you do what they assume you did?"

My stomach drops to my feet when he answers nonchalantly, "Yes. I killed them."

I stumble back until my winter coat scrapes the glass wall of the elevator, while mumbling, "Why would you do that? Why hurt innocent people—"

"Innocent?" he roars, his voice bellowing. "There was *nothing* innocent about them!"

When he spins to face me, I learn why he is talking so openly. The red light in the security camera is no longer flashing. His confession is only being heard by me—the person he married so he couldn't be testified against.

My stomach revolts as more truths seep through the confusion clouding my judgment. "Every time we were together was so you could have an alibi." When he remains quiet, I continue pushing. "That's what you told them, isn't it? You made out you were with me."

"I *was* with you."

I'm up in his face in an instant, stupidly unscared. "Before or after you hurt them, Maksim? Because you sure as fuck weren't with me when you... you..." I can't say the word. I can't picture him in that situation, much less speak about murder as if it is the norm.

"Does it matter?" Maksim asks, his eyes bouncing between mine like he can't understand the reason for the wetness brimming in them.

"Yes," I reply, nodding. "It matters to me."

"Why?" He truly looks confused, like he can't possibly understand why I am upset.

"Because this is the *exact* opposite of my beliefs. I'm a doctor. I save people's lives for a living and you... you take them."

After a disappointed flare darts through his eyes, he spins

back to face the elevator panel and jabs the button several times to hurry it along. He wants our conversation over, whereas I know it is only just beginning, although my next set of words are harder to speak than they should be. "Marital privileges are the spouse's choice." Cracks form in my heart when I say, "That means if I want to testify against you, there is *nothing* you can do to stop me," proving I'm not scared of the repercussions for threatening him. I'm petrified of losing him like I did my father, and in all honesty, I hate myself for that.

"I know," Maksim replies, his voice low and softly spoken. "But you won't."

I laugh like I am as loony as he is. "Don't be so sure."

"You won't." His confidence agitates me to no end. "But even if you did, you were not technically present, so your testimony will be pointless."

"You just admitted guilt. I could have you put away for life."

"You could," he agrees. "But you won't." He hits the emergency stop button before he turns back around to face me, his speed dangerously slow. "I know you—"

"You don't know shit."

"I know you," he repeats, moving closer. *Prowling* closer. "I know that even though your heart is telling you that testifying is the right thing to do, it is also cautioning you against it because it knows I wouldn't have done as accused unless I believed it was necessary." He hits me where it hurts. "Just like you know your daddy wouldn't have done what he did unless it was necessary."

He continues approaching, stealing the air from my lungs with both words and a soul-stealing stare that's full of silent apologies and begs for forgiveness.

"I know that you're upset now, but you won't be when you step back and assess things properly." He pins me between the elevator wall and him before angling his head so we're eyes to eyes, lips to lips. "And I know you're too smart to *ever* believe the connection we have could be staged. Fireworks, Doc. Tension so dangerous it broke through all the lies they told to try to keep us apart. Lightning on a pitch-black night. That's you and me." He licks his lips like his insides are burning up as furiously as mine. "Shit that potent can't be made up. Dynamite that powerful can't be manufactured." He tucks a strand of hair fallen from my bun behind my ear while murmuring, "You're just too scared to admit that right now, but you'll get there. Eventually."

"No, I won't," I try to deny. I say "try" because I need to work on the strength of my headshake and the confidence in my tone to make it more believable.

"Still a shit liar, Doc," Maksim murmurs a second before he seals his mouth over mine.

My insides naturally contract, my body choosing its own response to his kiss, but I keep my mouth sealed shut, refusing to give in. I'm hurt he lied and that his excuse mimics the ones my father issued when he was arrested for the murders of the men who brutally assaulted my mother. But more than anything, I hate myself that I still want him after everything he did.

"Don't." I moan the word instead of yelling it as planned when Maksim slides his hands behind my back and gropes my ass. "I don't want this. I don't want you."

My body calls me a liar long before my heart. It melts into his embrace when he curls my legs around him before he rocks his hips forward, grinding against me. My panties are so damp, not even my scrubs can hide their wetness. My body is attracted to this man, and so is my heart. It is just my brain struggling to keep up.

I guess that's nothing new.

Maksim licks my lower lip, and my resolve buckles. When his tongue slips inside my mouth, tingles race across my skin, making all logical thoughts nonexistent. Electricity races through my face as my skin burns with heat. I'm dragged into a lust storm I'll have no chance of surviving if I don't keep the playing field even.

"Promise me." His lips dust my ear as I fight to replace my

moans with words. "Promise me you won't hurt anyone else to protect me. Promise me you will always pick me first."

"Always first," he murmurs into my neck, his pledge given without a second thought.

Even with me pushing him back so I can check the honesty in his eyes, the throb between my legs grows, becoming unbearable.

There's a glint in his eyes that announces I don't need to hear his words to know I will always come first, but it isn't enough.

"When my sister died, my parents promised I'd never experience that type of pain again." Maksim's eyes bounce between mine when I choke on a sob. "They lied." I speak faster before he can interrupt me. "My mother had no choice. She was taken from me. But my father could have chosen to stay. He could have picked me over vengeance."

"No, Doc. He wasn't given a choice."

I act as if he never spoke. "Promise me, Maksim. Promise you will never do anything that will put you in a predicament where you could be taken from me as well."

"That won't happen—"

"Promise me!" I shout, my words on the verge of a sob. "Or I'll walk out that door and go straight to Myasnikov PD."

The slap mark on his face reddens when anger engulfs him, but he tries to downplay his fury. "Shit. Fucking. Liar. Doc."

Heartbroken, I push him back with enough force he crashes into the brash steel doors with a thud before I jab the emergency stop button. "And as I said, you don't know shit."

As the elevator jerks back into action, Maksim glares at me like it is taking all his restraint not to retaliate with the same level of violence I instilled on him. His fists are balled at his sides and his jaw is so firm it appears seconds from cracking, but the only time his resolve breaks is when the elevator dings, announcing it has reached the penthouse.

He blocks the exit with his burly frame for several heart-thrashing seconds before his standoff is broken by the person responsible for half of the confusion swamping me. "Missy Moo, the only sunshine in the world is you."

When I peer past Maksim's shoulder, I'm given an excuse for the wetness on my cheeks. My grandfather is no longer bedridden. He's seated in a bulky hospital chair only the wealthy can afford, smiling larger than the oxygen mask covering half his face.

Maksim stops me from racing to his side by snatching up my wrist. His hold isn't firm, but it announces his struggle to let me go is as tortuous as it was for me when I threatened to walk out of his life.

His chest inflates and deflates numerous times before he presses his lips against my temple and talks through their sternness. "Our vows said until death do us part." He inches back to ensure I can see the honesty in his eyes before saying, "But not even he is stupid enough to come between us. Remember that before you *ever* try to downplay what we have again."

He guides me into the foyer of my grandparents' apartment before he returns to the elevator and selects his floor.

When he raises his eyes, there's so much pain—so much angst. I almost race for him, but before I can, the elevator doors snap shut, and I'm left alone to battle through my confusion for the umpteenth time in my life.

CHAPTER TWENTY-FOUR

D r. Muhamed snorts when I purse my lips while reading my grandfather's latest medical assessment.

"I'm not saying your reports are inaccurate. It's just..." I'm at a loss for words now as I was earlier. My grandfather's health is going in the opposite direction a patient with stage four lung disease should. He is still a very sick man, but his oxygen levels are back to what they were at the beginning of the year.

I prayed for a miracle, but this is still above and beyond anything I thought I could achieve.

"The pharmaceutical company must have mixed things up."

"It could be the new trial medication..." Dr. Muhamed's words trickle to silence when I snap my eyes to him. He nervously shifts foot to foot at the end of my grandfather's bed. "I thought you were aware of his inclusion in the program. That's why I didn't mention it." He gathers a box from a medicine cabinet similar to the ones behind locked doors at Myasnikov Private. "It's a difficult trial to be accepted into, but for the right amount of money, Maksim found a way in. The results of the first-trial participants have been quite outstanding."

This is the exact reason my confusion is so high. Maksim has done so many wonderful things. When forced to remember the kindhearted, generous man who has spent hundreds of thousands of dollars on a stranger is the same man who can take the life of another with no remorse, my confusion becomes a slab of concrete I can't crack.

I'm so over my head instead of seeking a way out when Maksim left hours ago that I've done nothing but sit at my grandfather's side and relish his alertness. His cheeks have color. His chest represents the rattle of a baby's toy instead of the clatter of a train over old tracks. He's smiling and laughing, and as much as I want to take credit for his second grasp at life, I can't.

Nothing happening is thanks to me. It is all because of the money Maksim tossed into his medical care—money I am now skeptical came from real estate owned by Ivanov Industries.

I lied when I said I've done nothing but savor my grandfather's alertness. It was very much still on my mind while I researched the name the detectives tossed around as regularly as insinuations on Dr. Muhamed's Ivanov Industries–owned laptop, but it didn't have my utmost devotion.

My multifaceted search unearthed a legacy almost as impressive as the Ivanov name, but with a heap of murky undertones.

Maksim's father is the head of an Italian syndicate similar to the group that claimed my mother's life. Even reading about him in print couldn't alter my opinion of his personality. He is a tyrant of a man who ruled with an iron fist and not an ounce of repent.

Or should I say, he *was*.

He was killed eighteen months ago, and the young bride he wed mere hours before his death was in the process of being prosecuted for his murder when she vanished without a trace.

Part of me hopes she is still alive, but I'm doubtful. Bastian had many enemies, but he was protected under a law that has governed countries far longer than democracy.

He was sheltered under mafia law, meaning even if Maksim wanted to seek revenge for the numerous bruises and broken bones his childhood hospital records indicate were not accidental, he couldn't. He had to accept the unfair blows of life like the rest of us—by pretending they never happened.

I can't help but wonder if things changed because he took over his father's reign. It makes sense as to why he believes he can trial, convict, and penalize anyone in his realm. Low-ranked gang members can get away with murder—my mother's death is proof of this—but if they so much as give a papercut to someone high up in the underworld, there will be hell to pay.

Maksim's mother's time at Myasnikov Private was more damaging than a superficial wound. Do I believe the injustice deserves a murder sentence? I want to say no, but if you'd rather I be honest, I'll need more time. Alas, I'm too exhausted for a basic excavation, let alone the mammoth undertaking required to unravel a mafia entity cloaked in centuries of criminal activities.

After closing Dr. Muhamed's laptop, I place it on the makeshift nurses' station at the side of my grandfather's room and then twist to face Dr. Muhamed. "I'm going to call it a night. If anything—"

"Changes, you'll be the first I call," he interrupts before farewelling me with a chin dip.

He probably hates my extended visits. It is hard to do anything when you have a colleague breathing down your neck. My grandfather's last practitioner refused to let me sit in on their consultations. He spouted off the same excuses as Dr. Abdulov, saying that he was a professional with years of experience and didn't need the guidance of a second-year medical student.

Although we followed the medical plan he designed, I replaced him as my grandfather's practitioner shortly after that visit. I want to say I've given my grandfather the best medical treatment possible, but now I'm skeptical. Money is a prominent factor in any health care—regretfully—but perhaps if I hadn't always been so tired, I could have provided the same level of service as Dr. Muhamed.

I already hate myself, so you can imagine how bad my self-loathing becomes when I automatically hit the button for the floor below the penthouse instead of contemplating where to rest my head for a couple of hours for more than a brief second.

Maksim made it obvious in the elevator that I wouldn't get far if I decided to run, but I can't pretend nothing happened. He openly admitted to hurting three people, and he did so without remorse. I can't sweep that under the rug.

The elevator doors open barely a second before I jab the close doors button and then select the foyer level. Several men watch me when I detour through the foyer to the basement apartment I once shared with my grandparents, but none utter a word.

I'm reminded just how damp the conditions are when it takes me ramming my shoulder into the front door to get the lip unstuck from the doorjamb.

Mold and mildew engulf my nostrils when I enter. It is closely followed by a chill running down my spine. It is freezing in here.

"At least they kept the lights on," I murmur to myself while walking toward the lit-up nook in the corner of the living room I once called my bedroom. Since my grandfather was bedridden and my grandmother forever used her favorite recliner to sit at his bedside, I haven't made up the lumpy sofa bed in over a year.

A squeak pops from my mouth when a deep Russian accent says, "Do you want me to scoot over, Doc, or are you cool sleeping on top?"

My heart stays somewhere in the vicinity of my chest when a second lamp is switched on.

With my sheets thin, it doesn't take a genius to realize Ano sleeps naked.

"Why look away?" Ano asks when my eyes drop to the floor. "If I'm going to be killed through no fault of my own, you may as well make it worthwhile by giving my ego a quick stroke by taking a look and gasping in awe."

I don't know where to look, but my brain has no issues replying. Words leave my mouth before they're fully formed. "How can you joke about murder like it's funny?"

When silence is the only thing shared, I sheepishly raise my eyes.

Ano is peering at me with his brows crossed and his midsection exposed.

After a beat, he murmurs, "I'm probably not the best person to answer that."

I return my eyes to my feet when he scoots across the thin mattress, his modesty maintained by the scrunching of the sheet near his crotch.

I hear him walk away more than I witness it. His bare feet stomp the cold floors for almost thirty seconds before the door I forced closed is opened with less muscle.

Since I refuse to turn around, I assume I am alone.

Ano proves me wrong two seconds later. "Fuck it. From one orphan to another, you deserve to be told the truth." He waits for my curiosity to get the better of me before he says, "You're putting the men he killed on a pedestal they have no right to be on." Nothing but honesty shines in his eyes when he hits me with straight-up truths. "They deserved to die. Just like the men who raped and brutalized your mother for hours deserved to die. They got what was coming to them."

"You can't put what Maksim and my father did in the same realm."

Ano almost exposes himself when he holds his hands out as if to say, *Why?*

"Because they're not in the same domain. The men my father murdered had done it before. They'd tortured and raped dozens of women but continuously got away with it. They'd still be doing it now if he hadn't stopped them."

I understand Zoya's frustration when Ano asks casually, "And?"

"They deserved to be prosecuted for what they did! They deserved to die," I shout, finally speaking from my heart and my head.

I hate that I was left alone and that my parents didn't uphold the promise they made when Stefania died, but I never understood the pain my father was experiencing until I saw the hurt in Maksim's eyes a second before the elevator doors closed.

It cut me to shreds.

The anguish on Ano's face clears, making him look closer to his age. "Exactly my point, Doc. You're assuming you know who the villain and the hero of this story are, but I know you've got them mixed up. They both have power, but it is how they chose to use it that differentiates their titles."

"Maksim—"

"Protected the people he loves. That's *all* you need to know."

When I can't think of a single thing to say, he reminds me that the bar in the middle of the sofa bed is back breaking before he exits without a backward glance.

CHAPTER TWENTY-FIVE

"You've reached Zoya. Leave a message."

The pounding of my brain against my skull ruffles my exhale. "Z, it's me. I really need to talk to you. Can you call me back?"

I wait to see if our call magically connects before I hit the end button and dump my phone onto my bed. I had no clue how spoiled I've been the past week. The sofa bed springs are nonexistent, and the bar in the middle dug into my back all night.

I hardly got any sleep. An hour, two at max. My head is throbbing, and my stomach won't quit grumbling, but for some stupid reason, I'm more devastated about waking up in my apartment alone than anything.

It didn't matter how late Maksim came to bed, I always knew when he arrived because, as per our agreement, he slept inside me every night.

There's no denying how empty I feel this morning—both in my heart and between my legs.

I also couldn't stop the photographs of Maksim's childhood injuries from rolling through my head. They made me desperate to comfort him. My stubbornness just refused to listen to a single plea of my heart. It wants it to believe the events of our formative years don't shape who we are as adults.

I know that isn't true. I'm merely struggling to wrap my head around anything since I am operating on minimal sleep.

As I flop back onto my pillow, I throw a hand over my puffy eyes.

I honestly don't know who I am anymore.

How can you miss a man society deems you should hate? I should be on one side of the fence or the other—good or bad—not straddling my morals like my indecisiveness won't award me a nasty splinter. I just can't force myself to pick, because I know neither choice will protect me from my worst nightmare coming true.

That's all on my shoulders.

After a few minutes of silent ponderings that award me nothing more than more headaches, I throw off the bedding Ano left, then flop my legs off the sofa bed. My slow trudge to the shower mimics many I've undertaken over the past three years, but it feels different today. I feel like I've lost a limb, and the phantom pains are more tearing than the imaginary saw that hacked it off.

I'm halfway to the bathroom when my cell phone rings. Hopeful it is Zoya, I race back into the living room, snatch it up, and answer the call without looking at the screen.

"I am so glad you finally called me back. I'm dying here."

The laughter I'm seeking isn't close to youthful. "I doubt you'll be saying that when you arrive." Doctors being paged sound during Dr. Lipovsky's brief intermission to catch her breath. "I hate to ask this since you're not rostered on, but could you come in? We're short-staffed and run off our feet."

"It's not a problem," I reply, grateful for the distraction, confident it will make my guilt that I missed Maksim's presence last night not as heavy. "I can be there in fifteen?"

My reply sounds like a question, so she responds as if it is. "That will be great. Thank you so much."

"I'll see you soon."

She farewells me before disconnecting our call.

With my head in lockdown mode, I rake my fingers through my hair, twist it back, and then secure it with an alligator clip. After replacing the scrubs I slept in with clean ones, I race for the exit, completely forgetting about the horde of media camped at the front of my building.

Questions are tossed at me as I throw my hands up to protect my eyes from live-streamed TV.

"Mrs. Ivanov, is it true Maksim was brought in for questioning last night?"

"Do you have a statement regarding the joint operation of Trudny and Myasnikov Police Departments?"

"How long were you and Maksim dating before you wed?"

I'm clutched at the side just as the cameras damaging my vision are shoved out of my face.

"Keep your head down and your mouth shut."

Ano escorts me through the media so fast that I'm seated in the back of Maksim's SUV before another question can be fired.

"Fucking move!" he yells when they circle the vehicle like sharks stalking their prey.

He honks two times and almost mows one media duo down when they block his exit of the valet section of my building before he finally makes it into the opening.

I don't know whether to laugh or grimace when he connects his eyes with mine in the rearview mirror and says, "Still want to walk?"

Not eager to start a fight, I reply, "Seems like a nice day for a drive."

He drags his eyes over the foggy conditions before smiling. "Seems that way."

I last almost all the way to Myasnikov Private before my

worry about the first question tossed at me is exposed. "Is Maksim okay?"

Ano holds my gaze in the rearview mirror for what feels like a lifetime before he loosens the pressure valve in my chest with a brief head nod. "Might take a few days to sort out the mess, though." A *tsk* vibrates his lips. "The men you accused him in front of aren't fans of false accusations." I'm completely lost, but mercifully, he appears aware of that. "When you asked if he only married you so you couldn't testify against him, you ruffled more than just Maksim's feathers."

My eyes pop as awareness smacks into me. "I didn't realize they were law enforcement officers. The detectives yesterday made out they had already taken Maksim's statement."

Ano laughs. I have no clue what he thinks is funny. I am far from amused. "The men weren't law enforcement." He stops, pulls a face, then starts again. "Well, they kind of are, but not in the sense you're thinking." He flicks his eyes to the road for the quickest second before returning them to the mirror. "You good?"

I'd have given anything for a few more hours of sleep when he nudges his head to the building we're parked next to. It is Myasnikov Private Hospital.

"Thanks for the ride. I'll buzz you when my shift ends."

After farewelling Ano with a smile, I slip out of the back of the SUV and walk straight into pure chaos. There are more patients than beds, and every doctor on staff is rostered on, meaning the chances of me identifying the graffiti artist who vandalized my locker are poor.

Only two words are spray-painted across my locker door, but they're hurtful enough for bile to race to the base of my throat.

Dr. Killer

After shoving my purse into my locker, I scrub at the thick red paint with the cuff of my scrubs. The slur doesn't budge an inch. It remains as red as my cheeks when a familiar voice calls my name.

There's no hiding the frustration on my face this time, so I don't bother removing it before twisting to face the voice.

Dr. Sidorov takes one look at my burning cheeks and wet eyes before he demands the emptying of the locker room with two curt words. "Get out."

Once it is devoid of snickering laughter, he stops next to me before asking, "Who did this?"

"I don't know." I lower the rudeness in my tone to a manageable level before saying, "It was like this when I arrived." With my hurt higher than my morals, I ask, "Why didn't you inform me Dr. Abdulov is missing?" I almost say dead, but once again, I can't force my heart to admit to Maksim's crimes, even with him and my head having no qualms about doing the same. "I only found out when I was bombarded by two detectives yesterday afternoon."

He appears confused. I understand why when he says, "I was unaware of your involvement in his disappearance."

"I'm not involved..." My words trail off when I follow the direction of his gaze. He is staring at my wedding rings, which calls me out as a bigger liar than my head. I hide them by folding my arms over my chest before saying, "I just thought you would have informed the hospital staff of his dea... disappearance."

"It isn't something that needs to be openly discussed right now. The authorities are looking into his disappearance, but that doesn't mean it will be ruled foul play." His eyes bounce between my sweaty top lip and my crinkled brow before he asks, "Is there something you need to disclose, Dr. Hoffman? You seem a little skittish."

"I'm fine. I just..." My voice is full of a shame it doesn't deserve to hold. "Can this wait? I-I should probably get out there. It's pretty hectic."

"I don't see that being an issue." Once again, the ease of his tone doesn't match his pinched brows and soured expression. However, I'm too eager to skip his interrogation to investigate them further.

After ripping off my engagement and wedding rings responsible for my sloshy stomach and placing them next to the credit card that hasn't budged an inch in almost a week, I make a beeline for the exit.

When I break into the corridor, I think I am in the clear of more controversy.

I couldn't be more wrong.

Maksim's absence was felt this morning, but I had no idea that was because he wasn't home. He's speaking with two of the bigwigs of Myasnikov Private, and his commanding aura is noticeable even from a distance.

My throat works through a stern swallow when he suddenly stops talking and cranks his neck my way. I consider running until I realize the only direction I can take is past him. I'm in the open, so I am safe from being turned into putty by the hands and mouth of a genius, but you wouldn't know that when Maksim's eyes land on my empty ring finger.

He works his jaw side to side before he slowly, almost murderously so, returns his eyes to my face. His unspoken demand for me to place my rings back on is heard over the constant page of doctors being requested at the ER, but when a code blue sounds from the same ward, I act as if I am blind.

I sprint past him along with a handful of doctors, sighing when he doesn't stop me from doing the job I was destined to do.

CHAPTER TWENTY-SIX

Although the graffiti on my locker was scrubbed off by the time I returned from a double shift, even now, four days later, I'm still scalded with squinted glares and cold shoulders during the short trek across the assigned space for doctors to get ready in.

I assumed their narrowmindedness was because they'd heard about my run-ins with Dr. Abdulov in the weeks leading to his disappearance. However, I learned otherwise when I read the numerous headlines *Myasnikov News* has been running this week.

Instead of keeping readers abreast about three missing men, they've run a week-long feature on my nuptials with Maksim. Numerous images in their three-page spread included the videos and stills I stole from Zoya when I airdropped them to my cell phone.

To anyone outside of the Bratva world, I look like a gushing, loved-up bride.

From the response of my colleagues, I was the only fool

unaware of what the Ivanov name represented when I assessed Maksim's mother.

I stop staring into space when a kind voice asks, "Are you all right?" When I peek out from behind my locker door, Alla props her shoulder onto the doorjamb of the locker room and then offers me a contrite smile. "Don't let the haters get to you. Half of their snickers are because they're insanely jealous. He didn't shut up about you the entire time he was touring what will be the new wing earlier this week." An expression crosses her face I can't quite work out. "The way he growled 'my wife' any time you were mentioned... *damn, girl.* I almost fainted."

I smile. It can't be helped. That is precisely what Zoya would say if our calls lasted more than a few seconds. She swears she isn't avoiding me and that she's just busy helping Aleena with final preparations for the wedding, but I have a feeling she knows I know she is the source for *Myasnikov News'* latest feature.

My smile sags when Alla drops her eyes to my empty ring hand.

Every day before my shift, I remove my rings and place them in my locker, where I intend for them to remain. I don't put them back on. Ever. They just appear magically on my hand each morning when I wake up from an unrestful slumber.

I asked Ano about it yesterday morning. He laughed and shook his head before he returned his eyes to the road.

I want to believe Maksim is placing my wedding rings back on, but shouldn't I sense his presence?

Before his secrets were exposed, I noticed the most minor details.

Now I feel like I couldn't spot him in a crowd.

When Alla peers at me in silent questioning, I say, "It's complicated." I'm unwilling to open that can of worms at any time of the day, much less at 2 a.m. on a Sunday. "Are you on your way in or out?"

Her chest sinks as she exhales. "Out. Thank God. It's been a crazy house here the past few weeks. I'm beat." My heart melts when she enters the locker room, throws her arm around my shoulders, and then guides us toward the exit. "But not too tired to walk home my favorite doctor. I've missed you so much. It isn't the same place without you."

"I was planning to visit you on Donut Holes Thursday and then..." My words trail off. I'm too ashamed to admit two detectives basically interrogated me.

Alla is just like Zoya. She would never let me off so easily. "You got a visit from Tweedledum and Tweedledee?" When my sigh answers her question on my behalf, she bumps me with her hip. "They've been sniffing around a lot the past few days. The girl—"

"Lara," I interrupt, conscious she is terrible with names.

"She's good. Decent, even. But Ivan..." He must have rubbed her the wrong way if she remembered his name. "He's a snake in long grass."

"More like a bull in a China shop."

She throws her head back and laughs. "Just with smaller balls." When I roll my eyes, her laughter loudens. "He has major small dick vibes." Her voice suddenly turns husky. "Unlike your husband." She lassoes the air while galloping like a cowgirl. "I would have saddled up and rode him all the way to the altar too, even without requesting him to whip it out so I could check he was a thoroughbred."

"Alla!"

I can't stop laughing, and the more I try to discipline myself for its inappropriateness, the more it occurs.

I miss the playfulness of exchanges like this. More people surround me now than ever, but I've never felt more lonely.

That confession takes care of my giggles. They're under control and locked away by the time we arrive at Alla's car, parked a few spots up from the staff-only exit of Myasnikov Private.

"This is me," Alla says. "Let me put away my things, and then I'll walk you the rest of the way."

My mouth gapes like it hears the hundreds of cuss words tumbling around in my head, but it isn't willing to say them.

When Alla locks up her vehicle in preparation to chaperone my walk home, I say, "It's fine. I've got this. You go."

She fans her hands across her tiny hips before cocking a brow. "I don't know if anyone has ever told you this, but you're a bad liar."

I speak before my body can consider sobbing. "I may have been informed of that a handful of times."

She thanks me for my honesty with a smile before saying, "What's going on? You seem... scared."

I'm not scared. I'm just... *scared.* Ano is great, but I'd never want to be on his bad side. He has the same dangerous edge as Maksim but without the burden of being the head of a family. That level of freedom only ever ends one way—recklessly.

When Alla encourages me to continue down the truthful route, what should be a short sentence takes a long time to be delivered since I'm praying it won't make me sound like a snob. "I have a driver waiting for me."

"A driver?" She wolf whistles.

"It's not like that. He's a friend of Maksim's—"

"Who drives you to work every day?" When I nod, Alla says, "Then that makes him *your* driver, baby girl." She takes a moment to relish my grimace before she nudges her head to the entrance we broke through only minutes ago. "Go on. I'll wait for you to enter before I leave. These alleyways give me the creeps."

I see her fear worsening if she knew this was the alleyway where Dr. Abdulov lost his life, so instead of announcing that, I tell her to climb into the driver's seat and wind down the window.

"Don't act like your squeal isn't loud enough to alert everyone within five miles to any danger occurring," I say when she attempts an objection.

"Fine. You've convinced me." She unlocks her car door and slips inside before winding down the window. "But I'm going to start the engine too. Zero to sixty in under a second wasn't solely designed for race car drivers." Giggles bubble in my chest again when she scans the dark, dingy alleyway before saying, "This alleyway could do with a speedbump or two. It will stop the hoons."

"You're the only hoon I see racing up and down this street."

Her smile is brighter than the moon. "That is true."

I take a mental note to introduce her to Zoya before spinning on my heels and walking away from my apartment building. It seems stupid to return to the hospital and ride the elevator to the underground parking garage, but from the snippets of information Ano has shared with me over the past four days, Maksim has enough on his plate. He doesn't need me going AWOL added to the long list.

The night I confronted Maksim about the legitimacy of our marriage wasn't the only night he's spent at Myasnikov PD. He's been there every night since, and it has me worried I will be subpoenaed as a witness for the DA like I was for my father's case.

He told me to be honest on the stand, so I was.

I'm reasonably sure my confession pulled the jury over the DA's fence.

If I had lied, he may still be here, helping me wade through the mess.

Alla's toot as she drives past the entrance I've just walked through pulls me from my horrid thoughts. She zips out of the alleyway like she's as eager to be reintroduced to her bed as I am, narrowly missing Ano sprinting around the corner like it is faster to chase me down on foot than steer a bulky SUV up multiple levels of narrow parking.

He almost runs past me.

A quick glance through the tinted doors is the only thing that saves him from a predawn workout.

"What the fuck, Doc? Maksim thought you were running," he mutters breathlessly, joining me in the corridor outside the ER. "He's about to lose his shit."

"I wasn't running. I was..." Having a high IQ doesn't automatically equate to having stellar common sense. I am a prime example of this. "Why would he think I'd run now?"

I swallow harshly when my last memory rolls through my head like a movie. I testified against my father, my flesh and blood, so Maksim has every right to be worried.

I told him it was the spouse's choice whether they testified before making out that I could go against him without the slightest bit of remorse. I've never informed him any differently because I honestly don't know which team I'm meant to be on.

I always thought it would be with the victims, but my father's case taught me that that isn't necessarily true.

Sometimes victims are assailants too.

My issues stem more from their ability to alter my life course.

They can take more from me than the people they hurt. At one stage, they made me believe my life wasn't worth living. That's why I wanted Maksim to promise he wouldn't do anything that would put me in the predicament of him being taken from me as well.

I wanted him to uphold the pledge my parents didn't maintain.

Was that fair of me to do? No, not at all. But I have more abandonment issues than jealousy and vows I had no intention of speaking to advocate.

I am swimming in waters out of my depth, and the chances of my going under increase when Ano says, "I've got eyes on her. She's standing right in front of me."

Maksim is doing everything right. He is protecting me and sheltering me from additional harm, but can that excuse murder?

I honestly don't know.

Ano's eyes dart to something left of my shoulder before he shoves me back two paces. "Better?" I can't hear what the person on the other end of his earpiece says, but they must disengage their connection shortly after, because Ano speaks as if no one else is listening in while escorting me to the elevators as he has the past four days. "He's moody as fuck when he isn't getting any." I realize I have the situation wrong when he continues talking. "That's what I said. Some chicks dig somnophilia." His laugh bounces off the closed elevator walls and rumbles through my chest. "There's no way I could lay next to my girl all night and not touch her." I snap my eyes away when the reflective paneling of the elevator doors alerts him that he's caught an admirer, but I'm too late to hide my snooping ways. "We'll finish this later." He jerks up his chin like the person he's chatting with can see him. "I'd say under an hour. She looks zonked."

As the elevator arrives at the underground parking garage, he slides a bead-like device out of his ear and stores it in his pocket. "Best thing that ever came out of the US," he murmurs when he notices the direction of my gaze. "That and Hooters."

I roll my eyes before helming our walk to the SUV. I'm so tired that I don't wait for Ano to open my door, neither here nor at my apartment. I don't even guzzle down the vitamin water I consume at night to replace the electrolytes I lose during late shifts because breaks are minimal and snacks are hard to come by.

I make a beeline for the sofa bed, preferring it over the option Ano offered on day two of our unexpected roommate experience. He wanted me to sleep in my grandparents' bed. I couldn't do that. Not solely because it is hard and lumpy but because it is the bed my parents shared when we first moved to Russia.

It was the one thing that was solely theirs. They didn't have to share it with anyone, and I wanted it to stay that way until I found out a new mattress costs more than my grandfather's monthly medication.

Even with my grandfather in the forefront of my mind, I can't pretend my head isn't about to explode out of my nostrils. "Can you ask Dr. Muhamed to slide my grandfather's latest workup under my door? My head is thumping."

"Then you should drink something. You'll only make it worse by going to bed without taking something for it." Ano taps two headache tablets into his palm before he shoves them under my nose with a bottle of vitamin water from the refrigerator.

"I don't want to take anything."

"Doc—"

"The more you try to medicate headaches, the more headaches you get. Analgesics dependency is no different from any other dependency."

He's not up for a lecture, so he tries to take another route to drag me over my stubbornness. "Then drink some water."

"I will," I murmur groggily. "Later."

"Not later. Now." He unscrews the cap of the vitamin water while grumbling under his breath that he isn't dealing with the mess that comes from migraines. "I don't do piss, shit, or vomit. Those are my limitations. I'd rather clean up a blood bath than my father's stinky whiskey barfs any day of the week..." He freezes before his face screws up.

He's so deep in thought it takes me saying his name three times before he finally looks at me. "Was that your first memory of your father since your accident?"

I don't know a lot about what happened to Ano when he was sixteen, but I know his injuries weren't caused naturally. Someone struck him hard enough that they cracked his skull in multiple places. He didn't tell me that. I read it on his online medical record I unearthed when searching for information about Maksim's years of childhood abuse.

"Ano?" I prompt when he remains quiet.

"Yeah." He shakes his head like he'd rather get rid of the memory he just unearthed than encourage more like it before he places the open bottle onto the side table I'm using like a bedside table. "You should drink that, and I'm gonna... ah..." He flicks his eyes to the front door of my apartment before focusing on the one behind him. "I'm going to shower."

"Okay."

He smiles to assure me he is okay before he makes a beeline for the bathroom. I'm so tired I should be asleep before he turns on the shower, but I'm not. It takes several hours for my exhaustion to pull me under, and even then, it's cut short by the shrill of an alarm.

CHAPTER TWENTY-SEVEN

"Eventually, the long hours, lagging sleep schedule, and massive student loans will be worth it, right?" An interim doctor I've not yet met slumps onto the bench wedged between lockers before she carefully commences peeling off her stiletto. "And the blisters. We can't forget the blisters."

I hiss with her when the removal of her shoe unearths a massive blister. She's either never worn high heels while working or forgot to run her new shoes in before undertaking a double shift.

"Here. This will help." She stares at me peculiarly when I hand her a condom. "Condoms have many uses that don't involve the prevention of STIs and unwanted pregnancies."

She stares at the foil disc for a few seconds before seeking instructions.

"You just slip it over your foot."

"Over my *entire* foot?"

Her shock is understandable. Guys often pretend they can't wear a condom because their penis is too big. They're lying. You can wear a condom as a knee-high sock if latex is your jam.

When I nod, the intern I believe took my position on the surgical rotation last week twists her lips. "Interesting."

"The latex will stop any nasties from getting in the wound when your blister pops, and its natural lubricant will eliminate the rubbing that's causing the discomfort."

With her curiosity as high as her manicured brow, she slides the condom over the toes that are aching and red. When it offers instant relief, she shoots her eyes to me. "You wouldn't happen to have another condom, would you?" She gestures her hand at her right foot. "I went with this foot first because I wasn't sure I'd get my heels back on if I were to free the beast I feel growing on the big toe on my left foot."

I smile, loving the ease of our conversation, before opening my locker to hunt for another condom. "I should have another one here somewhere, but if I don't, there are condom dispensers in all the washrooms in the ER."

My rummage through my locker knocks out the credit card Maksim gifted me last week.

The still unnamed intern collects it off the floor before handing it to me.

"Thanks." Her curiosity is expected, and so is the unease of my reply. "It's not mine. A... *friend* gave it to me."

She waits for me to return the credit card to its rightful spot on the shelf—next to my rings—before asking, "If your friend has a brother, let me know."

I laugh like that introduction wouldn't encourage a heap of trouble in her life, before handing her a second condom.

"Who knew something so simple could offer so much relief." After ripping open the foil disc with her teeth, she peers up at me through a mop of curls. "Eva Mahoney."

I accept the hand she is holding out in offering. "Nikita." My pause to evaluate which surname I should use makes it seem like I am impersonating James Bond. "Nikita Hoffman."

Eva's dark brow shoots up high. "Hoffman?"

Either my stumble confused her or she paid more attention to the name on the credit card than she made out. It isn't in my maiden name. "It's a long story, and I'm already ten minutes into my miniscule thirty-minute break."

She smiles like she knows I'd rather cut off my arm with a blunt object than have the discussion she is trying to open. "Perhaps another time? I could bring whiskey-laced coffee. I've heard that's a hit with some medical officers around here."

My smile is genuine for the first time today. "It is, and honestly, I'm not sure I blame them anymore."

"It will be worth it... *eventually*," she murmurs again.

"It will," I agree.

I farewell her with a wave before exiting the locker room with more spring in my step than I entered it. Our conversation was awkward in places, but it was more enriched than any I've had the prior five days.

I'm still viewed as a leech by my colleagues, and Zoya's assurance that I am not isn't as well received over FaceTime.

I'm meant to be going to the cafeteria to rehydrate my veins with caffeine, but raised voices in the ER alter the direction of my steps.

Angry patients are nothing new in the emergency department, but this is the first time they've centered around a child.

"Mr. Petrovitch?" I ask when the side profile of the man shouting at the ward clerk to help his daughter registers as familiar.

My heart launches into my throat when Lev spins to face me. Yulia is cradled into his chest. Her cheeks are bright red, and her breathing is tachycardia. She looks seconds from collapse.

After checking her pulse and the reflexes of her pupils, I lock my eyes with the clerk so she can see the seriousness in them when I say, "She is going into ventricular fibrillation." When she stands there, gawping at me, my panic increases the volume of my voice. "She needs to be admitted, now!"

"She can't be assigned a bed. Her insurance has expired, and our previous claim was denied. She will *not* be admitted here today."

While Lev assures the clerk that his new medical insurance will commence next week, I snatch Yulia out of his arms, race her to the nearest gurney, and then wheel her into a cubicle with the equipment needed to assist a patient in severe cardiac distress.

"Dr. Hoffman, you can't do that. This patient has no insurance." As I commence placing defibrillation pads onto Yulia's chest, the clerk says, "A free medical clinic is five miles away."

"She won't make it five miles. If we don't restart her heart and achieve normal rhythm within the next few minutes, she will die."

Dr. Eiland enters the cubicle. She is the chief medical officer of the ER department.

Eva is close on her tail.

"Stats?"

Memories flash through my head when my reply mimics one I've heard previously. "Her pulse is over three hundred beats a minute, and eupneic breaths are present."

As Dr. Eiland gloves up, she asks, "Protein?"

I shake my head. "She hasn't been tested yet."

"Because she can't be admitted," the clerk interrupts. "She has no insurance, and her account is already tens of thousands of dollars in debt."

Dr. Eiland's wide eyes shoot to me. "Is that true?" I'm sickened when she steps back after I nod. "Dr. Hoffman, we're not—"

"I'll find a way to pay," I shout, too furious about profits being placed before a child's well-being not to yell. This is what happened to my sister. She got sick and needed an operation, but since we had only recently moved to Russia, we didn't have insurance, and her surgery was postponed. She died the following afternoon. "I will pay her debt and for any services we use today."

"That could be in the thousands."

Dr. Eiland appears seconds from announcing she knows that is an expense I can't afford, but Eva, who is assisting me in prepping Yulia to have her heart rhythm reset, endeavors to set her straight. "She has the means to back up her pledge. I saw her credit card. It has no limit." When her confession only pulls Dr. Eiland partly over the fence, she asks, "Do you know who her husband is?"

Dr. Eiland nods, her wordless acknowledgment matching the bob of the clerk's throat. "Yes."

"Then how about you stop fucking around and help us save this little girl's life."

Dr. Eiland is as shocked as I am, but since fear is the one emotion that can triumph over greed, she barks orders at the nurses and doctors surrounding us until Yulia's heart is returned to its normal rhythm and her life is saved.

"Thank you," Mr. Petrovitch praises me, mistakenly believing I deserve the credit for restoring the life in his daughter's eyes.

I don't.

It is the man I am already severely indebted to—the same man whose murky dark eyes and lazy smile popped into my head when I realized my private pledge to pay him back could be delayed by at least three years.

"We still have a long way to go." I guide Lev out of the cubicle and to the side of the nurses' station, where I am stunned to see Nurse Kelley working behind the desk. She hasn't been seen in the pediatric ward since our heated conversation. I assumed that was because Maksim had... *Nope.* My heart still can't put him and murder in one sentence.

"Dr. Hoffman?" Mr. Petrovitch dips his head, bringing his wet eyes to align with mine. "Is my little girl going to be okay?"

Even knowing I shouldn't give him false hope, I can't help but nod. "To return Yulia's heart to its normal rhythm, we had to shock her."

"Which made her better?" He struggles to speak in English

but understands it is easier for me to explain his daughter's condition.

"Yes. But her improvement will only be temporary if we don't unearth the cause of her recent spike in illnesses."

When he appears seconds from collapsing, I move him to a line of hard plastic chairs. Once he is seated, I give him a few moments to settle his panic before explaining the tests Yulia will need to endure to expose the cause of her sudden cardiac episode and the possible procedure needed to correct it.

"Bypass surgery?" His cheeks whiten as tears well in his eyes.

"That's the worst-case scenario. It could be as simple as administrating anti-arrhythmic medication, but we won't know until further tests are conducted."

"Okay." He takes a moment to sort through the facts before asking, "Will they be done here?"

"Um..." I wish I could give him a straightforward answer, but that is outside my means. Only a week and a half ago, I was barely getting by after paying for my grandfather's medication. Yulia's condition could end up being more costly than the end-of-life care of a stage four lung disease patient and over the amount I've been stashing away for three years to buy my grandfather a better ECOM machine. "I will try my best to have her admitted at Myasnikov Private, but—"

Again, he cuts me off with praise I don't deserve.

CHAPTER TWENTY-EIGHT

Afte ensuring Yulia is stable, I join Eva in the locker room for an impromptu patient debrief.

"That was..." Eva shakes out her arms and legs before breathing out heavily. "Whoa!" She peers at me wide-eyed and in awe. "We kicked ass today."

I laugh, loosening some of the heaviness on my chest. "We did."

The endorphins released when you save a patient's life are dispersed in a number of ways. Some interns cry, others holler and shout, and there are a handful who work off the excess adrenaline in a sexual manner—usually in the very room we're standing in.

Eva appears to be an intern who'd happily tick off all three items on the list. Her eyes are brimming with wetness, she's hollered a handful of times, and although there is no one to help her with the last item on the list, she thrusts her hips enough times to announce she needs a cigarette before she twists a recently opened pack my way.

I shake my head. I've not yet rolled through the emotions I'm anticipating to hammer into me at any moment because my stomach is too twisted up in knots to claim the victory we fought hard to achieve.

Yulia's blood workup showed no signs of the troponin T protein most heart disease patients have, which means it is unlikely her heart sustained any damage during her medical episode, but the cardiologist they brought in to conduct the tests is the best in the country.

I don't see his fees being close to that of the savings of an intern's salary.

My offer looks set to become extremely costly, but I'd be a liar if I said I wouldn't have done the same thing if I were offered to go back and overturn my pledge.

I wait for Eva to leave the locker room, before digging my cell phone out of my purse and dialing a number I usually only ring at the end of my shift.

It takes Ano a few seconds to connect our call. "Hey. Don't tell me you're finishing early for a change."

"I wish," I lie. My job is exhausting but rewarding—most notably when the whispered praise comes from a patient whose life is just beginning. Yulia was on the cusp of death only hours ago, and now she is smiling and asking what day it is. She became an instant fan of Donut Holes Thursday. "I need a favor."

Ano's pulse quickens so fast I hear its thuds in his voice when he asks, "Are you all right?"

"I'm fine. I just need something back at the apartment, and although I could go get it, I don't know if I'd make it out of here without a clerk and half the hospital's administration team on my back."

He laughs, but the lack of warmth in it exposes his unease.

I learn why when he says, "I'd love to help you, Doc, but I can't." Half of my disappointed huff barely rumbles up my throat when he doubles the output of my lungs. "If you're at the hospital, I'm at the hospital. Maksim would take my nuts if I left you unattended for even a second."

"Why? No one is out to get me. Especially here."

I freeze like a statue when he mutters under his breath, "Now." Before I can get a word of my shock out, he says, "Call Maksim. Whatever you need, he will get it for you."

"I can't call him."

"Why? Because you're as fucking stubborn as he is?"

Yes. That is precisely why. But since I can't say that, I settle on, "Because I don't have his number." I sound like a moron. Rightfully so. It is ludicrous to be married to someone and not know their cell phone number.

When I say that to Ano, he laughs. It is full of the warmth I was anticipating earlier. "Doubtful it's the first time he's slept with someone without giving up his deets." Jealously slices me open, quick and without mercy, but he covers up the gashes with flimsy Band-Aids by adding, "But it will be the last. You worked a number on him, Doc. I've never seen him like this." My phone pings, announcing I have received a text. "I forwarded you his number." I'm about to thank him, but before I can, he continues talking. "You're not gonna break up with him via text, right? I'm kinda enjoying life right now." His tone tips from teasing to seductive. "And the scenery is mighty fine in Myasnikov."

"I'm not breaking up with him," my heart answers before my head can object.

"All right." Ano appears eager to go, and it is proven without doubt when he disconnects our call half a second after telling me to buzz him the instant my shift is over.

After pulling my phone down from my ear, I stare at the screen for several long seconds, striving to build the courage to call Maksim. He could get any of his lackeys to do the heavy lifting for him, but since it is for me, I doubt he would.

He's wheeled meals to my apartment every night for the past

five nights—even when I hid in the bathroom and pretended I couldn't hear his knocks announcing it was time to eat.

By the time he left, the meals were stone cold, and Ano was staring at me like I'm a vindictive cow.

Since his assessment wasn't far off the mark, I ate my meal cold and climbed into an equally icy bed.

When my backbone fails to form again, I take the cheat's way out.

I call Zoya instead of Maksim.

"Why are you using the funds you set aside?" she asks after I explain the favor I need help with. "Maksim gave you a limitless credit card and permission to use it for whatever your heart desires. Use that."

"I can't."

"You can, and you don't have much choice." My silence leaves her the entire stage to work how she sees fit. "You have two, three nights' admission max saved."

"And?"

She *pffts* her dislike of my reply before saying, "And..."—she drags out the three-letter word as if it is an entire sentence— "during your two-minute rundown on what happened, you said the clerk announced the Petrovitchs were several thousand in debt." She lowers her tone, bringing it closer to the sluggish beat of my heart. "I don't think you have that much in your box, Keet. Because if you did, you would have purchased your grandfather's breathing machine with it months ago."

She's right. I would have. I counted the cash in the box under my bed every payday, hoping I'd have enough to purchase a new ECOM machine. I was still several thousand short before Maksim entered my life.

"I don't know what to do," I admit, my voice croaky.

"Yeah, you do." Her tone announces she isn't being pushy or mean. She understands this is hard for me, but she also understands I would have done anything for Yulia not to face the outcome my sister got lumped with. "Maksim gave you that credit card for a reason. He wants you to use it."

"That was before we..."

"We...?" Zoya encourages, incapable of reading my mind over the phone.

I swallow the lump in my throat before admitting, "We're kind of not on speaking terms."

"Huh?" Even the shortness of her reply can't hide her confusion. "Since when?"

"Since I threatened to leave him—"

"You what?" Her reply is so loud half the patients of Myasnikov Private hear her.

"Things are complicated." I sigh, not wanting to have this conversation at all, much less over the phone.

"Oh, I bet they are. Maksim is..."

Many words roll through my head when she pauses to consider a reply. They should be about his dark and dangerous side, but my heart wins the battle this time, and it has me expressing something I thought I'd take to my grave. "I miss him, Z."

"Then tell him that."

I slump onto the bench across from my locker. "I can't." Before she can call me an idiot, I express my biggest fear. "What if I lose him too?"

"Keet..." She stops to breathe out the laughter I hear rattling in her chest, shocking me. How is this funny? "I love you, girl, but sometimes you're so blind you can't see what is directly in front of you." I blame the adrenaline rush of my last two hours in the ER when a tear topples down my cheek. "Maksim would *never* put you in that position. He loves you too much to ever hurt you like that."

The tear flings off my cheek when I shake my head. "No—"

"He. *Loves*. You. That's why he is struggling to give you the promise you need to move past your fear that you will lose him too. He isn't a man who can sit back and let the person he loves be hurt because she wants him to promise not to retaliate. I don't know a single man who could promise that, let alone one who spent most of his childhood protecting his mother."

My voice cracks when I ask, "He told you about that?"

"No." Nothing but honesty rings in her tone. "But I know you, and I understand your fear." A shuddering breath fills my chest when she says, "And I also understand Maksim's. He doesn't want to hurt you. He wants to love you, but that comes with a prerequisite of protection. Everyone knows that. You just seem to have gotten the criteria a little mixed up since you've forgotten the love a parent has for a child is different from the love of a spouse." She hits me where it hurts. "Maksim isn't your dad, but I sure as fuck hope he loves and protects you as fiercely as your father did your mother, because that is the type of love every girl should strive for. That is *real* love."

The dam in my eyes breaks, and so does my stubbornness. For years, I only considered my feelings when my father chose revenge over me. I never once considered the hell I forced him to walk through when I demanded he pick me over the love of his life.

I am his daughter, his flesh and blood, but he chose my mother long before I entered the picture.

I am the byproduct of their love, not the source of it.

As I wipe under my nose to make sure nothing has spilled, I say, "Z, I have to go."

"Fuckin' oath you do." Jealousy burns up some of the wetness in my eyes when she says, "Give him a kiss from me."

She's still laughing about my grumble when I yank my phone from my ear, toss it into my purse, and then hightail it out of the locker room.

"Dr. Hoffman," the ER ward clerk shouts when I race past the nurses' station she's manning with the billing clerk from the administration team.

"Not now."

"We need to—"

My head slings to the side when assistance to flee without payment comes from the last person I anticipate. "Let her go. We will get everything squared up tomorrow."

I thank Dr. Sidorov for his assistance with a smile before I race through the staff-only side entrance. Ano is going to be pissed when my sprint past the security camera in the alleyway will force him to undertake a middle-of-the-day workout, but I'm too eager to get to where I'm going to wait in traffic.

By the time I reach the corner of my apartment building, sweat is beading on my nape and the chilly winds have frozen my tears to my cheeks.

With the media dwindling to two the past few days, the doorman spots my approach before I hit the driveway that leads to the underground parking. He opens the door for me and dips his hat in greeting.

I push through the door just as the elevator doors open, and Maksim races out. He's dressed to impress in a tailored suit and polished designer boots. He is the epitome of a successful businessman with an edge of darkness that should have exposed his necessity to protect those he cares about from the get-go.

"Nikita," he breathes out heavily when he spots me standing at the side of the foyer, gawking like it's the first time I've laid eyes on him.

He looks angry, furious, even, but some of the agitation scoured between his brows clears away when I push off my feet and race his way. He catches me in his arms, and when I seal my mouth over his, his shocked exhale flutters over my tongue.

As I lick the roof of his mouth, his arms come around me. One pulls me closer while the other weaves through my hair.

Our kiss is needy and hurried, and it makes me wet in an instant.

I'm not the only one excited. Maksim's cock is thick and braced halfway up my stomach.

"Not here," he murmurs over my kiss-swollen lips when I balance on my tippy-toes to grind against him. "If any of them saw you, I'd ki..." Untapped carnal desire scorches through my veins when he fails to finalize his threat.

He doesn't need words, though. His glare is enough for the men surrounding us to pretend they're needed elsewhere. As Maksim escorts me three feet to the elevator, they scurry in all directions.

Even the elevator attendant makes an excuse to leave his post. "I think I'm overdue for my break."

Maksim's smirk announces his ability to follow unvoiced commands will be significantly rewarded.

Heat sizzles through my body when he places his hand on the curve of my back to guide me inside the elevator. It is chilly today, and my scrubs are as thin as tissue paper, so the temperature shouldn't be as roasting as it is. It just isn't possible to be in the presence of a man with such an enigmatic personality and panty-wetting good looks and not get heated up.

I'm burning up everywhere.

"I've got her," Maksim says a second after selecting the floor below the penthouse, his voice sexy and raspy since it is brimming with lust. He works his jaw side to side before he drops his eyes to me. "I will tell her." He jerks up his chin a second before removing a bead similar to the one Ano wears out of his ear.

"Is Ano pissed?"

He rakes his fingers through his hair, adding to the sexed-up look I awarded it during our kiss. "He is."

When he twists to face me, my breath catches in my throat. He's so gorgeously tortured with kiss-plumped lips and narrowed, confused brows that a confession tumbles out of my mouth before I can stop it. "I've missed you."

With his mouth curved at one side, he cages me to the

elevator wall and burns me inside out with a searing gaze. "You have?"

The shock in his tone surges my confidence and allows me to speak freely. "Uh-huh."

One of his hands drops to my back, and as he yanks my hips forward to display how much my confession means to him, he asks, "How much?"

"A—"

He squashes his finger to my lips, silencing me. "Don't tell me with words, Doc. Show me."

He is so beautiful sprawled above me, so powerful that I let the last of my inhibitions float away before slanting my mouth above his. I'm desperate to kiss him, to feel the heat of his skin against mine, but there's no game if there's no competition.

"Did you miss me?"

His smirk announces he read my game plan a mile out, but he plays along like he has no chance of winning. "For every second of every minute." He breathes in my exhale when he murmurs, "Even the ones spent with a steel rod digging into my back." I'm already getting the gist of his confession, but he wants to make sure I don't underestimate his desire to be with me even when we're not doing anything sexually charged. "If you ever need space again, Doc, can you pick a more comfortable location? My back has been screaming all week."

His playfulness has me desperate enough to have him that I no longer care about our public location. My lunge for him this time is almost violent. Our teeth clash as violently as our noses, but I kiss him freely and without restraint.

And he kisses me back.

He rakes his fingers through my hair while exploring my mouth with his tongue. It is a wild, tender embrace that makes me needy with passion. I love how he kisses me as if it is as intimate and sexually gratifying as the sex it will forever lead to.

His hand slides down my back and cups my ass before he

encourages me to curl my legs around his waist. I moan when the crown of his glorious cock rubs at the entrance of my pussy.

As I lick, kiss, and nibble on his lips, I grind against his thickened shaft, doubling the pulses of my aching clit.

My needs become too overwhelming, and within seconds, I'm stroking Maksim through his trousers while wishing he was naked.

"I need you, Maksim. Please," I beg, too horny to care that I'm showing how weak he makes me. My clit is throbbing for attention, pounding as loudly as my heart. "I can't wait a second longer."

After cussing under his breath, Maksim places me back on my feet, leans over and jabs the emergency stop button on the elevator, and then tugs down my scrub bottoms to my knees with the same urgency I use to free his cock from his trousers.

He is as hard as stone, and the tip is weeping with pre-cum that drips onto my palm when he realizes how wet I am.

"Christ. We only kissed, yet you're already drenched for me." I arch up onto my tippy-toes when he authenticates how much his kisses turn me on by slipping a finger inside me. "You're so tight."

"That won't be an issue too much longer," I mumble while tugging him closer, notching the head of his glistening crown toward the folds of my pussy.

"No. Not yet." He pushes out like the words hurt him to express as much as they devastate me. "I need you wet enough to take me."

My disappointment is pushed aside for pleasure when he falls to his knees before he dips his tongue inside me. He tastes me with long, leisured licks, this kiss as confident and skilled as the one we shared earlier.

Within seconds, my core tightens as a wave slowly forms low in my stomach. My face flushes with lust as tingles prickle every fine hair on my body.

When his thumb rolls over my clit, I can't hold back my moan of delight.

"That feels so good."

"Doubt it is as good as you taste." He steals my ability to reply by gently sucking my clit into his mouth. My stomach spasms violently as my thighs struggle not to clamp around his head. "Do you have any idea how hard it was not to touch you?" His tongue thrusts into my pussy, teasing and needy. "I thought our wedding night was tortuous, but it had nothing on the hell I've walked through the past week."

My pussy convulses around his fingers when he switches from one to two. He thrusts them in and out, stretching me and making me moan. "Yes..."

"I knew how good you tasted but couldn't do anything to quench my thirst." His groan vibrates through me, adding to the sticky mess between my legs. "Not even my hand was good enough." He hits my clit with back-to-back licks before saying, "Don't ever do that to me again, Doc. Don't ever leave me hanging like that again, wondering who the fuck I am and where my loyalties should lie." He pushes three fingers inside me, curling my toes and burning my eyes with tears. He's not hurting me—physically. I can't share the same guarantee for my heart. He's so open and raw right now. So exposed. It is almost too much. "Promise me you won't ever do that again, and I'll do the same."

I shouldn't be able to think with how much lust is clouding my head, and I shouldn't be able to comprehend the complexity of his promise, but the glint in his eyes as he stares up at me is too strong to ignore.

He's willing to compromise.

Willing to try.

He's promising to put me first.

"Maksim," I murmur with a moan as a tensing and violent orgasm courses through me without warning.

Ecstasy spasms my limbs as pleasurable zaps of electricity race through my body. I shake for several minutes, my climax long and powerful since its arrival doesn't lower Maksim's dedication in the slightest. He continues massaging the tender spot inside me with his fingers while stimulating my clit with slow, teasing licks.

I can barely stand when the heat licking through me augments from him notching the head of his cock at the opening of my pussy. A gasp whistles between my teeth when he pushes inside me with one ardent thrust. He's so deep. So thick. I'm almost overwhelmed.

After taking a moment to acclimate to his girth, I clench around him, silently permitting him to move.

My muscles ripple and tighten when he pulls out to the tip before he slams back in.

I moan like I am possessed, loving how full he makes me feel.

"Christ..." Maksim breathes out through clenched teeth. "You feel so good." He pistons his hips on repeat, nailing me to the wall of the elevator. "You take my cock so well. You're going to make me come so hard."

Pleasure ripples through me as he plunges in and out of me hard and fast. He fucks me recklessly. *Possessively.* He uses every muscle to drive me wild, and all I can do is scream and moan.

I've never felt so taken... *claimed.*

He thrusts into me, his body moving like a well-oiled machine over and over again until I'm overcome with the insane need to climax.

I throw my head back and scream through an orgasm that is so overwhelming tears prick my eyes mere seconds before they slide down my face.

I'm a quivering, blubbering mess, but Maksim's pace doesn't slow. He continues to dominate my body, demanding every inch of its attention. He plows into me with enough force that my back creeps higher on the wall with every punishing pound.

My body doesn't mind, though. I grow so hot and wet that I slide up and down his lengthy cock with ease. I accept as much of him into my body as possible, and my acceptance is rewarded with another blindsiding orgasm full of heat and lust.

"Ah, Christ," Maksim grinds out, his hips as stiff and jutted as his words when the walls of my vagina squeeze around him.

His hips churn impatiently for several more minutes before the desire to mist his skin with sweat wins. He grinds into me another three greedy pumps before he buries his head into my neck and grunts through a brutal release.

My name rips from his throat as he comes. It is a feral, animalistic rumble that sweeps pleasure across my core as ruefully as his cum heats the walls of my pussy.

As the shudders of his release threaten to pull me under for the umpteenth time, he switches our position so his back is against the elevator wall and mine is open before he slides us down to sit on the floor, our connection never lost.

I brush my lips against his sweat-slicked business shirt before pressing my ear to his racing heart. We're almost still fully clothed—only the most intimate parts of our bodies are uncovered—but I feel raw. *Exposed.*

He knows my deepest, darkest fear, but instead of hiding from it as everyone else in my life has, he's trying to understand it. Possibly even lessen it.

Just knowing he's trying cuts my worries in half.

We stay huddled together for several long minutes, neither willing to break us apart first. I could stay immersed in his bubble forever, but regretfully, I can't. This is the only elevator in the building. We can't continue to hog it.

When I say that to Maksim, he draws me in closer, holding me with a tenderness a man his size shouldn't have, before he mutters against my temple, "They can use the stairs."

I peer at him, smiling when I notice how relaxed he seems. There are no grooves between his brows, no shadows under his eyes. He appears well-rested, which has me thinking back to his earlier confession.

"Did you really sleep with me every night?"

My heart thumps wildly when he tilts his chin so our eyes align. It isn't solely his nod responsible for the extra blood pumping through my veins. The raw emotion in his eyes is what my heart is paying attention to the most.

He doesn't want to hurt me. Not for a single second.

He only wants to protect me.

"What did they do?" I murmur, my curiosity too high for me to contain.

It had to be something mammoth, because I don't see this beautiful, gorgeous creature murdering three people for something minute and unmeaningful. His title in the underworld demands a level of fear, but this seems more important than that. It appears personal.

He brushes a damp stray lock off my temple before using the same fingers to increase the heat on my cheeks. He isn't distracting me, but he isn't racing to tell me the truth, either. He appears torn, like he's unsure of what my reaction will be to his confession.

"I won't hold it against you."

"I'm not worried about how it will have you looking at me." His voice is husky and lustful, and it makes me wish I could save our conversation for another day. My heart just refuses to listen to the prompts of my brain and body. "I'm more worried about how it will have you looking at yourself."

Me? How would the actions of others affect me?

Maksim appears seconds from answering my inner thoughts, but before he can, a familiar voice sounds out of the speaker above our heads. "I wouldn't bother knocking if the elevator was still rocking, but since it's not, I thought I should tell you that security has your 4:30 appointment in the foyer, waiting for the elevator." Even during work hours, Zoya still acts like a prepubescent boy.

"Thanks, Zoya," Maksim replies, miraculously standing.

I want to whine like a fifth grader when he carefully slides out of me after setting me on my feet. I just can't get any words through the lust clogged in my throat when I realize his cock never seems to go down. It is as thick and lengthy as it is when he thrusts it inside me, just a little floppier.

"If you don't quit gawking, Doc, I'm gonna clear my schedule for the rest of the day."

My eyes snap to Maksim before they shoot to the camera in the corner of the elevator when Zoya moans, "Keep looking, Doc. I'm about ready for round two."

The camera isn't flashing, and Maksim's grinding jaw announces he wouldn't even let my best friend watch our sexcapades, but that doesn't stop me from shoving my feet into my scrub pants and yanking them up like we have an audience before asking, "Were you listening in?"

"No," Zoya immediately replies, conscious of where my suspicions lie. "But I didn't need to hack into the building's servers to hear you. You were moaning loud enough for half of Myasnikov to hear." When my cheeks heat so fast she hears their boil over whistle out of my ears, she laughs. "I'm joking. I only joined the party two minutes ago because Ano was too chickenshit to interrupt you guys." I realize Ano must be close to her when she cups the microphone before repeating her statement to the accused. "You were totally chickenshit."

While muttering something under his breath about firing his staff and starting anew, Maksim hits the emergency stop button on the elevator panel, jolting it back into gear, before requesting Zoya have the security officers take his guest to his office. "Tell Francesca I will join her in the boardroom once I have Nikita settled."

"Francesca?" Zoya and I ask at the same time.

Maksim pays Zoya's grumble no attention. "Doc..." For one short word, he takes an extremely long time to deliver it. "I fuckin' love when you get jealous."

"I'm not jealous."

I glare at the now blinking contraption in the elevator's corner when Zoya's *pfft* rumbles louder than Maksim's grumbled denial.

Thankfully, I'm saved from the disadvantage of a two-against-one fight when the elevator dings, announcing its arrival at our floor.

I race out of the car that smells of sex and desperation, only just making it to the door of our apartment half a second before Maksim's sweat-dotted chest warms my back.

When his lips brush the shell of my ear, I'm putty in the hands of a sex god in mere seconds, so we won't mention how weak my knees become when he growls against my neck, "It's too late to run, Doc. I warned you the last time you got jealous that it would be the *only* time I'd fuck it out of your system in under an hour." His following sentence has a double meaning, making me more than eager to gauge its authenticity. "I'm a man of my word. It is about time you learn that."

Once we're in the safety of our apartment, he shreds my scrubs off me even faster than he did in the elevator. Then, just as swiftly, he falls to his knees and drags his tongue up the seam of my pussy, buckling my legs out from under me.

CHAPTER TWENTY-NINE

My eyes roll skyward when Zoya's breathy chuckles sound out of my iPhone.

"What?" she asks when I glare at her snickering face. "You're planning to stuff a dress that costs"—she ponders for a moment—"three to four thousand dollars into a knapsack that costs ten."

"It's a backpack." I freeze when my sluggish head finally absorbs the entirety of her statement. "How much did you say this dress is worth?"

I'm packing for Aleena's wedding, and although I could have rummaged through my clothes on the freestanding rack in my grandmother's room, my lusty head accepted one of Maksim's many offers to take some of the clothes he had purchased for me when our apartment was remodeled.

The dress I chose is gorgeous, but I can't wear it if it costs more than my first car.

What if I spilled something on it?

"Don't you dare," Zoya shouts at her phone screen when I

remove the red ensemble with a daring thigh-high split from my packing stack. "You'll steal the show with that dress."

"Even more reason for me to put it back. This weekend is meant to be about Aleena."

Although Zoya agrees with me, she will never not push me to accept more than I'm worth. Never less. "If you don't pack it, I'll tell Maksim that you put all your savings toward Yulia's hospital bill before paying the remainder with the credit card he gifted you."

"You wouldn't dare."

She glares at me as if to say, *Do you know me at all?*

"He'd have a fit." *Like I did when I discovered how generous my offer was.*

I didn't even have ten percent of the forty thousand Myasnikov Private was requesting, but Maksim refused to let me use even a portion of my savings to pay for some of the pledge I'd made.

Zoya hums in agreement. "And most likely go on another rant." Flashbacks of Maksim's response the day the credit card company called him to approve the amount needed to pay Yulia's outstanding medical debt roll through my head when she lowers her tone and snarls, "*Subsequent cardholder? You're calling my wife a subsequent cardholder. She is my wife, and you will address her as such, or I'll... I'll...*"

My heart melts into a gooey mess when we finalize Maksim's rant about the bank employee referring to me as if I were nothing more than the number on a plastic card at the same time. "*I'll transfer the equity of every asset I own to another bank.*"

"He was seriously hot that day," Zoya says, practically moaning.

"He was," I admit. "And he defended me without a single threat of physical harm."

"I bet that took a lot of restraint."

Shockingly, I laugh. "I'm sure it did, and how I showed my

appreciation during our drive home from dinner that night has me confident he will take that route more often in the future."

"So that was the cause of all those noise complaints the past two weeks?" Her grin screws up her nose when I poke my tongue at her. "I thought it was walrus mating season." She takes a moment to drink in my disgust before saying, "Whatever it was, you're still packing that dress."

"Z—"

"Don't Z me. That dress is the bomb. You're going to look smoking hot in it, and when your husband rips it off you in a jealous rage, you're going to ring your best friend and tell her she is a genius."

It would be nice to hand the jealousy baton I've been wielding the past few weeks onto Maksim, but I'm still on the fence. "It's a lot of money."

"Maybe to you, but to Maksim, it will never be close to the jewels he wants to drape you in."

"Talking about jewels, stop falsely dropping hints that I'm obsessed with diamonds." The tennis bracelet Maksim gifted me two days ago casts rainbow hues across the ceiling of my room when I spin it around my wrist. "Our plane will never make it in the air at this rate. The diamonds he keeps gifting me will be too heavy."

Zoya laughs. I wish she wouldn't. Maksim only needs to catch a whiff of her numerous money-inspired hints, and it is on my pillow hours later.

When she spots the plea in my eyes, she breathes heavily out of her nose before compromising. "Take the dress, and I'll make out not every girl needs a fairytale wedding. Drunk nuptials in a hotel chapel should be more than enough." Before I can scold her, she peers at someone over her phone, mouths that she will be a minute, and shifts her eyes back to me. "I have to go." She disappears from view for barely a second before her head pops back into the frame. "Pack the dress. I'm not asking. I am telling."

"Fine," I cave, not up for a fight.

The past few weeks have been amazing. I don't want anything to taint it.

Zoya smiles in victory before she farewells me with an air kiss, then disconnects our chat.

Begrudgingly, I return the dress to the top of the stack before trying to work out how to pack a suitcase-sized stack into a carry-on backpack.

I should probably unpack from my last weekend getaway before contemplating a restack.

My heart thuds in my ears when the last item I pull out of my backpack wafts up a deliciously spicy scent. It is the shirt Maksim left in the washroom, the one he was wearing when I spilled my drink on him. Except droplets of bourbon and coke aren't the only stain it is housing—tiny splotches of red dot the cuffs.

I work through a stern swallow when the familiarity of the stains smacks into me.

They're droplets of blood. In particular, the blood splatter that occurs during a knife attack.

I startle when a voice from behind me says, "I was wondering if you were ever going to get around to unpacking that." Maksim enters our room before lowering his eyes to the shirt that could convict him of murder. "I could have had it done for you, but then I would have taken the decision away from you instead of letting it be your choice."

"My choice...?" I ask, confused.

"On whether you want to stay with me or not." He smirks as if my daftness is cute before saying, "That is your ticket out, Doc. If you want to leave, and I'm too fucking obsessed with you to let you go, that's your ticket out." A flare of cockiness darts through his eyes. "Although I doubt even a life sentence could keep me away from you for long."

I still sound confused while asking, "Why give me an out for the very thing you married me for?" Rightfully so, I'm the most confused I've ever been.

"This was never about an alibi, Doc." A pinch of pain hardens his features. "I thought you would have realized that by now."

"I do. I just..." I don't know what I think. I'm so surprised but also so snowed under by this man that I'm constantly waiting for the other shoe to drop.

This can't be my life. It is too perfect. Too surreal. I wake up every morning expecting to find out it was all a dream.

I lean into Maksim's embrace when he cups my jaw before dragging his thumb along my lips. They're nude and cracked, dried from the number of screams he forced them to release this morning, but he stares at them like they're without a single flaw.

He bounces his eyes between mine long enough to send a needy current through my blood. "It'll make sense soon. I just need a little more time." We breathe as one when he tilts in close and murmurs against my lips, "*You* need a little more time."

Ano's fascination with threatening self-harm almost rubs off on me when he interrupts us a second too soon. Maksim's lips are only brushing mine. They're not wholly consuming them.

"Sorry." Don't mistake Ano's apology. He isn't apologetic. His stirring smile exposes this, not to mention how he rubs his hands while shuffling from foot to foot. "Just thought we should head off early since traffic is extra shit with the upcoming long weekend."

My eyes bulge when I take in the time on my phone. It is later than I realized. Since Aleena is at a final dress fitting, my chat with Zoya went longer than usual. I'm on the cusp of being late for the first time.

I point to the clothes I was in the process of packing. "They're mine, and if someone could grab my cosmetic bag out of the bathroom, I would love them forever." Maksim's growl makes me smile. "Figuratively." We haven't shared those words yet, but I feel them bubbling in my chest every time I am with him, so I don't think they will be too far off. "And you can keep this." I shove his bloodstained shirt into his chest. "I don't need it. I didn't back then, and I don't now."

I kiss him like we don't have an audience before racing for the door, hot on Ano's tail.

I'm almost in the clear when I'm stopped by the rumble that's toppled me into ecstasy more times than I can count the past few weeks. "Doc."

When I spin to face Maksim, my heart clenches. There's so much angst on his face, so much turmoil, so I anticipate for him to say something far more troubled than he does. "Don't work too hard."

My smile seems odd in the tenseness of our gathering, but I've held myself back so much the past nine years that I refuse to do it another second. "I won't."

It is difficult to walk away, but I remind myself that it is only for nine hours, and then I will have the entire weekend to smooth the deep groove between my husband's brows.

CHAPTER THIRTY

"It's quiet."

I follow Alla's scan of the near-empty OR while replying, "It is." I return my eyes front and center. "I guess we shouldn't complain." I pluck another donut hole out of the packet like I haven't eaten half a dozen already and pop it into my mouth. "We might have had to skip Donut Hole Thursday if we were still rushed off our feet like last month."

"By rushed off your feet, do you mean swept off your feet? Because from what I heard, you practically rode out of here on a white horse after your husband's *my wife* rant last month."

I chew my donut to mush, hopeful my gnaws will hide my smile.

When it only increases Alla's suspiciousness, I say, "You heard about that?"

"Ah... yeah. Everyone did." She leans in close so her following words are only for my ears. "I heard a few of the nurses used it for inspo." When I peer at her, lost, she makes vibrator noises Zoya would be proud of.

Hiding my jealousy is more challenging than my coyness, but

I give it my best shot. "Are you sure you were born here?" I ask, certain I am staring at Zoya's twin. Alla is a couple of years older, but her maturity level perfectly aligns with Zoya's. "They say everyone has a doppelgänger, but this is getting spooky."

"I wish I were born anywhere but here, but we're not all that lucky." She bumps me with her shoulder. "I'm still waiting for that invite, though."

"It's coming," I assure her. "Zoya has been tied up with her sister's wedding, but with that only two days away, she'll be back on deck full-time first thing Monday."

When she snags the last donut hole from the packet, I scrunch up the evidence of our piggish carb fest, then toss it into the trash. It rims the trash can before breaking through it.

I celebrate the victory with an internal jig, but Alla leaps into the air with her arms held high like I scored the game-winning point. "Why aren't you celebrating?"

I shrug before replying, "I reserve my cheers for real victories."

"Like when you learned Dr. Abdulov got his just desserts?"

I love Alla like a sister, but my feelings for Maksim exceed that. "Dr. Abdulov's disappearance is still under investigation. No one knows what happened to him. He could still be alive."

"Come on. You don't truly believe that, right?"

I must be learning the skill of deceit, because she looks surprised when I say, "Why wouldn't I?"

"Because he was a terrible man, and sometimes karma does more than bite." She eyeballs me for several uncomfortable seconds before she whispers, "You don't know."

"Know what?" I can no longer blame a lack of sleep for my daftness. Maksim ensures I am so sexually exhausted every night that I've been getting seven-plus hours each day. So I place the blame on sugar overload.

Alla returns to her seat next to me and says, "Dr. Abdulov was facing multiple malpractice suits before he disappeared. The claims against him were horrific. Families of his victims weren't solely accusing him of medical negligence. They said he murdered their loved ones."

"What?" That's it. That is all I can get out.

He's a doctor who recited the Hippocratic oath.

Murder should not be in his vocabulary.

I don't think I can be more shocked, but Alla makes a quick liar out of me. "Investigations took off when a handful of his patients' bodies were exhumed. Several were missing organs. Not all of them were registered donors." She leans in so close her breaths bead condensation on my cheek. "He was playing God. Picking and choosing who got organs and who didn't. I've heard rumors that money exchanged hands." She huffs. "It wasn't small change either."

It takes almost a minute for me to absorb the facts, and even then, my struggle to sort through them is heard in my tone. "I haven't heard a single murmur about this."

And I lose the ability to deliberate further on Alla's confession when my cell phone buzzes. It is from Ano, asking if I will be much longer.

ANO:

The jet is fueled and ready to go.
Maksim is already on board.

While nodding like he can see me, I reply.

ME:

On my way down now.

Too curious for my own good, and another emotion I can't quite understand, I say to Alla, "I need to go, but can you keep me updated on anything you hear?"

She immediately nods. "Sure, although I doubt I'll hear much. Things went quiet when Dr. Abdulov went missing."

"Still, I'd like to be kept abreast."

She nods like she understands my request has nothing to do with being nosy. "Anything I hear, you'll hear."

I smile in gratitude before exiting the storage room where hospital equipment is sterilized. With my shock so high, it takes everything I have not to stop by the computer in the almost desolate OR to do some research on Dr. Abdulov's former patients, but since I truly believe I will get more answers from my husband than a computer program, I return to the underground parking lot like my blood pressure isn't so sky high it is seen on my face.

"You all right?" Ano asks while opening the back passenger door of the SUV for me.

I jerk up my chin before replying, "I'm just dying to see Maksim."

Since it isn't a lie, it doesn't sound like one.

Maksim is on a call when I enter the private jet, so I mouth that I'm going to change out of my scrubs.

He tells his caller to wait, his tone clipped and full of authority, before he says to me, "Wait until after takeoff." Heat treks through my veins when he drags his eyes down my body in a long and dedicated sweep. I don't care what Zoya says. Maksim is more obsessed with my scrubs, makeup-free face, and messy bun than any designer dress she could force me into. "Then I can scrub the filth from your skin with my tongue."

I roll my eyes like I loathe his neediness before I plop into the first recliner I see and latch my belt.

"Thank you," I praise the flight attendant, who places down a glass of champagne for me. She isn't the same flight attendant as last time, although she is just as attractive.

"Double whiskey neat," Maksim requests from the flight

attendant a second after sitting next to me and gathering my hand in his. It is always the same hand. The one with the gigantic diamond my fingers struggle to hold up. "Before you ask, she would have more interest in you than me." His jaw tics, exposing his jealousy. "Mercifully for her, Slatvena is as possessive as I am."

It is the wrong time to smile, but I can't help it. I love his possessiveness. I just wish it didn't arrive with a ton of protectiveness that could take him away from me.

"I wasn't worried." I am honest, hopeful it will see him doing the same. "I was just wondering what happened to your last flight crew."

Maksim waits for the flight attendant to place his whiskey on the table in front of us before he twists his torso to face me. He stares at me for several long seconds, making my skin slick with sweat. "Is there something you want to know, Doc?"

When I sheepishly nod, he waves his hand across his body, giving me unrestricted access to the floor. It is the prime opportunity to ask him about Dr. Abdulov and his Trudny District counterpart, but you'll never triumph a wolf if you go straight for the kill shot. The slow, smart hunt always yields results, so it is the tactic I'll use.

"What happened to your last flight crew?"

Maksim takes a generous gulp of whiskey before the rattles of the jet whizzing down the runway can spill a drop, and licks the remnants from his lips before replying, "Although I don't believe they deserved another cent from me, they were offered a redundancy package."

"Because?" I ask, feeling like his answer is unfinished.

"Because although they were out of line"—his stare is almost too much. It is needy and lusty but also pronged with admiration —"you've proven time and time again that words can't hurt you, so I offered a rare leniency."

I smile, thanking him for his honesty before sliding toward

home plate. "I was informed today that Dr. Abdulov was under investigation for multiple malpractice suits." His lack of surprise indicates he was aware of his impending charges. "Is that why you...?" I still struggle to place him and murder in the same sentence.

"Yes," he answers after a beat, his voice barely heard over the roar of the jet's engine as it launches us into the air. "And despite the look you're giving me, I would do it again in a heartbeat if I was forced to go back."

"I'm not looking at you differently." I am, but not in the way he is thinking. "I'm just trying to understand." I scoot closer until our thighs brush. "If the law was already investigating the matter, why not wait until they reached a verdict before responding?"

"Because that isn't how things work in my industry. We're governed by a different set of rules." He seems more displeased by his reply than pleased.

His eyes snap to me when I say, "Mafia law?" I smile at his shock before muttering, "Not every book I read is fictionally based." I sink back to my side of our shared seat before releasing a slow, long breath. "A Bratva entity took my mother. When my father was sentenced to life, but they got away with their crimes with nothing more than a slap on the wrist, I researched them and anyone associated with them." Tears burn my eyes when I recall how unjust both my mother's and father's cases were. "They convicted my father because they said they had no evidence that my mother was assaulted." My voice cracks even though it is barely a whisper. "They lied. I took the samples myself. There was trauma no woman should ever face, and multiple indicators that exposed there was more than one assailant."

When I can't hold back my sob, Maksim undoes my belt and plucks me from my seat. A handful of tears splash onto his shirt, but for the most part, I keep it together.

It is a challenging feat.

Even more so when Maksim mutters, "The men who took your mother were not Bratva." He holds on tight when I try to wiggle out of his clutch, refusing eye contact. "They were part of a crime syndicate that worked out of the hospital that denied Stefania's operation. The same syndicate working out of Myasnikov Private until a few weeks ago."

The sheer bewilderment in my tone can't be missed. "But my father... he killed the men responsible."

"No," Maksim denies. "He killed the men who raped your mother and left her for dead." His heart thumps against my ear. "I killed the man who let her injuries overcome her before convincing her daughter that her legacy would live on if she donated her organs."

He holds on to me long enough for the truth to smack into me, and then he lets me go so I can make sure I have the facts straight by peering into his eyes.

"Dr. Azores."

I'm not asking a question. I am clicking on to the reason he killed the doctor on our flight, but Maksim nods as if I am. "He was the head of the surgical team at Myasnikov Private before Dr. Abdulov took over. He—"

"Encouraged me to donate my mother's organs." I knew I had seen him before, but the trauma of the day had my coping mechanisms making most of my memories hazy. I'd rather forget them than try to hold on to fragments that mean nothing to me. "Did they—"

Maksim's eyes fall to the floor, answering my question before I can ask it.

They didn't donate my mother's organs.

They sold them.

"How did you find out?"

He stares at me for several long seconds, gauging how I will respond to his reply.

He must see something profound inside my soul because my outward appearance shows nothing but a quivering bag of nerves.

After carefully placing me back onto my side of our seat, he removes a folder from a safe under a stationary bar. It looks like an official police document, but there is no department seal like most public service offices have.

"What the?" I murmur when he places a document beside his empty whiskey glass.

It is a contract for a sale, but instead of a new dishwasher or the latest model television being ordered, it is organs—vital ones patients can't live without.

There's no holding back my shock when the date and time on the ledger registers as familiar. It was the morning his mother was due to go into surgery—the exact date and time.

"She was meant to die on the table." Maksim's voice is a mix of anger and devastation. "And because she was an organ donor, no one would have batted an eye at them immediately removing her organs and shipping them to her purchaser instead of the people whose lives she wanted to save by choosing to be a donor."

I don't startle when he picks up his whiskey glass and smashes it against the wall. I want to hit something, and I've had years to process my mother's injustices. Maksim has only had weeks.

"If you hadn't fought for her, if you hadn't unexpectedly shown up at her room in the middle of the night, she'd be dead." He scoffs as if angry at himself. "Yet I still believed the lies they told."

I wait, praying he will relieve some of my confusion.

He does two seconds later. "Dr. Abdulov placed all the blame on you. He even doctored my mother's medical files so everything was in your name, and I stupidly believed the evidence."

"No, you didn't," I deny, speaking on behalf of my heart and my head. "Because if you did, we wouldn't be having this conversation."

Now his struggles make sense. Why he couldn't look at me. Why he wouldn't touch me even with the tension hot enough to scald.

He hated that he still wanted me even after all the lies they'd told.

"What made you realize I wasn't involved?"

"I knew all along. I just..." A deep exhale breaks up his reply. "I let them believe I was thinking with my cock." His expression takes on a serious note. "Then you offered to help me build a case against them before telling me about what happened to your mother and your sister." His smirk isn't close to a smile, but it is better than deepening the groove between his brows. "That's when the dots started connecting." He stares me straight in the eyes. "The benzodiazepine they gave your mother to make her unresponsive during her attack was found in the blood workup you were adamant my mother should get."

"I knew it," I murmur to myself. "I knew her soul left her body hours before her injuries claimed her life."

When Maksim inches closer, eager to wipe away my tears, I clear them with my sleeve cuff before signaling for him to continue.

He's not a man who lies, but he has no issues skirting the truth—especially if it can hurt someone he cares about.

That someone today is me.

But I need to hear this. We need to be honest with each other if we want to give our marriage a real chance of survival.

After ensuring my cheeks are dry, Maksim continues as requested. "The benzodiazepine was the cause of most of my mother's symptoms." I attempt to interrupt him, but he continues talking, foiling my chances. "She still has a B_{12} deficiency. You were right about that. But more was at play than a dip in vitamin absorbency."

Her condition is far worse than he makes out, but I save my lecture for another day.

"We assumed it was a rival." He laughs like he knows no one would ever be stupid enough to go against him like that. "We were wrong. They didn't know who she was. They were clueless because to my competitors, I am still *his* son, so I'd never operate under the maiden name of his whore." He keeps his eyes locked on his shoes as he licks his lips. "My mother traveled to Myasnikov to meet with a man who, even at his worst, would have treated her better than my father ever did, and almost lost her life in the process." His eyes are back on me, hot and heavy. "How fucking ironic is that?"

"Ironic or poignant?" My voice is jam-packed with emotion. "It brought us together, didn't it?"

He nods before reminding me of how stupid I have been. "And almost tore us apart."

"That's not true." I shake my head, disagreeing with him. "If you had been honest with me at the start, I would have understood."

My lips don't know whether to harden into a stern line or crack into a smile when he mutters, "Still a shit fucking liar, Doc." They choose the latter when he adds, "But it is one of the things I love about you the most, and the sole reason I won't give up on us. I'll never force you to do anything you don't want to do, but I sure as fuck ain't letting you walk out on me without giving this a real chance."

Love? He loves me?

"You fucking kneecapped me, Doc. From the moment I saw you, I knew I needed to make you mine. But I can't change who I am." He bangs his chest. "I protect the people I love, and I destroy the people who try to hurt them." His following words expose he is not a man who usually holds a conversation. He gives orders, and you either follow them or face his wrath. "But I'm trying for you, Doc. Every. Fucking. Day. I try for *you*."

My shoulders relax, and the pain that's been stretched across my chest for almost a decade eases.

He's fighting the same demons of his childhood as I am, pushing past the same neuroses.

And he's doing it for me as much as he is himself.

"I—"

Maksim pushes his finger to my lips, silencing me, before proving he will always be a man who operates on actions instead of words. "Don't tell me, Doc. Show me."

We don't make it to the bedroom before buttons pop and zippers are yanked down.

CHAPTER THIRTY-ONE

"That was..."

I don't have words to describe Aleena's rehearsal dinner.

The food was lovely, and the setting was romantic, but there were little conversations held between the Galdeans and the Dokovics before Kazimir arrived, and it nosedived to uncomfortable once the focus was directed to the groom who arrived an hour late for his dress rehearsal dinner.

Aleena did her best to bring the mood up. She introduced Kazimir to her family and friends with the gushing you'd expect from a woman in love and promised his grandfather a prompt and well-reared bloodline, but nothing she did helped.

The tension was thick enough to cut with a knife.

Even Zoya struggled to break through it, and she usually craves awkward situations.

"Have the Galdeans met Kazimir previously?" I ask Zoya as we walk down the corridor of the hotel hosting Aleena's nuptials, shadowed by the security Maksim was adamant I had to have since he needed to leave dinner early.

Maksim didn't say this is one of his hotels, but the opulence of the penthouse suite, and the proprietary name above the front entrance door, gives it away. I won't mention how the staff flurry around him to answer his every whim, or you'll think I am a jealous twit.

He didn't pay them an ounce of attention throughout dinner. His eyes were forever on me—as were his hands. I guess I could blame the stuffy conditions on my body's response to the briefest brushes of Maksim's fingers when they skimmed the skin high on my thigh. But I prefer placing the blame on others—*regretfully*.

I never thought I'd have the confidence to participate in a public display of affection, but I was five seconds from begging Maksim to slide his finger higher before a call stole his attention from me. The number on the screen of his phone was unknown, but Maksim's eagerness to answer it has me convinced he has the number stored in his memory bank.

"Who?" Zoya asks, drawing my focus back to her, still deep in thought.

"Kazimir," I repeat while scanning my keycard over the room lock of the penthouse suite. "Aleena's husband-to-be."

"Oh... yeah. *Him*." She enters before me before finalizing her reply. "I don't know. Maybe."

Her skittish response raises both my brow and my suspicion, but before I can grill her on it, a primal, visceral instinct to raise my eyes bombards me. I am sensing my mate, aware of Maksim's closeness, but something much greater is demanding my focus.

My heart launches into my throat when my eyes follow the prompts of my brain and heart. Maksim is in the living room of our suite. He isn't alone. A beautiful dark-haired specimen stands across from him, and his presence sends my heart into a flutter.

"Daddy!"

The shackles circling his wrists and ankles clatter when I throw myself into his arms before burying my head into his neck. He can't hug me back since he is restrained, but the words he whispers in my ear make up for a lack of physical contact. "Hey, baby girl. I've missed you so much."

When I inch back to thank the man responsible for my first meeting with my father in over seven years, a correctional officer I didn't notice in the corner of the room commences freeing my father from the restraints used to transport him here.

"I can't give you more than an hour," Maksim announces, his tone low like he's worried I'll be disappointed. "But I will, eventually. My lawyers just need more time to build an appeal."

"This is more than I could have ever hoped for." I kiss him, uncaring that the man who threatened every member of the opposite sex not related to me if they got within an inch of me is currently being freed from prison shackles.

And he kisses me back.

Although Maksim's kisses will forever set me ablaze, I pull back long before I've had my fill, mindful that an hour will never be enough for either task my heart wishes to undertake.

After squeezing Maksim's hand and removing the lipstick my kiss smeared on his mouth, I twist to face my father. He is no longer shackled, and shockingly, there isn't a single groove between his brows.

He knows as well as I do that this meeting would not have happened without Maksim. We couldn't even get phone privileges approved.

My pulse thuds in my ears when my father takes his time assessing me. I have the same shaped face as my mother, the same eyes, just a few shades darker since mine have speckles of brown throughout the green, and the same button nose. I was cut from her cloth, whereas Stefania was the spitting image of my father, just female.

It must hurt for him to look at me, especially since his last memories of my mother are of her bruised and mutilated body, but you wouldn't know that when he returns his eyes to mine and murmurs, "So beautiful. Your mother would be so proud of the woman you have become."

The dam I've been holding back for eight years breaks, and the deluge that comes with it is as shocking as the realization that I don't hate my father for leaving me.

I hate myself for selfishly expecting him to stay.

"I'm so sorry."

I'm growled at from all sides, and it switches some of my tears from sadness to joy.

"Ssh," Maksim murmurs, slipping beneath the sheets. "I don't want to wake you. I just want to be inside you while you sleep." He adjusts my knee like the sultry position I attempted to fall asleep in doesn't give him enough access to my pussy before he creeps closer. "Unless you're not tired?" He groans when the wetness that hits his cock's head alerts him to the fact I went to bed without panties.

My father left hours ago, and although I was emotionally and physically exhausted after our reunion, I had every intention of waiting for Maksim's return before falling asleep.

I had no clue he'd be gone for so long.

"Is everything okay?"

Maksim starts his reply with a moan. "Of course it is. How could it not be? Fuck, Doc. You're already ready for me." He runs his nose down the column of my neck. "Did you start without me?"

A giggle rumbles in my chest instead of the frustration you'd expect when you learn you're being monitored by security cameras hacked or installed purely to watch you twenty-four-seven. "Are you always watching me? Or just when I'm away from you?"

"Always," he answers without shame.

"Then you'd know the package Zoya left on my bedside table is unopened."

Pre-cum adds to the wetness between my legs when he replies, "Who said it was from Zoya?" He places his hand between my legs and toys with my clit. "Maybe I wanted a re-run of the night I watched you play with yourself while thinking about me."

"The night you couldn't see anything because I was covered by the bedding?" My words come out as moans. It can't be helped. Maksim is a genius beneath the sheets as much as he is out of them.

"Yes." After rolling me onto my back, he adjusts his position so he'll face no resistance sliding two fingers inside me. "But that won't be an issue this time around because my wife is a fucking goddess, and she is slowly starting to learn that."

He proves the lies in my head are false by yanking off the bedding covering us with his spare hand, exposing my pasty-white skin to the harsh rays of the lamp he just switched on.

I don't care that it casts an unfavorable hue across my body. Who would feel shame when a man who'd burn the world for you is looking at you like you're the most precious gem in the world?

He finger fucks my pussy, creating a delicious amount of friction, before he curls my toes by adding his mouth to the mix.

He swivels his tongue around my clit before sucking it into his mouth.

"Oh..." I breathe out slowly, already on the cusp of climax.

Pleasure scuttles through me when Maksim shifts the focus of his mouth lower. His lips are rimming the edge of an area no man has ever touched, but instead of repelling, I lift my ass off the mattress and rock my hips upward, encouraging his mouth to move lower.

"Holy hell," I murmur when his tongue flicks over my puckered rear, sending jolts of electricity through my lower stomach.

The naughtiness of what he is doing is as stimulating as the lashes of his tongue.

"Has anyone ever touched you down here, Doc?" Maksim asks as he switches the fingers in my pussy for his thumb and drops the slippery digits between my butt cheeks.

"No," I reply, my hips circling as wildly as my head spirals. His fingers are braced at the entrance of my ass. They're slicked with my arousal, and I'm suddenly feeling invincible.

The need in his voice when he asks, "Do you want me to touch you here?" has me peering down at him over my erratically panting chest.

I nod, doubling the lust in his eyes.

"We'll need to start slow. Your ass is even tighter than your cunt."

A girlie squeal rips from my throat when he flips me over before he pulls me back so my ass is thrust high in the air. It is replaced with unladylike moans when he buries his head between my cheeks with as much eagerness as he does when he eats my pussy.

I'm already an incoherent, blubbering mess, but Maksim pushes me toward full hysteria when he returns his fingers to my pussy and his thumb to my clit.

I shatter like glass, moaning and shouting his name.

"So close. So *fucking* close. But we can do better."

The thumb that hardened my clit to the point of pain is moved from the front of my body to the back.

"Relax, Doc," Maksim demands when the intrusion of his thumb in my ass causes me to clench. "I'll never hurt you."

Since I believe him, I loosen my pelvic floor muscles, allowing his slippery thumb fully in.

"I feel so full," I say, unashamed.

A heated hue creeps across my cheeks when Maksim replies, "Imagine how full you'll feel when you're taking my cock and my fingers at the same time."

He does the synced pressure routine he usually does with my clit and pussy until another wave crests low in my stomach.

"You're doing so good, Doc. I'm so proud of you."

He moves faster, harder. He steers me to the crest of hysteria before he ensures there's no other way for me to go but down.

I cry out when he slips his fingers out of my pussy a mere second before he thrusts his fat cock inside me.

The sensation of having two holes filled at once is almost too much. I'm so full. So taken.

So claimed.

I can do nothing but scream as ecstasy pumps through my veins.

"Maksim... God..." I grunt out when my blinding orgasm doesn't slow him down in the slightest. He thrusts into me on repeat, bringing my screams to an ear-piercing level.

"Better. Much better. But I still think you have more to give."

"I don't." Strands of hair stick to my sweat-dotted face when I shake my head. "I can't. I'm done."

"Shit."

Thrust.

"Fucking."

Thrust.

"Liar."

Thrust.

Thrust.

Thrust.

"Doc."

"Fuck. Christ. Shit." I mash my face with the pillow while a torrent of naughty, wicked words leave my mouth. I'm on the border of an intense orgasm, one I am confident will override the intensity of every one before it, but I need a little more to fully let go.

"Please, Maksim," I beg, unashamed. "Make me come. I need you to make me come."

"There she is," Maksim mutters seconds before he ticks off every fantasy I've ever had.

Hours after screwing me senseless, I lie with my head resting on Maksim's chest and his semi-firm cock still inside me. The rhythm of his heart announces he is awake, let alone the quickest pause of his breathing when I murmur against his sweat-slicked skin, "Thank you for bringing my father here." We moan in sync when I inch back, and the slightest movement grinds my clit against the impressive arrow of his V muscle. "I don't know how you did it, and I don't want to know, but you need to know how much I appreciate what you did for him..." I breathe out slowly before adding, "And me. I needed that closure."

I'm talking in riddles because I am emotionally drained, but Maksim appears to have no issues deciphering my gibberish. "You'll never get over what happened to your mother and sister, but with the right people around you, the blame will eventually shift to the people deserving of the guilt."

Several long seconds of silence pass before I break it. "I testified against him."

"Because you thought it would help him." Maksim isn't asking a question. He is stating a fact. "Your father's lawyer just failed to cross-examine you how he promised when he convinced you to be a witness for the DA." When I stare at him in bewilderment, shocked he hit the nail on the head, he mutters, "You're not the only one who can utilize Google." He tightens his grip around my waist. "Just don't tell Easton that. He needs his ego stroked as often as Ano does."

"I heard that."

Maksim's lips curl before his eyes shoot to the door of our suite. "Good. That's what you get for snooping."

Ano's chuckles trickle through the door. My disappointed groan replaces them when Maksim commences slipping out of me. "If you didn't have somewhere you needed to be, my head would be buried back between your legs by now." He lowers his voice to a whisper. "And perhaps I'd be claiming your virginal hole." He takes a moment to relish my blooming cheeks before nudging his eyes to the red dress someone at the hotel unpacked while we were at the rehearsal dinner.

It is a beautiful dress, but when my head is in a lust haze, nothing but my next climax is on my mind. "We could stay in."

"We could," Maksim agrees, the throbbing of his cock adding to the hope in his tone. "But we won't." When I pout like a child, he twangs my lip before saying, "This wasn't on the top of our list, but it is as important to you as every other item in the terms of our agreement." His expression takes on a serious note. "And Zoya was there for you when others weren't. For that alone, I will forever be in her debt."

I love Zoya with all my heart, but I can't help but joke, "I wouldn't let her know that. You'll be broke by the end of the week."

Determined to stand at my friend's side as promised, I shimmy off the bed and head to the bathroom, uncaring that I am naked head to toe and being eyeballed by my husband like there aren't multiple used condoms in the trash can of our suite.

The padding of my feet on the thick carpet pile almost drowns out Maksim's murmured reply when the heat of his eyes finally reaches my ass. "It'll be worth every fucking penny."

CHAPTER THIRTY-TWO

"Hold on. Go back," Alla demands, her eyes wide and mouth gaping. "Zoya objected to the marriage of her baby sister?"

When I nod, she couldn't appear more shocked—until I say, "And then took her place."

"What?!" Her voice bellows throughout the empty OR. "So she's married? Right now? She's shacked up with a stranger?"

I grimace, but since Zoya's story isn't mine to tell, I half shrug and half nod instead of shouting the yes bellowing through my head.

Alla's reply whistles through her teeth since it comes with a massive shocked sigh. "That's crazy."

"Yeah, it is," I agree, reclining back. "I'm worried for Zoya, but I also trust her intuition. She wouldn't have objected if she didn't think it was the right thing to do."

"Does Aleena think the same?"

I can't hide my grimace this time.

"Ouch."

Ouch doesn't come close to explaining the devastation Zoya

will be feeling for hurting Aleena. She will do anything for her—anything at all—that's why I know there is more to Zoya's decision than she is letting on.

"Anyway, I should probably head back. If I don't push pathology, who will?"

"Still waiting on Yulia's latest blood workup?"

I jerk up my chin, aware Alla is under the same NDA as the rest of the hospital staff. "It is so weird because she was well enough to be discharged before I went away, and now she is back to square one."

"You'll work it out." She rubs my arms supportively. "We don't call you Dr. Genius for no reason."

I sigh like I hate the nickname, but I much prefer it over the one that was graffitied on my locker weeks ago.

"If I don't see you before, I'll see you next week."

"You will."

After helping Alla return the chairs we borrowed from the nurses' station, I hug her goodbye before heading back to the pediatric ward.

"Are you okay?" Dr. Lipovsky asks when she spots my entrance to the nurses' station to gather a patient's file. "Too much sugar?" We crossed paths in the underground parking garage. I was exiting to collect supplies for Donut Hole Thursday from Ano, and she was arriving for her shift. "They smelled delicious. Though I'm sure my thighs would have despised every burpee required to work them off."

A laugh rumbles in my chest, but it is the fight of my life to let it escape my mouth when I notice a name missing from the patient board behind her svelte frame.

"Why has Yulia's name been removed from the in-patient list?"

Dr. Lipovsky mumbles something, but I miss what she says from my heels pounding the tile floor as I race into the room across from the nurses' station.

Yulia's room is empty, and her bed has been stripped.

Dr. Lipovsky rubs my shoulder when I fail to bite back a sob. "Why are you upset? You wouldn't have discharged her if she still needed monitoring."

"I didn't discharge her." Yulia's recovery after her medical episode was as fast-moving as Maksim's mother's, but she still had a little to go before she was well enough to return home. "I suggested to Lev that we could discuss the possibility of her being discharged for the weekend so she could meet her baby sister, but I hadn't commenced the paperwork yet."

"Oh." After checking Yulia's file, which has been placed onto the records officer cart to be collected instead of in the slot outside her room, Dr. Lipovsky says, "The paperwork states that you discharged her." She twists the discharge paperwork around to face me. "Is this your signature?"

I almost nod until I remember that I've been using my married name for the past week. I had nothing but words to thank Maksim for funding Yulia's medical expenses, organizing a one-on-one meeting with my father so I wouldn't be required to go to a maximum-security prison, and for every other wonderful thing he has done, so I've worn my rings every day since we reunited, and used the last name he chose to reinvent himself on every document I've signed.

Dr. Lipovsky appears worried when I say, "That is *not* my signature, but I have the means to find out who wants us to believe it is."

She watches me with wide eyes when I skirt by her, pick up the nurses' desk phone, and dial a frequently called number.

For the first time, Ano doesn't answer my call.

Upon spotting the concern on my face, Dr. Lipovsky stops a nurse whizzing past us so fast she is almost a blur by grabbing her elbow. "Who authorized Yulia Petrovitch's discharge?"

"Um." She looks worried, but since her concern is more based on Dr. Lipovsky's anger than the repercussions for snitching, she says, "Dr. Sidorov."

"Dr. Sidorov?" Dr. Lipovsky sounds as uneasy as her gaunt expression makes her look. "He hasn't worked in a ward in years."

"So why would he discharge Yulia?" I jump in, confused.

As quickly as my confusion rose, panic sets in.

What if Dr. Abdulov wasn't working alone?

What if he had a co-conspirator?

Anger envelops me when theory after theory smashes into me. Is this why he offered me a promotion that far exceeded my qualifications? Was he seeking a scapegoat—a fool he could puppeteer?

My brain is screaming yes, but my heart doesn't agree.

If Dr. Sidorov was a part of the criminal entity that stole my mother's organs and attempted to steal Maksim's mother's organs, why didn't Maksim take him down with the others?

I need answers, and since I trust my husband far more than I trust anyone else, I snatch my winter coat off the coat rack and then tell Dr. Lipovsky I'm going home because I am not feeling well.

She snatches my wrist as quickly as Maksim does whenever I lie. Her eyes bounce between mine, the wish to call me a liar beaming out of her. She just can't get her mouth to cooperate with her brain.

"I'll let you know anything I find out," I promise, finally clueing in to the cause of the worry blistering in her kind eyes.

Her nod is brief but full of punch. "Please be careful."

I return her hug before racing to the elevators that will take me to the underground garage. I want answers, but I don't need to get Ano in trouble while seeking them.

As the elevator arrives at the underground loading bay, I'm stunned to find men unloading produce from a truck at the central loading bay. They're veering straight past Maksim's SUV parked directly across from the elevator, but Ano's tall frame, which usually stands above any crowd, is nowhere to be seen.

"What is that smell?" I murmur to myself when an unusual scent impinges the air.

I take another whiff of the weird aroma before shifting on my feet to face the delivery truck. I almost slip when my stubbornness has my soleless shoes skidding over a shiny blob on the floor.

My wardrobe is brimming with designer clothes and shoes, but I refuse to wear them until Maksim allows me to contribute to the household bills.

It's been one argument after another for the past week, only ending once we've wrestled each other from our clothes and fucked the anger out on one of the many solid surfaces in our apartment.

My throat works through a stern swallow when I bob down to inspect the cause of my near slip more closely. It appears to be blood but has been watered down with something. It drips from the service entrance to the truck and seems to have been recently spilled.

I crank my head to the side when a familiar but not often-heard voice calls my name. "Nikita?" Boris's confused gaze bounces between me and the delivery truck for several seconds before it eventually settles on me. "What are you doing here?"

I don't know how catering operates at the hospital, but it seems weird that they're taking food out instead of in—particularly when they're using members of the pathology department to transport it.

Boris is carrying a box of bananas. It is leaking the same watered-down liquid that is dribbled across the floor, but he is heading in the direction of the truck instead of the service entrance.

"I could ask you the same thing." I step closer to him, whitening his cheeks more. "I didn't realize you had taken a position with food services."

"I-I haven't."

Suspicion colors my tone. "Then why are you carting boxes of bananas across a loading dock?"

"Because I... ah..." His eyes snap up for barely a second, but the widening of his pupils is all I need to know that I won't like what happens next.

They hold so much angst, and I learn why when a white cloth is placed over my mouth and nose a second after my feet are hoisted off the ground by the man pinning me to his chest and chloroforming me.

I thrash and kick, but within seconds, my limbs grow as heavy as my eyelids when I work a double shift. My throat feels like it is on fire, and my head is instantly woozy.

I am mere seconds from passing out.

When I no longer have the energy to fight, I'm lowered onto the cold concrete floor, where I drift in and out of consciousness.

I'm barely lucid when a teeming mad voice shouts, "What the fuck did you do?" Its owner's race across the floor is as frantic as my pulse as I slowly lose consciousness. Fingers press against the vein thudding in my neck before I'm roughly rolled onto my side so I won't choke on my thickening tongue. "Do you have any idea what you've done? She's Maksim Ivanov's wife!"

"I know who she is but I don't give a fuck. She isn't meant to be down here," says a second voice I'm certain I've heard before. "She saw shit she isn't mea—"

His reply is cut off by a crack similar to a fist colliding with someone's nose.

"She's sanctioned. We can't fucking touch her."

"Those rules don't apply to me!"

A scuffle breaks out, but I'm swallowed by the blackness engulfing me before a winner is announced.

CHAPTER THIRTY-THREE

A cold breeze blows through my scrubs, but for the first time since moving to Russia, I relish its coolness. My brain feels like it is on fire, as does every muscle I own. My symptoms mimic ones of severe dehydration. My mouth is dry, my breathing is erratic, and I have a fever. Drowsiness is also a sign of dehydration, but the wooziness in my head feels like more than a bit of confusion.

I feel similar to how I did the morning I woke up married.

The reminder has me opening my eyes too quickly for someone with no lubricant in their sockets. They burn from the width of their opening, not to mention my shock at the unknown location I am waking in.

I'm cold because I am outside, and the only thing protecting me from the elements is my surgical scrubs.

When I try to gather my bases, the lady seated a few spots up from me holds her purse close to her body while focusing on a bus approaching the horizon. She shakes like a leaf. She isn't cold. My presence is scaring her.

I understand why when I catch sight of my reflection in the

reflective material of the bus shelter. I look like a wreck. My hair is knotted, my face is covered with dirty stains, and my scrubs have seen better days.

"I... ah..." I clutch my head. It hurts to talk, but I push through the pain. "I need help." When she tugs her purse in tighter, still scared, I plead, "Please. I don't know where I am or how I got here..." I scan the unknown location. Even in the darkness of the night, its unkempt state can't be concealed. Several homeless line the streets, along with a heap of trash and cardboard beds. "Am I still in Myasnikov?"

Her nod is brief, but it offers me immense relief.

"My husband..." I take a break to lube my throat with spit, hopeful some wetness will ease my words out through the burn scalding my veins. "He will be... looking for me. Do you have a phone I could borrow"—another painful breath separates my words—"to call him?"

"No. I don't have anything. No phone. No money. No jewelry. I have *nothing.*"

As she returns her eyes to the bus, willing it to hurry up, the moon breaks through a stormy cloud. I squint when its bright rays add to the pounding of my skull.

"What time is it?"

When I shield my eyes from the bus headlights, the stranger replies, "A l-little after two."

"In the morning?"

Some of the fear she is experiencing trickles through my veins when she nods.

"I... ah... I..."

After drinking in the rock on my ring finger, then the emblem of Myasnikov Private Hospital on my scrubs, she scoots closer. My fear that I'm about to be jumped is unfounded when she whispers, "I-I can pay for your bus fare, but that's all I can offer you. I don't have any money. I just have a bus card."

After again scanning the street and noticing the stranger's eyes aren't the only pair gawking at me, I say, "Okay. Thank you."

It takes a mammoth effort to stand, so there's no way I will make it onto the bus without the stranger's help. Mercifully, she comprehends my struggles without me needing to speak. After banding her arms around my back, she hoists me to her side before she guides my ginger walk to the stationary bus.

"Mara, what did I tell you last time? No more druggies."

The lady placing me onto a cracked vinyl seat *pffts* the driver before scanning a transport card on the electronic scanner by the door twice.

"She's a paying customer," she replies to him in Russian. "That's all you need to worry about."

She's assuring him I am fine, but she still sits a couple of spots back from me.

Her trust is so low, when the driver peers at her in the mirror he uses to keep passengers in line several stops later, she pretends she can't feel the curiosity bouncing off him.

She doesn't move, speak, or acknowledge anyone until the Myasnikov Private Hospital stop has her reaching for the yank cord to tell the driver I want to get off at the next stop.

My head is still woozy, and my legs are unstable, but I make it to the front of the bus unaided.

"Thank you," I whisper to the guardian angel still watching over me.

Mara dips her chin before she shifts her focus to the window like I never said anything.

I barely stumble down the street two steps before I cross someone I know.

Eva sighs like I'm far more presentable than I feel before she cranks her neck to someone behind her. "Get Maksim."

In less than a nanosecond, an SUV pulls into the alleyway next to us, and Maksim races out. Sheer panic is scoured between his brows, and he looks exhausted.

I more collapse into his arms than throw myself into them, and then I bury my head into his pecs to drown out the frantic situation occurring around me.

I'm poked and prodded, all while still in Maksim's arms, before I'm asked a range of questions.

None I know how to answer.

"I don't remember anything. I'm not even sure what day it is."

I realize we bypassed the ER at Myasnikov Private when I'm placed onto a cool surface and Maksim inches back so we can lock eyes. We're in the security office of my apartment building, but it is far more fitted out than when I reported a suspected attempted burglary six months ago. The back laundry window had been shattered and opened, but nothing was missing, which led me to believe my return home from a late shift had scared the perps off.

"It's Friday morning," Maksim announces. "You collected donuts and coffees from Ano yesterday afternoon and ate them with Alla." He twists a monitor around to face me. It shows me sitting in the makeshift break room Alla and I set up whenever we're rostered on the same shift. "Do you remember that?"

He cusses under his breath when I shake my head. "I'm sorr—"

His growl cuts me off—*and makes me hot*, but I'll keep that to myself. "Don't apologize for something those fuckers did to you." The pain in his words cuts me deep, but it has nothing on the torment in his eyes when he asks, "Did they hurt you? Are you hurting anywhere we haven't checked?" The pure terror in his eyes asks the question he can't speak. He wants to know if I was raped like my mother was when she was taken.

"No, Maksim. I'm not sore. I feel perfectly fine." My quivering voice undoes the confidence I am trying to portray. "I feel like I just went to sleep and woke up."

When my words offer Maksim little comfort, Eva reminds me we're not the only two people in the room. "I can check."

"No," I shout a little too loud. "I'd know if I was hurt like that." Tears gloss my cheeks when I murmur, "My mother's injuries couldn't be hidden. She was torn to shreds..." When a sob replaces my words, Maksim wipes away my tears before shaking his head at Eva's offer, loosening the valve stopping my lungs from replenishing. "My memories will come back. They're just buried beneath a heap of fog."

I must miss a private conversation between Maksim and Eva as she objects to his silent denial as if they shared many words. I'd be jealous of their ability to communicate without words if there weren't a heap of similarities I had missed earlier. They could be mistaken as siblings.

"It could take a heap of weight off your shoulders, Maksim, and help us find Ano."

"Ano is missing?"

Again, Maksim doesn't look set to lie.

He merely continues to skirt the truth like he has our entire marriage.

"Do it." Maksim tries to cut me off, but I peer past his shoulder, stare Eva in the eyes, and repeat, "Do it. Do whatever you need to do to get answers."

"Answers that will leave me no choice but to retaliate," Maksim sneers. "Do you understand that, Doc? They took my fucking wife from right under my fucking nose. I can't let that slide."

"You can, and you will."

My head snaps to the side so fast I almost make myself sick. I don't know which way is up when Maksim's mother starts barking orders seconds after she enters the room. She takes command, making me realize Maksim isn't the king of his realm just yet. His mother is.

My throat dries even more when Mrs. Ivanov shifts her focus to me. She stares at me like she is assessing my soul from the inside out before she twists to face Eva. "Digestive benzodiazepine or injectable?"

"There are no puncture wounds in her arms or between her toes," Eva answers, alerting me to the fact she was the one poking and prodding me during our short commute to my building. "But I don't believe she ingested it either." Her next question exposes that her cover may not be fraudulent. "Rumors have been circling for some time that a biochemist has created a new drug that works as effectively as GHB, but it is dispensed as a vapor instead of a liquid. It makes it almost impossible to trace back to the source since there is nothing to compare it to. Vapors—"

"Burn off," I interrupt, too intrigued not to include myself in their conversation. "How long was I missing?"

"Nine hours," Maksim answers. His low tone shreds my heart.

I place my hand over his balled and bruised one resting next to my thigh and squeeze it before shifting my focus back to Eva. "There could still be residue in my nasal cavity or respiratory tract."

When Maksim's mother silently questions Eva, she takes a moment to ponder before jerking up her chin. "It will still be hard to trace since the manufacturing is being kept under wraps, but any sample is better than none."

"Do you have what is needed to test it?"

Eva almost shakes her head, but a second after her lips part, she waggles her brows instead. "I can have everything I need here in under a minute."

Mrs. Ivanov gives her silent permission to do what needs to be done before she devotes all her attention to me. Well, more my wedding rings than me as a whole.

"Mrs. Ivanov—"

"*Mrs. Ivanov?*" she interrupts, scoffing. "I believe the only person in this room with that title is you, dear."

"Ma," Maksim snaps out like his mother's tone is rude. It wasn't. She sounds more pleasantly surprised than frustrated. "She just got back from God fucking knows where. Now is *not* the time."

"Yes. I suppose you are right." It is a highly inappropriate time for me to smile, but it can't be helped when she adds, "I'm sure future grandbaby talks can wait. However, this can't." Her tone takes on a serious note as she twists to face Maksim. "She is here. In front of you. Safe *and* protected. So stop acting like she's not."

"She is *my* wife," Maksim snarls, banging his chest. "It is *my* job to protect her, and I fucking failed."

She acts as if his last four words didn't shred her heart to pieces like they did mine. "You have an entire team at your disposal—"

"It. Is. *My*. Job," he repeats, shouting.

There is so much shame in his voice. So much disappointment. He truly believes he has failed me. I know that isn't the case, but I learn where Maksim gets his spitfire stubbornness from before I can say anything.

His mother pulls him to the corner of the room without a single bead of sweat breaking onto her neck before she gets up in his face. "Your job is to protect her. I agree. That is precisely what you've been doing the past several weeks and the exact reason they let her go uninjured." Without taking her eyes off her son, she points to me. "If she were anyone else but your wife, she would be dead. You saved her, Maksim. You protected her as promised."

"If I don't defend her honor, if I don't respond to what they did, they won't stop. I'll be seen as a mockery, like a coward who can't defend his own wife. Is that what you want, Ma? Do you want the legacy we've been building since he left us to crumble back to the pittance he wrongly believed we deserved?"

She doesn't shake her head, but you can see the wish to do precisely that in her eyes. "You promised her there would be no more violence." I assume she means during our elevator reunion, but I am proven wrong when she says, "That's why she agreed to marry you." She steps closer, her expression nurturing, her eyes wet. "She picked you, warts and all. Now you need to do the same. What is more important to you, Maksim? Revenge or her?"

With memories of my confrontation with my father rolling through my head like a movie, I miss what Maksim replies, so I am eternally grateful when his mother asks him to repeat it.

"Her," he replies louder, the honesty in his tone unmissable. "It will *always* be her."

Irina's smile could warm the coldest heart. "Then do what needs to be done." After flattening her hand where his heart thumps, she aligns their eyes. "And trust your intuition that brought you back here time and time again."

They share a handful more unvoiced words before Maksim shifts on his feet to face me. I pretend I wasn't eavesdropping, but my ruse only lasts as long as it takes for the heat of Maksim's gaze to remove the chill of spending hours in the cold in the equivalent of tissue paper.

I return his stare, my heart squeezing when his eyes relay every emotion pumping through him.

There's so much hurt in his narrowed gaze, so much pain and shame, but since there is also a love I never thought I'd witness again in my life, I say the last thing I ever thought I would say, "Go." My words are choked by the sob I refuse to surrender when I add, "But if you don't come back—"

"I'll come back." He's at my side in an instant. His hand is in my hair, his lips brushing my mouth. "*Nothing* could keep me away from you. Not even the Grim Reaper himself is stupid enough to come between us. I *will* be back."

"Promise me?"

My words echo the ones I said to my father when I discovered him sneaking out of the front door of my grandparents' apartment, but since they're not coming from a man who just lost the love of his life, I trust them. "I promise."

I hold back my tears for the hour it takes Maksim's team to put plans into play while he showers and dresses me with a tenderness his agitation shouldn't allow. And I keep them at bay for the additional two hours it takes for Eva to administer medication we're hopeful will reverse the benzodiazepine I was forced to take. But I lose the ability the instant the elevator doors of my grandparents' new abode open, and my best friend walks through them.

I break, and Zoya holds me like she did when I lost my entire family within weeks of each other.

CHAPTER THIRTY-FOUR

A door creaks half a second before Zoya moseys into my grandfather's makeshift medical room. It is a little after four in the afternoon, but she arrives with a super-sized mug of coffee like it is hours earlier.

"Thank you," I whisper when she hands the mug to me, my head still too thumping for a more heartfelt response. It isn't solely being drugged that's responsible for my raging headache. It is the number of tears I shed last night.

Poor Zoya suffered the wrath of my downfall—again.

"About last night. I—"

"If you're about to apologize, my foot is about to land in your butt crack." When a smile tugs at my lips, she says, "Don't smile. I'm not joking. I even removed my shoes to make sure I wouldn't get anything nasty on my new pumps."

"You got new shoes?" I ask, happy to take the focus off my dread for half a minute.

"Yeah. Wanna see?" When I nod, she nudges her head to the elevator. "Follow me downstairs. There's an entire wardrobe of brand-new designer clothes and shoes that look like they haven't been touched." I roll my eyes, making her laugh. "If my new husband wants to gift me a wardrobe of designer babies, I'm not going to look at a single item priced under five figures."

The annoyance in her tone makes me realize I am one of those women who wrongly believe everything is about them, but Zoya smells my interrogation from a mile out and stops it before it can occur. "Any news?"

One simple question and my curiosity about her unexpected marriage is stored, and anxiety takes its place.

After glancing at my phone to make sure I didn't miss a message or call while I used the restroom, I shake my head.

I haven't heard from Maksim or his team in over twelve hours, and I'm scared shitless no news is no longer good news. I scoured online newspaper sites, the internet, and even reached out to some contacts I have at Myasnikov Private to see if there were any rumblings of a mafia war.

It is so quiet you'd be convinced not a single feather was ruffled in the Myasnikov District last night.

"He'll be okay, Keet," Zoya assures, mindful of where my mind strays when I go off track. "You'd need a tank to take him down, and it would have to be the size of a submarine to keep him away from you." She twists her lips before confessing to a sin that assures me she needs to speak with a shrink. "Not even the four deadbolts I installed on the servants' stairwell door could stop him." She laughs like her life wasn't in danger when she endeavored to put distance between Maksim and me. "What? He couldn't use the front door because it couldn't be budged without pounding the living shit out of it, and he knew that would have woken you, so I got inventive."

"Because?" I ask, happy for my curiosity to take center stage for a second if it will give my heart a little bit of relief.

Her next confession takes her a little longer to share. "Because I wanted you to know he wasn't giving up. He was just being a stubborn ass." She noogies my head. "Like someone else I know."

An intercom buzzes, sending my heart into a flutter, which the concierge flatlines two seconds later. "Mrs. Ivanov, I have two officers here to speak with you."

My suddenly wet eyes bounce between Zoya and my grandmother, who has just joined us, before I gingerly approach the intercom system to grant permission for the officers to come up.

I try to maintain a positive front as I enter the foyer to await the arrival of the officers, but it instantly crumbles when I'm hit with a flashback of me opening the door the morning my mother was killed and hearing my father's harrowing cries seconds after they asked to speak with him in private.

"If he's... oh god." I bend over, the pain ripping through me too much to bear. "I should have never let him go. I should have made him keep his promise. I can't lose him, Z. I haven't even told him that I love him yet."

"You won't lose him. It'll be okay." Zoya's grip on my waist is the only thing keeping me upright. "And he already knows, Keet. He saw it on your face every time you got jealous. Why do you think he loves it so much?"

I want to answer, but I can't. I'll sob if I speak.

When the elevator dings, announcing its arrival at the penthouse suite, I shut my eyes and say a quick prayer before slowly opening them.

I almost sigh in relief when the uniformed officers I am expecting are nowhere to be seen. It is the detectives I spoke with weeks ago, Lara and Ivan.

Lara looks remorseful for the interruption, but even with his nose splintered and a bruise he's poorly hiding with the wrong shade of concealer shadowing his left eye, Ivan looks as arrogant as ever.

His narrowed gaze and snarled top lip get my back up in an

instant, so before he can step out of the elevator, I say, "Unless you have a warrant, you are not welcome in my house."

Ivan proves a vicious tongue is necessary to deal with men like him. "Do I need a warrant, Dr. *Fernandez?*"

"It is Dr. Ivanov," I correct, "and yes, you do. My husband owns this building, so anything inside it is his possession."

"Then I guess it's lucky we're not here for him, isn't it?"

There's so much evilness in his eyes Zoya can't help but respond to it. "Call Raya," she instructs my grandmother before butting her shoulder with mine. "What is this in regard to?"

"Are you her lawyer?"

Zoya doesn't take her eyes off Ivan while answering Lara's question. "No, but I don't need to be to make sure she isn't rail-roaded by a chauvinistic asshole who thinks he's tough because he has a gun."

Our standoff reaches fever pitch before Lara finally ends it. "We're here in regard to your whereabouts between the hours of" —she checks her notepad—"2 p.m. yesterday afternoon until 5 a.m. this morning."

Before I can fall into the trap they're laying out for me, Zoya says, "She was here the entire time."

Ivan undoes her lie with a simple snapshot.

It is of me in the Myasnikov Private elevator. It is time-stamped within the range Lara announced.

"I arrived for my shift at..." I struggle to remember anything that happened since I slid into the back seat of Maksim's SUV yesterday morning. "I'm having difficulties remembering the exact time—"

"Another lapse in memory? How convenient," Ivan inter-rupts with an eye roll.

He doesn't deserve an explanation, but with my worry higher than my smarts, I give him one. "I was drugged with a benzodi-azepine that causes memory issues, so perhaps instead of wasting your time questioning me about my whereabouts, you should go search for the real criminals ruining this town." So much honesty colors my next statement no one could accuse me of not knowing where my loyalties lie. "And that person is *not* my husband."

Mercifully, Lara seems more interested in my rant than Ivan does, who's still glaring at me as if I am dog shit stuck under his shoe. "Do you know who drugged you or what synthetic they used?"

"No. We took a sample with the hope it would give us answers, but the results aren't back yet."

She jots down something in her notepad before asking, "Do you have an approximate time you were drugged?"

I shake my head. "I don't remember much from before I arrived for my shift yesterday. I remember driving there, and I think I entered via the underground garage elevator, but I can't be sure. It's all blank."

"Until what time?"

Ivan's sudden interest in my defense is shocking, but I don't realize it is a trap until it is too late. "I woke around two."

"A.m.?" Lara checks.

When I nod, victory gleams in Ivan's sable eyes. "So the alibi your husband's lawyer gave us an hour ago is false. He was not with you at all."

"Th-that isn't what I said. I said I woke at two. But he was with me the en-entire time."

"How would you know if you were passed out?"

Again, he doesn't deserve a reply, but Zoya can't cut down his attitude without words. "Because he sleeps inside her every night, and unlike the unfortunate women who have slept with you, she couldn't mistake his presence."

I assume I am imagining Maksim's deep, commanding timbre sounding through my ears when he says, "It's actually anytime she sleeps, but I'll save the details for someone more worthy of my time." But why can I smell his manly scent if it is an illusion?

I'm grateful Zoya still has me attached to her hip when

Maksim enters the foyer from the left. It appears as if he is exiting the main bedroom of the penthouse after a shower. His hair is wet, and his suit smells freshly laundered. It is just the tiredness in his eyes that tells the truth.

I wasn't the only one who went without sleep last night.

Maksim was right there with me.

After banding his arm around my waist, taking over Zoya's campaign to keep me upright, Maksim presses his lips to my temple before he shifts his focus to the detectives. "Is there something I can assist you with, Officers?"

With Ivan too shocked by Maksim's arrival to speak, Lara takes up the campaign. "Detective Lara Sonova from Trudny PD." After showing her credentials, she says, "We're here to verify the alibi Raya Hughes gave for Mrs. Fern—" She recovers quickly. "Mrs. Ivanov earlier today."

"Once she finalized her shift, she was here with me all night, as my lawyer has already stated."

Lara checks her notes. "And—"

"And if you have any further questions, they can be directed through my lawyer, as also stated earlier." I shouldn't love Maksim's arrogance, but I do. He is the ruler of his realm, and I am the woman he will protect until the end of his reign. "Is that understood?"

"Yes," Lara replies, nodding.

She shifts her eyes to me for the quickest second before she returns to the elevator.

It takes Ivan another thirty seconds to join her.

He keeps staring at Maksim like he's seeing a ghost.

There are a million questions in my head, but none will be voiced until I thoroughly investigate Maksim's body. I don't even care that Zoya and my grandmother are in the room with us. I tug his business shirt out of his trousers with so much urgency that stitches pop before buttons scatter across the marble floors.

I secure a full breath for the first time in almost a minute.

He is unharmed and beautifully humored by my search.

His laugh rumbles through my chest, shuddering out some of the calcifications his absence caused to my heart before it drops to an area far lower.

My pussy, to be precise.

"Ano?" That's all I can get out—one measly name.

Zoya sighs with me when Maksim replies, "He was found a few hours ago. He is a little groggy and sporting a handful of new stitches, but he's been through worse, so I don't see his recovery taking long."

"Is it...? Did you...?" I don't think I will ever be able to place murder and his name in the same sentence, so I try a different way to get answers. "Is it done?"

His eyes dance between mine for many seconds before he jerks up his chin. I assume that will be the end of his reply, but he shocks me by walking me to the corner of the foyer that hides me from the security camera before he says, "The faction working out of Myasnikov Private was more extensive than anyone realized. They weren't just selling the organs of legitimate donors. They were encouraging harvests."

I'm completely lost, but mercifully, Zoya seems more clued in. "With food?" When Maksim nods, she shifts her wide eyes to me. "That's why you kept bringing up bananas." Her focus is back on Maksim. "Her memories are still foggy, but she recalled seeing a crate of bananas being carried out of the hospital."

Maksim appears unsurprised by her admission. I learn why when he says, "They were poisoning members of the community through food banks, then plucking a handful of unsuspecting victims from the pile to succumb to the latest gastroenteritis outbreak ravishing the city. Their families had no clue."

"Then how did your mother end up on that list?" I'm not meaning to sound rude. I am genuinely curious because the Ivanovs are incredibly wealthy, beyond anything you could imagine, so there's no way she would be eating produce from a food bank.

Thankfully, Maksim understands my question is more inquisitive than an interrogative. "The man she came to see was a chef. With his business not doing well, he substituted some of his produce with supplies a charity worker was skimming from the food banks."

"The tainted food is why there were so many outbreaks over the past several months."

"And also why there was an increase in surgeries," I add to Zoya's statement, my heart sinking. With my heart in the vicinity of my shoes, my brain finally turns back on. "I saw bananas. They were being carried out of the hospital. Does that mean...?" My breath catches in my throat when the flood of information I've been overwhelmed with the past few days starts clicking together. "Yulia's father lost his job. He couldn't afford food. He was supplementing his lost wages with produce that was donated to him. That could be what is making Yulia sick."

I barely get two steps away from Maksim when he snatches up my wrist, halting my exit.

"Let me go, Maksim. I need to help her. There are ways we can reverse the damage of the poison."

The remorse in Maksim's eyes cuts me to pieces, let alone what he says next. "It's too late."

"No." Yulia isn't my sister, but you wouldn't know that from the devastation in my tone. "She can get better. I can help her."

The reason for Maksim's many quests to keep the truth from me is unearthed when he proves I'm not strong enough to learn just how cruel the world can be.

"My men found her this morning." A sob rips from my throat when he pulls me into his chest before he murmurs into my hair, "She was in a room at the back of the loading dock. Her organs had been harvested. There was nothing we could do." My sob almost drowns out a promise I had no clue I'd ever need until now. "We took down the people directly responsible for her death. We made them pay." Honesty rings true in his tone. "And I won't stop until *every* person who hurt her has paid."

"Promise me," I murmur, either too heartbroken to understand the depth of my demand or finally realizing if you don't fight fire with fire, you will never win.

Maksim inches me back before he lifts my tear-drenched face. "I promise. No one will ever hurt you like this again."

I believe every word he speaks.

It isn't hard since they are gospel.

CHAPTER THIRTY-FIVE

Maksim's eyes lift to my reflection in the vanity mirror when I say, "I should probably return to work soon. The wards are still overrun with poison victims, and I didn't take this much time off when my mother passed, so it seems silly to take this much bereavement leave for a patient."

He knows the real reason I don't want to return—I'm ashamed I didn't work out what was happening sooner since it was occurring under my nose—but he will never call me out on it. "If that's what you want, Doc, I won't stop you."

Smiling, I join him in the bathroom before assisting him in placing on the tie he's been fiddling with the past few minutes. It is black and pinstriped like his suit—the perfect ensemble for the funeral we will be attending this afternoon for a little girl whose life was taken too soon.

Once it's tied, I flatten it down like it wasn't starched to within an inch of its life by the dry cleaners, and then float my hand over Maksim's heart that should be too large to fit in his chest.

He will never admit it, but I know he paid for Yulia's funeral. The funeral home is usually reserved for the wealthy half of Myasnikov; her casket is the most expensive available, and her plot sits under a big old oak tree that will protect her from the elements no matter the season.

There's no way Mr. and Mrs. Petrovitch could afford such an elaborate farewell. I just refuse to call Maksim out on his generosity purely because I know he too is struggling with an immense amount of guilt.

From the rumblings of his crew, it wasn't Maksim's men who found Yulia. It was Maksim.

He tried to get Dr. Sidorov to reverse the procedure he had conducted in an unsterile training OR at the back of the loading dock, but with Yulia's organs already in transport to the new owners' hometowns, nothing could be done to save her.

She was gone, but that didn't stop Maksim from sitting with her until her parents arrived.

"Don't tempt me, Doc," Maksim says when I peer up at him with loved-up eyes.

I'm still grieving the unnecessary loss of an innocent child, but the way Maksim has helped me through my grief process over the past five days has made me fall in love with him more than I ever thought possible. He held me when I cried, washed my hair when I tried to drown my sorrows in the tub, and fed me even when I swore I wasn't hungry.

He looked after me like a husband would a wife and proved without doubt that he didn't marry me for an alibi.

"I'm already struggling not to touch you," Maksim admits, doubling the output of my heart. "I don't know if I will be able to hold back if you say the words I see in your eyes."

"I wasn't going to say anything."

Some of the hurt lifts when he murmurs, "Still a shit liar, Doc."

I try to pretend his words aren't gospel. "I wasn't going to speak." Now I'm honest. "I was going to kiss you since they'll forever relay more than my words ever will." I shrug before heading for the exit. "But if you don't want me to do that, I guess I will wait for you out there—"

He tugs me back in front of him so fast my words are forced back down my throat by the gust his pull causes, and then he cups my jaw as I've been dying for him to do the past few days before he seals his mouth over mine.

I melt into his embrace before I'm eventually wholly consumed by it.

Maksim knows how to kiss, and it has me suddenly knowledgeable as to why he's withheld them from me the past five days. He knows they'll lead to sex, and although he'd never deny me, he knew I needed time to grieve. Not just the loss of Yulia's life, but my mother's and sister's as well.

I wasn't given the chance to grieve back then.

Maksim would never allow that to happen again.

After nibbling on his lips, I inch back before locking my lusty eyes with his. "I love you, Maksim."

"Fuck, Doc," he murmurs, his chest heaving like the words are almost too much for him to hear. "I'm trying to be a gentleman, and you're making it real fucking hard."

A confidence I never anticipated owning shines bright when I lick my lips before lowering my eyes to the crotch of his trousers. "Who said I wanted you to be a gentleman?"

"Doc..." he growls in warning, his low tone announcing just how tethered his restraint is.

"I love you."

I inch closer.

"I need you."

Another step.

"But I can't tell you that with words. I need to show you."

He lunges for me so fast my pajama bottoms don't stand a chance against his rueful tugs.

I'm naked from the waist down in under ten seconds and being filled by Maksim's fat cock even quicker than that.

"Don't even think about it." Maksim's grumble ruffles strands of hair sticky with enough sweat that they shouldn't be able to move. "My cock loves being surrounded by your heat." I mouth his reply while he vocalizes it. "Even when we're not doing anything."

I pretend I'm not busting to pee by snuggling back into his chest and tickling his ribs with my fingertips. We were so impatient we almost didn't make it out of the bathroom. We stumbled as far as the walk-in closet before Maksim buried his head between my legs to feast on the dessert that will only ever be consumed by him.

Round two eventually saw us rumpling the bedding on our mattress. That was around two or three hours ago. I can't be sure of exactly how long I've been sheltered from my grief by Maksim's sturdy cocoon, because I collapsed from satiated exhaustion seconds after my name tore from his throat while his cum heated the walls of my vagina.

Our impatience to become reacquainted means we're still mostly clothed. Half of Maksim's trousers are huddled around his shoes, and the other half are sprawled across our bed. My pajama shirt is more of a belt than the ensemble I had hoped would entice my husband back to our bed earlier rather than later, and my lacy sleeping bra is still latched, but the cups are pulled underneath my breasts.

I stop fighting the smile I'd feel guilty showing after so many innocent lives were taken when my fingers flutter over a gritty lesion in Maksim's lower back. You can't fight something that no longer exists.

I'm too panicked to smile.

"What is that?"

"It's nothing," Maksim immediately replies before rocking his hips upward slowly, striving to coerce my curiosity to longing with his rapidly thickening cock.

"It doesn't feel like nothing to me."

We moan in sync when I yank him forward so fast the inches hidden by his seated position notch inside me.

Panic about how close I came to losing him smashes into me when I spot the cause of the gritty texture. Maksim's body has a number of scars and welts from the years he protected his mother from a monster, but this scar is new.

Numerous sutures are closing a fresh wound high in his gluteus medius muscle. The edges of the skin closed together with perfect butterfly stitches is singed and has a blast-like appearance. Whatever caused the puncture wound was hot and fast moving—most likely a bullet.

I missed it during my assessment because I only removed Maksim's shirt, and it sits around half an inch lower than the waistband of his trousers.

It also explains why Maksim only ever showered this week once I fell asleep.

Nothing but despair echoes in my tone when I ask, "What happened? Were you shot? Did someone shoot you?"

"It's nothing."

I never thought violence would be my go-to coping mechanism, but it takes everything I have not to bang my fists on his chest until it reddens from more than sexual exertion.

"That isn't nothing. You were hurt. Someone shot you. That isn't nothing!"

Anger overrides some of my fear when he throws his head back and laughs. He howls like a wolf staring at a full moon, reminding me that he is both alive and not a man who could be easily taken down.

The remembrance eases my hesitation by a smidge.

After a beat, Maksim murmurs, "You are so sexy when you're jealous."

"How am I jealous? I am mad." *And scared.* "So very mad."

"Still a shit fucking liar, Doc." He rocks his hips upward, securing the devotion of my eyes before saying, "But there is a way you can guarantee no one will ever have their hands on my ass again." Now I'm jealous. I didn't consider the fact he couldn't have been administered stitches where they are unless his backside was hanging out for the world to see, but I store my frustration for a better time when he says, "Come work for me."

I sound more curious than confused when I reply, "I'm studying to become a surgeon."

"And?"

After promising never to use clauses to encourage dialogue, I say, "What use would Ivanov Industries have with a surgeon?"

I realize this isn't solely about the real estate mecca he's forming when he answers, "Heaps of shit. Suturing. Medical procedures. Digging bullets out of backsides."

I don't pay the humor in his tone any attention. I only hear his admission that he was shot.

"Who shot you?" I'm not asking because I'm a nosy Nancy. I am asking because I need the name of the person who better have been issued a death certificate by now. "Is he dead?"

With my tone taking on a serious note, so does Maksim's expression. "I don't know." My pledge for revenge takes a back seat when Maksim responds in a way I never anticipated. "I was more concerned about getting back to you before you heard the rumors than getting immediate revenge."

"Rumors?" The anger in his eyes answers my question on his behalf. "They thought they'd taken you down?"

He jerks up his chin before brushing off an attempt at his life with humor. "They could never be so lucky." He tucks a strand of hair behind my ear. "And neither could you."

"This isn't funny, Maksim. I could have lost you."

His eyes spark with so much love it makes it hard to breathe. "You didn't."

"But I *could* have."

My teeth grit when he says, "But you didn't."

Frustrated, I attempt to dismount him.

He refuses to let me go. He tugs me back onto him, forcing a moan to ripple between my lips.

He gives me a minute for my head and heart to reprimand my body for how easily it gives in to him before he aligns our eyes. "You didn't come close to losing me, and you never will if you take Eva's place on my team." My confusion is only seen for two seconds before he tries to smother it. "You thought she was just an intern?" He smirks like he thinks my lack of smarts is cute. "She is almost as brilliant as you, Doc." Before jealousy can engulf me, he adds, "And just as fucking stubborn. She wants to go home. She's missing her family, and she is willing to do anything to get back to them." My heart pains for Maksim's team during his following sentence. "But she goes where my team goes, and my team goes where you go. For now, that place is Myasnikov. But it doesn't have to be for Eva if you take her place. She can go home, back to her family."

I'm being hammered with a heap of emotions I don't know how to handle, so I shouldn't be surprised by my next question. "You know this is emotional blackmail, right?"

"Is it?" Maksim attempts to pull a face a man as shrewd and cocky as he can't pull off. "I thought this was negotiating. But what would I know? Supposedly I'm not well-versed on how they're meant to be just and fair."

"Maksim—"

"I want you at my side, Doc." I laugh, assuming he is joking when he says, "If I have to buy a hospital to have that, so be it. I'll buy every fucking one in the country." But the absolute truth in his eyes reveals he isn't joking. This is how badly he wants to make me happy. This is how much he wants me to be a permanent part of his life.

He is willing to give me everything, but the only thing I want is him.

When I tell him that, he says, "Then accept my offer, and you will have me twenty-four-seven."

I want to. Yes is sitting on the tip of my tongue, but if I don't keep things even between us, I will be eaten alive. So instead, I say, "I will consider your offer after reading a properly drafted contract—"

"Twice," we say at the same time.

When I recall the last time I shared my mother's recommendation for any legal document, my mouth falls open.

Maksim's lips more twitch than part, and they announce that he's been watching me for longer than we've been married.

His smirk merges to a sultry grin when I ask, "Exactly how long have you been watching me?"

He rolls his hips, mindful my anger never lingers for long when I'm horny, before saying, "I could tell you, but then you'd know all my deepest, darkest secrets—"

"And I'm the only one that privileged."

I giggle at Ano's interruption—Maksim growls.

"You better have a damn good excuse for interrupting us."

"It's the traffic, boss. It is as unpredictable as your moods when you're not getting any," he answers through the double doors of our bedroom, enlarging my smile. "Thanks for taking one for the team, Doc. I was getting so desperate for a Maksim mood lifter I was about to offer up my services. To you, not him. Nothing gets a man's mojo back faster than a brutal bout of jealousy."

I can't tell what thumps louder. My clit when Maksim's race to shut Ano up with his fists frees the last two inches of his cock hidden by his seated position, or Ano's feet when he realizes Maksim's threat won't be idle this time since I couldn't hold back my moan.

They're both loud and desperate.

CHAPTER THIRTY-SIX

The cuff of Dr. Lipovsky's blouse tickles my wrist when she slips her hand into mine a foot from Yulia's coffin. She doesn't say anything. She offers me silent support until the baton can again be handed to my husband.

Maksim was my rock throughout the service, never leaving my side until Ano whispered something into his ear a second before the assembly of people paying their respects to Yulia slowly filtered toward her coffin.

He initially told Ano to wait—but then he saw the urgency on his face.

Whatever he had to share couldn't wait.

I told Maksim to go before waiting at the end of the line.

There are so many people in attendance it has taken almost forty minutes for me to reach Yulia's coffin. I place down the dusty-pink rose the funeral directors handed every attendee upon entrance a second before Maksim returns to my side.

I smile when he places his rose next to mine before sneaking a bag of donut holes into her coffin.

I told him how much she loved them after her first discharge.

That is the only time they were mentioned, yet he still remembered.

I couldn't possibly love this man more if I tried.

"Is everything okay?" I ask Maksim upon noticing the zigzag groove between his brows.

When he jerks up his chin, I almost call out his lie, but the approach of two parents who have every right to hate me shelves my reply.

If I had just stayed by Yulia's side or transferred her care to another hospital, they wouldn't be burying their little girl today.

Maksim's fingers flex on my hip, soundlessly acknowledging he understands my guilt before his lips brush my temple. "Nothing that happened was your fault." He peers at me for several heart-healing seconds, mending my heart as he has the past five days before he strays his eyes to Mr. and Mrs. Petrovitch. "They know that. *You* know that. You just need a little more time for your heart to forgive your head."

I should hate how easily he can read me, but I don't.

I feel guilty about what happened because if Maksim's team hadn't altered everything back, my family name would be stained with more controversy than a man protecting his wife.

My concerns I had before I was drugged were spot on. Dr. Abdulov wasn't working alone. Multiple doctors and medical staff at Myasnikov Private were part of an illegal entity that netted over seven million dollars in organ sales in the prior twelve months alone.

Over three million of those dollars were made from the sale of Yulia's organs.

A high-up dignity in the Russian political scene was desperate to save his son's life, and when he warned Dr. Sidorov that there would be hell to pay if he canceled his order, Dr. Sidorov stupidly believed his wrath would be far worse than Maksim's promise of retribution if any organs were ever sold out of Myasnikov Private again.

He was wrong.

An exact number will never be disclosed to me, but while searching for information about Yulia's service, I noticed online funeral notices rose by at least four hundred percent the past week.

Knowing patients were left to succumb to illnesses that were curable before their organs were harvested without consent was already shocking, but the angst deepened when Maksim announced how they tried to cover up the blunder of his mother's near-death.

Dr. Abdulov and Dr. Sidorov didn't solely prepare to throw me under Maksim's bus if Irina's true lineage was ever unearthed. They sprinkled my name throughout every horrid crime they instigated—crimes I would have paid for by now if Maksim hadn't married me.

As believed, and even while not operating under his father's surname, Maksim and his family are protected by mafia law. They're untouchable, so if it were ever discovered that a recently formed sanction had "killed" the once matriarch of the Fernandez family under the guise of natural causes, heads would have rolled.

Dr. Abdulov and Dr. Sidorov knew theirs would be the first on the chopping block, so they doctored paperwork to shift the focus elsewhere if the truth was ever discovered.

For the past six months, I was their scapegoat.

That is why Irina's surgery was placed under my name and why my credentials were tossed at Maksim left, right, and center when he sought the truth behind his mother's admission.

They didn't solely tell him it was me and hope for the best. Everything was altered—including Irina's online paperwork when I stupidly forgot to log out of the HIS system during my last shift at the ER.

They were so thorough, if Maksim's IT guy wasn't the best in the business, I doubt anyone would have believed that I hadn't tried to steal and sell Irina's organs.

Well, everyone but Maksim.

He trusted his gut, and although occasionally the grief he was almost forced to endure had him second-guessing his intuition, he has assured me time and time again that I was never the first name on his hit list.

He will never admit to my next admission, though.

I know he initially married me so I'd be protected under the same laws that shelter his family, but I will ensure he stays married to me for completely different reasons.

The people who ran the operation out of Myasnikov Private were pissed they had been placed under Maksim's spotlight. He was too powerful for them to push aside like they had other sanctions. When his interrogation into their trade arrived with a ton of attention they didn't want, they sought revenge on the person they believed responsible for his interest in Myasnikov.

That person was me.

How do I know this if I've never met the people helming the sale of organs on the black market? The scar on the jaw of the man who woke me in the middle of the night, drenched with sweat, was extremely telling.

My memories are still hazy from the day I was drugged, but the occasional memory breaks through the fog—usually when I'm sleeping. The man who said I had sanction before his fist cracked into another man's face had the same scar along his jaw as the man I saw gawking at Maksim and me in the poolside cabana Zoya hired for Aleena's hen party.

I'm also reasonably sure he's the same man who placed me on the bench at the bus shelter, but those memories are hazier since they occurred directly before my memories were stolen by a secondary benzodiazepine.

Maksim's response last night when I woke up gasping for air and with a ton of unlocked memories exposes that he wouldn't have offered the scarred man a second leniency even if my memories had arrived earlier.

Leaving me defenseless is as bad as hurting me in Maksim's eyes, and the rules that stop rival families from wiping each other out agree with Maksim, leaving him free to prosecute without fear of punishment.

Although Maksim hasn't openly admitted that he killed the people responsible for my kidnapping, I don't think he'd lie to me if he were asked outright.

He has no issues being honest, particularly when it comes to his protectiveness of me. It is merely his belief on whether I am strong enough to hear the truth that guides his replies, hence me only learning about the organ sales being placed in my name days ago.

I'm drawn from my thoughts when Yulia's father stops in front of me. "Dr. Ivanov, this is my wife, Agafa." His voice is low and on the verge of breaking. "Agafa, this is the doctor I was telling you about. The one who helped our baby girl when no one else would." He chokes on his last few words.

I squeeze his hand, soundlessly promising him the pain will eventually lessen. It will never go away, but it will get better. I shift my focus to Mrs. Petrovitch. "I'm so sorry for your loss. Yulia was..." I struggle to find the right words, so I settle with one. "Perfect."

"She truly was," her mother agrees, burning my eyes with new tears. "Thank you for helping her." My tears almost tumble when she drifts her eyes to Maksim and praises him for not leaving her child alone in the cold. "Knowing she wasn't alone makes the hurt not as devastating."

Maksim looks prepared to say he doesn't deserve her praise, but a baby's coo stops him.

My lips quiver when I drink in the tiny features of a newborn baby in a stroller at the end of the pew. She is the spitting image of her sister, just several years younger.

"I'm sorry. She is due to be nursed." When Agafa returns her eyes to me, it dawns on me why my parents made the promise they did when Stefania died. They were returning the silent pledges I shrouded them with when I gave them a reason to hold on. They wanted to perish with Stefania, but they lived for me. "Please excuse me."

When Mr. Petrovitch attempts to follow his wife, instincts have me snatching up his wrist. He looks as broken as my father did the night following my mother's death, and as hurt as Maksim was when he wondered if I had been injured the same way my mother had been, and it unlocks the words I couldn't find only seconds ago.

"Nothing that happened was your fault. Yulia's death isn't on you."

He shakes his head, sending tears tumbling down his cheeks. "I gave her the food. I fed her their poison."

"Because you placed her first." His sunken eyes and the looseness of his skin announce he went hungry so his daughter wouldn't. That makes him a man—an honorable one. "Don't *ever* feel guilty for doing that."

"She was my daughter. My baby girl," he murmurs, his heart breaking before my eyes. "It was my job to protect her, and I failed." He tosses over the holy water at the edge of Yulia's coffin, startling the people who have yet to file out of the church before he falls to his wife's feet to apologize for a wrongdoing that doesn't belong on his shoulders. "I'm so sorry. I'm so fucking sorry. It's my fault. Our little girl is dead because of me."

CHAPTER THIRTY-SEVEN

Hours later, Lev's tearful plea for forgiveness at the feet of his wife is still playing in my mind. Agafa immediately denied his begs for redemption before she told him in no uncertain terms that Yulia's death was no one's fault bar the men who poisoned the food of people down on their luck, and then wrapped him up in a hug that was so warm it heated my chest.

It's hard to concentrate on anything, so it takes me longer than I care to admit to realize I don't recognize this part of Myasnikov whizzing past my window. I'm seated in the back of one of Maksim's many cars, being driven to an unknown location.

I told Maksim I didn't want to go out, but he was adamant. Not even a promise to sign on as the Ivanovs' chief medical practitioner could persuade him to stay in. He said I need this closure as much as Yulia's parents do, and although he'd never force me to do anything I don't want to do, this is one thing he won't let me back out of.

I peer at Maksim in confusion when Ano pulls to the curb at the front of a restaurant that has seen better days. Several tiles on the roof are cracked, the wood siding is moldy, and every surface is paint peeled.

"Maksim—"

"No questions, Doc. Not yet."

He tells Ano to circle the block before he guides me up the rickety stairs.

The inside of the restaurant isn't as worn as the outside. Patrons fill the tables, and the aromas wafting out of the kitchen are almost enticing enough to encourage the most grief-stricken people to eat.

"Thank you," I murmur to the hostess when she hands me a menu after seating us near the back of the restaurant.

We're right next to the kitchen, and although the food carried out by servers gives reason for the number of people eating at the rundown location, it isn't as appealing as it should be since we're also near the restrooms.

The only advantage of this table is that you can take in the entire restaurant. It is almost like we are at the king's table, and everyone below us are the paupers.

I've barely scanned the top line of dishes on offer, faking that I plan to eat, when a friendly voice greets us, "Hello, I'm Felecia. I will be your server this evening. Can we start you with some drinks?"

I nod, eager for alcohol to numb the pain in my chest, but Maksim requests to be updated on the chef's specials before I can order the strongest bourbon on offer.

"I'm not exactly sure what they are today." If my jealousy weren't suffocated by grief, I would take offense to the long stare she gives Maksim before she asks, "Would you like me to check with the chef?"

"Please. I heard the potato and leek soup is to die for here."

Maksim's reply barely leaves his mouth before Felecia snatches up our menus and skips into the kitchen. Her chipper personality would usually rub off on me, but I'm not in the mood today. Yulia's sendoff was beautiful. Maksim didn't spare a single expense, but I can't stop pondering ways to make her father realize her death isn't his fault.

"Can we please go home? I don't want to be here." I sound like a spoiled brat. Rightfully so. I am whenever I am in Maksim's presence.

"Soon," Maksim promises, his tone lowering from the bark he uses on his staff to the commanding rumble of a husband trying to force his wife back to the land of the living.

After squeezing my hand in silent support, he watches Felecia float across the room. She drops off a bowl of soup at the table near the door before collecting the tab from another.

When I signal for her service, still desperate for a numbing agent, she stuffs a handful of bills into her waitress apron before returning to our table.

"What can I get you?" she asks, forgetting she's meant to update Maksim on the chef's specials.

Again, I am interrupted before I can place my drink order. It isn't Maksim. A waiter at the front of the restaurant is shouting for help.

"Is anyone a doctor? We need a doctor."

Instincts have me shooting up from my seat without a single thought crossing my mind, but before I can get two steps away from the table, Maksim snatches up my wrists. He doesn't pull me back into my seat, but his eyes silently plead for me to consider the consequences of my actions before jumping into the deep end without a life jacket.

"Please," the waitress shouts, shifting my focus back to her customer. "He's choking."

Bile burns my throat when she commences conducting the Heimlich maneuver on a man with a headful of gray hairs and an arrogant expression even while being offered assistance.

"Get off me!" His voice is so familiar it features in my nightmares every night.

None of my dreams in the past week have featured anything but my kidnapping and when Maksim told me I was too late to save Yulia. They all centered around the death of innocent people, not the man who is meant to investigate and arrest the bad guys, so why was Detective Ivan's voice included in the flashbacks of me lying semi-unconscious on a cold concrete floor?

My pupils widen when Ivan tries to pull away from the server trying to help him. His bruises have healed somewhat over the past five days, but they still reflect the damage a fist would cause to someone's face when punched.

"I'm trying to help you," the server curled around Ivan's back announces when he rears up for a fight.

The waitress is doing everything right, but Ivan pushes her away from him and commences shoving his fingers down his throat like he knows the foamy white substance bubbling in the corner of his mouth won't asphyxiate him.

His crimes will.

It takes several long seconds for the dots to commence connecting, but when they do, I'm hit with a savage amount of anger, not solely from how long it takes me to unearth the truth, but from the brutality of it.

"That's why he looked at you like you were a ghost," I murmur more to myself than Maksim. I lower my eyes to my husband, gasping when I realize he was almost taken from me by the very people who are meant to protect him. "He shot you."

Maksim nods before he adds words to his nonverbal reply. "And he drugged you because, according to him, he doesn't need to follow mafia law since he is the law." The pain in his eyes cuts me raw when he murmurs, "He was going to kill you. He was going to kill my wife." I can't tell if he's angry or relieved when he confesses, "But mafia law saved you." I realize it is both when he sneers, "*His* name saved you."

"No," I deny, grateful for the latest splurge of memories. "*You* saved me. The man who rolled me onto my side knew I was *your* wife. That's why he let me go."

Before he can confirm or refute the sheer honesty in my reply, my eyes shoot to the front of the restaurant, where the waitress is squealing. Ivan is on his knees, and a puddle of vomit next to his shiny shoes announces he could be saved, but even with Maksim freeing me from his hold, I can't force my legs to move.

He hurt my husband.

He hurt the man I love.

He almost took him from me.

If that isn't bad enough, he drugged me so I wouldn't remember that Dr. Sidorov had discharged Yulia until it was too late. Her organs were halfway across the country by the time I woke, and her body was cold when Maksim found her.

That is unforgivable, and I refuse to pretend it isn't.

"Ma'am?" Felecia says, shifting my focus from Ivan's rapidly whitening face when he spots my gawk. "Was there something you wanted to order?"

I'm so stunned by her nonchalant reply to a customer she recently served being on his knees, fighting for his life, I sound in a trance when I reply, "No." My tone improves somewhat when I return my eyes to Maksim and say, "I think we should eat in tonight."

He takes a minute to assess my soul from the inside out before he asks, "Are you sure that's what you want, Doc? I'll never force you to do anything you don't want to do."

I scan the other restaurant-goers, who appear as uneager to help Ivan as I am, before nodding. I'm not the only one sentencing him for his crimes. Most of the patrons in the restaurant were victims of his. I recognize almost every one of them since I never forget a patient or their family members' faces.

"Yes. I'm sure."

"All right." Maksim excuses the waitress from our table with a tip far too generous for general service before he guides me out of the restaurant via the kitchen instead of the main entry Ivan's rapidly dwindling frame is blocking.

My heart whacks my rib cage when our veer through the kitchen has me stumbling onto a profile that's had my grief in a constant state of despair the past six hours. I've struggled to move past my sadness since Yulia's funeral, so I have no idea how Mr. Petrovitch arrived for his shift today.

Guilt crashes down on me when I remember the tiny little cherub nestled on his wife's chest when he took the blame for their daughter's death. Just like me after my mother was murdered, he has to work.

You can't choose not to when you've already spent the money that has yet to come in.

Lev never shifts his head my way, but I know he feels my watch because the heaviness weighing down his shoulders shifts as much as mine does when the frantic shouts of the waitress for help silence at the same time Ivan's chest stills.

One of the men responsible for the murder of his daughter is dead, and he is as relieved as I am.

After staring up at the ceiling long enough for my heart to recommence beating, he pulls a bowl of potato and leek soup off the serving counter. "Don't serve that," he instructs a sous chef before he moves a soup pot off the cooktop and pours it down the sink. "I think some of its ingredients curdled. I'll make a new batch."

As he scrubs the pot to ensure not a single residue of the poison he used to avenge his daughter's murder remains in the pot, Maksim places a suitcase I didn't realize he was holding until now onto the stainless steel counter between Mr. Petrovitch and us before he ushers me outside.

I rear up to protect Maksim as ruefully as he will forever protect me when our exit is eyeballed by the second half of the duo investigating the wrong people. Lara is standing next to an unmarked police cruiser, scanning notes in the notepad she is rarely without.

When she notices she has caught my watch, she stores her notepad away before straying her eyes to Maksim. The interrogation I am anticipating doesn't happen. She accepts Maksim's chin dip as if he spoke a thousand words before she calls in a possible officer in need of assistance on her radio.

Her words aren't hurried, and neither are her steps when she approaches the restaurant where one of her colleagues lies slayed.

"She knew you weren't lying about being drugged with a benzodiazepine," Maksim murmurs as he signals for Ano to pull up at the curb in front of us, "because your symptoms mimicked hers to a T." As he assists me into the back seat of his ride, he says, "She got too close, and Ivan wouldn't let anyone stand between him and his share of the proceeds."

We make it halfway home before my bewilderment lifts enough for me to speak. I don't take our conversation in the direction you'd anticipate for someone who took the Hippocratic oath. "How much of a tip did you leave the chef?"

Maksim smiles like he's as obsessed with my nosiness as he is with my body before he replies, "Enough that he'll never have to work another day in his life if he doesn't want to." When I rest my head on his shoulder, needing his closeness, he tugs me over until I sit side-straddled on his lap. "It won't ease their pain, but it will give them time to grieve."

When he lifts my head and our eyes lock, I fall in love all over again. He isn't solely offering the Petrovitches a lifetime to grieve. He is giving me the same crutch, and although there will be times when I will believe I'll need more than a lifetime to get over my losses, the burden will never feel as heavy with Maksim carrying a majority of the load.

When I say that to Maksim, he twists his lips. "You'd have to hand over some of the load first, Doc. I don't think you're ready for that just yet."

"I am. I have no issues accepting help." He almost calls me a liar, but I continue talking before he can. "I'm even considering taking you up on your offer. There are just a few matters I need to take care of first."

He waves his hand through the air, giving me the floor. I'm reasonably sure he did the same when trying to convince me to marry him, but the memory is still a little cloudy.

"I have to finish my studies. I didn't come this far to give up now."

"Not an issue," he replies without pause for thought.

I doubt his response to my subsequent demand will be as carefree.

"I want to finish them at Myasnikov Private." His growl sets me on edge *and dampens my panties*, but we will keep that between us. "The patients there deserve better." Since he can't deny my claim, he remains tight-lipped. "It is also a ten-minute walk from our apartment, and since your security team hacked into the surveillance system the day we met, it will almost be the same as having me at your side twenty-four-seven. You can spy on me as often as your heart desires."

He maintains his quiet front, announcing what I've always known.

He's been watching me from day one.

Aware my demands are not yet over, Maksim says, "And?"

"And?" I pause to build the suspense, boiling the tension that will never evaporate between us. "You need to leave my alarm clocks alone. I set them for a reason."

He laughs, but instead of remaining quiet like he did when he couldn't deny his security team hacked Myasnikov Private's servers, he says, "I learned from the best."

It takes several long brain-frying seconds for me to unravel his riddle, and when I do, my jaw drops.

My grandmother greeted him like she knew him because she did.

They'd met previously.

When I stare at Maksim, demanding an answer, he smirks before revealing, "She snuck to your bedside to turn off your alarm clock the night we met. I didn't think she could see me in the shadows, but she told me she'd kill me if I hurt you. I believed her enough to play nice."

His chuckles rumble through my chest when I murmur, "You're a shit liar, Mr. Ivanov."

He hits me with a frisky wink before murmuring over my lips I'm praying are about to become kiss swollen, "I learned that from the best too."

EPILOGUE

Six years later...

"Not too much longer, sweetheart, and then you will feel much better."

Beautiful, big brown eyes peer up at me as the anesthetic pulling Veronika under lengthens her blinks. I brush back the locks that snuck out from under her hairnet before lifting my eyes to the lead surgeon on this case.

"Ready?" Eva asks as she heads toward an OR nurse with her scrubbed-to-within-an-inch-of-their-life hands held in front of her.

Once she is gloved up and ready to operate, she spins to face me.

I nod, words above me.

Today is a big day for Veronika's family, and one they would have never seen if it weren't for the generosity of Ivanov Industries.

Although I didn't allow Maksim to buy every hospital in the country, much to his dismay, he secured our charity organization the right to operate in almost every one of them.

We don't undertake surgical procedures solely on children with neurological disorders. Our help extends to all forms of medical assistance, and our patients don't pay a single cent for the healthcare they so desperately need.

We're bridging the gap between wealthy patients and ones with no insurance one case at a time. To date, we've helped over seventy families with lifesaving surgeries they were previously denied and hundreds of less complicated procedures.

I was meant to lead in Veronika's surgery today, but with my stomach as swollen as a beach ball, I chose to sit it out. A standard craniotomy takes three to five hours to complete, but Veronika's is more complicated, so I couldn't risk needing to hand over her care mid-surgery if I were to go into labor.

"She is in good hands," I advise Veronika's parents when she is wheeled away from them. "Dr. Mahoney is the best neurosurgeon in the country."

Maksim's deep rumble rolls through my ears as I direct Mr. and Mrs. Bordoza to the ICU waiting room. "Still a shit liar, Doc." He props his shoulder onto the doorframe of the OR's nurses' station before he drags his eyes down my body in a slow and dedicated sweep. "My wife is a fucking genius." He returns his now hooded eyes to my face. "And she's sexy as fuck too."

I try to act unaffected by his presence. It isn't my best effort, but once again, if I don't keep things even between us, he will eat me alive. "What are you doing here, Maksim? I thought you were helping my father and grandmother move into their new place."

My grandfather lost his fight five years ago. It was six months after my father was released from custody to await a new trial. The evidence was still damning against him, particularly since he has always admitted his guilt, but when the jury was finally informed of the extent of my mother's injuries and just how brutal her assault was, his sentence was reduced. With time served counting toward his new conviction, he was able to sit at his father-in-law's bedside during his final weeks.

"They're all settled, so I thought I'd come check on my stubborn wife." His eyes lower to my stomach, his lip hitching higher like he's obsessed with how its roundness fills in my scrubs. "You're nine months pregnant, Doc. You shouldn't be standing all day."

"In these shoes, it feels like I'm walking on a cloud." He smirks, cocky he won our shoes and clothes debate within the first two months of our marriage. "Besides, I only have another..."—I cringe when I check the time—"seven hours until I am on maternity leave."

"That's one of the perks of being the boss. You can give yourself an early mark whenever you want." He pushes off the door and heads my way. "But since I know how important this particular case is to you"—Veronika has the same brain tumor Stefania had—"we'll compromise." My knees pull together when he states his terms. "I'll take you out for lunch, make you scream my name twice on the drive back to check in on your patient, and then I'll rub out your aches in the tub after your shift."

When he cradles my head and brushes his lips against my temple, I take a moment to relish his hand in my hair and his minty breath in my nose since he put cigarettes on the line while negotiating for me to ditch contraception, before saying, "You still haven't learned the art of negotiating, Mr. Ivanov."

"I haven't?" When he inches back, bringing us eye to eye, I nod. "How so? Did you miss the part about you screaming my name...?"

"Twice," we say at the same time.

He smiles, loving how well we still gel after six years.

The past few years have been relatively smooth, but we faced a handful of bumps our first year of marriage. Don't misconstrue. We were rock solid, even after learning he didn't solely marry me so I'd be protected under the same laws that shelter his family. He did it for the exact reason I tried to strip from him when I thought he married me so he'd have an alibi.

We exchanged vows so he couldn't testify against me—no matter which court I'd face charges from.

But the laws that protected us almost took us out when the boss of all bosses learned it wasn't Maksim's father's new bride who killed him.

It was Matvei—Maksim's younger brother.

Hell rained down on us, and I learned hard and fast that there are more things that could steal Maksim away from me than his protectiveness.

My stubbornness was at the top of the list.

Remembrance of that makes my following sentence so much harder to articulate. "I should stay. Veronika is my patient."

"You should," Maksim agrees, shocking me. I blame pregnancy hormones for my stupidity when he adds, "But you won't."

"Maksim—"

He guides me toward the exit before half his name leaves my lips. "You need to eat. My baby is hungry." Heat roars through me when he murmurs, "And so the fuck am I."

"You ate this morning," I reply, no longer fighting his brisk strides to the closest exit, mindful his hunger has nothing to do with food, and too horny not to portray a lust-fueled idiot. "And I'm sure you'll eat again this evening."

"Fuckin' oath I will," he agrees, shadowing my panties with more wetness. Even after six years, we still can't get enough of each other. He also still sleeps inside me every night. I've not yet had the heart to tell him that won't be possible after I give birth. "But wasn't it you who said three meals are the bare minimum a man should consume per day?"

He has me over a barrel, but I try to act like his hold over me isn't as strong now as it was the day we met. "I meant actual meals, as in food."

He stops walking, twists to face me, and then flares his nostrils.

I'm putty in the hands of a genius two seconds later when he says with a moan, "Still a shit fucking liar, Doc." His tongue delves out to wet his lips when he steps closer, and he growls, "I can smell how aroused you are. You're as hopeful now as you were when you negotiated that I eat *you* a minimum of three times a day once I knocked you up with my kid." His eyes bounce between mine, as lusty and commanding as ever. "And because I promised my wife to do exactly that, I'm going to keep my word because it doesn't matter the where, the what, or the how, she and her needs will *always* come first."

We only just make it into the back of his SUV before buttons pop and the bottoms of my scrubs are yanked to my knees.

Continue for bonus chapters.

The End!

The next book in the martial privileges series is Zoya and Andrik's story. You can preorder it now.

If you'd like to read Maksim's POV of their first met and the "shower incident" click here for two bonus chapters!

Facebook: facebook.com/authorshandi

https://BookHip.com/XGLQVZM

Instagram: instagram.com/authorshandi

Email: authorshandi@gmail.com

Reader's Group: bit.ly/ShandiBookBabes

Website: authorshandi.com

Newsletter: https://www.subscribepage.com/AuthorShandi

If you enjoyed this book - please leave a review.

ACKNOWLEDGMENTS

This book has been a long time coming. The past eight months were the longest I've gone not writing. It was pure torture, but it was also good. I needed time to fix past stories, work out my action plan for upcoming stories, and improve what I already had.

All books had a handful of editing updates, and a select few had a complete overhaul of edits. We found promotional material for each series and brainstormed ways to get more readers.

It was a tiring eight months, but it was good for business.

I hoped Doctored Vows would be an easy book to regain my writing mojo.

Maksim had other plans.

He fought me tooth and nail and kept his cards in close to his chest. He didn't want to share a single detail, so I stumbled whenever I tried to force his words onto paper.

Ultimately, I gave up and wrote what I was hearing. It was all from Nikita's side, but the story flowed the instant I stopped trying to force Maksim's POV. I got words, lots of them, and I loved them.

So, yeah, this book was a single POV book, but that's okay. It keeps the intrigue high and the surprises secret.

You learned who Maksim was *with* Nikita.

It made it all that more special.

Well, it did for me.

I guess I should move on to the acknowledgments now since

this is the acknowledgment page. As always, I must thank my husband, who has never stopped supporting me. He is my rock and will forever be my number-one muse.

I love you, Chris.

Lauren... the dedication is spot on. Thank you for listening to me ramble about these two for weeks on end. The words we share led up to the perfect writing days.

I'll be forever grateful to Lacey from Crossbones Editing for squeezing in a final proof when a double booking left me high and dry. Courtney Umphress and Lacey have made Doctored Vows extra sparkling, and I'm hopeful the book is as shiny and error-free as possible.

I struggle with editing, so I rely on my team to make my manuscripts sparkle. Then we have the whole issue of trying not to input errors while updating the final file.

It's a tricky feat for someone who just wants to write.

There's so much more to this author's life than just writing. My prior eight months prove this more than anything, but writing will always be my main focus. I missed it, and I have no plans to stop now that I've returned after a lengthy (for me) hiatus.

Until next time,

Shandi xx

ALSO BY SHANDI BOYES

Denotes Standalone Books

Perception Series

Saving Noah *

Fighting Jacob *

Taming Nick *

Redeeming Slater *

Saving Emily

Wrapped Up with Rise Up

Protecting Nicole *

Enigma

Enigma

Unraveling an Enigma

Enigma The Mystery Unmasked

Enigma: The Final Chapter

Beneath The Secrets

Beneath The Sheets

Spy Thy Neighbor *

The Opposite Effect *

I Married a Mob Boss *

Second Shot *

The Way We Are

The Way We Were

Sugar and Spice *

Lady In Waiting

Man in Queue

Couple on Hold

Enigma: The Wedding

Silent Vigilante

Hushed Guardian

Quiet Protector

Enigma: An Isaac Retelling

Twisted Lies *

Bound Series

Chains

Links

Bound

Restrain

The Misfits *

Nanny Dispute *

Russian Mob Chronicles

Nikolai: A Mafia Prince Romance

Nikolai: Taking Back What's Mine

Nikolai: What's Left of Me

Nikolai: Mine to Protect

Asher: My Russian Revenge *

Nikolai: Through the Devil's Eyes

Trey *

The Italian Cartel

Dimitri

Roxanne

Reign

Mafia Ties (Novella)

Maddox

Demi

Ox

Rocco *

Clover *

Smith *

RomCom Standalones

Just Playin' *

Ain't Happenin' *

The Drop Zone *

Very Unlikely *

False Start *

Short Stories - Newsletter Downloads

Christmas Trio *

Falling For A Stranger *

One Night Only Series

Hotshot Boss *

Hotshot Neighbor *

The Bobrov Bratva Series

Wicked Intentions *

Sinful Intentions *

Devious Intentions *

Deadly Intentions *

Martial Privilege Series

Doctored Vows *

Deceitful Vows *

Made in the USA
Las Vegas, NV
14 November 2024